THE
LAST BOY
ON
EARTH

THE
LAST BOY
ON
EARTH

WEST AMBROSE

Queer Space
New Orleans

Published in the United States of America by
Queer Space
A Rebel Satori Imprint
www.rebelsatoripress.com

Paperback ISBN: 978-1-60864-371-4

"To The Wanderer
who is yet to trap Love in
Beauty's rose-garden"

The Above
The Shallows
Guyot
Indra-1
The Below
Corallina
Clarel
Snideshead
Eaumarseilles
Illyrial
Peusouci
Vinesdam
N
Shell Bed

A witchcraft drew me hither.
That most ingrateful boy there by your side
From the rude sea's enraged and foamy mouth
Did I redeem…

DRAMATIS PERSONAE:

The Below

The Below/The Endless Deep
A realm far below the attention of The Above. It is said that The Below contains many magical linguistic tides of knowledge. While The Below and The Endless Deep are often used interchangeably, there are parts of the sea where The Endless Deep starts to become more appropriate in vernacular simply because it is so unknown, even to those who live there. The Below changes the very nature of linguistic flow in and of itself.

Julian- A boy in search of a narrative. His narrative.
Adrian- A sea-captain in search of a boy.
Dimitri- A navigator who is lost. They can make any map but one.
Batiste- The ship's armorer. A boy who knows his blades and shades. A refugee from Peusouci.
Pierre- The ship's gardener and Adrian's confidant.
Ernest–A bookbinder.
Pericles– A bookbinder's reefmate.
Vico– The foundling child of Ernest and Pericles.
Henry– The pâtissier's apprentice. Purveyor of sweets and Vico's best friend.
Thaddeus– A weatherman from Eaumarseilles.

Tutors, Courtiers, Pirates and Artisans, and the various other creatures of The Endless Deep.

The Shallows

The Shallows
The Shallows is a place between The Above and The Below, where wayward creatures, and occasional folks from The Above wander on occasion. The Shallows are are polluted by the air of The Above. The most chemically laden part of the ocean, it is often used as a meeting point for bustling ports of trade so that Denziens of all three regions may meet to some level of [dis]comfort. The Shallows has a culture of brisk trade with The Above and sometimes parts of The Below as well.

Eric— A maker of deals, working in trade and travels on various ships.
Florent Sage— A media expert with little expertise.

Nurses, Doctors, Bonesaws and Thieves

The Above

The Above– A world after the Anthropocene. A land of plenty, overcomodified and over-identified. The Above encapsulated any part of earth that was not tossed into the sea and transformed into the undefiable and monstrous. Those from The Above cannot tolerate the living conditions from The Below. In the same way, true creatures of The Endless Deep cannot tolerate The Above.

Vern– A boy in search of a kingdom.
Mx. Herbsmith— An influencer and business savvy associate.
Land denizens made up of a variety of folks. Though, notably, no boys.

CHAPTER 1

The last boy on earth sat pretty on his gilded throne.

Men came from miles to admire him—women, nonbinary folks, trans, and cis, and robots, and humans, alike. Of course, he liked the men best. His eyes flashed when the cameras swarmed, dazzling golden-brown in each refracting, longing lens. He was always surrounded; when he was driven to his mansion before sunset, to lay his head on damask and laurel covered pillows and piles of love notes overflowing onto the lace-trimmed linens and rippling duvets. When he sang, low and sweet in stadiums filled to standing capacity; *Who will be my baby, tonight, who will get to know me, get to show me how to feel loved?* When he hummed under his breath; *Ave, Ave Maria,* after a press conference with scientists and influencers, morticians and businessmen and other cartographers trying to map his genealogy, his birthplace, the traces of his name. When he found himself in the corner of a glamorous party, letting languid harmonies float over the balcony, hoping to be caught below; *dance the hours away, who can say, what an hour means when it is shared?*

"You will grow, won't you?"

It was nine o'clock in the morning. The first enquirer smiled. They had a yellow stain on their front teeth, a tight bun and the news reporter's habit of hunching even when they were not trying to intimidate.

No *Good morning, Vern.* No *How are you?* He could be straight to the point, too.

"I will exist, in space and time– why certainly, Mx. Herbsmith!"

"Yet…" Herbsmith clicked their pen trying to get the wording exactly right. "You show no signs of aging."

"Precisely."

"You will be twenty next year—"

"No, I will be seventeen, same as I was the year before, and the year before that, and the year before that and…"

"So, in our years, though, you'd be twenty-two, or so?"

"Around that. But physically, I can not be."

"Can you die?"

"I do not know, sir. I suppose I am not immortal. No one is…I am just a boy, after all!"

"There are no more boys after you? Everyone has looked?"

"Oh, yes. Thoroughly." A counselor behind him pushed over some papers to show the proof; numbers and charts and lots and lots of data—he never had the head for it. He knew what they were all really asking; was he made in a lab or was he grown, organically, sexually, mistakenly? Was he an it, a they, or something, *something else*, really?

"No further questions. Thank you," The interviewer said, a grumble hidden somewhere under their politeness.

Busy. In a rush. Vern thought. *Impressed, but busy.*

He had time before the second interview, but only for idle thoughts. Soon, there would be time to get ready, bathe and dress before the party tonight. *Perhaps I will read some Goethe, or some Virgil. No, Plutarch! There are so many poems to practice reciting for the gala next week,* he thought. *I shall do it while drinking champagne in the bathtub…*

The second interviewer took his seat. This one, too, was nothing spectacular.

This will be easy, Vern thought, already occupied with the white-grape and rhubarb millefeuille being prepared for a late lunch. He was already dreaming about the classical music they had asked him to curate for the party…

"…And where were you born?"

Ah, I've not heard that one in a few months!

"I do not remember. I was found with a head injury. I am so thankful that I was saved."

"You mean *preserved*."

The man had on a simple linens and dark robes. He did not meet Vern's gaze, too busy writing in his jade-colored notebook, bound in embroidered cloth.

"I meant *saved*. Do not mince my words, thank-you."

"And you are trans, right?"

"Cis or trans, what does it matter? I am a boy."

The man continued to scribble.

"Well, you have *boyparts* and speak *boyspeak*, right?"

Vern smiled, a rippling circle across an ocean's wave; effortless, light and playful.

"Oh, of course, *sir*. But I would much rather speak about Romance--" he felt the silky words, practiced and studied, over and over, flow from his poised throat. "Romance and Love and Art—all things of Beauty in this world *must* have Art, and so they must be free to create it as they are free to love."

"What do you mean?"

"If only we could fill the air each day with bird song and love letters. It's what makes the world go 'round–Don't you think the world would be a better place then, mister…" he paused. "I am *ever* so sorry. I didn't quite get your name."

"Julian." His voice was clear.

"I see, *Julian*." Vern made his own voice sweeter, out of spite.

"Are you gay?"

"What do you mean?"

"Are you queer?"

He raised an eyebrow.

"Isn't everyone, a *bit*?"

"Are you a boy, then?"

"Of course."

"Cis or trans? Human or—"

"*Boy. Thank-you.* Now, like I said, these matters do not hold my interest, but if you would like to discuss Plutarch…"

Julian flipped to the next page, apparently unhearing.

"Can I sleep with you, even if you are not, say, attracted to someone like me?"

Vern was not too offended, as it was a question he had been asked plenty of times before: how many holes did he have, did he feel pleasure, did he feel pain? How many partners? Have they ever seen or felt or touched where he was born, made…*created?* The choice word never landed right on their tongues.

Vern did not say *Silly thing, no one can sleep with me. I am the last one— it is in one of my new contracts.*

He did not say *Silly thing, not in front of everyone.*

He did not say anything. For a moment. Then, he collected himself and went back to one of the dozens of fail-safe cues he had learned.

"Romance is a universality; roses in one language blossom as pomegranates in another, seasons change and so do they—what's any of it mean without a *proper* translation?"

He did not say *A pretty face does not hurt.*

He did not say *Smile. Keep smiling. Do not make it seem forced at all.*

He did not say *You are hiding something and I taste it, I taste it between us here and now…*

Julian rustled some of his papers into a neat, brown satchel with a long sigh. He looked too young to sigh like that. The thought startled Vern.

"I never knew Earth had such a history; love and peace for all."

"Well, they are—" Vern felt his mouth go dry and corrected himself. "*We* are many different things."

With serene politeness, Julian leaned forward to fold his papers. His hands moved with steady, winsome grace. Their closeness felt deliberate somehow, but Vern could not catch the meaning.

"Take care, Vern. Thank you for the meeting. It was very kind of you to also take the time to talk to me. Thank your associates, too. For me, please?"

Julian opened the door to let himself out, and it hit Vern *why* he had leaned over so far; the scent of his cologne lingered. It was the bitter Vern noticed first, wrapped in the plush, heady silk of a tiny, star-like blossom—*a clementine*, the variation of a plant which had died out on Earth in a Winter blight.

"Is something the matter?" one of his associates asked.

"No, I am…a bit famished, is all. Thanks for asking, though."

They believed him to be sincere. It was good enough. It would have to be.

CHAPTER 2

Vern soaked himself in the pink-petaled tub. He savored the blush of grapes on his tongue the way he savored Murasaki and Lorca—he flitted the perfect, creaseless butterflies of his hands across his body and hovered; *Who are you, stranger, and why do you darken my doorway so? Why do you tell me tales of woe instead of tales of diamonds and violins? Where do you want me, when you imagine me floating at the edge of your bed; reading about me, seeing my face on a screen—what do you think you really know about someone like me?*

He decided on the Valentino suit. It was last minute but would work without a hitch—gorgeous in its vintage nature.

His associates were not truly his keepers. He had built his brand and then voided contracts that were not ethical. He bought his lawyers and then bought them out. He kept doing it and he would *keep* doing it until he found something *better* to do with his time. At least, that is what he told himself. He was no one's victim. Never again. And yet…

There were still *too* many rules for his taste. The limousine ride made him nervous like it always did. He tried not to think and focused on the rain drizzling over the newly tanned moon as he hummed; *Who will be my baby, by daylight, who will get to know me, get to show me how to feel alone? Ave, Ave Something…A drop of water, the little boy was looking for his voice…*

The party was the usual routine; camera flashes, a toast or two, some waltzing…

More Verdi, for monsieur? someone asked. Vern's thank-you bubbled in the glass of Champagne then fell flat as he walked away. On the white-arched balcony, he stared up at the stars, back to the crowd. Finally, he could cry now. He could cry and cry and cry without causing a scene. The stars blended into drops of petals and yellow paint—he saw them as they really were; desperate and dying icons of a time that no longer existed. The distance is what existed—distance that burned his lungs; distance that left him retching the fragrant dishes into a clawfoot toilet on his knees, curled for days in bed.

"I did not mean to interrupt." The voice startled him; it was too familiar, all bitter-bloom and phosphorescent rain.

"Oh!"

"The stars are not roped off. Anyone can come see them—" Julian did not say *Anyone can see you cry if they just looked for you,* though he might as well have. He stared at Vern for a moment before he spoke again.

"He listened, and he wept, and his bright tears went trickling down the golden bow he held…"

Vern swallowed. He knew that one. Of course he did. He answered in the only way he knew how—a gift for a gift.

"Tears like mine, will keep thy memory green…"

"Do they know?"

"Know what?"

"Do not play games with me, not now…"

Julian leaned in. He was wearing a white, loose linen shirt and a pair of brown trousers that fitted him expertly. He dressed plainly. It made his slight and striking features even more noticeable.

"How do *you* know you are the only one of your kind?"

"You m-mean a boy?"

Julian said nothing more.

Is he wearing some kind of glamour, Vern thought sharply. *Is he…like me?*

"You mean young, ah well—I told them, they ran what tests they said they could predict that sort of thing, they said…"

He did not say *They would hurt me if they knew what I really was.*

He did not say *You will hurt me when you know what I am.*

He did not say *You already want to hurt me because you know me. That is how wanting someone works. That is Love.*

Julian was about his height, too. He had brown eyes, reflecting back Eternity—a dream that fell on its own sword and drowned as a myth, long forgotten.

Vern started to cry again. He did not say *I never cry in front of them. I have to be strong. So, I weep to myself, for myself, for you. This is holy, this new, this is the appendage of ghost, bleeding Summer and ivory. I will be the soft petal your thorns tear through. I will lay down and I will give you a place to lay. I will be everything and anything, if only you tell me why I am crying...*

"You will be an experiment to them, if they—"

"They will not. *Trust me,*" Vern pleaded. He felt dizzy.

"I do not know you, sir."

"Do you?"

"Do *you?*"

It was Vern's turn to be taken aback; did this man see him as untrustworthy? Vile, somehow, by that same nature? Why did he sound so miserable, so violated when he said *'I do not know you, sir'?*

"You will be sold off and, and—" Julian fidgeted. His hands were mesmerizing. He wore no jewelry. It made him seem even more luxurious. "And do you *really* want to be sold?"

He did not say *I did what I did. I am well off now. Alone and well off.*

He did not say *Am I running out of time? Oh, am I running out of time?*

"Do you know what people do once they get what they want? They discard you. I promise."

"You want me..." he breathed out in disbelief.

"I want things different than you see them. Where I am from, no one is owned. No last names signify a connection. We are all of an artful grace, an individual freedom that is as foreign as it is sovereign. Here, you are looking at being kept. Treated..."

"I am treated *well.*"

Julian stretched against the railing and lit a long thin cigarette which plumed with lavender-bronze smoke. His movements were less practiced, now—Vern could see how he limped. He could see the odd motion behind such fluidity—he wondered if he had the scorching pain Vern did, the infections and endless ailments from this planet's air. Julian shifted and while Vern watched, blowing circles in the smoke. His lips held secrets meant to deceive no one. He was the most dangerous person Vern had ever met.

"A strand of opals behind glass— tired, even as you keep dusting it off, one day it shatters…"

"On Earth we are *all* free to–"

"Do not tell me of *this* place, until you let me tell you about another one. Please, let me tell you about mine."

His voice had the allure of an evening vesper, a quiet command without any violence.

"*There,* each man is free; well and truly free—Every man is a Prince, he lies with who he likes, when he likes, however he likes. He loves amorously and wholly and never worries who has his heart and if he's hurt a lover—he is forgiven, mostly, but never lightly. There the houses are not built to keep one in and the people do not wait for the faces of strangers to fill their screens and clamber for a glimpse—there we don't dress as if we have to conceal and there is no concept of partners; no man belongs to another—when we lay down we get up the next morning with whoever and however we choose—we wander, but we have no intention of vagrancy because there's nowhere to go *back*, only *to*; I go to you as another might go to me, sweetly, helplessly, bravely seeking a friend in the night; it is always *your* choice when you go and when you stay, who you are and where you are that person because there, *there* every man is free… to love himself."

Vern swallowed around the lump in his throat until he could speak.

"There, our bodies are…changed. When we give ourselves freely, when we take as freely, we change things. There is a transference that reshapes the nature of each dwindling flame and passing wave. We exchange kisses and can move continents. Do you know what I mean?"

"You are…using someone else's parable, surely—"

"And *you are* undying."

"Undying?"

The word was glass in Vern's velvet bed of a mouth. He really looked at Julian's eyes, and found they were the same as his, rings of glittering aureate amidst pools of deep, golden brown. The same as the band on his finger but not mined and broken into any mold. At least, not yet.

He was young. He could be a boy.

He did not say *I remember when they found me and ran tests—We have no such proof of aliens. . How they turned me over, poked and prodded at my skin— too dark and light at the same time. The machines are probably confused, just be happy it is a human boy. Keep quiet and we will help out. You will cross all those borders we have tightened with ease. Everyone will see you, everyone will know exactly where you are…*

He did not say *I remember the lilac moons— Do they still shimmer so?*

He did not say *It is such an imperfect memory, it feels like a dream. Is it a dream, stranger, mercurial and tide-sung. Are you exactly like me, lost in earthly reveries, longing for a home that floats?*

The last notes of a requiem bathed Julian's skin—Vern could not think about anything but the man before him. He did not want to.

"Alright, for starters…I am a bit younger than you, but not by much," he heard himself admit, as though by automation. His smile wobbled like a simple wooden top.

"What gives it away?" Julian had a boyish grin. Nothing could hide it.

"You have only wandered here now. I think…I was an explorer once and I went very, *very* far. Too far. I can not quite remember."

Julian glanced around, brushing his sleeves in a hurry. He came off shy and delicate in a way Vern had never seen before.

How could we be so similar and yet…

"So, they really do not know about—"

"No, they do not," he was too quick to assure. *I hope.*

10

He did not say *I am alien enough down here. There's only one, so they want me. Two and they will kill us. They will want to see where your scars are, and where your chest ends and your boyhood begins. They will want to know how you have sex and if you even like it. If you are too sick or too well, or where your body works and where it does not. You deserve to keep what they want, dear boy. Keep it all. I am not alone, not really, even if I am the only one. Run from this place and do not ever come back.*

He did not say *I want to hide you away and I want you to make me invisible. Let no one see me but you, give me no eyes but the ones that look exactly like mine. Let your soul sear into mine and start fire after fire after fire; when it burns, it is real, when it burns down, we move faster; chase me, taste me, crease me in the centerfold of your wonder; completely Yours.*

He did not say *Earth has changed me. Now I want to belong to someone—could it be you?*

"Vern?" Julian asked. He was still leaning and it made him seem smaller. "Have you ever been kissed, properly?"

Vern blinked, head swimming. Julian's words seemed to levitate in front of him like snow.

"...take you upstairs...take you far away from here...treat you right..."

He wanted to say *Yes,* anything but could—his hand brushed the other boy's. He was no longer here; he was upstairs, he was across the dance floor, the continent, soaring, he was leaving, falling again, watching the vibrating purple rings of those...moons. He was sure that is what they were without remembering. Then, he was underneath Julian; he was over him, pressed against the other boy's back, hard—*Please,* he heard Julian say, his voice was closer to a whisper then, the will o' the wisp of an aria's ending, tipped his head back and he spilled a thousand *I love yous,* floating, floating, floating...

I know you, He heard himself say through the thick milky waves of Not Here.

And I know you, He heard the words drip back into his own ears, honeyed and blooming, in the sweat of his hair and the saturnalia of his skin.

11

His dreams changed color; baby blue and swimming with waves, salt-loved and tender…

But what did it mean?

Julian brushed him away. He was still talking. He was fully clothed, and the curved arches of his spine were cloistered by fabric and confusion.

"…Somewhere no one else would hear. I cannot stay here too long or I…"

The air. He wondered if Julian could adapt to the atmosphere. It was almost impossible. He wondered if *he* was no longer anything worth retrieving to such a marvelous place because he had lived and breathed the filth here so long. He wondered if he had killed Julian through the sheer journey of, what he now assumed, was trying to find *him.*

Oh, he thought. *No, not that…not after so long…*

"Please…"

He did not say *I am not worth any of this trouble. Take the last breath from my lungs and start again. Destroy me. Destroy me, instead. Break these petty perceptions and I will walk on a new planet for you. Forever and ever. I will relearn the history I never knew I had.*

He did not say *Let them hear us. I am so tired of this exorbitant life of hiding.*

He did not say *Leave now. If…if you still can.*

He turned and saw the crowd dancing through the doors. Someone would see them alone, eventually. It was a matter of time. And then what—who was safe? Who was *really* safe? Was he not already ending Julian's life one precious second of treacherous air at a time?

He did not say anything.

Julian reached for him, and he slipped past, through the crowd, his bodyguards, his groupies and stalkers, through the quarter notes and rests, the cello strings and harpsichord arpeggios, the limousine doors and the croak of his own voice begging *Drive faster, please—*

Vern did not look back to see what his security detail made of the boy who looked just like him, who had come too close and made him scared. Vern knew he was the rarest and most constant of cowards, it was a fact of nature akin to the schedule of tides.

He would double the driver's salary to ignore the hysterics creeping into his voice. He would drive himself–goodness knows, he always loved to. It helped him ignore the torrent of tears that hit the windows from inside the glass. It helped him to ignore the way *Please* had rung out; so similar, so *familiar…*

He threw open the doors to his house. The rooms were lined with turquoise and cream-colored wallpapers, half a dozen peacocks, statues and taxidermy and living, too. He rushed past them into one of his bathtubs. He scrubbed at his body, bruise after bruise after bruise. He wanted to rip the skin off until he could taste his own blood; *would it be Julian's?* The thought hit him square in the chest, he tried to sing, tried to produce something, *anything* of Beauty; it came out a stain—A silent, ghostly stain upon his quivering lips, untouched.

Ave, Ave… He thought, forcing his lips to move. *Something.. Anything. Please, please…!*

They did not. They could not.

The word followed him, winding around every high ceiling through the rafters of each cold, echoing corner of the house; *Please, please…*

He ran out in one of his long, white robes, trailing bathwater down the marbled halls. He opened one door after another; the ballrooms and kitchens and greenhouses and sitting rooms and observatories and conservatory after conservatory; the windows where paparazzi cameras would flash for a glance to peer in; past the parties and businessmen and all the past events that turned his very dwelling into a mausoleum; down here he had everything, everything a human being could possibly want…*who will get to know me, get to show me…* the bedrooms were immense and grand and totally empty; the four-poster beds and chairs and closets; he could not hear the sound of his own footsteps any longer. His knees gave way. The perfect curls of his hair locked into place. He fell down and shrieked, a piercing cry with no sound…

dance the hours away, who can say, what an hour means when it is shared?

He did not say what he felt.

He could not. The air turned his body to gold and sealed his very nature as a secret.

He remained slumped over until morning, a crumbling monument, calcified. *Please,* he ached to be split open by the softest graze of a whisper. He sat there, refusing to move or eat or sleep. The world no longer gazed. If they did, he was unaware. He wondered when his heart stopped beating; he wondered if they would ever find Julian or if he got away, after all. He wondered and stared and posed all alone, saying nothing.

The last boy on earth sat prettily on his gilded throne; devastated.

CHAPTER 3

Julian was wrapped around his own existence, willing another level of nacre to protect and memorialize him.

You were so small, Julian, why do you want to be smaller?

He remembered being asked that once, by a dear childhood friend or perhaps a tutor, whose name now slipped his mind. But he remembered the answer.

That way I will be the tiniest boy in existence. And when someone loves me, they will know it right away…I will fit in the palm of their hand. On the dandelion seed they blow, I will be the breath of each and every wish, loved.

He sighed. He was, after all, masquerading as a man now. And common men died all the time. What was a common man here? Well, what were they all *not* like? They were not like Vern. That was a start. They did not have the security or the glamor to preserve themselves in gold, and seldom did.

"…Awake?" He heard a voice, gruff and brisk with worry. "I am sorry you did not get your golden boy."

Julian tried to focus on the voice; he was handsome. Solid. He did not look anything like Vern. He was quite large, long dirty blond with a beard to match. He had eyes the color of lightning bolts piercing disturbed seas and his broad chest breathed easy, no catarrh or asthmatic wheeze. Above the curve of his full dark lips was a pale scar, centered as though it was a star.

"Pardon me?" Julian said.

"You…really do not remember, do you?"

"Sir," he began, looking around. He was surrounded by fine pillars carved of coral, posts for a bed plush with thick, blood-red quilts. He swung his legs

15

over, noting one was bandaged. As he straightened himself out, he felt the floor beneath him sway; the other man caught a cup before it slipped off the bedside table.

"We are on a ship," he stated, dumb with shock. "We sail beneath the waves!"

"Yes."

"You…do not know him, do you?"

"The person you keep referring to? No, I cannot say that I do. You kept mumbling about 'a boy with a heart as hard as gold.'" He sat down in an armchair across from the bed. "I am Adrian, by the way. You know that gold is not that hard, right? Even human teeth can dent it. Mine do."

He smiled to demonstrate. A gold tooth with a ruby inset glinted its welcome at Julian.

"I am…" he paused in a panic. *Do not say Joules. Do not say Julian. Say something, anything else!*

"Well, you are *Sebastian*. You told me as much."

Adrian was trying to be helpful, concerned wrinkle creasing his forehead like the title page of a book; he thought Julian had forgotten. Julian laughed it off.

"Ah…yes. That is right."

He peered into the looking glass catty-corner to the bed. It was encrusted with giant black pearls, still embedded in their luxuriant shells. All real. Julian examined his complexion. He was a shade paler from fright and his curls were unruly and frizzy. Most of his physical change seemed to come from injury, the bandages all around his torso and upper leg, and yet…he felt different somehow. He felt *shipwrecked*. He bared teeth to his reflection, not caring if the other man could see. They were sharp as needles. *Enough hiding!*

"So, good man, er, *Adrian*, what happened to me?" he said with a brusque shake of his head. He looked right into Adrian's eyes. He would not back down.

Closer up, the scar above Adrian's lip curved like a fish hook. He stood, much taller than Julian from his sickbed, but seemed to be uneven somehow. At first, Julian thought it was the nature of one of his legs, a weathered wooden thing—but he stood straight. There was something else to it, like looking at a double image; he could imagine Adrian younger, sweet-faced and churlish, yet he could also imagine him ancient and monstrous, without a definable shape at all…

"You were being dragged to a dock," he began matter-of-factly. "Men, guards I think, were dragging you, bound and limp. I thought they had killed you because you did not struggle. Then I thought you were playing dead, but they pushed you over and you did not resurface…I fished you out and brought you aboard.."

Julian tried to take everything in, horror and confusion ebbing under his trying to make sense of anything.

"Why did you help me?"

"Because they are utter barge rats. They work for Olive Branch, beauty company run by his nibs." Adrian rolled his eyes. "I am surprised they did not want you for different reasons."

"Different reasons?" Julian's voice faltered, alarmed.

Adrian let his gaze linger. He said nothing. Julian felt his cheeks flush.

"Mining for beauty…using their proprietary methods," Adrian offered after a while.

But Vern might be in trouble…No, he decided. Vern was not ever in trouble; he was always the *cause*. Now Julian had made himself known out of some dullard protective impulse, and *he* was the one who was in trouble.

"I do not see it that way," he said, wobbling back to the bed. His throat was parched. *Water*. He needed to drink it down. He needed to be surrounded by it. He would re-drown himself if he had to!

He grabbed the elegant glass before him and poured from a crystal vase which would have been better suited in a castle than anywhere it could have been mistaken for a chamber pot. Swallowing felt a herculean task…Yet even that, somehow, was also a relief.

"Is it safe? No tricks?"

"Of course it is safe." Adrian blinked, having the gall to look hurt. "And besides, why the devil aren't ye resting?"

"Rest won't mend me, I need…"

To throw myself back overboard.

"Look, I see you and I are from very, *very* different worlds but those people, you do not understand. I do not believe you have ever met them. They are powerful beyond belief *and, and…*"

"Spit it *out* man. I was a journalist before this, I have heard woolier yarns from saltier sailors. I can handle it."

"You were not breathing and then…there is no getting around it. I pulled a dead thing onto my ship. I expected to give you last rites as is the Captain's burden, take your boots and rings as is a pirate's burden, and throw you back over. You had no pulse. Then your wounds closed as though you got into a scuffle, not even a swordfight. Care to explain that? Creatures do *not* simply self-resurrect here. My men do not. I know even the spryest boys on my crew do not. Undying is one thing, but…"

"I made a wish when I fell into the sea. Perhaps, someone, somewhere, made the same wish, and it came true…Or maybe I am composed of the sea now. And it is the sea's wish that commands."

How many Waterhouses and De Morgans and Ettys could he pore over—but he had never seen a sailor who had drowned a siren instead.

He assessed Adrian's ship once more. Its walls twisted like the inside of a sea-flower, wide and deep teal. Everything about its filigree-adorned surface, the fresh paint on the walls, the bespoke sleigh bed and abalone writing desk, the gilded books and oil paintings, were all things of pure luxury. And yet, there was a darkness…He took a deep breath and Looked. He loathed the Looking. Sometimes, it made his head ache terribly. Sometimes, it sent him seizing until he passed out. Other times, it led to injuries like his torso, his leg. Still, he had to know. A dim glow emitted in front of his eyes, pale cornflower and warm and quite beautiful:

18

"You were a curiosity to this Eric, and never more than that, though you thought he wanted more, that you were protected by some errant desire of his. You realized your folly after you learned how dangerous he was. You fled with your life and nearly nothing else. There was a price for the body you so wanted to give back. Your body wraps around and is infinite. towering. horrifying. There *is* something else. You…are of the sea. You smell of jasmine and irises. Just like, like—wait. Oh! Did you say *boys?*"

Adrian did not move.

"What did you just say?" he retorted between grit teeth. His shaking hand touched the hilt of his sword.

Julian felt afraid, suddenly, but moved past the feeling.

"No, you misunderstand. There is no time for fussing and fighting. If there was time to waste, I would have drawn a sword at the first and we would now be engaged in the sweetest swordplay rather than these tiresome orisons. I do not even remember half of what I said, it does not work that way, so please, *please* answer me."

"Yes, aplenty!"

"You said creatures, men, and boys…Such as myself?"

Boys? he wondered. *And how am I breathing, after all?*

"There is many a boy under the sea, though none are like you! *You* are a terror! I hardly think there is another like you in this whole universe."

From Adrian's lips, it was not a compliment.

"And where in this wide, wonderful universe are we?"

"As you said before, we sail underneath the waves."

Julian smiled. For the first time in a while, he felt disbelief in kindness.

I could go home, he thought, tears brimming to his eyes.

Adrian was no longer sitting in his chair, so content.

"You have some explaining to do," he stated. He moved his hand away from his sword, but that did not make him any less fearsome. Julian had Seen him slice for tiny transgressions and slights.

"Adrian, I must apologize—Any strange gifts I possess can be explained,

I assure you."

"Aye, you are an *excellent* liar."

"It is no lie; this is not where I last woke up. But it is a wider world. Safer, even."

"I do not quite understand."

"You go to The Shallows sometimes–that space of dirty grey waters over-wrought with trading ports, hollowed-out moss-rock dwellings, and dead coral repurposed for other means. You peek up there to The Above, do not you?"

"Occasionally," he mumbled.

"It is only my twin who is in such danger," Julian continued. "And my twin is also in no danger. He is a perfect fit in whatever world he chooses. He is a coward at heart. A *bloody* one."

"Your twin?"

"I…cannot say. Surely he has perished. Or turned into something else for his punishment. And if he has not, all the more grief for us."

"Would you not grieve for a boy whose very likeness was on your dying lips?"

Julian sighed. The broken-hearted were the best company for such af-fairs—but could he trust him?

"Loving someone too purely…it does you no good. Let's say you do. Let's say you follow love everywhere, even to the most dangerous and lofty places—and then love leaves you to drown, what then?"

"Are you sure you did not tangle with Eric?" Adrian raised an eyebrow.

Julian laughed good-naturedly. The scene before him was clear now.

"I am quite sure. I did not know him," he said. "Or think to love him, like you did."

"How…?"

"The Sight I am gifted with has come with a terrible price. As do other things. My twin…"

"Is your twin your true brother?"

20

"Of course. We were even born the same way. I wanted to bring him back here. I wanted to make sure he was alright. He was dealing with some pernicious folks from The Above."

"What would they want with him?"

"He marketed himself as the last of our kind in The Above."

"Why would he ever want to go there?"

"I do not know."

"But you are here."

"So I am, and that's where the problems begin," he faltered, wondering how to explain. "I think he washed up on shore by accident but then wanted to go home and could not. He wanted to get lost in The Below and took a wrong turn and…he must have been terrified. Or so I thought. I was looking for him. He was…different when I found him. He wanted fame and to capitalize on his beauty and whatnot. He could twist things and make them his own. I thought he was being preyed upon, but now I see…he was preying upon others. Down here, I shudder to think of what he is capable."

"He is very powerful?"

"Yes. He is like me, in some ways."

"In some ways?"

"He does not believe in…in what I believe. Not anymore, at least. He does not have Sight the way I do. Though, he is very gifted. No one knew when I was younger that I could…" Julian looked at his hands. He inhaled, once, twice. Then he started fresh. "He does not know how to use a sword because he never thought he needed that kind of protecting. Not like me. I have never felt safe. Not once in my life up there."

"But, you did not learn to fight up there?"

"Something in me yearned for it. I wanted to learn to wield as I wanted to learn Latin and French and Portuguese. It is in my birthright to know."

Adrian took off his coat. In a dark green shirt and neat black trousers, he was tanned and strong and really…he was just a man. The observation made something in Julian's chest ache.

Adrian reached out and poured more water. It was filled with little camo-mile flowers and petal-like cubes of ice suspending tart pomegranate seeds. Lingering, he placed the glass into his hand before sitting beside the exquisite writing desk that overflowed with ornate stationery. Ink ran in blackest lagoons of regret, swirling from where the moonshell design of sad blues and opals ended.

"Are you afraid of me, boy?"

"Sir, I hardly know you…"

"I see," he replied. "But from what you have gleaned of me…am I worthy of your company?"

"I *promise* you I do not intend to pry. I am a bit rusty and went too far. Nothing could move me from this ship. Perhaps my stars shine darkly over me, but…I would like to find the place I am thinking of. With or without him."

I think I have remembered where I am from. A little. After all this, it would be a simple and profound joy to return…

"Keen on staying?"

"Yes, sir."

"Would you like to be an apprentice—" at the same time Julian blurted out "cabin boy" and Adrian laughed. It was a full, rich sound. It bellowed.

"An apprentice it is then. When you are fit to stand for more than a minute or two."

"I…alright." Julian agreed. For where else did he have to be? For once, what was expected of him, whether it be others or his own moral compass? Here was someone who did not wish to throw him to the wolves. He had that, for now. It was more than enough.

"I have one more question, if I may."

"Please."

"You spoke about mirrors in your fits? Should I cover ours? Something about 'finding another or fracturing…'"

"I do not think so. I was mostly concerned with him. My twin, who

22

is now long lost amongst The Above—how do I explain? My twin could feel what I could feel, sometimes, or I could feel what they feel rather…but when they died, I did not. And when we were young, we were told that--" he stumbled, unremembering. "That if the person or persons someone loves no longer loves them, it is a kind of death. So, I must be cut off. Cut up. Unmirrored. Shattered. yet…I did not shatter. In fact, I feel stronger than ever. I feel like…me."

"Can that bond ever be restored?"

"No."

"Can it…ever be made again? Or be…wrong? forged? stolen?" he asked, a tinge of something in his voice Julian did not recognize.

"I doubt it. I do not know. Besides, my twin…he thinks we are from another planet. Not quite. We are from the sea! I did not have the heart to tell him, I could not. You lose your memory, and you think 'ah, the stars, how beautiful!' But crashing does not work like that: The world is beautiful because we are truly from it."

"The sea is another planet, is it not?"

"In a way. But he is mistaken, and he thinks we are from up *there*," he waved a hand to demonstrate, half-heartedly. "I imagine there's things he cannot handle in reality. The Above…it is so much simpler than The Below. Base and coarse and miserable."

"The Endless Deep?" He sat down next to Julian. Julian did not mind at all.

"Mhm. I bet you have seen things. Creatures that can turn into other things, surely?"

"Evil things that masquerade as lovely ones. I should let you rest now."

"No! Tell me. Please. I want to know what I have missed since being away. My useless excursion did nothing for me, after all. I can hardly remember, and pray it all comes back."

Adrian rose to dim the sun panel. He did not leave. Instead, he went to the abalone writing desk, swirled in elusive blacks and blues, ending where the ink stains began. It was exquisite as it was dark; its scrivener almost seemed a part of it in the gloam of the light. From there, he picked up a large Captain's log as if ready to explain a steady routine. The prospect of steady work and a new life to throw himself into excited Julian greatly. Over the edge of the page, Julian could see a shadow-hewn sketch of someone…

"Even if there is someone else just as you are," he said, flipping to another page with haste. His tone changed, and he avoided Julian's eyes. "You must believe me when I say this: I have *never* seen someone like you…at least, not since I was quite young."

A fragment of *something* flashed through Julian's head: *One of Adrian's thoughts? A dream, or a memory?*

The phrase itself was clear enough though:

Won't you call me, Joules, like before? he almost said, taking every ounce of composure to stop himself.

Julian pursed his lips and said nothing. He listened to the Captain with patience, anticipating the water-logged night ahead.

CHAPTER 4

There were lucrative opportunities under the sea, for those who could suppress the full body shudder at five hundred and forty-six fathoms. That was where the sun became a stranger and one's eyes could not adjust from the lack.

Pierre was not like his plants; he had not ever been a sun-lover and thought nothing of leaving the Shallows for voyaging and wages. He grew up in Eaumarsailles, shimmering kelp vineyards and sea-side surrounding his cottage in The Below. There, he perfected the art of germination before he could perfect a love letter.

This was much better. The ship made its own sunlight in helpful lamp panels that resembled terrestrial greenhouses and the phosphorescent hallways. For a true-blue deep-sea fish, the Captain had a real feeling for illumination and its necessity. This gig was nothing like other barges Pierre had found himself on, the gloomy and cheaply powered mining and extraction rigs deep in the aphotic. Pierre had done catering for miners for five cold dark years and had been two seconds from running loony into the decompression chambers without a helmet the whole time. Nowadays, whenever Pierre felt claustrophobic, shut up in the premature tomb that was the ocean, he could retreat to his impossible orange grove, hide in a hammock plant and let its psychotropic slime give him meadows and breeze and the voice of a friend…

Someone unzipped his hammock and he blinked the goo from his eyelashes before glaring at the intruder.

"*Poisson vipére!*" he said. "I was watching my stories."

"Sorry, Pierre."

Ernest did not *seem* sorry, but he was excited.

"Here for your pigments?" he asked, his strong freckled arm fishing into the leaf-strewn wooden crates for Ernest's latest whim.

Ernest's slit pupils expanded at the prospect of new indigo. He could see colors in colors that Pierre could not even dream, even with the hallucinogens at his fingertips.

"You know, I never did hear of people with color emergencies before I met you and Pericles."

"We are illuminating the manuscripts," Ernest explained. "So the emergency is inherent. I woke up with an adorable critter in my head who was born for marginalia..."

Pierre liked the art talk on this skiff, the way the whole crew contended with idleness and stress with impossible feats of creation. Pericles and Ernest churned out books, paintings, and restored artifacts, which they wrapped in silky waterproof packages and buoyed to the surface for a king's fee. They made everything using compressed boxes of double walled glass with holes for rubber gloves, as though a book were a premature mammalian. *A true labor of love,* he thought, *and they would not be able to do it if they were on any other ship.*

It was worth dealing with the other stuff, the unsavory side of the business—all of it was worth it for the true freedom of this life. Though lately...

"Dimitri and the Captain are still into it," Ernest sighed.

"I thought Shallows-leave was going to straighten some of that out," Pierre said, concern flitting through some of the kelp that grew along his arms, and up the back of his tensed neck. He wasn't ancient, but he sure felt older than the Captain and the navigator, who at each other's throats, in every literal and figurative application.

"They get out from under each other's feet and then it is all rose-blooming and honeymoon again with those two!" In Pierre's ad hoc capacity as medic he had mended many a broken bone from one of their famous fights.

Ernest shook his head in agreement. He gathered his tail with worry.

"Shallows-leave made it *worse* this time. Henry told me the whole thing when he came by with Pericles' lunchbox. Batiste did not come back from The Shallows with everyone else. Captain gave him a *task* the first day they made port without telling anyone. Dimitri feels punished."

"Why punished?"

"They have a," Ernest paused. "*Crush* sounds juvenile, it is really something you have to see to believe, the navigator was a couple bouquets short of courting the armorer in the old fashion. And this was not like the other ones. At least I do not think so. But now…"

"I did see some of that. It was cute," Pierre said with practiced blandness, glancing at the unfinished bouquets in the florist fridge. Best to get rid of them so Dimitri would not see them on their next visit, perhaps dry them for some stock paper.

"And there's something else. Apparently, the Captain went fishing."

"What? That does not sound like him, he's cold as anything…"

"He went *fishing*," Ernest insisted, "and he got a bite. So now there is *someone* in Batiste's room and…"

"I should have jumped ship with *Batiste*," Pierre groaned. "Dimitri is going to steer us all right into a mountain! Some navigator!"

"Precisely." Ernest looked gleeful for someone who was facing certain death. "You should have *seen* them at breakfast. Dimitri brandishing the samovar they reserve for Captain's ashes, Captain standing with espresso all over his shirt. Not a word out of either of them. *Glaring.* Nobody dared get a danish until Vico ran in and stole the whole plate."

"Spectacular. Can't have a single normal day on this ship, not even a fucking danish. Thanks for filling me in. You got everything you need, Ernest? Indigo, brush-plants? Whatever is left of my morning mood?"

"Do you have more ultraviolet mushrooms? My old ones are fading," Ernest requested. His Endless Deep deadpan was not penetrated by Pierre's sarcasm at all. Ernest was, after all, from a coral-reef that had seen even less sun than the Captain's bluest moods. This no-doubt was as frightening as amusing to him and Pericles.

Pierre plucked some of the mushrooms from a log, putting on gloves first so he would not touch the rotting wood. He sprayed them in a protective coating and then stuck them in Ernest's basket. He waved Ernest away, disposing of his gloves after and trying to clear his head of hurtful thoughts. Opening the florist fridge, he removed the bouquets from their buckets, and stuck them in the garbage port, closing the lid with a final clatter.

Over him, Pierre could already hear raised voices and sighed. *So much for peace and quiet.*

It was one thing to scuffle now and again with the closest thing to a first mate the Captain had; there were instances where differences of opinion could be articulated with a quick fight, or fuck, especially this far below the surface. The Endless Deep was filled with bioluminescent temperaments those closer to the sun had a hard time dealing with; endless riches, beauty, exploration, art…such passionate and extravagant tempests were naturally made. Most could not take a swim around the ship and come back with a clear head in the occasion of distemper. These were the creatures of opera and ballet made quotidian, the very paintings Pericles and Ernest loved to frame.

The sad truth was for the Captain and Dimitri, the fights were not achieving a more fragrant vine of metaphor, they were climbing into tsunamis without release…

He could tell this latest 'fishing expedition' was going to break a lot more than glass.

Something had changed.

Pierre left the fridge and took a deep breath, taking in the smell of orange blossoms and mulch. He would be alright. The ship was in excellent shape and the waters were fair to sail on. There was still time for the morning to redeem itself. He had a couple hours before potions were to be poured and seafruits checked for holding temps. He hopped back into his hammock, whispering a calming mantra to himself before the voices beyond the tendrils of lotus and sugar kelp unfurled, continuing the mesmerizing leaves of melody for him.

CHAPTER 5

It was a bleak scream that woke Adrian from an unwanted rest. He jerked from the table in the canteen he had rested his head on and looked around, gritting his teeth from the usual pain in the leg. On checking his stump that morning, the dressings were soaked with blood and there were fresh splinters from the prosthetic, even though it had been painstakingly varnished.

Evil old thing, a familiar voice in Adrian's ear whispered, and he shook his head, irritated. *Better off as driftwood. Maybe you are, too.*

He would go to Pierre for the compound he had devised, meant to promote fibrination and synergy between wooden leg and his waterborne self. A month under the sun and regular vitamins meant scurvy could not be the cause. The leg was not the issue, it could not be. Perhaps he was just getting older.

Or perhaps this was a punishment. Punishment for *what*, Adrian could not admit, and when he tried to think of it his head turned into a writhing mass of logical knots he could not cut. All Adrian knew was though he sailed an endless voyage and was loath to make port, something of his past had found him at last. Perhaps his fresh wounds presaged the blood that should follow.

He had left his Captain's quarters long ago, no huge loss as he could not remember the last time he had spent a night there. The privilege of sleeping through until morning was forfeit along with the luxury of sleeping in the nude. The Captain was always to be dressed and alert, for the sake of the crew. Especially with mysterious fish aboard.

Adrian pursed his lips, made eye contact with Dimitri, his beast of a navigator, who slept about as easy as he did.

"Strange passenger," Dimitri muttered, jerking their head down the hall. They had a cut above their eye from their fight this morning, where Adrian had hit them before taking off his rings, but they were not spoiling for another round. Adrian was grateful; if Dimitri fought him in this moment, he was not sure he could best them. "*Your* guest, Captain."

"My guest, on my ship," Adrian agreed with good cheer. "All appears to be as it should."

Dimitri's brow was furrowed in a thick line of concentration over their messy worktable. Their stocky frame gave the impression of a guard or enforcer, yet they had taken to mapmaking their whole life, nearly a divine vocation. Quiet and nomadic, Adrian could place them by the leather-like patches of turtle shell adorning their flesh, but knew nothing of the lad's lineage from their own lips. They rolled the sleeves of their navy-blue tunic over and over, stimming on the fabric with alarmed aggravation. Their hair was cut shorter than most other young men these days. Their tattoos crawled up the span of their arms, with a few curious ones on their back.

Adrian thought he knew what a few of them meant, but as for the rest…

"Did you see our course, then?" he asked. They shoved the scroll in his face, pointing at the spot they had pointed to several times that morning.

"Interesting game, to give me the same coordinates as before."

Adrian sighed, exasperated. "We will make it through." Several pots of ink had spilled on Dimitri's desk, never near the maps. Not Dimitri's style. When they joined the crew, they had been newly dispatched from a job as a barge handler for being too unruly, too quick to anger—But now, if Dimitri was not working on maps Adrian almost never saw them.

"So, tell me how the rest of the crew fares?"

"The skeletons you keep, Captain? The catfish and kois? They are all light and easy from such a generous Shallows-leave. The crow's nest is rich with sea stars to gaze at through the gauzy petals of sails on either side, when they are not trifling over their bindings and paints. I am sure the generous salaries push them to work harder."

Adrian frowned. "It is not about making them work harder, it's about making sure everyone can manage while they are here with…"

With nothing, the thought clung to Adrian's head with such sullen rage. *With a monster, on the outskirts of civilization, searching night after night for what? A myth.*

"Did you happen to hear from Batiste?" he asked, ready to leave Dimitri to their own devices. Their shoulders hunched inwards. A scowl as sharp as lightning pursed their lips.

"Batiste, who was that again? Red hair, scarlet temper? The armorer, with his fabrics and forge? Returned to tear down half the ship? Not bloody likely."

"Yes, well…if he should reach out, we will have a new crew member who needs a first fitting. And a sword."

"I will, if he ever bothers to write. I'm busy ensuring you do not collapse the ship into another deep—"

Adrian closed the door. He could still hear Dimitri's occult and mumbled warnings.

Can't be getting in a damned whirlpool. Again! And who got blamed for that, Captain or navigator? You want to damage the hull until we are stuck to the bottom of the ocean?

Adrian walked down the corridor. He had been sailing for seven years now; it felt like a minor eternity. Each of his crew had signed on for some reason or another; he was a fair enough Captain, and he liked to think that most of them respected him. However, no one knew *why* they were sailing, or where their final port was. He had promised them riches, but never had the heart to tell them what he sought. Perhaps Dimitri suspected, but everyone else either did not know or did not care. Adrian haggled and bargained and played shipwright so the vessel was fit to sail. It did not matter how hard the life was or how unfit he felt to command. He knew it was this or swim sunwards until he hit the surface, lay out on the sand until he could no longer breathe.

Adrian made a few more rounds on the ship, passing the crow's nest and the hammocks, the hull and the upper decks. Everyone was either working as they should in these midnight hours, or asleep. Maybe the noise had been in his head. He knew it could not be Julian, fresh from fever and working on some middling task, perhaps a spyglass that needed fixing...

*But now...*Adrian tried to put the past few days together without luck. *How was any of this possible? How is he even here? He is supposed to be long dead, long mourned, but does not seem to remember...*

The bandages around his waist were off and the scales were iridescent as they were impossible. Still, the boy did not fathom his own depths...

He heard that same bleak scream and quickened his pace and turned to the quarters where the boy had been.

Julian writhed on the bed as though seized by some invisible storm, making the bed shake with his narrow frame.

Automatically, Adrian rushed to his side.

"You promised! You fucking promised me, you little traitor!" Julian screamed, with wide, unseeing eyes. The centers had gone from glittering brown, to inky black.

"What?"

Julian's whole body jerked up. In a moment, his limbs twisted, his mouth hung open as though he were capable of being drowned.

Adrian went to shake him awake, when his eyes opened once more, rolling back, then blinking.

"A-adrian?" Julian whispered. He reached out, as though seeing for the first time. "That you?"

Adrian protectively bracketed the boy's knees and waist with his arms until Julian spoke again.

"I am fine, the pain is excruciating—but otherwise, I am *fine.*"

"You might want to tell me what the hell is going on."

Julian motioned to the bedside table. He fumbled for a glass of water, until Adrian poured the rest and placed it in his hands. He was about to finish the sentence when the glass dropped from his grasp, and he kneeled over the side of the bed into a washing basin and wretched. The awful sensation that he was choking on his own vomit was enough to make Adrian hover like a nurse. Yet, the worse the shaking became, the straighter Julian stood. He waved him away, irritated.

"Your navigator is lost and I am…ill."

He clutched the basin as though it was a child's toy. When Adrian reached out a hand, Julian grasped at it, pulling him closer. Adrian stroked the boy's hair.

"I am assuming someone aboard feels as though you have reached to fiddle with their gullet. You can reach into people's heads with this marvelous Sight, and it wrecks you!"

"Do not talk to me about being wrecked! I thought I would die up *there*." He clung to Adrian's side; his tears fell like so many pearls. "They did not know *anything*. I thought I would go mad; avoiding doctors day and night, another machine, another IV full of blood–all pointless, I am breaking down from how the air touched my lungs! Down here, it might get better—at least, someone would know how to care for me. At least, I thought…"

Julian struggled for words.

"How did you get that limp?" Adrian asked, seeing more of the shimmering scales, the webbed skin at his hips under the billowing nightshirt he was trying to sleep in.

"I do not know." He thought of Vern, and wanted to ask Adrian suddenly, about his leg, but his mouth went dry. If Julian asked, he worried he would find out more than he wanted.

"You said you thought your twin was not gifted like this. But you supposed you were not the only one, regardless?"

"Yes!" Julian moaned, fear gripping his stomach. He reached for the basin, pushing Adrian away as if he had burned him. "I do not understand it fully, too shaken from everything to try. You think me to be a rational creature, that might go on in this life forever content without answer! Without

34

self! What is the meaning of all this!"

Adrian took the basin from his hands and caught the boy as he crumpled forward. Julian sobbed into his chest, not caring who could see. The waves of boytears came harsher and Adrian, after muttering every consolation, could not think of another thing to do. He kissed Julian's forehead, pressing his hands to his cheeks before he realized he was crying, too.

"You must stop this, Julian," he whispered gruffly, giving up the pretense of the moniker 'Sebastian.' *Julian* was the name that had come to him from his shallow dreams, and he believed it like a memory. "I want to help, I want to. Show me how."

Julian lifted his arms and pushed Adrian away with enough force that he felt as though he was wicked; *had he harmed him? Had he come too close?* He moved away as quickly as he could.

Julian was about to say something, when a heavy swing to the door startled them both. Dimitri stood there, face drained of all color. As they took in the scene, their eyes held a sharp, dangerous quality Adrian had hired them for, and now despised.

"Your *guest,* Captain," they said, looking right at Julian. "Has some explaining to do."

CHAPTER 6

Vern's long eyelids fluttered open. He felt cold–too damned cold!

"I have always wanted a statue of a handsome dead boy. And now I have the last one!"

The sentence stuck in his head. Now fully awake, he remembered things in flashes, which came back too willingly: someone had put a bounty on his head–then someone rescued him! Someone much more adept than Julian! That idiot boy! Vern had been doing *so well*, Above and away the Depths which had been Julian's fucking farrago—he had been free! These people wanted to help him. They were slippery but so was he!

And he was *home*. He stretched from the wide, sleek bed with its yawning mouth of white sheets. The room looked more medical than bedroom, yet it still was comfortable.

A man with black hair long as his confidence and wicked eyes was watching the ocean outside. He turned when he heard Vern's slight movements, smiling wide.

"Welcome back," he said. "Name's Eric. I've been your technician, or specialist or whatever. Not a doctor though, definitely not a doctor. I'm here to make sure that your passage from one element to another was, er, successful."

"Enchanted," Vern said, the timbre of his voice hushed, but ever so sweet.

This will be easy, he thought. *I already know what he wants.*

"I heard that you were trapped Above. A rough deal, to be sure," Eric continued. "Perhaps we could help?"

"Such a grand rescue, and no strings attached?"

"Rescue…" Eric chewed the word over. "Well, that's one way to put it."

36

"How else do you like to put things?"

"Would you agree to a partnership?"

"Of course." Vern said smoothly. The language of commerce was as common in The Above as the witticisms and wooings down Below. Vern took comfort in it; here people always spoke their minds instead of layering it with poetry. "So read me the pretty terms and conditions, Eric, but first, do tell me where I am."

"You are back in The Below."

"The palace?" he asked, a little confused.

"No, this is my ship—I'm head of OBCO, one of the largest trade conglomerates in all the seven seas."

Eric's teeth seemed almost as though they'd been sharpened, a little less *sea* and a little more *monster*. Vern would deal with that. He was too busy taking in the details of his suite; high, marbled pillars and glass cases filled with medical products, displayed like they were precious and ancient. In the adjoining room, everything looked a little less clinical, but no more controlled.

"And what is it you trade in?"

"The last thing worth getting in business for: Beauty, with a capital B. No one here is worried too much about extending life, so it's important to keep up with the other stuff, quality of life, looking like you've got time…"

"Of course." Vern nodded along. He had played his cards right Above, disgraced or not, he had come back valuable.

"There's a couple forms which you'll need to sign for me, but you'll be our spokesperson, essentially."

"Essentially?"

"There's a few other, trifling tasks." He shrugged it off, but his left cheek twitched. Vern grinned.

"Contractual trifles nonetheless," he said, and swung his legs off the table. "I am not going anywhere, and I have nothing better to do than hear you explain it."

"You'll have to come with us to procure some of the materials we need for…but not for testing purposes, of course! We operate humanely, well we *are* certified humane in any case," Eric said, hastening to explain with the flusterment of someone who was never asked to elaborate. "Procurement is a particular *challenge* in my field. Different environments and far-flung cultures which are difficult to navigate. You know beauty, appearance is everything, and first impressions are…well. I have lost many partnerships to careless faux pas; my expeditions end in catastrophe for my PR and research departments both. I *know* that you would be an asset in civilization or in the wild. *You* are special that way."

"Do not flatter, I have had enough of that for an age and you have not the touch. I am not afraid of hard work, if that is what you mean by procurement. And, to be clear—I am a contractor, free to come and go as I please. My compensation will be…" Vern broke off, thinking of a proper pied de terre, and acreage. Addictive land. "Yes, my own landholdings, and a percentile of profit from items procured with my aid."

Eric scribbled furiously in his notepad. "A finder's fee," he said, biting the end of his expensive ballpoint pen while he mulled it over. "Yes, I think there's language allowing for this in the contract already, but I will put a clause in. Forty percent sound fair?"

"Do not insult me, dear—that must be worse than the flattery. Seventy percent, to be dispensed each quarter regardless of actual profit," Vern countered. Eric was doing the sums with such intensity they were almost visible over his head. Vern held up a languid hand to explain in plainer talk. "Seventy cents on the dollar without an advance. If I bring you something worthless then I eat the risk."

"Oh, yes, that is…more than fair."

"Wonderful."

Eric smiled, no doubt that he had run this right, somehow. Vern was better at understanding the men of Above now, what he needed to say to make them feel strong and stay in the superior position. He looked over the contract and turned over the thick sheaf of paper out of a force of habit, to make sure nothing else was written on the back.

"I will not sign of course," he shrugged, to Eric's profound confusion. "Well, I never leave my name in my own hand, 'tis beneath me. It will be enough to take me at my word, yes? The word of a Prince?"

"I'd have to run that by Legal."

"That would be a grave insult, where I am from."

"Well, *someone* ought to sign the contract, surely."

"You have *your* pen. And there's the dotted line," Vern prompted, a little condescending. He watched the Adam's apple bob in Eric's throat, and blinked slowly, realizing he was possibly on the verge of something else the man wanted, not in the contract or their conversation. "And then you can tell me all about the far-flung voyages and rich foreign people we are to meet, darling."

"Darling?"

"Sure," Vern agreed, unable to divine what he was agreeing to. "But only if you sign."

Apparently, that was all Eric needed, and he flourished his signature on the dotted line without hesitation.

"I am excited to do business with you," Vern assured. "And I feel so much better even since moments ago. Whither are we bound?"

"Deep Below, for a spell. There's a shell bed in the Abyss we'd long been trying to locate, and now my best oceanographers have at last confirmed the location beyond a reasonable doubt. Northeast, under an auspicious star. Hidden from modern detection, but using the old ways, one can barely discern the shadow of its own obscurity. We are putting a crew together, and soon we will be able to descend. There's a couple of specialists joining us from the nearest port before the voyage."

"A pearl," Vern repeated, trying not to betray the sudden panic that clung his heart. Eric looked put out.

"It is not just any pearl, though I know someone of your standing must have seen many remarkable gems. This pearl is the root of all things that

39

interest me. Beauty and valor, youth and dazzlement. And if I can synthesize it, then I change the world. We, I mean, as partners. We change the world."

Vern swallowed. He did not say *I feel very, very ill.* He would take care of that on his own. He had work to do—he had to figure out how to get off the ship immediately.

CHAPTER 7

It occurred to Vern, after the sudden feeling of mortality which gripped his heart at the mention of a pearl, he was free to move about the ship, but that did not mean he was free. He had spent hours stalking the hallways in his pajamas like Little Nemo, far enough from civilization that it would not matter if he was seen clawing at the walls like a trapped animal. He could manage his own image afterwards, but escape was the priority, not doing it with style or grace. He could not be like *Joules*, so resigned to some sort of poetic destruction; stark, beautiful, so tragic in its finality.

He liked the idea of living! What was so wrong with that?

On Vern's third turn around the research ship's common corridors, chewing a piece of breadfruit in his hand, he finally saw what he was looking for. More accurately, he heard it.

"Excuse me, nice doctor, perhaps you could help me?" he asked a passing scientist, gesturing above his head with a segment of mangled breadfruit. The scientist paused, thrown by being addressed as though he was a safe adult. "Why does the ship groan like that?"

The scientist blanched, and hurried away from the childish smile in Vern's eyes.

Vern could see the way the walls concaved at soldered seams, he could see haphazard posted signs, in all big letters so even Vern's eyes, which tended to shuffle words and make new, could not mistake them: NO COMPRESSED GASSES IN THIS AREA. NO RUNNING IN THIS AREA. NO RADIO OR SHOUTING IN THIS AREA.

DO NOT TOUCH THE WALLS.

DO NOT TOUCH THE WALLS.
DO NOT TOUCH THE WALLS.

"Do not *touch* the walls," Vern repeated, looking at his outstretched hand and imagining the effect of sudden brutal decompression on his newly fleshy body. He was already accustomed to the pressure of the deep sea, but he half-recalled a tutor explaining about gas conversion, the frailties of bodies in the elements. It was a big risk, but a high reward, which made it a *Joules* plan. He should resist it, but still… "Do *not* touch the walls. Do not touch the *walls*."

"It is good advice."

Vern turned around and looked at Eric.

"Why can't I touch the walls?"

Eric waved the question away.

"No shipwright am I. I just pay the bills. It is an experimental craft."

You pay the bills, Vern thought skeptically, and looked up at the high ceiling, looking for a hairline fracture, listening to the deep groan of the oceans pushing down on them like a headache. *Do you?*

"If that is the sound this vessel makes before we have even left sunlight's reach," Vern pondered, charmingly. "Why, we will not find pearls. And nobody will find us. How inconvenient."

Eric fiddled with a ring on his left hand, a black desiccated tentacle wrapped around his index. Vern found he was looking at it quite a lot, despite his manners. He had never seen such a ring before and wondered if it was made of real octopus. Barbaric if it was, and in bad taste to wear in front of an undersea Prince regardless of its material. Whatever monster he had found himself accompanying leagues below the sea, it was clear that he could not stay.

"Inconvenient? For…?"

"Debt collectors," Vern pouted. Eric stopped spinning that unnerving ring. Vern wanted to rip it off him, finger and all. "Do not look so shocked."

"I suppose I am surprised that you would think such a thing of me. That I would be dishonest in our dealings."

"I am often dishonest," Vern admitted. "I would be a fool not to expect it from others. Where is your diving bell? I like an intimate honeymoon. Granted, the location could be better."

"Diving bell? There is no diving bell."

"How do you plan to escape then?"

Eric looked surprised, and then Vern truly felt fear.

"There is no *escape* from this, beautiful boy. I am ruined by immoderate dealings and even if my body cannot be found, the debt collectors would need to find it to close the case. So, death, entombed with my treasures, and my work."

"That is very *boring*," Vern sighed. "No doubt you think it is profound, but it is so unforgivably boring. I did not agree to death in our contract."

"The science is sound," Eric changed the subject. "That spot, deep in the ocean, has *the* pearl, the ingredient I need to change everything."

"But you ran out of capital," Vern smiled, taking Eric's hand in a false, mothering comfort. "The information came to you too late, when you were still pretending everything was alright. And now your greatest expedition is your tomb. Everything you wanted is inches out of your reach. Or have I missed something, *caro?*"

"I could not have put it better."

"I could have. There's a terrestrial poet who wrote on this subject, but I am not prepared at all, I have forgotten it. I do not eulogize *peasants* anyway." Vern dropped Eric's hand with disdain.

Reddening, Eric opened his mouth to answer, but he was interrupted by a long scraping over the top of the ship. *Not a bad sound, not a sound presaging destruction,* Vern thought, and before he realized it his legs were carrying him up the stairs, slipping in his stocking feet until he found himself in a receiving dock. **DO NOT TOUCH THE WALLS** yelled every sign he passed, and he started banging on them as he ran to the dispatch vessel, no doubt one of the specialists Eric had decided to take with him on his thanatic voyage.

I cannot die now, I am the youngest, Vern thought. *I am no common fish, swimming to the place where I was born just so I can die. And I am not a shabti for this man's tomb. I am not even a commemorative statue, not anymore. I am a Prince, I am a boy. I have people to kiss, I have things to do. I am the youngest, so he must die first. Though I do not plan on that happening to either of us. And besides, I would not know where to go, if it was me first.*

I do not know where to go.

I want my brother.

"Vern," Eric yelled at the bottom of the ramp to the vessel. "Do not *leave* me here."

Vern grimaced at the order and turned the wheel on the hatch. He slipped through the door, letting the doomed specialists pass him with a deep and courteous bow. It felt like the end of a party that had gone too long, and if he kept on telling himself that, he knew he could depart without a scratch.

"I am not leaving you anywhere. When I am gone, you will not be anywhere at all, according to your own wishes. Thank-you for giving me life. Your intentions were monstrous, but I must thank-you anyway. So, thank-you. I am ever so sorry I cannot stay."

Without looking at Eric, Vern shut the door with all his strength and disembarked the doomed research vessel. From his vantage point, he could see her from the outside and could see her name: *INDRA-1*. She looked almost organic, revealed to be deep green when her failing lights flickered from the portholes. She was longer than she was wide, and in her belly, wide motor wheels like a mill's ground with a great noise which must have terrified those inside. She shook like an eel writhing in toxic shock in a brine pool. She had held together for Vern, but she needed to break apart now, too burdened by the mere world to carry out what she was made for.

I am sorry. Vern thought to the ship, hoping she could hear, somehow. *I am the reason you were created. I fear your name will be ubiquitous with disaster and hubris, no -2s or -3s after your line, and I am the unworthy soul who gets to know you were kind.*

Vern found a digital camera on the control panel and shakingly held it at

44

arm's length, taking a picture with his precious eyes closed so he would not seize from the flash. When he opened his eyes again, he had a picture of *IN-DRA-1*, but there was only black ocean before him. He could not see detritus, nor could he hear the vessel's groans. He cried at the control panel, lit up on autopilot and making its way to a safe place above five hundred fathoms. He would have liked to stay, however nonsensical the notion. He missed the noble ship already and felt as lost as she.

As the docking pod lumbered through the deep sea of its own accord, Vern upturned drawers and boxes, looking for food and distraction, trying not to get overwhelmed by the expressionist blurs of memory blooming in his mind.

"I have a brother," he shared with the docking pod. "A twin. Maybe you do too, both built in the factory on the same day? Sorry I came on board so abruptly. With no host gift and a nothing of an introduction to announce myself. I have been a beast, not a boy."

Beeps and whooshes were all Vern received as response, and he beeped too. Finding someone's stash of expensive shoreline snacks, he grazed while looking through a large black museum box, getting crumbs on the contents. There were clothes inside, and a beautiful jewelry piece that he pulled out with sticky hands.

"That is familiar," he mused, looking at the black pearl in the middle of the ornate choker, surrounded by strings of smaller pearls. "Little boat, can you play me a song? I hardly wish to cry, you see. This feels like it should be happy, but I keep feeling things wrong…"

Soft piano piped through the speakers, and he felt less frazzled, studying the black pearl as though trying to place a face. Digging through the remaining clothes, he found they all fit. Some pieces he even remembered wearing, once upon a time.

Perhaps then, this is my trousseau, sent for by Eric before our union in death, Vern thought with a shudder.

The mechanism of *marriage* was a foreign one to him, contained in the sinister penny dreadfuls he devoured when he was Above. Vern remembered that in Illyrial, none could be promised under such duress. In practice, he thought it must be something like the contract Eric showed him. Words that made him a thing, with other things to match. How could he have consented, even in bad faith, even without signing? He felt ashamed. He felt *bad bad bad*.

Vern put on the choker, pulling on a shirt of fishnet and shell after, and then flowing black trousers and matching robe. He felt more like himself now, finally free of itchy satin pajamas, and wandered as much as he could while playing with the pearls around his neck. He found the document which accompanied his trousseau and tried to read it before giving up. He was too tired, and the print was too small—the letters jumped around like shrimp on the reef.

"Little boat, can I have bedtime lights and a song?" he requested. "Can I have soft blankets and a voice which is familiar? Can I have my brother back, and his friends? Can I apologize to them for what happened to me? Can I ever go back or is it all ruined beyond repair?"

The docking pod did not answer, but the lights dimmed, and a little cafe jazz started playing. It was effective in lulling Vern to an uneasy sleep, despite his heavy tears.

When he awoke, there was no more music, and the docking pod was blinking at him. He could feel a drop in temperature which indicated a failure of some kind in the system already spinning its gears for far longer than it was made to do. Vern could sympathize. Systems failure would not be fatal to him in this sort of vessel, which had been turned to hybrid air/water systems before he had even set foot on the craft, nixing the fear of decompression sickness. But he wanted to help the little boat, *INDRA-1* still heavy in his heart. If there was a saltwater leak, corrosion would be intense, nearly immediate, and difficult to correct. He could see the vehicle used electricity, but that did not have to be the case. He could rip out circuits and replace them with saltwater mechanics if it meant a better voyage.

"We will get you home," he murmured. "What hurts?"

"Status report for new user," the computerized voice said. "There's a breach in the fuel reservoir. We are too far below sea level to boot solar back-ups. Hatch integrity is compromised. I am unable to send a homing signal. Autopilot is compromised. Our counterweights are not sufficient to stabilize an upward trajectory against the mass of the sea at this level of submersion."

"That is harrowing, but succinct. Thank you. And how are you feeling?"

"Operating systems are otherwise functional."

"That is wonderful news. And we are still *moving*. We are not going down?"

"I do not understand the question."

Versus the smothering seas, Vern did not think a banker's box of silk and snacks would correct their course, and opening the hatch to jettison ballast seemed foolhardy.

"Let's not worry about that."

"New user, are you passenger or crew?"

"*Cargo* would be more accurate."

"I do not understand."

"Neither do I."

"Would you like music?"

"Yes."

Vern listened to the soothing and generic classical music from somewhere in The Above, shuffling through the banker's boxes which constituted his trousseau. *Despair does not suit you,* he remembered someone saying, could not quite place if it was meant as a compliment or a critique. For now he would take it as truth, and try not to despair.

"Do you know where Illyrial is?" he asked a few hours into the docking pod's uncertain voyage. The computer's silence meant no, he assumed. Shame. If he had been able to chart coordinates, then he would not have minded being sunk to the bottom of the sea. It would have taken an age, but he would have been able to come home, or to the memory of home, would have been able to be set right in his incorrigible ways by people far wiser than he. Perhaps he would have stood a chance of seeing Julian again.

"How do homing signals work?" he asked, after a restless night where all he did was try to read the map included in his trousseau but ended up replicating it perfectly instead. "Why can't you send one? Malfunction or something else?"

"Systems override. Authorized by verified user Duke Eric."

"How can I override the override?" Vern asked, feeling his spine prickle at the unwelcome name.

"Do you know the password?"

"No. But I am a Prince, and a real one at that," Vern grumbled. So, Eric got the last laugh after all; nobody could have left his pity party, even if they'd been fleet of foot and made it into the docking pod and tried to turn around… "What an odious man. At least I have my health."

Vern folded his new map into a binder with the old one. He still could not read it, and knew he was too upset to even try. He pulled the ring from his pocket and looked at it in morbid fascination. This too was familiar, though he could not guess why. There was a name at the tip of his tongue, and the more he studied the ring, the more he was convinced he thought it would come to him. Something to do with Julian maybe, though he was sure Julian would never wear something so upsetting. Not his ring, then but…

The tentacle twitched in his hand and he nearly hurled it across the pod with a shriek.

"No!" he yelled, to the ring or to his own addled mind. He did not like to raise his voice, and said the next part in a hysterical whisper. "No, *thank-you*. Absolutely not! How dare you! Computer, what are the carbon monoxide levels?"

"CO2 is normal. Filtration is not yet compromised."

Vern clamped his lips together to avoid screaming and reexamined the tentacle. He was seeing things, surely, and if he understood that, he could use reason to fix his temporary lapse in sanity. With a deep breath, he tried to recall the earthly art of psychoanalysis. Some of the most entertaining conversations he had in The Above were with the magicians and headshrinkers who asked him about the mother or monster under his bed. He could pray at the altar of cigars and anima if it meant regaining control. The tentacle did not *move*, obviously he just remembered a time where he had seen a tentacle–or *somezing much like a tentacle*, as Doctor Freud-Helsing would surely interject with a waggle of his massive eyebrows. Vern had proceeded to sublimate it onto the sad calcified fragment in his hands, a child-like product of id and *jouissance* or something along those lines. He just wanted Adrian to be here because he was scared and lonely and usually if he could find Adrian he could find…but who was *Adrian*?

"Er…Adrian?" he finally asked after a long confusion that was not helped by extended musings on Winnicott or *différance*, and he prodded the tentacle in his hand. Perhaps it *had* moved?

"Password accepted," the docking pod said. "Homing signal sent."

"Oh, most wonderful," Vern felt more doomed than ever. "Where was this signal sent?"

"Home berth."

Panic gripped him but resisted the urge to ask the docking pod to rescind the signal, too eager was he to live. He felt foolish, as though he had walked into a trap. He certainly had, or worse, sprung a trap for someone else. Either way, he'd made some kind of ruinous indiscretion, blurted out a name which was not his to say. A fool! Once again played for a fool all the while thinking he was *so fucking clever*.

And he would not be going home, would he? If the docking pod wanted to go *up* so badly, he was bound for the surface. He crouched, grasping the ring in his fist and hiding his face in his knees, trying not to vomit or cry.

Ruined it again, he thought. *Have not a clue how not to ruin. Just want to go home.*

Light-headed, Vern asked for carbon monoxide levels. They were dropping now, and the docking pod indicated a decline in breathable oxygen with little to recommend the passenger apart from taking shallow breaths and hoping for help. He curled up and started breathing from his gills to limit his consumption. His nictitating membranes, which he long ago forgot he had, slid over his precious eyes to protect them from irritation, and he tried to summon Princely thoughts.

Against the odds, Vern started to remember. Too little too late, like Eric's trip to the shell bed, but at the very least he had context for his own disaster. Vern remembered he was a Prince, truly, something he had known without remembering before. He once had everything he pleased, but some flaw in his own nature prevented him from taking it, perhaps a crack in the pearl that had birthed him. And he had forgotten, like a fool, everything of worth and all that made him unworthy.

"Despair does not suit you," Julian had said to him once. Vern had not known what it meant then either, and never asked, choosing to brush it aside like a stray eyelash. He never thought to ask for what he needed. It never occurred to him he could *try*.

There was a hiss accompanying oxygenated water, from The Shallows by the stench, pouring in and displacing what was inside. A hand reached in and effortlessly pulled him out, like a cold bar mollusk from the denuded shell. He looked up, confused and hazy, at a man.

"What the fuck?" the man yelled, as though Vern was something unspeakable, and calmed himself. "Do you *speak*, little fishy? Or are you for eating?"

"M'not speaking to *you*," Vern slurred, before his common sense could prevail. He bit his tongue and blood started trickling down his lips, on the man's ugly wellingtons.

"So, where's Eric?"

Annoyed and ashamed by this man's irreverent, hungry stare, Vern flopped to the side and tried to get up. His entire body was seizing still, even as he gasped as much good water as he could. He wanted to swim but he could hardly twitch his fingers.

"Went fishing, and I got a boot," the man grumbled, as though Vern could not hear. "Oh well. We can find some other use for you. You know you look just like that Last Boy on Earth?"

CHAPTER 8

Dimitri stood silhouetted in the door, wounded.

"Why not tell me! I know exactly where to find your, well, your *Batty.*"

Dimitri flushed to the tips of their ears.

"I…" Dimitri stopped themself and shot a venomous look at Adrian. "You! You are out of your *mind*! Every time I think you top yourself, you do something so unspeakably cracked…When were you going to tell me? Or anyone on the ship? Security is lax at the best of times, and your guest is…"

"You know who I am!" Julian cried. He wiped off the remains of his own sick and stood with any poise he could muster. He gave Dimitri a little bow, sick still dripping down his chin, standing prim as a petal.

"Y-your highness, please," Dimitri stuttered, a hint of horror etching into their usually impassive features. They bowed back with wonderful grace. "Of course I know you, how could I not? And how do you, I mean, about *my* friend—"

"How do *you* know? About me?" Julian asked.

"That is quite simple. I shall explain to you over strong coffee, if the hour is agreeable, and—" Dimitri's tone softened a considerable amount.

"Am I the only one here who does not know a single thing that happens on my own ship?" Adrian inquired, offended.

Dimitri looked at Julian, then back at Adrian, hazel eyes crinkling in a slow smile. "I think *so*, Captain."

Julian frowned at him once more–with such disdain!

Adrian collected himself and with a great huff, left them alone.

"He has not told you yet?" Dimitri laughed.

"He is so tight-lipped, it is absurd! I do not think he knows any more than me. Besides, it would be one thing if he were quiet, but the man is loquacious, without saying a thing."

"It is worry, maybe guilt. I think whatever happened to you, he had a hand it in it."

Julian made a little *excuse me* gesture, then washed his face in the filled basin and discarded the rest of the clothes. With a swift fling, he emptied out the vile smelling liquid into the nearest porthole, then closed it.

Dimitri led him out the room and onto the winding decks until they reached a narrow alcove with over-stuffed sapphire velvet armchairs and a pretty white and navy-blue kitchenette.

"Is this the kitchen for the whole ship?"

Dimitri laughed again. It was a lovely sound. Julian wanted to make Dimitri laugh all the time.

"No, this is a humble coffee nook. The Captain cannot stand a day without good coffee," Dimitri explained. He procured a fulsome quartet of madeleines from the icebox. Julian got a whiff of heady coffee and lychee-rose.

Julian sat and watched, giddy, as Dimitri produced a strong, heady cup of espresso. He was so entranced by the spectacle he forgot the drink was meant for him and pushed it away with regret.

"It smells marvelous, but I am afraid I cannot tolerate caffeine. Do you have camomile?"

"I am guessing not a lot has changed about you."

Dimitri poured the remaining hot water into a delicate white cup with a handle carved from blue-purple pearls. The casual glamour of such a cup floored Julian, but he was distracted by the scent of the flowers in the tea. The teabag floated momentarily before sinking to the bottom, and Dimitri slid the teacup over with surprising grace for their strength.

In the moonlight, Julian took in Dimitri's statuesque features. He wanted to reach out and run a hand through the grain of their hair. He wanted to see if the marble would melt into ebb-flow, if he would transform under the right touch…

He wanted to ask about the many gold hoops along one of their ears and the swirling lines of tattoos down their arms. They seemed almost star-like, tangled in some kind of language or floriography Julian could not recognize.

"You, my boy," Dimitri said, taking a sip of the steaming coffee. "Are a Prince. One of two, which I suspect you know."

"The second part, yes. The first…"

"I have charted so much of the sea. I have never been to Illyrial, but…I would know its Prince anywhere."

"Illyrial!" Julian tried to say anything else coherent but was too struck by Dimitri knowing the name of the place in his thoughts.

"Do you know where you stand, in the throne's succession?"

"No, I am afraid I do not. I have a blur where I ought to have my past."

"So like him."

"My twin?"

"My Batty." They looked down into the cup. "*Bastard.*"

"How did you know I like camomile?"

"The Captain stocks one tea more than anything. I think he's been looking for you. It is as though you were separated at birth."

"I do not think we were, but I do think you are close. We knew each other; he was looking for me. Did he ever say where he knew me from or…?"

"The man is tight lipped as he is ferocious."

"Well, if I am a *Prince*," he chewed the word over—it fit in his mouth, and yet it did not at all. "Where is the castle? The king and queen?"

"I draw more maps than gods do fates, but even I know not where Illyrial is. You are the first true mystery aboard the Clarel. And its first true answer."

"I am from another part of the seas, towards the Northwest. Frost-swirled and fabled, my people told stories before paper ever existed to draw a map… though I wandered from ship to ship, place to place after that. I have seen cathedrals like coliseums and coliseums like hyacinths. I am afraid all I know about the principalities here since moving with the sea-winds is the outskirts and whatnot—except, what the Captain has told me. Until…"

"Until?"

"A few months ago, Batiste and he were arguing in some furious way. 'More swords! More swords!' He seemed on edge. He's been verklempt since I have known him, but it is much worse lately…"

"You think it had to do with finding me?"

"I do."

"And Batiste?"

"Batiste makes clothes, dreams them and weaves them from his head. But he…he can make *more* than that. He designed all our armory and weapons, which had a great deal of their own strength, until—" Their mouth hardened into a thin line. "Adrian needed something…"

"He needed something?"

"He was *looking* for something. He always is, even when it is not you he searches for. A type of mineral, a chest of treasure, I was not allowed to know. I told Batiste not to go, I was afraid…"

"*You* were afraid?"

Dimitri laughed. Then they hung their head. Along their left arm, some of the squiggles turtle-shaped and jade-colored, seemed to move…

"I should have gone with him. I was afraid. Batiste was steadfast as usual, a boy of steel and hilts. I should have expected no less. Fear and Regret are such constant bedfellows these days…it is almost comfortable, something like self-pity. I try not to encourage it."

Julian listened to them explain. He listened to them talk about before, when Batiste was there and better times upon the ship, in general. *Batiste embroidered these darling golden flowers onto all our vests, Batiste knew how to embroider precious, poisonous plants into armor should we need protection…Batiste with his wild hair down to his hips, running around the deck with Vico and Pierre, trying to get them to stay still for measurements. Batiste on the sails, trying to rescue a stray angelfish, with Ernest and Pericles, all the rest of us underneath with nets, ready to catch the poor creature…*

"It has not been the same," Dimitri said after a minute. It was not a confession, so much as a statement of fact.

Julian could sympathize.

"I see. I want to apologize for prying in your head so…"

"I was angry with you at first." Dimitri lowered their voice, hand tense on their cup. "Then I realized…you might be the first person in ages who knew where he was." They broke off, too close to tears.

"I want to help."

"I do not want to risk your health."

"I risk what I please. Besides, it seems Batiste is touched somehow. Like me, yes? Is he from Illyrial?"

"No, I do not believe so. Though, he might know more about where it is."

"The way I see it is we could help one another. At least, in the absence of a forthcoming Captain…"

Dimitri grunted. The sound was rough and despondent. It made Julian want to gather the man into his arms and console them.

"He would work himself into a frenzy on his pieces, For him, each embroidered thread is a piece of vision, when gathered…He only understands what it is all about when he's finished something, I think, when it is beautiful."

"Then why can't I reach out to him, using my Sight? And why doesn't Vern, my own brother…" Julian stopped himself before he became too upset.

"Boys, when they are young, have their own sensibilities…perhaps your Vern possesses something else. You and Batiste, you have this other way to look at people," they said, toying with the handle of their cup. They tapped a small, repetitive pattern onto its edges, little bubbles of spume in the seafoam.. "It is like you know already…how is it? He never could explain it. I do not think he wanted to! I did. I want to chart everything in this wide world. To make it known to others and to know."

"Some things you just know."

56

"Yes, that too I know, though I resist it."

Julian did not understand the man. He could wade through not-knowing as others might tread water. He simply let go, the teabag in the cup, both sinking and floating, forever suspended.

"I will teach you how not to know and you will teach me how to know, let's call it that, then? If these things must be even."

"You do not wish them to be even?"

"My help does not come with a price. My heart is not..." What was he to say? Strong enough? Too strong? He could not place it. He was not quite yet himself.

"Yours."

"What?"

"What boy has a heart that is ever truly his? Hearts are made to be in a state of constant transit; floating, far and away, for someone else. They do not have borders. They are not meant to be contained to the paltry parameters of paper. A map is exact but also a best guess."

"Is that why Illyrial is so hard to find? Because it is no defined borders, you cannot know where it starts or ends? Never truly?"

"That is what I have heard, your highness."

Julian thought on such matters. Then, there was the pleasure of earnest conversation he had missed so much. No one Above had made him feel so at ease. And lately, no one Below either.

Dimitri collected their cups and went to clean them in a quiet, content manner.

"May I continue to speak to you like this, your highness?" they asked, setting the cups in the drying rack. "I do not wish to presume."

Julian fumbled for a towel to dry the cups, at pains to be considered a proper guest.

"Yes. Dimitri, I would like that ever so much."

Dimitri handed him another cup, and Julian dried as they continued in rapturous conversation.

CHAPTER 8

Over the next few weeks, Julian fell into his new life as though he had never left it. He moved from one area of the ship to another, enjoying the newness of everyone's routines and passions. He wanted to meet all the lovely people, to throw himself into anything and everything. And yet, the ache felt familiar. This doubleness that he lived with, he relished.

From the crow's nest he could see the wide-open seas; the churning waves swarmed over the water-lily shaped sails of The Clarel, billowing around their open petals, covering the sails. He could see the sprawling deck, wider and more magnificent in daylight. The crew were delightful; Pierre showed him the cultivation of his glowing kelp and vines and strange, luminescent seagrass; he lingered over the saplings, the sweet buds of pale lavender searoses, and let Julian sit in on his demonstration of how topaz and tourmaline corals changed when replanted to different reefs. Pierre was laid back, but diligent in such a way that Julian suspected demanding the man move any faster would only result in the loss of all the delicate and lush vegetation upon the ship.

Oftentimes, Julian left the gardens with a basket full of oranges to take back to his quarters. He marveled at the joy of eating them while reading from the many books that Ernest and Pericles kept. Adrian had neglected to mention what his crew did for trade; paintings, bindings, antiques and rare objects, and the acquisition of anything related to art.

"Catch," Ernest said, and tossed the half-finished embroidery to the other man across from him. From across the table, Pericles caught it with one hand, never looking up from what he was fiddling with one of the bindings he was currently working on.

"Fragile things, all of us. Now, just a minute…"

"Do you need a different color?"

"Hardly, though I might luster it with gold later."

Pericles pushed the thick square glasses up the bridge of his nose. He unwound the embroidery, a piece hung in his lips, then he pressed it into the stitching where the book had been made. He was shorter than Ernest and moved in a way that recalled mice in The Above. Julian watched, fascinated by how he could see the slices in the crumbling margins and know where to put new stitches. He wanted to ask what they were doing with the stacks of paintings in one corner, their gilded frames sparkling, when a boy with broken shell still behind his ears raced past them. He was using a pair of paintbrushes as a makeshift gliding toy.

"You already met Vico, yes?" Ernest said, moving another stack of frames. "Vico is a boy in the child sense and will come to learn whatever trade he desires when he is a bit older."

"Is he…yours?"

Pericles shrugged. "Not in that sense. Not like in The Above, it is…we found him floating, belly up like a dead fish one day, and when Captain could get him to breathe under here, well…we could not let him go. He likes *us*, so he stays around the bindings and paintings on this side of the ship."

"Does he have anyone else?"

"No, anyone else is long gone."

"Or never existed to begin with," Ernest added.

"Dimitri, did they—were they found like that, too?"

Pericles stopped stitching for a moment. "Did Dimitri tell you that?"

"No."

Pericles did not look up, but he frowned. "Then you should ask them about it."

Julian promised to visit them again soon, but he did not want to disturb their work. Pericles and Ernest ushered so many different books filled with paintings into his arms that he felt spoiled. He kissed them each on the cheek and produced a basketful of oranges for Vico. As the weeks grew longer, he marveled at all he did not know; he never asked Adrian what on earth all of this was all far, what all these *beautiful* things meant.

And what did Adrian do in his spare time? What did he want to do with his life? All these marvelous people—his function seemed constrained to giving orders and staying shut in his quarters, with books and endless cups of coffee. They seldom passed each other in the hallways, and if it was not about how Julian was acclimatizing, then they did not speak. A brisk, polite nod—and then, it was done. At night, Julian wondered: when he first was rescued, did Adrian want him on his crew or did he want him because he liked to collect artifacts fished from Above?

Julian kept busy in a hundred other ways. What if he blushed each time Dimitri showed him one of their intricate maps? He knew the man's heart belonged to another. He heard it in their pulse, even when he knew he should not. He was observing them without the hope of touching.

Dimitri never shooed him away when he stopped by their cabin. Slowly, he began to take coffee with them more often on the airy, ivy-coiled balconies of the top deck. There, they gazed upon all kinds of passing fish, plant-life, and wave-patterns that swept up shimmering bubbles in their wake. The voyage was peaceful then. Almost.

On one of Julian's evening visits, Dimitri's hands were stained inky blue, and they were curled by the right side of the bed. Julian stood in the doorway, holding a lantern. He was wearing a white nightshirt, borrowed from the Captain's closet, and felt underdressed. He had been wandering the ship, head adrift with nightmares and saw the navigator's light was on.

"Ah, your highness, I am just redrawing some lines on this one. Do come in."

Julian put his lantern down and sat at the foot of the bed. Dimitri looked up.

"Will you sit like that and make me very nervous, or will you make yourself comfortable?"

Julian adjusted himself, trying not to think about how close they were. He watched Dimitri draw careful, exact lines over longer swooping ones. Once they were dry, he retraced them with his fingers; once, twice, three times caressing the spot.

He wanted to ask *Where does that one lead, over the meridian, is it somewhere we are going soon?*

He wanted to ask *Do you know what to do with your hands ever since he's been missing?*

He wanted to ask *Can you touch me like you touch that sprawling, stained parchment and show me where I should go?*

Dimitri lingered on a curve to the right—it was near a cluster of islands but seemed to go nowhere.

"What is it?" Julian was confused. "What do you keep tracing and retracing?"

"Where do you think it is?"

"A special place. An important one?"

"Not quite. It is a place I do not know how to draw, not yet. The image eludes me; will we sail there one day? Will I see it with him or alone? Will I find it, only knowing how to see what I have already seen, unable to capture its present essence? How will others find it? Will I regret showing them? Will I long to draw the world and no one hungers to see me but the sea?"

Julian's pulse thrummed hot as blue flame. He heard the murmurings of it since he came aboard, and here it was; *boyspeak.* The most precious language of his kind—

"You make these splendid things, but you have trouble living day to day."

"That is the curse of our kind—to live forever, young and undying, and also so very alone."

"Where did you come from, before this?"

Dimitri put the pencil down. A certain darkness passed over their features which made them seem older than Julian for the first time. But it did not frighten him, like it did with the Captain.

"I was floating to the surface. The seas were rough, they had been for some time. I found myself too exhausted to do what's natural and swim—with my first and last breath I saw the stars, through the waves and the clouds. It was marvelous. I have been fascinated with them ever since."

"You almost died, when you were…" Julian tried to put the pieces together. "Dimitri, how are we made? What puts us together in the sea? It is not like The Above, it is not…is it?"

"No, dear," they answered. "Not at all."

"You were not scared?"

"Not really. I think some of the folks on the ship…" they sighed. "I think they feel bad for me, maybe for Vico, too—but we are all born in different ways. Although I do not wish to walk in the company of those Above, I value the stars and their light for charting, and I would like to see them again."

"I could walk Above."

"And it almost *killed* you. It broke your body down, organ by organ—"

"Was I sick before then?"

"I suppose. But sickness is not the same here, you will not worsen, not if we take care of you…"

Take care of me? Julian gripped the side of the bed, suddenly dizzy. *Who ever thought to take care of me?*

"If you say you are fine, I will get the Captain in here myself. I do not want to do that." They said the last part in a pinched way.

It made Julian feel warm.

"All I wanted…all I *ever* wanted was to be here! And now…"

"Now you do not know what to do, getting what you want?"

"I fear it was the taste of a wish, after wandering a wasteland."

In the light of their sun panel, running down from lack of charge, Dimitri's eyes sparkled. "Now you get to find out. What you are, what you want… is that the worst thing?"

"No…" Julian shook his head. "What if I cannot remember Illyrial? You

62

speak of it so naturally. Yet, you have not been."

"The Endless Deep is not so defined. More of us come and go as we please, and each place is defined on its own terms. We do not own down here, not the way they do in The Above. But what always stood out about Illyrial is that it was truly borderless. Not just in terms of The Above and how they drew lines, but in terms of everything else. Does your heart have any natural closing?"

"No."

"Then why does it hurt you so, to think of such matters?"

"I am not afraid," Julian answered, in an instant. The memory burned, even now, of Vern on the terrace, all the rotted smell of earth roses around them, dying in a way that stuck.

"Yes. You are very brave. Have you been that way your whole life?"

Julian thought, murky images floating through his mind.

"Yes."

Dimitri reached for his wrists with blue-stained fingertips.

"Do you think I am afraid?" they asked, voice hushed.

Julian wanted to reach out, to cling to them, but…

He wanted to say *I am monstrous. Teach me how to kiss the stars into your mouth. Seek me in your long, lonesome nights of swimming astray.*

"Above, I told Vern when we engage in such a pleasure…"

"Illyrial has its own powers of transformation. That of pure desire. Change me tonight, little Prince," Dimitri danced Julian's palms across the topography of their dorsals, fingertips to heartlines.

Julian's head filled with images instantly, a channel opened as easeful as the flowing sea themself; *Dimitri curled around themself, opening to the night sky, Dimitri swimming from some unfamiliar kingdom; Dimitri working on ships, coast to coast, clinging to the masts, daring themself to chart the stars; learning to map, exact, occupied with the desire to reflect the whole, real sea, bursting as a citrus in their palms; the fierce, inimitable determination to create so that when they risked gills and limb to see the stars, they could be at peace; stars upon stars, glowing behind their eyelids even when they were in the hull of deep, seafloor cargos, stowing away...*

He felt candlelight pulse through him. Dimitri was in the burning wick of his frame, a mass of flames, unfurling, diffusing, devouring; *blue, blue, blue;* he wanted to push into their thoughts until he no longer felt his body; *images of those they had met before; boys, men, creatures of all kinds; nameless, shapeless kisses photosynthesized into an ecosystem of pleasure and power; the many tangled limbs of foreign, rough aches; burning, burning, burning; then, the images became familiar; Batiste, Adrian, Vern, until each saw themself, floating in between the sequences of transforming Memories...*

Julian reeled.

Little Prince, you went above to find yourself but you never gave others the constellations by which you may be found– Dimitri's words played in Julian's head, flute-tipped and gorgeous. They tasted of heady, honeyed salt-brine.

Dimitri gathered him to themself with sweet, open kisses.

You want me to be him. Julian was not offended. *It makes you interesting. Your absence, I long for it, too.*

Do you wish to call me Vern?

Sometimes.

Sometimes? Dimitri grinned. They cocked an eyebrow. *Dazzling boy, come here!*

Julian grasped Dimitri's hands downwards and straddled them.

Sometimes, I will be him, and then—he murmured into the other's mind. *I will be something new, beyond that...this is where we decide what we feel for one another...*

Dimitri unlatched the porthole.

"Come adrift with me," they said. Julian took off his nightshirt, enchanted.

He followed Dimitri through the porthole, momentarily frightened for there was nothing rigging them to the belly of the ship. But Dimitri swam with ease. In their wake Julian could follow, until they were both shielded by the broad hull. There was no cause to be quiet, and in the sea depths Dimitri teased soft sounds from Julian which sunk to the thick forests of seaweed beneath them. They licked Julian's gills until Julian was tasting their scent directly and arching against them. He wanted to go mad by swallowing seawater and Dimitri, the way lovelorn sailors did in fanciful siren ballads from Above, felt he was close to such consuming madness already. He gasped in half-drowning and hooked a leg around Dimitri, groaning deep, trying without success to make friction in the seaborn weightlessness.

The dusk-lorn blue surrounded them, and Julian felt his new scales tickle in the breeze. His legs moved with more ease, and his body embraced the water naturally.

"Not all at once, my Prince. You know I will give you all," Dimitri said, lips still latched on Julian's gills and making him moan with the profound sensation.

"Then give me all. Do it now. *Please*," Julian commanded.

With a bitten off groan Dimitri held Julian around the waist and guided him down, until he was anchored and secure around their length, filled all at once with impossible heat. He cried out, the sound swallowed by Dimitri when they kissed him and started to move in him. Dimitri wanted this, and *badly, since that first terrible nightmare on the ship…* Julian realized somewhere, as he felt a knot begin to unfurl in his stomach, long tied. *When I had entered them, unaware yet totally and completely penetrating…*

The heat sung, sweet and voiceless, notes on the scale of an aria, before the sound overtook him.

For a moment the singing hushed and he heard, but also saw: *Batiste in a sparkling array of light, dancing, surrounded by sleek, white pillars.* The room changed, down the halls, he saw something he never thought he would; *Vern, back under the sea, also at the party…* But what was going on in the tangled web of images meant almost nothing to him.

Dimitri had been right. They both were. The thought, gone before it finished, he did not know if Dimitri could hear it.

Dimitri's strong hands resumed clutching his waist, his mouth sucking up the expanse of his exposed chest, caressing, caressing...

"Your highness, I..." Dimitri broke off, but Julian could hear the anxious question in their besotted thoughts. Julian wrapped his other leg around their waist and clenched hard.

"You do not want to spill your common seed in a Prince? You find such a thing improper?" he asked. Dimitri's eyes widened, with scandal or lust, and he continued. "More improper than presuming to deny me?"

"No," Dimitri choked. "Thank you for the privilege."

The sea went foam-white. The water shuddered. In Julian's head the notes sung loud enough to pierce.

They drifted together after, buoyed by the ship's wake. In a dream haze, they exchanged long, unhurried kisses as they drifted back inside. Julian traced the trails of Dimitri's swirling tattoos, which in the water seemed to be cast from celestial light itself. Eventually Dimitri swam them back through the porthole and kissed him on the hand in the chaste manner of the court.

"Would it scandalize you if I rested in your bed?" Julian asked, pulling on his nightshirt.

"There is no scandal in my heart, your highness. It would be an honor."

"And if I were to take you in my mouth while you lay there like a Prince, would you find that to be an honor as well?" Julian was already nuzzling at their lap. "Shall I honor you in that manner?"

Dimitri swallowed and made several attempts at an answer before they hid their hot face in their hands and spread their legs instinctively.

"It does not hurt, does it?" Julian asked, blinking his eyes up.

Dimitri shook their head.

"T-too good."

"Alright, your grace," Julian teased.

He did not stop until he could feel Dimitri's hands trembling in his dark curls, and he lay with his wet lips pressed in regal triumph. Dimitri was plush and warm to rest against. They pulled the coverlets up and stroked Julian's hair until he was asleep, voice thrumming through his skin.

The next few weeks continued much in the same tender rush; new people, new places, new ways to wrap oneself in the arms of a stranger. Julian had found his sealegs, after all. Finned and fanned and more tail-like by the day, but he had found them. In passing he told Dimitri about where and when he had seen Batiste in his mind's eye. From that precious information, the rest of the crew had known where to sail to at once.

Course was set and reset. What the Captain thought, Julian could not guess. Instead, he busied himself with the rush of his excitement and new-found health. At small trips to port, he was delighted by those he met and they were delighted back. Lazy mornings and afternoons were filled with reading, writing, music, and looking over the paintings that Pericles and Ernest labored over while Vico triumphed in his own nonsense. Sometimes, he popped into the extravagant gardens, where Pierre was always ready to talk his gills off about the cultivation of exquisite buds and vegetation. In the evenings he wandered the decks, singing lilting tunes, drinking tea and getting used to the fresh sea air. Oftentimes he wandered into Dimitri's quarters with the intent of practicing Sight, instead tumbling through the hot press of their kisses before either could speak a word aloud.

One evening, Julian was lost studying a book of deep-sea cave paintings, from primordial times. He was picking at the rind of a ripe blood orange and so lost examining a phantom spiral in a hunting scene (which could have been accomplished with hands or brush or tentacle) that when Adrian knocked into him, he yelped. The man was half-frozen, smelling of desperation and wine. Julian wrapped the silks of his night shift tighter around his shoulders against the frisson which ran through him.

"Good evening, Captain."

"Only Adrian to you."

"I am fortunate to be on such a ship, but I would not flout its order and call you anything other than Captain."

"I see."

Adrian had long disappeared in Julian's mind and he had welcomed the absence. Now, he was harder and more closed off, a shadow of anger etched into his otherwise amenable features. It made him grotesque, somehow, the way he held himself. Adrian reminded Julian of the terrible loss of memory, the ache of his fall back into The Below.

"Goodnight, then." Julian was already walking on, ready to lose himself in cave dreams.

"Have I offended you so?" he asked.

For a moment, he was tempted to use his Sight but thought the better of it.

No, if this man does not want to tell me a damnable thing about anything, then what should I care what other detritus litters that head! he thought. *No more chasing down every wretched corner for something which should be given without fear! I will go to bed, and I will look forward to a new day that I can scarcely believe is mine to cherish...*

"I am about to retire for the night."

"I do not wish to offend you. I merely..."

"Indeed, *Captain.*"

Adrian shuffled in such a way that it seemed the boat thumped itself in rage. Julian shivered and glared at the man. How he loathed him then. Julian continued despite his good sense.

"Because you are lying to me. All these men, they are telling me the truth—and you have the nerve to lie to one of your oldest friends! Apparently. It is not a lie, I wish to retire from this conversation *immediately.*"

Julian looked and Looked. He Saw nothing. He did not want to.

Adrian stood back, as though he had seen a ghost. Centuries could have passed before he spoke again. Julian's legs ached from standing on the deck and he fought a rising tide of syncope.

"I have thought of you often."

Julian remained silent.

"I will tell you what you seek. All I know. Tomorrow night." Adrian's jaw clenched, brow furrowed, and he withdrew even more. He seemed to loom, too large and venomous. A beast trapped within a tiny frame, ready to lash out at the slightest provocation. "But you will not like it."

Julian stood his ground, though he felt lanced through the side. He saw Nothing. He would not. The orange rinds stained his fingers a blood-smeared pink. But he felt the sea around him turn crimson and ice-cold, and he wanted to scream...

"If you tell me and it is not *true*..." He remembered this feeling before, for this same man. He wanted to cast Adrian down from where he stood. He wanted for his crown and all. He raised his voice as though he was giving a command. "Then I shall regard you as 'Captain' always. I did not come back to be made something other than what I am. I shall not be afraid of you. I shall have my own wishes to pursue and in time, when I leave, I have a kingdom to go back to. I have an underworld to see. I will, of course, thank you handsomely, but...I will *no longer* be beholden to this treatment."

Adrian swung at him, managing only glancing blows, and then said nothing. When Julian did nothing, he put his hands around his neck. Julian flailed, finally extracted himself in a helpless fit.

"Do not approach me again. Not now. Not ever. Know your *fucking* place!" he spat. Adrian recoiled, and stalked off.

Julian laid down in bed for a half hour. He was bruised but he did not feel it. When he found his boytears staining the paintings, smudging them, he kept the books open until he could not see.

Ruins! Ruins–all of it, he thought. *Will I ever be allowed any measure of peace?* In the dark he wept until the tangle of his thoughts, all the nightmarish images conjured fell into a ball of stinging, empty threads. His sobs emptied through his chest, echoing down the halls...

Dimitri found him, choking on his own saliva. Without a word, they ungrasped Julian's bone-white knuckles from the rippling blankets and carried him to their chambers.

For once in your life, you will stop putting others before yourself. Enough of

Sorrow! Enough of Worry! Dimitri's firm, rough voice rang through his head. *Do you feel ill? We can spend the night quietly, or did you lose your footing...*

No. I did not.

Then what?

He swung at me. Hard. He...I could not breathe.

Fuck's sake. Dimitri's kisses halted with his thoughts. *You do not know the rough little games we play here...Do you remember anything like this in Illyrial?*

We were free to do as we please, Julian frowned, trying to think. He was from a country of peace and swooning words, or so he thought. *I...I do not recall that kind of roughness. Why?*

Disregard such a foolish question. It is something I have heard from Adrian and never understood. Though he is in far too much trouble now!

There were no pretty swords. His bare hands and nothing more.

Oh! No honor indeed. My Prince, if he ever tries that again, I will stab him myself. Through the heart.

Julian said nothing, but let Dimitri take him apart, over and over until he was melting into seawater, open-mouthed and gasping until dawn.

CHAPTER 9

When Julian was deep asleep, worn out from tears and Dimitri's tireless mouth and hands, Dimitri slipped out of their shared bed and dressed. Without a sound, they pulled out a box from under the bed and opened it to check the two blades within, black and glinting. With a light foot, they slinked into the kitchen.

There, the dread Captain sat, drinking his black coffee, looking a mite hungover. When he saw Dimitri, Adrian frowned, eyes growing stormier than even before.

"I suppose the little Prince has come crying to you."

"No. I had to rend it from him, in our bed, where he should be thinking of nothing but his pleasure, you hateful man."

"Ah, you have been bedding him. Of course," Adrian said with a sick smile. Dimitri took his coffee out of his hands and poured it on his lap. Adrian looked straight ahead without flinching, and Dimitri threw the cup into the sink. "I never took you for a *knight*, Dimitri."

"You do not take me for *anything*," Dimitri retorted, uncaring of how much of a wound the stark statement revealed. "Or perhaps that is only been true recently. Though time was when you had interesting people on your ship you would take interest, instead of pretending not to notice when I slept with them, instead of swatting at them like a blind ship's cat. Time was, you moved a little quicker than that, and with more charm. You really are getting old."

Adrian glowered, and Dimitri laughed.

"*That* is what raises your hackles, eh? Being called old? Feeling finite lately, *Adrian*? Feeling pointless? Out of fashion? Maybe there's a reason for that."

Adrian rose to his feet, still unsteady from liquor. Dimitri easily stepped to the side and watched the other man hit the full sink with an almighty clatter. Dimitri laughed nastily, and set the box of blades in the cupboard, for now. Adrian did not yet deserve such a wound.

They rolled up their sleeves and evaluated Adrian with an unbothered glance. He was listing starboard, favoring his wooden leg which was, despite all, immune to the effects of alcohol. But his gaze was focused now on the prospect of a fight. However mean a drunk the Captain was, his strong body was faster than most potent liquors, and his mind quick to follow. If anything, he would not feel blows which could fell lesser men, and then Dimitri would have the disadvantage.

"Alright," Dimitri said, very calm, and unbuttoned their shirt. They did not want to ruin it. "Have at it. Show me what you were going to do to a boy half your size. You have more cause to throw me around than him, do not you? You know I am more likely to forgive your loutishness, accustomed as I am to your insensate rage. I think the only problem here is I do not make you feel as small as Julian, I do not know what it is about the Prince, but around him, you must feel so..."

Dimitri's sentence was cut off with the air to their diaphragm, for Adrian had thrown his entire weight against them. They gasped before their left hand raised by instinct and closed around Adrian's lower jaw, pulling down. The unexpected grapple caused Adrian to lose his footing before he gripped the counter, kicking out blindly. Dimitri grabbed a large mug from the dish rack and broke it on Adrian's head; the handle remained intact in their fingers, and they gripped it so they could wield the jagged edges. Adrian's free hand found its way around their throat.

Go down, they thought with red rage, uncaring of who heard.

"Go down," they repeated hoarsely, and brought the broken mug on Adrian's knuckles, white on the counter. Adrian released their neck with a silent shout. "Go down, you fucking beast. If I beached you and left you for crabs it would be too kind, compared to the destruction you have courted for yourself."

Adrian said nothing, but he went down. Dimitri followed, winded and still so upset. The two sat in tenuous silence amidst the broken plates and cups until Adrian had the nerve to speak.

"Not all of us are raised in castles, which is not the first thing I would say in my defense, normally. I am just mentioning this very briefly because–"

"Because you are a self-pitying fool," Dimitri interjected. They stood on no ceremony; they could not think of calling Adrian 'Captain' and meaning it. Adrian conceded this with a shrug which infuriated the good navigator even more. "What fucking castle am I from? You have hurt the boy. He's the one who's hurt. Not you. He is not like us."

"I am not old."

"You are not young. You are not a boy. You *hurt* him."

Adrian put pieces of crockery together on a plate so nobody would cut themselves, a shadow of regret crossing his face.

"I am not a boy. I hurt him."

"Any man worth his salt would apologize," Dimitri concluded.

"Do I answer to *you*?"

"You can hardly answer to yourself," Dimitri said, voice raising. "You may as well do as I do, you—"

"I am still Captain of this ship—"

"Yes, and I am still a strong swimmer. I will think nothing of exiting this wreck should you find yourself incapable of apologizing to a boy you consider a *guest*—"

"And abandon your *latest lay* with such a beast?"

"I will fucking *kill you* first—"

They were interrupted by the canteen door swinging open with a bang. Dimitri saw Julian and felt discomfited for a moment, sitting on the floor with fresh bruises and cuts blossoming on their arms and face. Out of the corner of their eye they could see Adrian cringe. Julian took in the spectacle of them with a wild stare, and then sat in a kitchen chair as though it were a throne.

"Which of you will explain this?" he said, and waited. "How my rest has been disturbed."

"I beg your pardon," Dimitri said immediately. Adrian snorted, and Dimitri glared daggers at the feckless man. "I was speaking with the Captain about what happened earlier tonight, and the conversation grew...*spirited*."

"I did not ask you to talk to someone who cannot listen, Dimitri," Julian chastised with a frown. "I wanted you to stay with me."

"I apologize, your highness."

"You are forgiven," Julian allowed, and turned a cold gaze to Adrian. "You. I suppose you're still *drunk*? Or mad."

"I am ready to explain, as we discussed earlier," Adrian said, without a lick of apology.

"And do you even know where we are going, since your crew members are missing, along with whatever mission you sent them on?"

Adrian's jaw set. "I assure you that has been taken care of. In my hours of not disturbing you, I have seen to it–"

"I will confirm it with others on my own time. But I do hope you have not already wasted so much of theirs," Julian dismissed.

"Why would you doubt my skill at—" Adrian did not finish the sentence, his audience had already turned away.

Julian scowled, feeling childish and small, and helped Dimitri to a chair. He sat on their lap and counted the new marks on their flesh, in danger of crowding out the tattoos and scarifications. He kissed Dimitri's cuts and scratches, assuring them all was forgiven in their head, that they would not be banished from the Princely bed for attempting chivalry. Privately, darkly, he thought on how he would make Adrian answer for such injury, and did not hear the beginning of the Captain's tale.

CHAPTER 10

"I know I was a child, once. I lived a stone's drift from the castle. Your castle, to be precise." Adrian said this last part to Julian, who looked to Dimitri to see if this was some captainly lie. They were already settled for the sordid tale, though they had heard it before. No dishonesty, just a blinkered narrative entrenched as another line on Adrian's seaworn forehead.

I apologize for his poor entertainment, my Prince, as I know he would not. It will be like listening to the only tale the Shahryar knows, no matter how much a street urchin he fancies himself. Yet I do not know if I can do this for one of a thousand nights.

Julian felt the sharp disappointment as though it were his own.

Not anymore.

Dimitri's thoughts turned to a frustrated jumble where they touched on the Captain, treasured memories conflicting with the agonizing present. Julian stroked their hair, and turned to Adrian, who looked between them as though he could see their conversation.

"And did we know each other?" Julian prompted impatiently. "Me on a balcony, weeping and seated at my harp while you swept kelp and broken shells from the great marble steps? Or was I one of those diaphanous symbols of affluence you ceaselessly pursued, even as you grew to be self-made and newly rich, handsome and so lonely? Did the one with my face break your heart into little pieces, and do you yet rake them from the depths like so much seaglass? Land's sake, what is worse than a man with an explanation?"

"A man who lacks one?"

"The man who lacks explaining may yet fill the sweet air with no thing, e'en several nothings. Sooth, tell me about when you were a *boy*, and how from this pip you grew to be a *fool*."

"I did not say boy."

"What *thing* then?" Julian frowned, not understanding. Dimitri coughed delicately, and Julian sighed. "Or beast?"

"I was the eldest of several," Adrian explained. "And when the whelps were all old enough to steal and lie as their parents did, I entered the castle as a scullion. I thought of advancement."

"Oh, but you could *read*, Captain," Dimitri reminded, and turned to Julian. "Your highness, I will give you the summary or we will be here until the oceans dry up. Our fearless leader's journey from scullery to skullduggery in as many steps as an elegant pavane into the deepest trenches of infamy: Adrian learned to read as a not-boy child, and such an unexpected talent got him fine new shoes and sweets, and he became a castle *pet* of sorts until he wanted what he could not have…"

"Me?"

"Not *quite*, your Highness. But he was thus expelled from the royal home without a reference. This was an exquisite burden for someone who looks for sun rays in the currents and never loose change in the silt. Eventually, he came to outgrow his shoes, and he neglected to read any more books, except the ones which told him what he already knew; there are places exceptional persons go to succeed, and he was exceptional, or at least felt as though he ought to be advanced some kind of exception on the promise of *potential* as a return. And so, a clever teenager became a dull and grasping twenty-year-old, and…" They turned to Adrian, eyes wild and unforgiving. "What was the story after all that, Captain, in the few years ensuing? Did you make anything of worth? Did you discover a fount of gold? Did you ever get what you wanted?"

Adrian opened his mouth, but Dimitri was faster.

"Or are you here, plugging all the holes in your ship and your lies even as you long to sink and take us with you? Nursing a bad leg and a grudge against the first man who saw you exactly as you are and could use you thusly?"

"Eric?" Julian asked. Adrian, quiet still, looked away from them at the name.

"Who else?" Dimitri said in a low, unsteady voice. "Even now, he *tries* to be his own man, but all he does is follow the Duke's steps, like a worker bee."

"That is enough from you, you mutinous cur. You have never understood," Adrian snapped. "You think you know about me because you're near me, by my fucking grace alone!"

Julian realized he was all that stood between them on the deck. He did not want to be stuck in the middle of one of their cataclysms, torn collars and skinned knuckles, but if he moved…

"I understand more than *you* ever can. Even if you have forgotten, I am a *navigator* and I do not truck in the febrile nonsense that charts your stars!" Dimitri snarled over Julian's head. "While we are on the topic of grace; you have crossed me so many times, *Captain*. More than the occasions I have contemplated the incredible wreck I could make of this place, with a careless brush of ink. Were it not for the souls aboard I hold dearer than *yours*…"

"What did Eric do to you, then?" Julian tried to ask; raising his voice over them, he felt as though he was being swallowed by the waves around them. He was not sure either of them heard him until Dimitri crossed their arms, reticent and retiring.

"Damned pointless to ask any of this. *That* is a different story every time, and very poorly rehearsed to boot. Why not ask him about the castle again!"

"He took something from me," Adrian offered up. Dimitri's forehead smoothed in surprise.

"And…what might that have been?" Julian asked, now able to get a word in edgewise without yelling.

"If I *knew*—"

"A bloody narrative convenience," Dimitri dismissed.

"I owe you an apology, *Mitya*," Adrian, still glancing anywhere else but Dimitri and Julian, moved to the edge of the ship. "I do not think you have ever known me at my best. Not really."

"Then how have I known you?"

Adrian mumbled something, looking for the first time *young* in his abashment. Julian and Dimitri waited for him to repeat himself.

"I am changed," he stated. "It may be easier to simply..."

The ship creaked ominously beneath their feet, and at first Julian did not understand why. Then he heard Dimitri's sharp inhale of breath, their strong hand clasped on his shoulder. Adrian winced, and Julian saw him then, unfurling into a grander shape than the sparing, paltry form to which his crew was accustomed. Long spirals of phosphorescent blue lit the deck to the exclusion of the stars and Julian could not find Adrian's eyes in the remaining, seething black mass.

"Dimitri," Julian whispered.

"It is all right."

Dimitri was not afraid, and from that Julian found that he could not be either. In front of them, Adrian or whatever it was began to fold back in, wrapping until he was once again just a man in a long coat. He removed the coat, beneath was a thin white undershirt and his pants. His hair stood up on end, all disheveled; his organic leg trembled as though he were about to collapse, the arch of back peaked through his night clothes.

And when had I ever seen him out of this garb? Julian thought. He had felt confused as the ship shook, but when everything stilled, when he saw how the tentacles squirmed, how large and electric blue they beamed...

When I was first sick, I was rescued a brief time back. But there was another thread tugging at it, another time he had seen Adrian like this, all rumpled and vulnerable...

He felt that same overwhelming despair on the night when Adrian had accosted him; something in his mind clung to him, it formed shapes; senseless blobs that tugged at one another, twisting and overlapping until they formed outlines; Adrian kneeling, surrounded by velvet curtains, the shape of strange beds, the feeling of being so very high up, the heads of meadow flowers, lush petals dropping to the floor; other places, other times; who could say

78

if any of it belonged to them now?

"I do not," Adrian could not finish for the tears.

Dimitri unbraced himself from Julian's shoulder but did not go to the Captain, who, flesh and bone and seemed too small for his frame; it was as though he had collapsed into himself.

"Adrian, why would not you say—?"

"I do not know what it is *I* am anymore. He took it from me. How can I explain when I can nary fathom it myself? There are all these things I remember which do not belong to me anymore, from when I was a man. And everything after is not…real. Or lasting. What was *before* was real."

"Tosh," Dimitri snapped with shocking vitriol. "Tosh and fiddlesticks. What did he take from you except any sense you may have previously possessed? Come on, Captain. The crew can not see you beside yourself like this."

"I am sorry, Dimitri."

"*Shut up.* Let's have some tea and then we will have it out, the way we used to before you resorted to your seclusion and a preponderance of misery. Julian, *your Grace,* I mean, can you find my good teapot? Also, may I shed blood for your honor?"

"Whose blood?" Julian asked. He followed the two of them in a whirlwind.

"Depends." Dimitri smiled.

Below deck, in the kitchen, Julian took the large sleet samovar from the shelf while the kettle began to whistle and dance. Perhaps imprudently, he looked at Adrian while he scooped delicate leaves into the samovar's depths, trying to understand where all of him was kept.

"Drink," Dimitri said to them both, curt and kind. "No milk in it, not before a fight. The strong, brave liquor unadulterated is what's warranted."

"I do not want to fight you," Adrian whispered.

"So you'd forfeit and eat the shame of it?"

"I do not forfeit. Nor do I accept."

"It is never that simple," Dimitri said. "Drink the damn tea, Adrian. Then fight me like you used to. The same terms."

"What are the terms?" Julian asked, taking a long sip of tea.

"A mere bauble," Dimitri said.

"It is obscene," Adrian said at the same time.

For once, Julian understood. At least, he hoped he did.

"I think you should fight them, Captain." He put down his cup and catching Adrian's nervous glance. "And if it is not improper, I will add my own stakes. The privilege of hearing your given name on my lips again, if you are the victor."

"Not improper at all," Dimitri said, with a sidelong glance at Adrian, who was examining the bottom of his teacup. "What says the Captain?"

"By cock and pie, I say you have a bloody nerve," Adrian answered. "Dictating terms to me and including *him* in this…private matter. Swords?"

They donned long padded vests and let Julian pin garish red hearts to their sides. Julian kissed Dimitri on the lips and graciously permitted Adrian to kiss his hand before standing out of harm's way. The swords, short and ceremonial, were produced from the cupboard.

Julian could not remember the last time he had seen two men stare at each other so intently, despite trying not to touch. Dimitri's not inconsiderable height and heft made them a formidable foe, but Adrian was light on his feet and smiling and comfortable with a blade in his hand, maybe more comfortable than Julian had ever seen him. Their hearts stayed pinned to their vests, and while their swords sliced through the air, neither managed to sever the flimsy paper from the chest.

Then Dimitri jabbed, abandoning their hitherto courtly style of slicing and corralling, just as Adrian reached out with his swordless hand to rip. The heart on Adrian's chest tore, half on and half off, and Dimitri's was flung in a ball to the ground. It was a perfect draw, though the duelists had not finished. They grappled, weapons now thrown to the side with a clatter, until they were on the floor, breathing hard and drawing blood.

"This is better," Dimitri bit out, fist bunched in Adrian's hair. "You have

80

the air of being above it, but *this* is the only way I have been able to respect you."

"Because you are a fucking barbarian," Adrian retorted, wooden leg in Dimitri's thigh, scratching down his back.

"And what the fuck are *you*?"

Instead of answering, Adrian kissed Dimitri with sanguine teeth and tongue, hands digging deeper into his back. Julian could smell their blood commingling and sank fast.

"Gentlemen, I…"

Julian faltered, his vision went white, and felt the air thicken like it would before a storm. Then he fell into an aquavernal meadow of anemone and coral, seeing the distant sun from several fathoms below. He was breathing hard, and his sword lay beside him, a cloud-blue ribbon wrapped around its handle. He watched Adrian, he thought it was Adrian, cycling through his stances, martial and straight-backed.

CHAPTER 11

Adrian turned to him with a careless grin that Julian wanted all for himself. Julian held out a hand to pull him down.

Is this a memory, or wishful thinking? The thought floated away. He could not fathom anything else—the change was jarring, but faded like music from a distant orchestra.

"You have been practicing," he said, pushing a curl from Adrian's forehead. "Your form is so much better."

"I have a good teacher," he responded, averting his eyes in that habit he had from when he was possessed of true humility. "A good…patron."

It was late evening. They sat in a meadow filled with an abundance of seaflowers and fruits; bioluminescent orchids and roses amidst the glowing algae; above the low hanging branches, swirled with coral and crystal leaves, grew sweet berries plump and iridescent as pearls. The water was pushed around them by warm, light currents. He could taste the dulcet waters; he knew he was in his fine jewel-strewn robes that kissed his knees, a curve of gold crowning his dark, rich curls.

Adrian was younger, more rounded out. Maybe a boy, or maybe a man who was trying to hide the fact he was still a boy. His beard was still coming in, and his light hair fell in unbound tresses, the shadow of a braid coming undone from the tide. He was dressed in fine silks, a waistcoat encrusted by so many emeralds, and held a long, thick sword.

"Embarrassed by a Prince's favor, still?" Julian asked, with a carelessness that felt foreign. The pain of it was glancing, though it was…*old*. Antiquated, even. Prince though he was, he had never been embarrassed by any of the company he kept. And yet, he sometimes felt Adrian's hesitation when he put a flower in his bonny hair and called him *darling*.

"Not *embarrassed*, Highness," Adrian said, chastened.

"Just Joules, silly."

"Your brother…"

"What of him?"

"His Favorites will be…" Adrian found himself stymied. "They will be made of finer stuff."

"Brother *Vern* likes to scour the finishing schools and all the royal courts abroad for his coterie of sycophants and pretty faces. We are Princes of a kingdom! How many more are out there? He knows, by their royal favors,..by their royal voices! Oh! I cannot bear that lot. It is so easy for me to love, and yet…well, never mind. He cannot bear to be alone, so he is not. Low effort, high reward. He's always been like that."

"Not like *you*. You make things hard on yourself," Adrian said.

"Indeed. The day is sunny, the field remote, yet my knight has not yet taken advantage of my unguarded state," Julian breathed, flopping onto his back with a sigh. "Instead, we are talking about my brother and, oh—You are shy as ever! What kind of ruffian are you?"

"*Yours*. All yours." He moved from where he had propped his elbow up with a slow graceful arc, and pressed Julian to him.

"*This,*" Julian murmured, allowing himself to float a bit. "*This is my kingdom.*"

Adrian scooped him up by the waist and they drifted.

"What does it matter? We shall sail together. And you will always be my Adrian and I your Joules—there will be terms to decide such a union but that."

"Princes in other kingdoms, you know…"

"*Illyrial* is self-serving nation, born from my brother and myself—"

"You do not have to treat him as an equal."

"What would I be if I did not?"

"Joules…"

"Every man is a Prince, he lies with who he likes, when he likes, however he likes. He loves amorously and wholly and never worries who has his heart and if he's hurt a lover—he is forgiven, mostly, but never lightly. No man belongs to another…"

"When we lay down, we rise the next morning with whoever and how-ever we choose," Adrian laughed, taking up the speech with mirth. "We wan-der, but we have no intention of outcasted vagrancy because there's nowhere to go *back*, only *to*; I go to you as another might go to me, sweetly, helplessly, bravely seeking a friend in the night; it is always your choice when you go and when you stay, who you are and where you are that person because here, here every man is free…to love himself."

"He knows them as well as I do—though maybe he does not honor them the same way."

"*Your* words, my dear boy."

"But he is better at giving speeches, we even each other out. He is good for staying at the palace, too—when he is not away, he loves having his men over. Me…I do not think I even want to stay here, opulent as it is."

"Why?" Adrian leaned over him, his lips hovering on the edge of Julian's cheekbones, nose, before touching the corner of his mouth.

"Because there is a man who is not from Illyrial, who lives by its tenets, and I wish to follow him through all the seas. If he is so set out on finding who he is, then I may follow if I so like…"

Julian pulled him down. He tugged at the flowing locks of his hair, twist-ing it in his hands until Adrian moaned against him. He felt overwhelmed, blossoming as one of the searoses, coming undone in the arms of the white-capped tide. He floated, twisting around Adrian until he straddled his waist, his lithe, frond-like sea-legs weaving.

My boy, my boy, my boy, He heard him. There was no trying; the connec-tion was instant. *How do I deserve you? How had I wandered from the wasteland of my days to you?*

In his head he felt more than the words Adrian said—he felt as he was feeling, he was a series of vibrations, ever tuned towards the point of song. He was in love, truly and completely.

You are my Captain, there is no other Captain for me to chart such a course with, he pushed the heavy coat off Adrian's shoulders and slithered around him.

In the dim, long strides of starlight falling from Above, he stripped Adrian down until he was warm and naked underneath. Adrian was unaccustomed to being undressed by another, and momentarily shy, he bit his lip.

"Do I please you, your highness?" he asked, resorting to court protocol in his timidity.

Julian reached between his legs as a response and he squirmed.

"Oh!"

"You are always *pleasing* me," Julian assured, and stroked up the plain of Adrian's stomach, his chest. He pinched one of his nipples, teasing a needy sound from Adrian's precious throat. "But what pleases you? What would jolt you from your admirable manner and such ironclad bloody chivalry? What should I do to make you forget I am a Prince so you will treat me like a lover?"

"How should I forget you are a Prince?" Adrian asked, trembling hand stroking Julian's cheek. He was tense and arching into Julian's touch.

"If I commanded you, you would have to," Julian said with a sharp smile. He was straddling the lad now. "If I told you to forget any *Prince*, and think instead of your hard cock, how I would feel around it…you would have to."

Forget your Prince, Julian responded, lancing the gouache of lust he found there with his thoughts, spreading it like marbling on an end page. *Make me yours instead.*

Adrian's gaze darkened, and to Julian's utmost delight he grabbed him hard around the waist before flipping them so his head was surrounded by dripping meadow blossoms. Their combined weight crushed the little night-flowers and released a beguiling scent intermingled with Adrian and the tones in their thoughts. He gasped when Adrian pushed in all at once until he was

85

fuller than he had ever been in their hurried encounters in corridors and under balconies. Adrian did not stop until Julian found his breath and moaned cut-off pleas, pulling his Favorite's hair, demanding *harder, more, until I am buried in the petals.* He bit down, tasting blood without a care for where he left his mark.

"Does *that* please you?" Julian asked when he could speak. Adrian's tongue flicked between his gills in response, and they tumbled into another fugue of speechless noises and the heady smell of night-flowers. Hours passed and Julian scrambled after Adrian, wishing him closer, closer. After, they lay together and looked up at the waves.

"What is it?" Adrian was bitten all over. His skin was a bruising gradient of scale-like marks shining down his neck and chest.

"I had learned and studied and loved every day here—but until you showed up…was I even alive? Was I even truly a boy? How could I be myself without you?"

A shadow passed over Adrian's face and he did not answer. He was hesitant, still.

"And I cannot find fault with him, or anyone else on such an evening." Julian lay across his lap, arms flung out as if trying to touch the light of the stars above. "And to think, in just a few more turns of the glass, we shall set sail!"

"I can hardly believe it myself. The ship…" Adrian sighed, a dreamy look in his eyes.

Julian had helped design some of the Clarel's aspects, but he could not take all the credit. He knew that it was Adrian's gilded project, a dazzling creation that would take them anywhere.

"I will be down at the shipyards in a few turns of the glass. But I have to be away for a few hours this evening. Some of the doctors at the palace…"

"Do you think it is getting worse? Should I stay with you, or wait in your quarters?"

"No." he pulled Adrian's hands together, gathering them in his own grasp.

"Please, do not worry about me. They want to make sure we can pinpoint what we can before we sail. Our good-hearted tutors simply wish to see us fit to thrive, and think to send me with all the vials and potions they can! For any foreseen illnesses and unforeseen disasters."

"And we will find out a way to help, to make sure you are in less pain…"

"To cure me?"

"No darling. I would never wish to change you in a way that extracts you from yourself."

"Nor I you…I know we do not speak of it often, I…" Julian knew he should tell Adrian the last part. "Some suspect it was the way I was extracted at birth, and ever since, well, Vern is healthy. But me…"

"My boy, you are fragile, it is no shame. You are as a jewel is; sparkling, terrifying, possessing a rare quality that is uncommon…and for that you pay a price."

"My most gentle friend, it is not that I am ashamed. It is that I simply long not to rest so much, to do all I long to do—and the many creatures of these other kingdoms…what will they think? All the troubled, many nights I put you through here! Oh! Tell me you do not mind, and I shall call you a horrid liar."

He thought back to how much grief he had brought Adrian; all those nights in the palace together, in his chambers ailing and shrieking and hung his head.

"Enough," Adrian said sharply.

"I shall want to spar with you ever so. I long…"

"To sword fight and sing amongst the many foreign kingdoms! Then, you go to your doctors, and I shall be at the shipyards. After, I shall meet you… we shall recover together." He helped Julian with some of his buttons on his tunic. He gathered the last of his clothes and stood. He looked as though he was going to say something else, then stopped.

"It is not like The Above," he said. "That is the one dry, dead region with none of our kind. Besides that, we are safe to travel and travail Beauty together."

"Oh, I am glad—I would only like to navigate The Above for abandoned times, so that we might put on our floating helmets and see the stars."

"Indeed, all the machines and whirring…when there are endless king-doms in The Below."

"Thank goodness. Oh! And speaking of," Julian in a flurry of excitement, floated down a bit to his opal-sewn satchel and pulled out some papers. Amongst them were several maps. "This kingdom over…here! It looks like the food is divine. They have some of the largest libraries, besides Illyrial, of course. And I heard there is a man there who plays the castanets with such ferocity that dances last for days."

"That does sound fun."

After they scoured the maps with joy, each said their farewells. Adrian clung to his shoulders tightly when they parted, a kiss burning on his lips as he left.

Julian heard his thoughts, even though it felt too far away for it to be pos-sible: *Joules, what have you done to me? Why can I not give up on the chance of our happiness? What will you do with me when you know what I am?*

CHAPTER 12

Julian turned back, gathered his satchel, and looked at the palace. Where the image of glittering pillars should have been, and the answer to Adrian's thoughts, was instead a blinding strike of pain. The room was pitch black. He cried out into an abyss.

He was waiting, waiting, waiting…but when he turned back, he was out of the field. Instead, he was back on the ship, and Adrian was trying to stay his killing blow with a trembling hand. Julian's blade was inches from his throat, and yet Adrian was smiling up at him like a fool, gold tooth glinting ruby and blood.

"I yield," he breathed.

"Oh. Oh my," Julian said, and dropped the sword. Adrian's hand stayed above his neck for a moment and then fell to his side.

"Fuck me," Dimitri said in pure shock. Julian looked around, jolted; the kitchen was a mess, tables overturned and crockery in pieces, crunching underfoot. "*Your Highness.* I have never seen something so beautiful in my life."

Julian staggered to his feet, leaving Adrian crumpled on the floor with a disdainful glance. His sword felt like a natural extension of his royal self. He did not ask what happened. He did not ask if the man at his feet was hurt. He felt like a Prince, a Prince who would be king, and that was all he needed to know.

"I win," he said. Dimitri and Adrian looked at him, confused, and he elaborated with an impatient gesture. "The duel. I win, yes?"

"Yes," Dimitri said.

"You may do with him what you like," Julian said to Dimitri. "Attend to his hurts first, make sure he is not disgraced before his crew, unless disgrace is a storm his authority can weather. I care not what comes after."

"I am not hurt," Adrian protested, his labored breath coming in harsh whistles. Julian looked downwards, baring his teeth, resisting the urge to put a fine foot on his bloody chest and push.

"Do not use that tongue to lie to me, not ever again," he said, without the intention of repeating himself. "Or I promise you shall not use it for anything after. You should have been my tribute. My Favorite. A diadem enriching my coffers and my name. Instead, you acted dishonorably in my absence, like a spoiled brat who cannot be good when he is unwatched. You conceded the will of another man before mine, so faithless and crass are you. And then you *lied* and pushed me around as though you meant to kill me. You are for the navigator now, if they still want you. I am sorry to give a worthy man such a gift."

The deep silence that came after was gratifying, as though the seas themselves had stopped moving. Dimitri executed a half-bow, and Julian gripped the sword tight, found the door and left. He could hear Adrian's harsh breaths now, pricked with tears, Dimitri mumbling something inaudible which could have been a comfort or an insult. He wished he had been more cruel. He returned to his own quarters, upset and exhausted.

As he slept, Dimitri attended to Adrian's wounds.

"Stop crying, it is not all ruined," Dimitri muttered, pressing an unguent on Adrian's cleaned chest. They wondered which medicine in the cabinet would patch the hole in his lung. "If he was really *finished* with you, you would be split in half."

Adrian did not respond, which was a mite worrying, but took the potion. The ragged whistle in his throat ceased and his shoulders relaxed, though his tears were still free-flowing.

"I reckon you will want to sleep," Dimitri said. "My quarters are closer."

"*No.*"

"I insist," Dimitri said firmly, and softened at Adrian's miserable resignation. He was a sore loser, always had been, but tonight had been so *different*. "Only sleep, Adrian. I will hold you to our terms later."

"Life has touched me in ways which are strange to him," Adrian mumbled, half asleep already as Dimitri bundled him up.

"A fine riddle, Captain."

"I was better once."

"He seems to think so."

"Do you think he will ever forgive me?"

Dimitri wondered how to answer, but Adrian was already asleep before they could settle on *No, of course not, but you can still ask the boy for the privilege of making him laugh.*

With the clinical movements of a field nurse, Dimitri undressed the Captain to his skivvies, pushed his hair out of his face. It was too long; in his more pleasingly vain moods, Adrian would thread it into braids and wrap them around jewels and flowers to weigh against the current. He had not had those moments of late. Dimitri pulled off the Captain's ornate rings next, too easy to pry from thin fingers, no rich saffron dye on the tips or deep red varnish on the bitten nails. Adrian's gilded ship, extravagant in its charms, had long lacked the Captain to match.

With care, Dimitri unbuckled his wooden leg and set it to the side but paused alarmed when their hands came away stained with Adrian's curious amaranth blood. Still asleep, Adrian whimpered through parted lips, like a child in a nightmare. Dimitri worked quick to replace the dressings on his stump, worry growing when Adrian did not rouse, although the closure beneath the dressings was raw, unhealed despite the age of the wound. It must have rubbed his mind to pencil nubs which scraped the knuckles to use.

You consented to duel me in this *state? Was I to be your executioner? What punishment do you think you deserve?* They felt tricked, cheated of a satisfactory win. The prospect of an unequal fight shamed them, and it was apparent, to an insulting degree, that this duel had been a farce.

They pulled a blanket over Adrian, an ornate quilt in dark jewel tones, embroidered with earth birds and moons. The Captain himself had bought it for them in softer days, when he still went to port for pleasure. He once had kind words for them and learned with patience the ways to unroll Dimitri like a parchment to read their body like a map. He once called them *Mitya* more and made them feel so cherished. It was a joy to sail with him then, and a keen hurt to remember now. They kissed the Captain's forehead, if only to find fever, then stood, ramrod straight.

Even if it meant they must fritter away the days of privilege allotted to them from this hollow win, Dimitri vowed to get to the bottom of Adrian's sudden decline. No one thing or person could be responsible, and they would pull the truth from him like a signet from his emaciated finger. That would be revenge enough.

Dimitri left to meet the morning, locking their chamber from the outside.

Pierre was already in the kitchen, a vein in his forehead throbbing while he swept up broken porcelain.

"Dimitri!" he cried, and gestured with his broom. "Look at this fucking mess! The blood is going to take an age to clean and I have never seen such finely ground teacups. And pray tell, what the *fuck* happened last night between you and the Captain? Vico woke up in the night and had to sleep in my room, he was so scared. Do not tell me you two have finally…?"

"Do not be daft," Dimitri said, eyes narrowing. "Captain took a bad fall during his rounds and needs to recover, without any gossip. Clean this up and be quick about it for once. I will replace the tea service at the next port. And Pierre—what the blazes do you mean by *finally?*"

Pierre buttoned his lips and kept sweeping. Dimitri turned on the kettle and made smoky tea with a twist of lemon.

Julian slept two turns of the glass more than his custom, then met Dimitri in the map room. He had not lost any of what Dimitri had seen in the night, studious and royal and dangerous. He pointed to the maps. There were a few notes from Pericles about *what* routes to take and where one might go for the quickest escape, accentuated by confused scribbles from the Captain: *Found notice here, in one of my drawers, but did not remember the address, had to do a little digging—why would I send someone here? Unless we were all going together, what did I think was so dangerous, or something Batiste alone would be able to procure?*

"Your Batty," Julian exclaimed after reading everything over. "My brother. Can we make it there in three days' time with these headwinds?"

"Oh," Dimitri said. They had not been expecting *this*. "Both of them? A rescue?"

"More of an abduction, I fear. No doubt Vern will be enraged by my reappearance."

"You think Batty is there?"

"I know he is, sweet man. I remember him and I remember his clothes, at the party."

"And I checked, your highness, yesterday before all of this. He *did* know where it was, after shuffling through papers, and whatnot…he did not remember much beyond that, but…" Dimitri felt smarting tears. It was too much to figure out, to hope for.

"We will need the Captain to make himself scarce, if we are to make port," Julian said. Instinctively, a hand went to his neck, then his bruised cheek. It would fade soon. Besides, Adrian looked even worse. "His is another known face."

"He is scarce, no cause to worry about that," Dimitri promised. They thought briefly of Adrian, locked up and recuperating from the sudden alleviation of his black moods. Yes, alleviation was the right word.

After a few days, he will be better. Not good, but better.

"What *are* the terms of those sacred duels you two share?"

"Sacred…?"

"What does he lose? What do you gain? And vice versa. If he has ever bested you."

"It is indelicate," Dimitri said with a cold smile that told all. "And he has won but once."

Julian sat silently, happy to wait for an explanation. Dimitri blushed, newly interested in the mess of maps between them. They wondered if Julian thought it provincial, or lowly, if 'sacred' was an arch appellation to dismiss uncouth practices. It was difficult to explain how Dimitri and the Captain dealt with each other in a way that did not sound gruesome or gratuitous.

"We start with tea, and then swords," they finally said. "You saw that part, hand cut paper hearts which we must brush off by blade. And then our fists and teeth, until one of us yields. Once there is a victor…"

"Then you fulfill terms," Julian prompted Dimitri, who had paused again with the task of describing it.

"Yes, they are as such: For a period of three days after, he who yields must work to satisfy the victor according to certain terms set before, to the exclusion of his regular duties. That last part is important. After three days, satisfaction is considered attained and all injured honor restored. Me and Adrian, we have a more carnal and immediate view of *satisfaction* compared to that of high-born duelists. Perhaps the custom is not quite how you know it."

"I enjoy this iteration a sight more. It is less sad," Julian confessed, remembering young men banished over thrown gloves or misinterpreted looks in concert halls. He looked fondly at Dimitri. "T'was a fine thing, to see you fight in my name. I am happy you have not killed him."

"I do not like to kill," Dimitri agreed. "It is enough to draw blood."

"So, he must do your bidding for three days, correct?"

"He must. Though, *you* were the victor of last night's duel, your Highness. It is to your will he bends."

"Without my stir, you would have triumphed. So, your will or mine, without complaint," Julian reiterated, gesturing to the map, and Dimitri agreed. "A perfect time then, for *this*. When the Captain is new imbued with great sense and drive. I recall he was clever once."

"*Adrian* was?"

"The Captain was quite capable, and found cause and pleasure to use

94

his brains, when he was young." Julian's lips thinned. The memory, sweet as it was, stained his tongue with a metallic taste. "He could invent a country noble out of a bolt of satin. On a whim, he built ballrooms from deep sea caves and tenement hallways. He fashioned sonnets and *candles* from dead white coral and loose shale, unearthing treasures from common things as though they had always been there, only neglected by the gaze of all. *Candles* in the deep sea, Dimitri. I was possessed of such radiant colors for the first time because there was a lad below who taught things to burn. I daresay he was someone to admire and even covet. Once. That is the fellow I need right now. Tell the Captain to resurrect such a man if he can, and tell him why."

"Men do not simply self-resurrect here," Dimitri reminded.

"Why, he said that to me too."

"Was he wrong?"

"He often is. Would you like to be in his company?"

Dimitri shook their head, feeling the sudden danger even as Julian remained nonchalant.

"I will speak to him. What should he make for you?"

"I need flowers. Candles. In a discreet book, hand stitched and written, there are to be ciphers for luck…" Julian paused, considering. "And a good-bye book. Not a book of the dead, a good-bye book. Be clear on that. He will understand, if he remembers anything of import."

"Your highness, are you *sure* he can do it…in three days' time?"

"He could do it in a single evening, were he to apply himself! I have seen him write a symphony in the morning and conduct it that night! Make sure he has everything he requires and then furnish him with his commission."

"How long of a good-bye?"

"He does not need to know that." Julian shrugged. He was already thinking upon another strategy for their rescue mission.

"I do," Dimitri blurted out, and bit their lip, realizing they were on the brink of impudence. "If it pleases your highness to say *when* you would return from The Above."

"It does not please me," Julian muttered, and met Dimitri's teary gaze. He tried to keep the thought hidden, but Dimitri, Sight or not, was clever enough to follow his line of thought. "To wander willingly from happiness in search of some other necessity. To stay as I am and see old friends turned into pawns and monsters with no recollection of our love. If we met again, Dimitri, I hope you would know my face, as you did when I first came aboard."

"But how could I forget you?" they asked, stunned and hurt. In silence, Julian looked around, at the ship built from Adrian's ignorance, the maps to nowhere.

There's no malice in it, he thought, less to Dimitri, and this time, in some lone, agonizing corner of his brain. *He has just forgotten the true feeling, tells himself memories like they were fairy-tales learned by rote. I loathe him all the more for it.*

Though he swore he was thinking about Adrian, as he pushed his shoulders back, head held high to prepare for whatever was next, it was not true. Instead, for the first time in a while he thought of Vern.

CHAPTER 13

"Adrian," Dimitri said, key in hand. "You have been very quiet today. Thought you could escape my notice, perhaps?"

Adrian looked up from the book of poetry he had taken from Dimitri's shelf, double shelved and supported by yet more stringently collected tomes. He was wearing his golden spectacles which had the curious effect of making him look younger, and fragile. Ever since Dimitri had known him, Adrian had refused to wear his spectacles except in private, for books. On returning his leg to its case, they'd retrieved the glasses from a neglected shelf and left them by the bedside, and they were momentarily heartened to see he was reading.

"I slept 'til aft," Adrian admitted, brushing his hair from his face. Behind his spectacles, Dimitri could see his eyes *were* less sunken, tracking more steady than last night. "I was…I was tired in my bones. Is *Julian* all right? I acted infamously to him. It shames me… and you, *sir*."

"My Prince makes his schemes," Dimitri responded. "And your *shame* remains your own."

They continued to evaluate Adrian. Lurid bruises spackled his bare chest and the handkerchief on the bedside table was spotted purple with aspirated blood, yet he seemed better already. There were strong potions in the portable apothecary, most made by Pierre, but a surprising amount had been concocted by Adrian, himself. In hindsight, Dimitri could understand if Julian considered him to be a Renaissance man.

"Are you still tired, or have you slept enough?" They took the slim book out of Adrian's hands, shutting it and putting it on the shelf.

"Yes, sir. I have slept enough."

Dimitri held Adrian's head by the chin and caught his anxious gaze.

"This is *not* how I would like to deal with you, Adrian. You have a patron who showed me the wisdom of this arrangement, the selfsame Prince whose authority you flouted. You are very fortunate in that regard, for if my will was all my own, you would not be put to such fine work."

"Fine work, sir?" Adrian repeated, swallowing.

"Fine work indeed," they said in a distant tone, producing the scroll with Julian's commission. "Read it and tell me what you require."

Adrian read through the elegantly written note, then looked up.

"Mitya…"

"Who?"

"*Sir*, most of this is beyond me. I would not know how to start."

"That is not what Julian thought." Dimitri watched Adrian's face for any hint of deception. "It stands to reason that you are mistaken, as usual. Tell me what you would need."

"He may as well call on me to fly," Adrian muttered, too peevish for Dimitri's taste. They twisted a lock of his loose hair around their finger and pulled smartly. Adrian hissed.

"Well, if he made such a request, I would still expect you to comply without shaming me," they said with easy firmness. "This seems like less of a chore than flying, do not you think? Pretty words, on paper. Flowers. Candles. It is almost a party."

Adrian frowned, still absorbed with the note. Dimitri remembered Julian's confidence that Adrian could remember and work quickly, pushing their own doubt in the project to the side.

"May I tell you what I need by sunrise?" Adrian asked after a moment, gaze downturned.

"Will you know by then?"

"Yes. No excuses."

"Would you need your sight in the acquisition of this knowledge? Would you need your hands?" Dimitri prodded. Adrian froze, cheeks coloring.

"I happily leave that to your judgment. Sir."

Dimitri took off Adrian's spectacles. They pulled the restraints from the cabinet and Adrian let them bind his arms behind his back with strong knots twining up to his elbows and leaned into the silk of the blindfold with graceful complaisance.

"The door will remain locked, and I have the key. I will return in two turns of the glass, to feed you. You have been remiss," Dimitri murmured under the shell of Adrian's ear while they secured the blindfold, braiding painstaking black knots in his long blond hair so it would tug and pull at his scalp with the slightest movement of his head. "You are weak. I believe you yielded to another man's blade because you are not attending to yourself properly."

Adrian's lips parted in a half-formed protest and he tried to turn his face to his navigator. Dimitri put their thumb on his lip again. *Quiet.*

"I have already asked you not to lie. I know what you like to eat, and I know we had to make port this morning to get it because you had forgotten or neglected it in the ship order. To a man, all other crew members have access to what they like, I have checked. You are fastidious on their behalf but you have missed out yourself. Do you understand that it looks deliberate?"

"Yes sir."

"I think there's many things you have forgotten or neglected in the last year or so. When I return, you will tell me some of these things between bites."

Adrian's lip trembled, but he said nothing. Dimitri braced him to the headboard, looping a final rope through the bedpost to secure him, making sure he was comfortable and buffered by pillows so he would not fall off the bed even if he struggled.

"Rest now and think deep on all my sweet Prince asks of you," Dimitri commanded, and pushed the beeswax into Adrian's ears and then kissed him, hand between his thighs. They tasted tears and desire and pulled away from their captive before they got too deep into the sensation, relishing the sound of protest they wrenched from his throat. There were three sunsets ahead of them and Adrian felt best when he was forced to say please. They could afford to take their time.

Locking the door quietly, Dimitri walked down the hall to Julian's quarters. Julian met him there with a soft embrace.

Thank you, he said. *Does he bear it well? Is it at least a pleasure to watch? Does he remember?*

I think he may.

Julian cast his Sight like a net to try and find the elusive Captain, surprised at the ease of it. Adrian writhed in blackness decorated with sharp flashes of remembered candlelight from the blindfold pulling his hair, interspersed with images of something greater. The sea loomed on his blocked ears like a heartbeat while he tried to calculate time and gave up in seconds, moaning something with a semblance to Dimitri's name, head thrown back against the headboard. He was not focused now, far from it, but Julian could see the rolling clouds of calm on his horizon.

It is my wish that you leave him that way.

Dimitri followed Julian, knelt at his bedside and begged him to fuck their mouth until his back was arched like a bow. Soon Julian was wailing, an unrestrained clear sound that echoed down the hallway and made Dimitri's lips grow lax around him, pulling their own length from their trousers. They crawled onto the bed with Julian and kissed him, but paused when Julian stilled, eyes wide.

"Julian?"

"You taste of him."

"Is that…" *bad?*

Neither bad nor good but thinking makes it so.

I can wash my mouth, if it offends you.

No, I—

Julian pulled Dimitri closer and pushed his loose collar down to bare his gills. Dimitri understood, and sucked there, enough to leave molecules of scent under the spiracle which lanced the side of his neck. Julian shuddered and kissed them again on the mouth, hard and desperate. There was a name stuck in his throat, a name which he would not say, or even think.

"You miss him," Dimitri said, after. Julian scoffed.

"He is just down the hall. Do not be absurd," he said, and turned away. "There is nothing to mourn and nobody to miss, dear man, not when I am in your bed. And besides, we do not have the time to count such losses. We have other precious things to save."

Dimitri could hear music in the air, but they knew it came from Julian rather than any instrument aboard. They helped him get dressed for the evening.

The evening was for dinner and reading, in an ornate room near a kitchen where the chairs were overstuffed and comfortable. Vico wandered freely and stole choice morsels from people's plates. Ernest dashed out twice, to bring Pericles full plates of sumptuous, savory tartlets and greens. The Captain's absence was noted but nobody seemed to miss him overmuch. Julian sat on Dimitri's lap, and they shared a plate before the hourglass emptied and Dimitri left the table.

Julian watched Ernest and Pericles argue over the properties of a rare finishing varnish for picture frames. Later, Pierre came down and joined them. He fished out a copper-tined mandolin and Julian listened to Pierre's absent-minded song while he played with his food. Others came and went to grab snacks for the watch, to sit and talk. Music played in a pleasant, jovial way, and people spoke to him in besotted tones, but he could not enjoy the conversation or follow the tune.

"Julian," Dimitri said, sitting beside and taking his hand. "Was I too long?"

"Not at all. How does your patient fare?" he asked politely, handing Dimitri an orange to peel for him. It smelled faintly of vanilla when it was opened, one of Pierre's delectable creations.

"He is taking solid food now. Finally. I dare say he is much restored since the afternoon."

They handed him a long black cloth without explaining, and Julian put it in his pocket.

"The medicine is taking," Julian said with a small smile Dimitri returned. This visit had been more like a game, and little excited flashes of the encounter lit up like terrestrial fireworks between them. Adrian's head resting on Dimitri's chest, fed from their fingers while Dimitri spoke sweet cruelties to him and made him beg for who knew what until he wept.

"Captain needs new medicine?" Pierre asked, half interested.

"Now who said *new*? Is there old?" Dimitri frowned, and Pierre produced a glass jar of large lozenges from his beard like a magic trick.

"Exactly," Pierre said. Julian got the sense he was aware of more of the truth of Adrian's sudden indisposition than the rest of the crew and had been for a while. "And he *is* needing his pills, if he has not got new. Has me concoct these for him every fortnight and he did not pick them up before taking his 'bad fall'. But I thought he would have told *you*, Dimitri, as you are his devoted nurse these days. Or whatever it is you are."

"It must have slipped his mind," Dimitri said, eyebrows knitting together and letting the crack slide. "What are they for?"

"The old broomstick," Pierre responded, and saw their matching expressions, confused and mortified. "I mean his *leg*, you heathens, the one that is missing? I do not know what he takes for his cock. If he takes anything for that! Anti-rejection drugs, I reckon. That thing was hewn from a tree, you know, those monstrous tall plants from above."

Aggravated, Julian felt a rip in the back of his head, the falling star of a migraine. He hid his face and waved at Dimitri, trying not to snap or sob.

"Take the medicine to the Captain. Make him take it. *Now*."

"Yes, your highness."

"Ensure he will not forget such a thing in the future. Ensure he knows what I am owed and he cannot shirk," Julian added darkly. *If he wishes to die make sure he's not in debt when he does.* Dimitri hovered and Julian gritted his teeth. It was not Princely to yell, not at a friend. "Do not *hang* on me. I am fine. Attend to him."

Dimitri exited without another word and Julian squeezed his lids tighter. Trying to stay sitting upright and poised.

"Your royalty-ness," Pierre said, uncomfortable to address Julian without Dimitri. "If I may?"

Julian cracked one eye open and saw Pierre was holding a small black bottle of liquid. Of course, a doctor with a cure for mental anguish.

"Thank you, kind sir," he said quietly. "But I cannot tolerate anything derived from the lotus root. Perhaps you can take me to my quarters. And there I will take a few doses of whatever can relax without addicting me to an ersatz sensation. I need to keep my wits about me, you see. I cannot live in some happy fog forever."

"Should I find Dimitri?" Ernest asked, drawing curtains over the sun panels. Julian shook his head minutely. Dimitri would return soon enough. "Then I will stay with you, your highness, if you will permit me. Pericles has these storms, too, and the moss do not touch them. I have told Pierre over and over; he should not have offered that to you."

"He means well." Julian was in too much pain to be angry. "I am sure it must soothe some."

"Yes, it soothes," Ernest agreed sadly. "It is a palliative. A trick to play on a dying body in mercy's name. But you live, Julian."

The muscles in Julian's cheeks singed lightning strikes into his brain; he was smiling. His hand found the long strip of cloth Dimitri had handed him at supper in his pocket, and he realized it was a blindfold, one of several to contain Adrian's nervous and distractible gaze. Curious prophecies indeed. He pulled it over his eyes with Ernest's help, and for a moment he fancied that he saw as Adrian did. Some pain abated, and he sighed.

"Yes. *I live.*"

But Dimitri did not come back. In a few minutes Julian asked Ernest and Pericles to escort him to his cabin, then ushered them out, making them promise not to worry themselves any further with the matter. Once alone, he vomited once, twice, and passed out. On waking again, he adjusted the blindfold and curled into himself. The seizing would begin. He would be alone and terrified. He would have no control over his limbs and could not cry out for help.

CHAPTER 14

Dimitri paced outside their own chambers like a jilted suitor. The ship rocked gently on the calm seas and sun panels the color of dripping honeycomb were dimmed for the late night. The navigation room and adjoining chambers were at the tip of the ship, where often wind and intense tide could batter and break precious things, if they were not secured by an adroit hand.

Sometimes, in rough weather, the bow would tip close to the surface, to avoid deep sea benthics. But while everyone else gripped for their lives, in Dimitri's cabin all was bolted and rolled, and they could float to their port-hole without being clobbered by detritus. Free swimming, they could glance the cloudy skies, and see stars that way, a precious gift from the storm. They never slept better than that, could never be cradled in the security of the stern during such a night, along with the children aboard and the *Captain*.

Dimitri was trying to think without thinking, annoyed by the effort, so generally angry with the Captain they were sorely tempted to cut him loose and then cut him properly, until he did not mend. Duel be damned, Prince be damned, fucking ship be damned…

How can you make me feel this stupid? Why? They covered their mouth like they had spoken and looked at the medicine in their hand, discerning what it really meant. Adrian would rather die than have them in his confidence, dishonorably, of sepsis and fever, the wonderful thoughts in his head all frittered away from pain. *Undying*, and he would rather die.

Dimitri gritted their teeth, bit the inside of their cheek until they tasted blood. *They* were not a cipher, the problem had always been that no one chose to read. They were not like Adrian, who resisted each glance, every question, and was still constantly interpreted. The simple things that Dimitri required were plain to all, but never in reach.

Dimitri's Prince had asked but one thing of them, and they could do it. They could have the Captain explain the regimen. They squared their shoulders, and opened the door, quietly.

"You are a *right* bastard."

Adrian heard Dimitri's voice first, far too early from the last visit for it to be morning. He pulled his head up as much as he could in his current state.

"Sir?"

"Do not *sir* me. Do not address me. Nod if you understand."

Adrian nodded, feeling a pit in his stomach and twisting at his bonds. For once he did not know what he did wrong.

"You did not tell me you needed medicine. You've never told me that."

"I…"

Dimitri's hand jammed against Adrian's mouth, more than a warning. They were angry, Adrian realized, angry and afraid.

"Shut up. Did you forget about the medicine?"

Adrian shook his head after a small hesitation.

"You decided not to take it."

Adrian nodded and felt their hand lift from his mouth.

"Why. Explain. Do not lie or I will muzzle you."

"It is poison," Adrian said hoarsely, and swallowed. He had been sweating and crying for hours now and it hit him that the well of sorrow and desire was not quite infinite. "Sir, can I have a glass of water? Please?"

They sat him up and Adrian felt the cool glass at his lips.

"You do not think this water is poisonous. Or if you do, you still drink it. So, you are not paranoid, or you do not mind the prospect of such a dispatch, not really," Dimitri reasoned after Adrian had finished. "You think nothing of gambling your life away with any other kind of drug, or alcohol, so…I do not understand what's wrong. Explain."

"It is the leg that's wrong! My body rejects it because it is going to kill me," Adrian explained in a rush, and felt singular clarity upon saying his quiet suspicion out loud. "I need it off me. It is extraneous anyway, you have seen how I really am. The leg is *cosmetic*."

The last word made him nauseous for some reason, and Dimitri stroked his hair while he struggled against the urge to vomit on their lap.

"Why do you commission Pierre to poison you, then? And in secret?"

"I do not *know*. I just need it off."

"Julian thinks you are suicidal, and who could blame him? I think he's…" Adrian could hear their jaw set, listening. They were in congress with the Prince at this moment, a fact which made Adrian wish he could wrap his arms around himself. He resented being tied for display, vulnerable and unhidden. "I *know* he is pained by this."

"He does not think about me."

"Sure."

"I need it off."

"It is not on."

The leg had long been uncoupled from Adrian's thigh, no doubt stowed in its custom case at the foot of the bed in the Captain's quarters. Adrian shook his head violently, frightened at the prospect of ever putting it back on, only calmed by Dimitri's hand on his shoulder.

"Use your *words*, Adrian. Come on. Do not make me guess."

"I meant off the ship, sir. I do not want it near me."

"What if you are wrong?"

"I can get another one. I can *make* another one. I will take the drugs I need for it, and I will be good. But it cannot be *that* one. Please." Adrian wished he could see Dimitri, wished he could gauge how mad he sounded from the navigator's reactions. He knew he was on the precipice, obsessing about the malicious leg at night when he could not sleep, but the more he spoke of it the more he was convinced. "I am not using it right now."

"You are right about that," Dimitri sighed after a moment. "It upsets you."

"Yes, it *does*." Adrian realized he was weeping, in terror or relief. Dimitri's hand was in his hair, his head was on their chest and he did not move away. He did not want to. He trusted Dimitri and if *they* determined he was mad, then he was. If they put the pills in his mouth he would take them, if they latched the leg back on he would wear it. But he was so scared... "It does."

"Were I to throw everything which upsets me overboard it would be a very light ship. You'd be watching me go and marveling at the speed."

"I know sir. I am sorry."

"I will discard it. I will tell Pierre you do not need the medicine anymore. Do not worry about it."

"*Thank you.*"

"There are no other secret medical regimen you need to jettison?"

Adrian shook his head quickly. After this there was nothing.

"And what will I say to Julian?" Dimitri asked, then sighed at Adrian's confused silence. "Adrian, am I to believe you are in *any* condition to be doing as you should? There was a trifling matter of flowers and candles. Tell me if you cannot."

"I have not forgotten, sir. I can still meet his mandate without shaming you," he promised.

He felt Dimitri lift from the bed, but Adrian did not ask them to stay, though his mind was running circles. He had already asked them for too much and could bear the remainder of the night with his disordered thoughts, trying to contend with the instructions he had been given. Dimitri had Julian for company, a fine boy who needed care but not babying; Adrian's wretched self seemed a very sore substitution.

"Good man," Dimitri said, and stroked his sweaty hair out of his face. Adrian leant into the touch and the hard won praise with a shiver, yearning for more but still too stubborn to ask for it. "But do not disappoint him. You cause so much trouble as it is."

✳✳✳

Julian wandered the ship in the early hours, in a light fog he could push through enough to think, but riddled with excruciating pain. He met with Pierre to gather ingredients for the rescue, and to pick up a new concoction for this new ailment. He would check in when he was not scrivening, or convening with Dimitri about the rescue. He did not say what happened, and swore anyone who knew to secrecy. They had to get through the next evening, and would not be the cause of everyone's grief. After he handed off what he needed to Dimitri and Adrian, Julian worked to exhaustion, often slumped over a pile of books until the first rays of morning would wake him. Dimitri attended to Adrian and that it was rough work. He did not wish to further burden them.

But he was sick and could not hide it well. He told Ernest once more to distract Dimitri with tasks, to make sure they took care of Adrian. He did not explain; for the next forty-eight hours agonizing pain leapt from his head and spine to the very roots of his ankles. His limbs and his gills all thrummed with strange frailty, as if each time was the first. He lay there alone.

Hours passed in the dark and turned into the next evening before he knew it. He hazarded a walk in the weak sun, head compressed from bed rest. He walked the deck, salt-winds and gray breezes perfuming the air; *too strong, it is all too strong…*And with the first strengthening of his body, he felt images come; *a holding cell, a boy, the flash of blood upon glass, a man's hand upon his waist, carrying him…*

The ship rocked. Julian vomited over the side until there was nothing left in his body and sank to his knees. He dreamed of a cocoon of arms which conveyed him back to his warm and dark quarters. When he awoke, he picked himself up as though it never happened. The lights under the deck were dim enough that they did not burn. In a mechanical turn he found himself at the kitchen, struggling to make tea. Two broken cups later he managed

109

some warm water and leaves in the porcelain. It would have to be enough. *It is alright, it is already better here. Days here, but weeks, sometimes months up there.* His muscles ached in their familiar way. He took a sip of tea and closed his eyes.

He wandered without thinking, and found himself at Dimitri's cabin. *Should I tell them what's going on?*

No, he could not, at least, not *now*, when so much depended on them... But to his surprise, Dimitri was not there, drawing their maps. He gasped softly.

Adrian looked as though he had passed through the upcoming storm, weathered, but more open. His hair, usually pushed back in a semblance of half-neatness, was out of its pins and ribbons, an earthly feather quill the only thing that kept it out of one side of his face. His head leaned forward, heavy with grief, upside-down on a tarot card. He was not wearing his prosthetic leg, though this did not seem like a punishment from Dimitri; Julian did not know if he could trust someone who would think of doing such a thing. There was another leg on the table, under double-walled glass to protect it while it was refined. The room smelled of the different fabrics and books he had out, and a strong, unavoidable scent of ash, as though something was burning...

"Good evening, your highness," Adrian murmured. He studied the floor instead of looking at Julian. He rubbed the rope burn on his wrists.

"Yes, it is. Where is your warden?"

"My master rests," Adrian said, eyes flickering to the closed bedroom door. "They told me to finish my work before I came to wake them, if they do not rouse before."

Julian looked at the mess around him; books, bottles, vials, powders, a frightening amount of plants, mixed with several pots of paint from the lower decks of the ship. Salts, crystals, and seashells; the shells were in various states of breakage, some open on hinges, some torn in two; others were cracked and then refragmented, or ground down to a fine powder. He wanted to feel hatred for this man, but instead he felt awe.

"Have you been behaving yourself?"

Adrian colored, unsure how to answer. Julian took a deep breath. He saw the things he saw in his dreams for a moment, sparkling…then they fell away like the shimmering snow from Above. He felt the things he felt now…*they* did not sparkle. Not at all.

"Everything else is nearly ready," Adrian finally offered.

He did not say *Why do not you ask me what it is for?*

He did not say *Do you remember what I remember or is that lost on you, too?*

He did not say *Have you truly known me that long? How could you have been my own true heart and treated me as this, so cruelly? How can you be the same, if it is to be believed…*

Adrian motioned to the left with his head. As he did, Julian could see the bruises all down his neck. The wounds were only faded to lavender in their newness.

"Over there."

"W-what's this?"

He saw the parcels that he was supposed to collect. And yet…To the side of them was a stack of yellowed pages, a slip of a photograph underneath.

He picked it up and turned it over. Then, he meant to gasp, but no sound came out.

"*What* is this?" he breathed, finally. On it, he saw his own likeness and Adrian's, together. In the same meadow as he had Saw in his visions.

"That is the picture of someone I lost," Adrian began. The words passed through his lips as though they were grits of sand. "After I sailed on my own for a while, I met Eric. I believe he took something from me, though lately I am not so sure what, if anything; at first, I thought it was my other form, or he had created the monster that I am, but now…"

You think he took me? Somehow? The thought throbbed in his head. *But I am right here.*

Adrian felt it. He reached for it as though it was natural. He did not have to practice like Dimitri did. Shivering, Julian moved towards Adrian as if in a trance, gripping the table. He did not bend down, but reached out, tracing a hand through Adrian's flowing locks, the side of his wounded cheek until he reached under his chin.

What I saw when I passed out, I could have died.

What did you see?

What do you remember of me?

Almost nothing. A mere imprint, a photograph of someone I knew. But inside my head. And it is buried under a lot of fuzz…

I…

Hey!

What?

What're you doing?

Impudent. You have pretty thoughts right there. Nice green leaves, the frills of a ballroom— what is that from?

There's a door. Do you, do you see it?

Yes! Shall I open it?

Try. Please.

In his mind, Julian pulled at the memory, tugged and tugged, but nothing happened. He lost it and felt a wrath like no other come over him. His whole body tensed again and he growled. Adrian opened his mouth to explain and Julian raised a hand to quiet him.

"Memory is just memory! The man before me…you are not him," he could barely get the last part out.

"If I was the last man on this ship, would you not even regard me?"

"I would not regard you if you were the last man on *earth*!" he cried out. He loathed himself then! Adrian and the lot of them! The move from Above to Below had been too much! All of it, and waking up in his arms, rescued by this man, no—this beast! He shuddered. No, it is not that he was grotesque to look at, it is not that he would be unpleasant to kiss, but it was the way he spoke of the past, it was the very nature of his heart…he had been utterly twisted beyond recognition!

He sighed, tears dripping down the still-warm curves of his cheeks.

Dimitri had entered the room at some point. He did not hear their thoughts. He did not hear much at all.

"We have a party to get ready for," they said grimly, looking from Adrian to Julian and then looking out the porthole. They spared another glance at Julian, a shadow of worry over their features, but held their tongue. "And we would not want to be late."

Julian agreed, in a daze. He gathered his belongings and the new ones given over, heading for the door. Only as he picked up the ornate little box of things Adrian had made, did he stop. A chill ran up his spine.

No, I am not well enough for this to be happening. No, no please—The room spun. One touch and he already felt the stabbing pain settling back, bright and sharp agony.

"No, wait…" he murmured, falling back. He did not know if he was speaking out loud or through his Thoughts to them. Dimitri and Adrian scrambled to his side, watching in horror as he crumbled to the ground.

CHAPTER 15

The room melted, wax down the spine of a candle. Julian was no longer in the recent past, but further. He could make out rose and ivy encrusted laurels over his bed, the sea hyacinths on his bedside table. The bed was massive, shimmering around the edges like a pearl, careening with white sheets. A few low-lit coral chandeliers cupped dim blue lights in their grasp. From the far side of the room towering windows were opened, and curtains billowed from fresh seabreezes, salt-stricken with Summer's delicate air. Julian sat in his bed, unharmed and unhurried. Yet he felt anxious. He was unwell, though he was stable since the tutors had attended to him with purposeful apothecary measures.

Vern hovered in the doorway for a moment.

"How do you fare, my dear Prince?"

"Quite well, *nacreum*," Julian hid a cough in the pages of his book.

Vern wrinkled his nose. "I worry; you only lie to me when you are sick... I hear what they whisper—your vitals destroyed! Your spine tingling with magma, your ever-shaking hands—blind from pain in your head, then nothing! Nothing! I am kept out of this? Why?"

He was not upset with Vern. Distant. But not upset. *How strange!* And Vern looked distraught as a lover!

"Worry not. Do not you have your little party of the week? Are not there sweets and dances and strangers for you to delight in? Do you really think I would make you worry over this?"

"Yes, I...yes, your grace."

"You do not have to, Vern. C'mon."

"It is your rightful title. I am away to my parties."

"To rule. To please yourself sweetly. Have fun."

Vern sighed. "I will. But tomorrow, I shall not budge from your side."

They could hear the noise down the hall, and Julian dismissed his brother with a thin hand. Vern hurried away, looking radiant in his dark-green suit, but so worried.

Now alone, Julian continued to sit and read, taking a tablet of medicine every now and then. A puffing machine would cleanse the water around his bed and gurgled at regular intervals with the task. His lungs burned with every breath. His legs, when he moved towards the windows, shook. Above all, it was his head that felt odd. Beyond memory, it pounded through the images...

From the decadent balcony came a loud, cantankerous thud. Then, climbing upwards was a creature with perfectly pleasing tentacles, and a bag filled with many books. It was Adrian. His beard had not quite come in yet. His hair fell beneath his ears, on its way to getting longer. His sword dangled from the loop of a thick, seashell-studded belt. He looked ecstatic yet apologetic...Julian rushed to him, gathering the tentacles and all. He would have fallen, had Adrian not scooped him up like a child.

"Hello, darling!"

"I should apologize I have been so long, Joules." Adrian's low, rough voice sounded melodic. "You do not know me very well and your kingdom has been so kind to me—"

"Nonsense. You made sure I did not die at my very birth! That is quite enough! I sit here and mope for you while my twin runs reckless—"

Coughing, he pulled Adrian onto the clean, white sheets, grit from the road be damned.

"You never stay long enough to explain. This time, can you please?"

"W-why?"

"Because I am unwell. And because I have missed you. I have everything here, or so I thought. As I go through with my lessons...I have not the teacher

I truly need."

Adrian laid his sword down and gently began to massage the boy's back. He exerted great control over the swirling mass of limbs, willing them to float *ad nauseam*. The tensed, spasming fans of Julian's gills were cracked, dried blood along their seams. Julian looked in a mirror, and the memory scalded him. There was a creature as lovely as Vern, yet consumed by illness, drained of all life. The arm that held the gilded, round frame was taped to several IVs wrapped around the full-mouthed roses on the bed.

How sick was I, even then?

"I am better when you are here. I know that."

"My boy, I do not think I can cure you."

"I did not mean *cure*. But in Illyrial, we are connected. What you did, when I was born…you before Vern even, would be able to help me, somehow…"

"Joules? When you are not scribbling at this, or practicing your singing or dancing or sculpting, what do you wish to do?"

"It is silly." Julian felt hot tears sting his eyes in an instant. "I wish to go with you. This life is not for me. I want to explore. Sick as I am, I wish to see new places and delight in new things…"

As Julian said it, he felt ashamed. He broke from Adrian's grasp and promptly fell off the bed. He could have used the cane lying next to one of the canopies but opted not to. Instead, he curled around himself and howled. Adrian's tentacles slithered down and retrieved him. His brow knitted together in worry and…love.

"You could. It is…what I want to do. Every time I am here, I…you are unlike anyone I have ever known."

"I am not. I am just—a mess! I am going to be the first dead in a world of the undying. What a hideous precedent."

Adrian pulled him closer.

"I…thought you would thank me and go on. Where I am from, it is not the same. I am not the same. How I was made…it is not like this," he blinked,

116

his suckers pulsing with trepidation. "No such sweet creatures fighting to flood their pearls with cracks and sea salt."

"I do not know what you are talking about—" Adrian pulled at his knotted muscles, engulfing him with such tenderness it hurt to feel, and he recoiled. "Are my virtues reason to loathe me?"

"Never," Adrian replied, sharply.

"When my tutors have gone at my final command and Vern is off gallivanting as usual, I feel as though I shall die. I am already so alone, so fastidious in my learning—that is a pleasure. But in these hours, as I grow into my own crown—"

Adrian untangled himself a bit. "What would you have of me, then?"

"That you stay, that you come to know me as I long to know you; that we will become, as in our marvelous talents, infinite. In our reckless ailments, stronger when we lay together in love…" He kissed his lips, fresh tears in his eyes. "I am sorry. I know you have never wanted this of me, I know it is because of *how* I am…"

I am a fool! I have ruined it! This rare creature who saved my life—he will think that I am seeking one thing only! Somewhere in Julian's head, the thought twisted another knife; how gentle we were! How like lovers on tarot cards! Who turned us over and sent us to our ruins? When will we ever get the image returned to its proper orientation?

Minutes, maybe hours passed. Then, Adrian picked him up, as though he were a petal on a stray current. He kissed the tears from his cheeks. Then, he dipped below to Julian's lips. His body felt warm and vital and suddenly, just a little well.

"My sweet Prince, your own assumptions blind you," he said, tugging at Julian's night-clothes, the thin, linen cloth in light blue, kissing the older needle bruises down his arms. Julian flung his arms around him, IVs and all, pulling him down onto the bed.

The image iterated over itself, copied and copied again, as though saving into his bloodstream *to remember…*

***

"I think he is waking up."

Dimitri sighed with relief, stroking Julian's curls. The seizing had stopped, and the boy's lips were parted in exertion. They looked at Adrian, who had knelt across with great effort when Julian had dropped. His face was clouded and unfocused. It was clear he needed a task or he would do something regrettable.

"The last time this happened, he nearly killed you before he came to himself."

"Yes, sir," Adrian said, hand unconsciously drifting to his ribcage.

"So, absent yourself. Dress in something that would please him. I expect you know what that might be," Dimitri muttered. "And get your hair out of your face. I have told you before. You look a fright."

"*Sir*, I…" Adrian fumbled with his protest before Dimitri had to warn him. "Of course, sir. I apologize."

"It credits you that you are…concerned for the Prince," Dimitri said, and wrapped their free hand around Adrian's neck, pressing only a touch. "I will not punish you for your reluctance. But you forget that you are still *mine*. You will do as I say, and you will stay out of the way if I think someone else will lay a finger on you. Even if this is the harm you wish on yourself."

"I do not—"

"I want you gone. So go."

Adrian struggled with his speech, before nodding silently and getting up, hand gripping the table to balance himself. He grabbed a nearby cane and his new leg as he left.

CHAPTER 16

Julian returned to Dimitri's cabin with a thud. Dimitri held him, shielding his head from sharp corners. He did not see Adrian as he got up. He could not bear to face him, not after all he had seen…

"Will you be alright to…?" Dimitri asked.

Julian sighed. The room looked as though it was wrapped in cellophane, and he hurt in ways he could not describe. His mouth tasted of lead.

"It is going to have to be."

Dimitri dressed him in careful, precise strokes of their hands. First the buttons of the elegant, toga-like garment were undone; the clasp shuttered in Dimitri's hands and they draped the fabric, shimmering over his shoulders, until it flowed like water over his very essence. He did the clasp, the gold teeth of a fine thorn inside the center of a ring of petals; though the fabric was cream and plain, the detailing on the single shoulder and borders was anything but. Rows of silver embroidery were placed to look like currents; seashells bloomed from the heads of bud-like corals. A harness of gold was dipped over his head, swirling design matching that of the anklet on his left foot. And of course, he wore a crown, a diadem of pure pearl.

"Dear boy," Dimitri said, sweeping the last of his dark curls away from his face.

"I must look ghastly," Julian replied. Ripples of Woe were draped in elegant folds over his frame. The ghosts of intravenous drips shadowed his wrists.

"I do not think anyone could believe that," Adrian said at the door.

Julian blinked.

Adrian's hair had a subtle shine to it, bound by a series of handwrought gold bands. His polished boots were tanned bronze with knotted bows, in the imitation of something both floral and terrestrial. A long, green jacket that fell to his ankle, sewn from jacquard, imprinted with the silhouettes of Juliet roses and broken petals. The colors were so rich, they almost hurt to look at; emeralds, jades, and lily-pad all blending, popping into view when the head of a jewel-pattern sparkled before falling back into the fabric.

Of course he still favors green for himself, Julian thought, momentarily unguarded, and Adrian's eyebrow raised.

Still?

Get out of my head with those dirty feet. Know your place.

Sorry.

You look good.

Dimitri looked between the two of them again. They retreated to the corner for a quick sweep of the desks. *To make sure everything is ready to go. That we left nothing behind,* they thought, though it was a weak one…

"Err," Julian began, then found his sentence had no end.

Adrian shrugged, the gesture turning into a small bow at the very end. His brow furrowed at the unconscious gesture.

Was he remembering? And what of his memories did they share? The thought hung in the air. They had thought it at the same time and marveled at its sameness.

Was it perhaps my twin he sought? No, no of course not? But them…together, Julian saw fragments before him, neither pushing nor pulling at them. Instead, he felt, and he was not so confused anymore. He was walking on the un-mended pieces of his own haze; intrigued, pitying, reeling…and a little bit desiring.

Did we wake up to love in our hearts as though waking up to Spring? Julian thought. *Must it always happen all at once, a bloom pushing through heavy, icy-tinged rains and slate-strung winds? And will it make us better to love, or much worse? Will we be forever lost in a place between loves, believing the worst in ourselves until it is too late? Why not rejoice in our tender aches together, like*

120

a ship built from ecstatic whims of Fancy, like a map full of stars to our stolen Youth; Who stops us, stripping down all our bygone graces, to remake this bed, our sempiternal palace of the Deep; Is it not ours to claim; this one true origin of Love?

He picked the remaining objects folded over into an envelope. Carefully, he tucked them into his pocket, hidden until needed…

Dimitri dressed much quicker in a neat, black ensemble, adorned by a few silver pieces on their shoulders; epaulets in the shapes of stars and moons that made them look almost as a knight would. They were pleased after adjusting the silk lacing on their boots, and followed Julian to the ship's deck. Before meeting with the crew, Julian fussed with their razor-short hair, not even snagging the earrings on the top of their ear when he did.

"Your own finery?" he asked. "Or was this a gift?"

"I have but one gift from him," Dimitri said, shyly pointing to the silver arrow which pierced the helix of their left ear. "He did it himself. Hurt like the devil."

"Why an arrow? Does he have the bow?"

"Bow, and quiver," Dimitri responded. "And he has many arrows. I just wonder if he remembers where he left them."

They went in together. Adrian had passed them in the hall and was already speaking to the crew, assembled as they were for the first disembarking in what felt like an age.

"…Do not rush, do not fret. Only a couple of things must go right. Everything else is fun. Treat it like a rehearsal for shallows leave," Adrian smiled, gold tooth glinting. "It is long overdue."

That got a few titters. It was as close as the Captain ever came to apologizing for the unpredictable stretches at sea. Adrian shifted, leaning slightly on his new leg, elegant clockwork protected with tempered swirling glass, and continued in a serious tone.

"Protect the ship. Leave port if the landing party signals. They *are* rich, but we are wrong to presume the rich are soft or unwary, however often that turns out to be the case. We did not choose this place because they are uncareful, but because they have already hurt one of our number."

"Does he know we are coming?" Pierre asked. Adrian blinked.

"Batiste knows we would not leave him," he responded to general approval. Pierre glanced at Dimitri, whose thoughts lay on his mind like a fraying blanket. "Any other questions?"

"Where did your leg go?" Vico asked, having considered all possibilities over without a satisfactory conclusion. Pericles hissed his name with a shake of his head, but Adrian laughed.

"Shark food. Dumb shark."

Adrian stopped Dimitri and Julian before they left with the rest of the crew to the top deck.

"Flowers," he pronounced, and held out two identical parcels for them to take. Neither bore a receiving name, but both were signed by him. "Candles. *Book.* Do not open them before you breach the surface. Especially not the book. Do not drown the book."

"Captain," Dimitri muttered, crossing their arms. Adrian froze and they jerked their chin up. "It is sunset."

"Oh," Adrian said, distantly. He looked at the surface. "Yes. I guess it is."

"So, you do not have to…Are you still giving this to me?"

Adrian swallowed but Dimitri broke eye contact first. Julian could not discern the meaning.

"Stay close to the ship. If you can. Please," Adrian said, and absented himself.

Adrian's thoughts were obstinately fortressed when Julian Looked, obscured in impenetrable paper like the waterproofed packages in their hands. With a sudden jerk like a fish hook in his gut, Julian realized, and then wondered if Dimitri also understood. The Captain had chosen a sole recipient for his parting words, had constructed it with care so Julian would not hear his voice last. He turned to say something along those lines, but Dimitri was crying, angrily swiping their face as though that would stop the tears yet to be shed.

"I hate him," they wept. "I hate him so much. *Why* can't he just…"

"Dimitri?"

"I want him to win, sometimes," Dimitri admitted in a shaky voice, still wiping at their face, trying to stop the heaving gasps. "I want to let him win. Is that stupid? I feel so…"

They snapped their mouth shut as the ship snagged on the teeth of reef-adorned rocks, surrounding the long, winding docks to a villa. It glimmered underwater, windows filled with swirling lights and sounds, flooding through the glass. They were closer to The Above here. Julian did not know what to say but held Dimitri's bunched hand until the craft came to a full stop.

Another itinerant heart, he thought, watching Dimitri ready themself afresh. *Wounds all glancing but there's a quiver of endless arrows, and one mark. I am sorry, Dimitri.*

If Dimitri heard Julian, they did not acknowledge him, and Julian wondered how to fix it, whatever it was between them and the Captain. He could imagine Adrian in better spirits, hiding away less in his own quarters, giving Dimitri the attention they had to fight for. To Julian, it was clear *he* had upset such a cozy accord. Burdened all, with his presence…

Or maybe it is not your fault, The thought hit him like a sword. It was not his own. He looked across the deck at Adrian, and could not find a suitable response.

The floor beneath him thudded once, twice. The landing party waved to the rest of the crew, secured what they needed from the armory, and disembarked. From the narrow, dimly lit corridors of the docks, they ascended to the floating island, an overgrown mansion tethered to long, winding bridges. Now they were in The Shallows; the place between The Above and theirs. As they swam, Julian noticed marvelous lights, torches upon torches of magma flowing through the high, doric-shaped cylinders alight with crimson. The water smelled stranger here; it was not easy to take in, not like being choked to death on land, but it carried a semi-sour taste, acrid as dried seaweed.

Once inside, a man with a luxurious dorsal fin offered to take their coats.

However, Julian declined, insisting The Shallows gave him such a chill. There were scores upon scores of people; land, sea, and other...everywhere! And how they danced! Music floated through the waters from large, conch-crooning bands. It was all so different from The Above! Had he thrown parties like this? Grander and more dazzling for anyone who wandered by? Or were they intimate, reserved for the inner chambers of Princes' bedrooms...He wondered, watching everyone dance, mingle, pick at long flutes of alcohol from their glass stems. He felt sick but pushed on.

Amongst the swaying crowd was a boy with long, wild hair filled with silver-dusted dried anemone. His eyes glistened green and his lips floated into a smile the way ribbons tie and untie. He was dressed elegantly, loose, puffy sleeve shirt under a tight vest, and a pair of lace-stitched trousers. His shoes were slipper-like, but were strewn with metallic spikes, creating the effect of something soft but untouchable.

"Shipmates!" Batiste took in their expressions, positively giddy. "What on earth is your problem? It is a *paaarty!* Lighten up!"

Batiste, beautiful, sunny boy, had *too* much of a flush to his cheeks. He would be the perfect picture of health if not for the line of fishhooks that snagged at his billowing sleeves. They were shot through the fins on his arms, fastened there...Julian did not dare ask what all *that* was about. He had not considered this would change him and Dimitri. He thought it would all work out, that there would be more mouths to kiss, more limbs to caress in the night. Now...

Dimitri lunged forward to grab Batiste, but then fell forward, stumbling, arms empty.

"I...thought you would want to see me."

Batiste's long dark lashes, mismatched from the beautiful shade of red he had chosen for his hair, fluttered. "I see you, do you want something? They are *loaded* here, there is everything someone could want, from Above or Below. Why is Captain hulking around like a sullen trod? Did his hair get *longer?*"

Dimitri shuddered as if the hooks were piercing them too. They reached for the nearest tray of drinks. "W-what happened to you?"

"Nothing, you like me when I am working! You never come to these parties…"

"You never invite me. Who is throwing this one, anyways?"

"Some fancy influencer friend of the Olive Branch Company. A Florent Sage. Works behind the scenes a lot, into the industry side of industry, if you catch my drift… He is renting the place out for the night. At least, that is the gossip. Who would not want to come to a place like this for the evening? Everyone's here! And everyone wants something from someone, *mon cher*! So do you wanna…" Batiste motioned to the other creatures he had been dancing with.

Dimitri took another swig of champagne, for fortification. "Pass."

Batiste smiled wider, noticing Julian for the first time.

"But I see you have been *fishing*! Who is this *divine* little creature! And *who* is his tailor?"

"I am a—" *Prince!* Julian wanted to scream. For the first time in a while, he wanted to assert himself for the good of another…but Dimitri stopped him.

"This is the noble textile merchant *Sebastian,* he is here with us for an evening of…"

"Enchantment." Julian finished, flying by the scales of his back. "I am out for my own pleasure."

Batiste extended a perfumed hand, but Julian did not take it. He waited with a practiced cold fish expression until Batiste took the hint and brought his hand back with an unoffended laugh.

"You definitely remind me of *someone*. Are you sure I have not seen you before?"

"Quite, I am not from here. Not really…"

"You seem familiar, yet utterly foreign! One ought to know where such a boy is from!"

The description made Julian feel lightheaded. He had been from so many places after all, and some of them unknown, who would accept him now? Who would see him as one of their own? As men built allegiance to countries and forms, old and new, who would take in a Prince with no origin?

"Well, if you'd like to rejoin us," Dimitri began, but not before Batiste could pull them in, swaying until they felt sick…The kiss on their cheek felt cold. They had waited for the perfect boy to return and found he had changed. And now those lovely nights of anticipation had meant less, reduced to scraps of fabric in the overstuffed wardrobe of Batiste's mind. Batiste would atone for it, somehow, but rules or not, he no longer cared for Dimitri as they had hoped. Dimitri was devastated.

And yet…

"Pardon me, I have got to attend to other business…" Julian began formally, in case anyone overheard, giving Adrian a firm glance.

"Alright, what shall I do? Follow you? Guard you? Cause a distraction with—"

They both looked over at Dimitri.

"Adrian, see that they do not lose their head. They have been used poorly. If I ask for a distraction, a scene to be caused, you should *both* be quite ready! Is that clear?"

"Yes, your highness."

"And Adrian…did you know about *this?*"

Know that Dimitri's heart gets knocked about like a clam in a benthic? he thought, and Julian caught it as though a butterfly landed on his outstretched hand. *No, I did not. I thought they enjoyed the chase and did not mind the brevity, the chaos, the…Well, I figured they must like heartbreak. I have been so distracted.*

I did not know either. They never let on…

Memory is imperfect, when it yields to the heart's want.

Is mine imperfect because it yields?

Adrian shook his head. *We share the same defects; we feel under the haze of duress…*

What does it all mean?

I hope, but I do not know.

That is for later then, Julian thought and he could see the Hope threaded along the thought, glowing warm and gold as Adrian received it. Adrian took a deep breath, then looked at him.

"As you wish," he replied out loud. Then smiled. *Your grace.*

The words melted through Julian as though they were fire. He tried to keep himself from showing how surprised he was.

"They were always so open compared to Batiste," Adrian added, talking conversationally as they moved to the side of the room, to make Julian's slipping away unnoticed. "Batiste looks fragile from afar, but Dimitri…I could never send them off for something like that. I only sent Batiste in the first place because he seemed to *relish* the extra shallows leave. I suppose it is tiresome to be in Love, when one lives forever."

"I suppose." Julian said, thinking. "But that is not a problem for me…"

"Why?"

"All my stolen years have taught me," he sighed, tilting his head towards Adrian as though seeing him for the first time. He swayed as though they might dance, moving to the side further. "That endless time is time made for pleasure and change."

When Adrian turned to say something, Julian was already gone. He watched him weave through the crowd, before disappearing altogether. If he had a thought he wanted the other to see, he did not share it. No, he could not, for fear it would make his heart shatter.

We can start anew. We can leave what we have forgotten and start as strangers. I hope this can be.

CHAPTER 17

The more Dimitri spoke to Batiste, the darker their thoughts became. They were not connected to Julian, nor even in the same halls of the grand party, but he could feel them flowing, as if these thoughts had to go somewhere; to be heard, to be found, to be *protected*...

Why would you do this to me? I waited all those weeks for you. I thought you were hurt, but you were just too busy. Why do you treat me as if I am something to set aside for a spell, a replaceable toy, a mannequin to dress up and discard, not a real man for your pleasure. You changed. And though I am in agony, I cannot say that is all I feel.

"Dimitri," Adrian said in their ear, hand on their shoulder. Dimitri had not even heard him approach. "*Mitya*, we have got to—"

"Do not *call* me that, what do you think we are doing right now," Dimitri said, without bite. Champagne had soured in their mouth, and their head already hurt from the excess of carbonation and sugar. They felt like a fool. "Where's our merchant friend?"

"He was called away on family trouble," Adrian said smoothly. "Like we thought he might be."

"Oh," Dimitri replied and looked around as though they might still see Julian. When Adrian spoke they almost did not hear.

"He's not careful with you."

"Neither are you," Dimitri said, not bothering to ask who Adrian meant. A parade of beautiful people over the years, and the statement applied equally. No doubt they would meet Julian's brother and the whole dance would recommence, infatuation and feats and fallout. "And neither am I. But that is of no import. *Careful* is for finer folks, Captain. *Careful* does not apply to me."

Adrian did not answer, and Dimitri crossed their arms, watching the ball-room as though they were on another planet. Neither of them could dance, Dimitri realized with a sick feeling. Adrian's leg was still new to him and Dimitri had never learned the moves. They were stuck here together, miserable wallflowers, until a sweet-faced boy came to collect them.

"You have forgotten something," Adrian said after a long silence. Dimitri glared at him, wishing ardently for a duel and enforced silence. If they ever made it off this floating island, that would be the first thing they would do to heal the yawning gap inside. "We are pirates. We steal what we do not deserve all the time."

"What I want I cannot steal," Dimitri countered, throat tight again. It was a nightmare trying to say this to *Adrian*, awful and unpredictable and irretrievably someone else's problem. Handsome for the first time in an age but only because a Prince had crooked his finger at him. He had never spoken to them this way before, and after tonight, Dimitri warranted he never would. Backlit floor tiles started pulsing like the death trap of a cuttlefish. "If I could, I would not want it. I want someone to *give* it to me."

"What is it that you want?"

"I cannot explain it to *you*, Captain. How can I, when it will become another precious weapon in your hands?" Dimitri paused, noting their shallow breaths and trying to avoid the ensuing panic attack like they would dodge a fencing parry. It was not working, and they found they were still talking, saying things they could never take back. "When it marches the same way every time, and I would have to see you every day after and…*fuck*. Adrian, I just *cannot*. It's not paper. It's not paper!"

They were pointing obliquely to their own heart, tears streaming down their cheeks. The music kept playing and they slid down the wall into a crouch, hiding their face.

I did not mean to tell you, they wanted to say, but could not get the sounds out. *Remember you do not care, or better yet, pretend that you did not ask. Keep it like how it was yesterday, before sunset. Take away your secret packages tied in ribbon and your kind words, I know they are not for me, I know they are to prove a point to someone else and…I do not want you to prove that point because if you do, you will both leave me forever.*

"Get up, navigator," Adrian hissed. "I cannot join you down there."

Dimitri stood, wiping their face with the heel of their palm and trying to regain their composure.

"Sorry, Captain," they said, standing up shakily. "I have had too much to drink."

"You have not," Adrian said, and cupped Dimitri's cheek. Dimitri did not brush his hand off, did not want to, and met Adrian's gaze. "Not too much for this."

Dimitri did not know what was happening until they were in the kiss, hidden by Adrian's coat and melting into the sensation. Adrian deepened the kiss and they felt Adrian's other arm around their waist, clutching his collar as though they might fall. The other man only broke away because his new prosthesis whirred under the strain of the position. Adrian cursed under his breath, and Dimitri staggered.

"You are a damn fool," they said. Adrian took this to be the highest praise, calibrating the leg with a screwdriver he had pulled out from the hem of his coat along with an assortment of small black screws. "You will break it."

"The leg? Or your heart?" Adrian asked. Dimitri shrugged, shrinking. It was too much for one night, it was more than the last seven years put together. "Sit with me, Dimitri. Let me kiss you again."

"Why?"

"Because the dance floor is full, and we have had enough to drink. Because I *want* to, and you are so handsome, and you have been miserable tonight thinking we do not know it."

"Who's this *we*…" Dimitri started and laughed through bitter tears when they realized. "You do not mean *Sebastian*."

"Of course I do, Dimitri. You act like you have lost him already; you have mixed him up with someone else. You are rushing to the end but it is barely begun. He is still for you, and you for him."

"And what about you?"

"I do not know who I am for. I like kissing you. I like being in your bed."

"Then why are not you kissing me and bedding me more, if you like it so much?" Dimitri asked, stung.

Adrian closed the panel on his leg, sliding its elegant latch shut. He put the silver-tipped head of the screwdriver back into his coat, but did not close the pocket.

"Same reason I cannot eat food I enjoy," he said. "Or read books for pleasure. I tend to forget until *you* make me do it."

"I cannot do that for longer than three days. I wish I could. I'd make you, and unmake you until you were…"

But I cannot be that lonely all the time, Dimitri thought, and surely, *somewhere* the thought must have gone…*I cannot be so lonely anymore.*

They wished Adrian could reach into their mind, just once.

"Until I was what?"

Dimitri shook their head, then sighed.

"I do not know, Adrian. But to my consternation I have thought about it a lot, how I'd like us to be. Until doomsday, I would strip you down and build you up if I had the time. I want to tie you to the mast in a storm and provoke your other form to the surface so I know what it is like to be under and above you at the same time. I want to service you while *he* watches and realizes how much I like the taste of your cock. I want you to *fuck* me, you hardly ever fuck me because you *are* a pillow Prince and you have a sweet ass, so I do not complain, but enough! It is driving me nuts because you should be *fucking* me. I want…*is this bothering you, wage slave?*"

This last part was snapped to a shell-shocked server sidling up to them with canapés. Dimitri's head whipped around as though they were the one with tentacles, eyes piercing. Adrian's mouth dropped open, nonplused and possibly amused.

Dimitri took the entire tray of mini quiches and glared until the server ran away. Dancers who'd caught part of the outburst were smiling to themselves but mostly stayed lost in each other's bodies and eyes.

"Drugs, booze, and blades at this joint, but frank sex talk is over the line," they said furiously. "I *hate* the Shallows. I think these have bird in them."

"The eggs served this close to The Above are usually from birds," Adrian confirmed. Dimitri, shocked from this revelation, dropped the entire tray into a garbage receptacle, and glanced over at the nearest chaise. They decided to sit on the velvet fabric, stomach too-empty, as they motioned for Adrian to come over.

"Revolting."

"Everything else you said, I did not know," Adrian mumbled, and saw Dimitri's frown. "I know you would prefer that I do not. I am not sure I can forget on demand."

"Could you try?"

"No."

Sighing, Dimitri took the lozenge Adrian gave them, another pill to offset latent oxygen poisoning. They were close enough to the surface that they could feel the tightening in their lungs already; their body had always preferred Below, the deep where the air was untainted; all the pollution of the air, even the notion they were closer to it, made them feel as though they might stop breathing without hope of resuscitation. If not for the stars, Dimitri would prefer to be where they could breathe, where they could survive without hives clinging like barnacles to their trembling, hot lips.

The lozenge dissolved, tasting like sugared seagrass and they immediately felt better.

"What's that?" a passing dancer asked curiously, and sat with them to rest, sweat dripping in glittering sugar dragees off his bare shoulders.

"It is molly," Dimitri said in perfect deadpan, playing stoned earthling to the tilt. Adrian hid his laugh. "You want some, handsome? I have got lots."

"I try not to take designer drugs from the 20th century. Hurts my tummy. But thank you, Doctor Zhivago," he said with a toss of his pretty sequin-studded locs, and then kissed Dimitri on the cheek, leaving a smear of retro plum lipstick on their cheek. "And I hope your Lara fucks you hard on that vintage ecstasy. Bottom rights!"

They watched him drift away, impossibly graceful.

Dimitri stole a glance at Adrian, and realized he was looking at them with the same questing glance; trying to figure out if Julian was talking to them and not him. He pushed a braid out of his face and looked out at the ballroom instead.

"Wish we were dancing."

"Me too," Dimitri said, tangling their hand in the other man's hair to remind him to be good. Waiting was its own special torture for both, though Dimitri could endure it better than Adrian, whose thoughts turned apocalyptic in a queue.

"We could. Dance."

"I do not know the steps, and you are…"

"I gave it a little upgrade," Adrian offered, tapping the leg. "I will lead, and if it winds down, I will crank it up again."

"Sure," Dimitri scoffed, and gasped when Adrian swept them to their feet. "*All right.*"

Adrian did lead, he led marvelously. He smiled in their ear while he explained the steps when needed and murmured *left, right, back, there's a good lad* until Dimitri's cheeks glowed. Dimitri felt graceful, did not feel stupid, did not stumble when Adrian's hand caressed the small of their back and let them drop just a moment, still secure in his arms.

"I did not know you danced," Dimitri said, their head resting on Adrian's chest during a slower song. The steps for this kind of dance were immaterial as they could float, sensuously bearing each other's weight as equals. It was a common dance from the Deep and one which the guests from The Shallows watched with awe and perhaps envy.

"I could not before," Adrian responded, hair drifting freely. "You…"

He lingered on the thought happily and Dimitri remembered his leg then. They held him a little tighter, free hand brushing down Adrian's thigh. He was not trembling with exertion, he did not lean on Dimitri more than the dance required. Dimitri had given him back dance, and Adrian had given them his first since the awful wound.

"I hope you danced with him before," they murmured. "It feels so good."

"I hope so too," Adrian said wistfully, and kissed Dimitri full on the mouth before whispering the next on their parted lips. "But I hope we two have many more, *Mitya*."

✳ ✳ ✳

Meanwhile, Julian wandered from the crowded ballroom to the less populated halls of the fine venue. The kitchens were preparing all sorts of delicacies, but most of the wait staff were resting their gills. He smelled the lingering scent of Above food and was instantly nauseous. Too many dead things on the plate, flayed and skinned. It made him feel panicked. He quickened his pace to a series of corridors, perhaps the private quarters of whoever owned the venue?

Julian waded through the crowd. The hallways were much dimmer. From them, he could only half see where he was going. Turn after turn, he tried to call out, to see if he could hear a single thing—the harder he tried, the more his head filled with static and pain.

Then, from the edge of the looming darkness, a pair of hands came and covered his mouth.

Adrian! He thought, as though it could be heard across the whole party, before the room sank into total blackness.

CHAPTER 18

The boy searched for a blade. Any sharp object that might be hidden would do; a flint of glass, a broken shard of a recycled canape tray. He knew, under the dirt, there must be something of use to him. He would use his bare teeth if he had to. The bars of the holding cell were wrapped in crumbling iron and covered in rows of thick, yellow-white barnacles. The floors were thick and muddy, not stable enough to tunnel through. Inside, the boy lay next to him, a sweet mirror who looked utterly slain. He fished around for something in the dark. He had been in binds like this before. The memory was not clear, yet it also was not singular and no longer induced panic but rather a fascination with escape that made the whole scenario *fun* in a way he could not articulate. He rocked back and forth onto something sharp; once, twice…*snap!* The tight, scratchy ropes fell away. His makeshift blade was part of a broken vanity tray and still smelled vaguely of garish perfume. He wrinkled his nose, and worked on his feet, trying his best to ignore the bruises. To ignore the other fellow across from him…

"Julian?" Vern whispered. *"Joules."*

No answer. Julian sat there, slumped over, unconscious.

Is he…? He looked for the breath in his body, he looked for any sign he might stir. His chest was as still as a porcelain doll. For a torturous moment, he imagined burying him, placing a kiss on his mess of dark curls, then never getting up again to see anyone, a living *gisant* for the boy he killed.

As Vern undid the last of the bindings from his ankles, he heard a sound like a wasp's wing passing over a petal.

Julian was awake, sitting up, perfectly untied. He was knotting the ropes into origami. He was covered in no fewer scratches than Vern could feel on his own body; his lily-like hands were cut-up, and a gash on his right shoulder looked as though a hook had gone right through it. His face was bloodied but seemed no less angelic by the rivulets of crimson streaking down his ruddied cheeks. A few freckles stood out on his nose: a half-moon crescent on the left side of his face, just under one eye.

Vern raised a hand to his own face in an involuntary motion. He felt the constellation of raised bumps there, too. He felt breathless.

"Are you alright?" he asked. "We should find—"

"The hell *we* should," the boy spat. Julian looked radiant, especially in his anger.

Vern could have cried. He jerked back. *Ah, my twin,* he thought. *My own ilk after all.*

"What a golden god you tried to be."

"Me?"

"You. My enemy forever! Why? Because *you* have decided so!"

"As if you are not a Prince!"

"I am a Prince, so are you. I cannot change that. But first, I am a godless little boy, and my love knows the boundaries of no kingdom."

"Listen to yourself."

"Surely, it is you who is out of your mind!" Julian stuffed the ropes in his pocket. "Look at yourself!"

Vern wanted to weep. *I am! I am out of my mind with grief. I have spurned you. I see you before me. And you are hurting because of me…*

"How are we so *different*," Vern said, his words dripping with ice. "How and why would you even come here to—"

Vern stepped back as though he had been burned. For one aching moment he stood across from Julian as though he was looking into a mirror. Then, the glass rippled. He lunged forward and kissed him in an agonizing desperation. Julian gathered him in his arms.

They kissed. The frisson felt like an electric spark. The meeting of a mirror to a mirror, magnified.

"I wondered when this would happen," Vern said, lilting and lyrical as ever. He traced the curves of Julian's bow lips, pressing at the open scrapes there with gentle fingertips, then kissing over them.

"What on earth happened to us?"

Vern sighed. "It is kinda, well—" His voice cracked. "All my fucking fault."

"Your behavior is, but what brought you there was not. Come now. We will figure it out together…"

"It is not like anyone is looking for us." Vern said, suddenly.

"What?"

"They think we are helpless. We are boys, after all. Men prefer tales of rugged older fellas who can get themselves out of any scrape. But when boys do it *their* way, well…"

Julian leaned back. "I am listening."

"Joules, it was *me* who got our memories erased."

"You! You put us—put *me* through all this! *Not* Adrian?"

"Oh please, your brawny beloved blond, the *sea Captain*? Who wrote you sonnets and built arches of flowers where'er you walked? Adrian of the ruined capes over the treacherous bridges under your slipper shod feet? Who could *always* tell us apart, no matter how I tried to trick him for a kiss from his whiskery lips? Nice Adrian–*That* Adrian? He would never ever, he would kill himself before. Poor lout probably got his leg taken from him—"

Julian's eyes widened, '*how could you know that*' on his lips. Vern waved his hand nonchalantly; he had not fixed that suspicion, but Julian's reaction was all he needed to confirm at least one part of the gruesome tale in his head.

"W-what was I like, what were any of us like?"

"You were *you* Julian, so easy to love. But as a result, your enemies found you easy to hate," Vern began. He played with the cupid's ringlets around his face, nervous that he had to explain anything like this to his older brother. It felt like a test he had not revised for. "I may never have been a duelist, and

137

I never ruled by the sword, but I saw the trouble that surrounded us. I was always much better at coffee tables and boardrooms. That is my nature. For all the good you did, sweet Prince, I had to send twice the guards out to make sure you could do more. Your enemies were reviled by how we, and by we I do mean mostly *you,* ruled with such an honest and delightful soul…"

"You called me Joules, too?"

"Everyone did. You preferred it. Do you prefer it now? Or is it…" *Is that another thing which has changed forever?* He thought, crushed.

"I would like it if you called me Joules."

Vern looked down at his own scraped up hands. His outfit was intact for the most part despite everyone being so rough with him. On his throat he wore his choker with many strands of white seed pearls interspersed between various sea gems. In the middle sat a perfectly formed shining, black pearl.

"It all came back to me, here—it was my fault. I made a deal with Eric, I thought it would for the good of Illyrial, or for my own good. You were leaving on your ship and…and I was heartsick."

"But it is not just my memories, Vern. It is Adrian's too."

"I did not do that." Vern looked away Julian. "When he went looking for *you,* like he was some shameful banished boy of old Illyrial, he must have… not known the way. Oh, quite, quite forgiven! In my ledger anyway, if he's had rough dealings with you since then I shall not forgive him, until you say I can. But I think *Eric* has been playing tricks on all of us. I think when your Captain went looking for you, that is when it must have happened. Covering his tracks! Naughty, naughty! *Not* forgiven! We shall fix all of it, there is time yet."

"Fix, Vern—*How?*"

"My memories came back in here because I was on the brink of finding what I needed. What I loved. I suspect when you and Adrian make amends you will have that same stroke of change."

"Vern?"

"Yes, Joules?"

"You *love* me?"

Vern pulled at his curls. In the shell-dust of the dungeons they were in, he truly did seem a boy. He warmed to the tip of his gills.

Under the sensitive, tight skin just behind his ears, a pair of semi-translucent teal fins shimmered, fanning out like wings. Julian whimpered. Vern's came out behind his ears, twitching in response.

"This bond is different than between other boys—for you and I share a throne, so alike because we were from the same shell. Do you understand? We shall part ways again and again, but they shall always know us by our bonnie features."

"And why are there no boys Above?"

"That is *our* kind, Joules. Above, ones that might have a glancing feature in resemblance were all killed; destroyed, or forgotten…"

"Forgotten?"

"Forgetting up there is not the same. It is as good as being dead. It does not come back. Not like here," Vern took Julian's hand and placed it over his heart.

"Boys, men, creatures…I still do not understand. I am afraid I will need you to spell it out."

"Our queer kind, some stay boys forever, some are already born little men; some men regain a boyhood later in life, and some boys can grow a beard if they so choose; and creatures! Well, as I have said, how, where and why one is born is as different and multiplicitous as the wide, wide sea; coral reefs, asexual reproduction, seahorses with broods, boys born from the foam of a white wave blessed by Venus themself, men from the metal of ancient diving helmets; octopuses and squids, snail beds and shell beds…you name it!"

A shell bed. Julian grasped at the pearl collar on Vern's neck and bought him flush to his chest. Vern was messy and powerful. Julian would never forgive him. He did not need to.

Julian tried something, then: *You who share my every molecular being. My twin, in your own way you tried to protect me...*

In an instant, Vern was shedding tears.

"You got it back?" he said, excited, touching Julian's temple.

"Yes! And...Can you?"

"I am on a few things that would prevent it regardless—suppressing the earth air and what not. I should, I should switch to something a bit safer, actually, but err...no. I never showed your natural talent, and I did not try in class. I think if I could be damned to try...who knows! My gift must lie elsewhere."

Julian kissed deeper and started rubbing his thumb between two gills, making Vern whimper uncontrollably into his mouth from the new sensation.

*All of those parties, all of those fancy courts, but...*The thought floated between them.

Julian guided Vern so he was turned from him, clutching his waist to his own and hooking a finger under his collar. A bizarre deja vu overtook him as he stroked his other hand up Vern's spine the way others had done to him. He watched Vern arch in the same way he would, his shallow breath hitch before he gasped, dorsals fanning while Julian pushed splayed fingers against their grain and kept a firm hold of him by the neck. The things Julian had to instruct others to do, a thousand secret things most did not even know, he knew by instinct for Vern, and the realization made him hungry.

"*Nacreum,*" he said, and Vern moaned at the pet name, head turning though his eyes were squeezed shut. "How do you usually...?"

Vern blushed deep.

"I do not know," he admitted. "But I..."

Teach me the way to please you, the way only I can. The intoxicating thought passed between.

"How many boys have you fumbled with since we last met? How many *men*?" Julian asked, hot under Vern's ear. Vern stuttered, biting his lip when Julian stroked his cock slowly. It did not feel at all like his own heated touches, he jerked into his brother's hand and whined. "Answer your *Prince*, boy. I want it spoken, so anyone can hear."

"Wanted you to *rule* me. Could not let anyone else…"

"Do you think this is a pleasure for me, to teach one so very green?" Julian scolded with a smile, watching Vern tremble before deciding on a story to tell him. "When I was first taken, the poor lad above me had to push me open with his thick fingers for hours before I could take his cock properly. He was not much bigger than we are, but it did not matter. It almost drove me mad; I was so tight he could not move in me before spilling his seed. He stayed inside and stiffened again and then he could fuck me, *finally*, and I could not stop clenching…"

"Joules…"

"But what will I have to do for you to sheathe me, ungrateful boy?"

"Please do anything you need to me. Please fuck me," Vern gasped, tears in his eyes, shocked at how fast he was reduced to begging. "Please, my Prince. I was made to bring you pleasure, to be your companion ever, equal in birth but beneath you always. Please make me fit you…"

"I do not need you to fit, dearest," Julian explained coolly, pushing a finger inside. "I prefer if you are gripping me too tight, struggling to take me every time. Afterwards, I would so enjoy offering you to my closest friends and Favorites, to make you heavy with a sterile clutch, lavish you with plush tongues and kisses until you are able to accept such a gift at your Prince's whim. 'Consort' may suit you better than 'crown Prince,' if you could do such a thing for me. I would be most pleased."

Vern's back arched, thighs shaking.

"But I *could not*," he whimpered, touching his tight belly, trying to think of where a clutch would press against, and moaning when he imagined Julian instead. "I would break."

"I did not break, when I tried it," Julian said, pushing deeper and with more fingers while Vern clenched around him. "And I do not think you would, you are made of stronger stuff. So enough holding yourself at an arm's length, boy, you have let your sole duty fall to the wayside and it is a disgrace."

"My sole…"

"Princes are made for pleasure, as I have told you over and over." Julian remembered, and all at once the feeling came back to him; everything in Illyrial he longed to remember in his past began to come back. "Their own and that of their subjects. Can you remember that lesson this time?"

"*Joules.*"

"You will kneel before anyone I command," he said into the quiet cell, and thrust deep. "And like now, you will stay there until you need your gills to take a breath, until the lucky men I choose for you are sated and helpless to groan your praises. You'd be cruel to withhold this from anyone who asked. You are not cruel. I will not allow it any longer. *Use that tongue.*"

Vern did as he was told, and with great pleasure.

"On my lap. Now," Julian purred. There was a shadow of protest before Vern remembered himself and scrambled into position, arms wrapped around Julian's shoulders while Julian guided himself inside. He *was* tight, and Vern grit his teeth when Julian pushed all the way in.

"*No,*" Vern shook his head emphatically, pupils blown. His voice was only a little roughed from Julian's cock. Next time Julian would have to put him to better use.

"You were silly for denying yourself. Such a beautiful boy. Anybody could have been your first, anyone you desired."

"Not anyone. I did not want it to be just *anyone,*" Vern admitted shakily, grinding down as much as he could on Julian's length even while Julian thrust up and made his legs shake. "I just knew you were for others, and I…never thought I could ask you, Joules, I am sorry…"

Floating through the water, yet restrained perfectly in Julian's embrace, they looked as some new creature; merged; Vern's ass pressed to the cusp of Julian's hilt; twin shells of pleasure, hinging and hinging, opening and closing with each cohesive thrust. Together, their bodies grinded, mid-water, as though trying to press back into one another and form, whole and pearlescent, once more.

"I am for everyone I want, everyone who will have me. So are you," Julian said, and Vern, dubious, opened his mouth. Julian quickened his pace in response, hand rough around Vern's cock. "Don't you dare contradict me."

"N-no," Vern stuttered, and held on tighter around Julian's back. "I will ask you *first* next time, I will…"

They kissed, moaning into each other's mouth as they released together. Julian held Vern close and let their consolidated thoughts pass without shape for seconds or minutes. Vern, throbbing pleasantly around Julian still, nuzzled into his neck and they both writhed in the afterglow.

Does it feel like that every time? Vern thought, giddy and overwhelmed. While he processed, a jumble of memories and fantasies poured from his mind, like papers from an overstuffed drawer or mattress. Julian saw new things to try, deep-guarded desires tasting just a bit of shame, naive questions and hopes, the shape of people's lips, friends and strangers and his brother, speculation on the taste of a heavy cock or two… *Oh Julian,* can *it feel like that every time?*

Vern untangled himself slowly, moaning as Julian slid out. He looked at Julian and wanted to touch him, to reach out and make sure he was real. Seized by a new desire, instead he reached down between them and touched where Julian had spent himself inside. He marveled at the sticky, white iridescent substance and sucked on it, before pulling Julian in for a watery kiss.

Taste yourself, He beckoned, and Julian kissed him deeper, sighing. This boy he had traveled to the above and back for, here, wanting of him, impossibly… *Taste what we have, the sameness of our very beings, and then taste of me.*

"What are we to do now?" Julian asked, remembering *where* they were, and why they were there. "Flee?"

"You have what I came for." Vern said slyly. We can go back now."

"How?"

"Illyrial can be remembered now, for its Princes have…" He blushed, pausing with gravity. "If we had not, then Illyrial would remain shrouded as ever. Not one new inhabitant would make berth there, not even if we found exactly where it was marked on a map. If you did not rule me and I did not honor your rule, Illyrial would be forever cloistered and virginal."

"What about Eric?"

"And Florent, one of his naughty press secretaries, and everyone else here…well, we shall simply devise a plan," Vern smirked, pulling his clothes back on. "Here is what I remember; you and I, when we are at peace with one another, could do *anything*, unfathomable as that seems right now."

Vern sat up, head clear and pulled Julian up next to him. In the middle of danger, he felt complete, somehow, entirely found.

"Now, Joules," he stood, facing him once more with a wicked look while he took something out of his discarded jacket pocket. "What is this *book* Adrian gave you?"

"Hey!" Julian cried, grabbing it from Vern's hands. "Do *not* open my letters, Vern, it is such a…"

"Bad habit, I know."

"I am sure I have told you—"

"It is a good-bye book, is not it? It is precisely what we need to bid adieu to this place."

"*Yes*, but not just now. Not all at once," Julian said, flipping through it gingerly so as not to cause a spark. It *looked* right, but the state of Adrian's mind… "You read it, I presume. Does it make sense?"

"I never had a head for all that, but it looks like the other ones I have seen, more or less. A little nicer."

"Was there anything else included with *my* correspondence?"

Vern turned out his pockets sheepishly. Among other pilfered treasures lining the young Prince's pockets, endless flowers and a handsome bundle of candles were produced. An additional note, still sealed with Dimitri and Julian's name on it, sat on the floor between them, and Julian took it in his hands.

"But who's Dimitri?" Vern asked. "And why do *you* get to open *Dimitri's* mail?"

"Vern, shush."

"Can you read it to me? Adrian has the *nicest* writing voice. It feels like tingles, all the way to my toes."

"Vern, my love. *Focus*: Dear Dimitri, and dear Julian," Julian started, raising a warning eyebrow at a vibrating Vern so he did not burst out. "In case of my absence from you, I have enclosed instructions on how to light a candle. It is not commonplace knowledge nor is it instinctual. From the book, pluck a page and fold it left to right, so the rough side faces itself. Each page produces a different fire, read carefully and choose. Take a candle and place the thinner end in the fold, close like a kiss and then rub. The open flowers are for burns, to be placed between closed lips and swallowed. White soothes the pain, red heals the wound. The *closed* flowers are for—" Julian continued, scanned ahead, and swallowed, deciding to improvise. "The closed flowers are to be opened upon your safe return. Yours, Adrian! What a nice letter, and informative too."

"That cannot be how it ends, that does not sound like him at all," Vern frowned, put out. "Where's the overarching metaphor, the approachable and considered sentiment? Whither the lengthy postscript? Wherefore can I not hear the teardrops on the page?"

"He has been unwell," Julian explained, folding the note with haste before Vern got suspicious and tried to scan it for himself. Then he sorted out the flowers from the pile, white and red in one pocket and closed in the other, with the note.

"That is not an excuse, Joules. When has he *ever* signed off with 'Yours, Adrian?'" Vern cried in indignation. "And he was so strong at the start; the page plucked and folded, the *rough side facing itself*. The flower is implied but not yet present, did you mark that? Most beguiling! Opening and closing, flowers and books, paper and flame! Two sides of the same coin, for the two recipients, such generous romance in its even hand. *Everything* indicates a happy climax. But then! Just as we are about to be delivered to our blissful apotheosis! It sounds as though the writer gets up for a snack rather than finishing the thought. Badly done, I say. Maybe his worst, only saved from infamy because I have read his shopping lists...I mean, this scribble is on its way to *sabotage*! Does he even want you to come back? I get no sincere sense of a 'safe return', whatever that might mean. Does he restrain his formidable gift to please this *Dimitri*? Or does willful mediocrity please *you* now?"

"These are not the questions we should be asking, Vern. Come on, look through the book with me and figure out what flame we need for doors. You can ask him what on earth he was thinking when we see him next."

"And I will! You know as well as I that letters should be a sacred pleasure, to write and to read, not an onerous chore..."

Vern continued his outraged prattle, a pleasant and familiar accompaniment while Julian scanned the good-bye book's perforated pages and found the one he needed.

"...If someone sent *me* a letter like that and made me the proud recipient of a plumber's requisition rather than tender words from a lovely friend, I would weep for a fortnight before endeavoring to find consolation in the arms of another," Vern concluded with a soft sigh, and stood with Julian. "But water over the boat, I suppose. Let us see if the plumber's candles are any better..."

"I have missed you so," Julian laughed, and lit the candle as instructed.

A harsh blue flame flared from its tip and turned the page to ash that floated to the top of their cell before dispersing like snowflakes. Carefully, Julian pointed it at the lock of their cell, which popped and sparked before it was no more. The door drifted open from the flame's force and Vern pressed his palms together in silent glee, understanding the need for quiet before Julian could remind him.

The Captain's not totally cracked, then, Vern thought with palpable relief, and could not know how close Julian's thought was to his.

CHAPTER 19

Through the basement of dungeons and boiler rooms and wine cellars, Julian followed Vern. Vern moved with newfound energy and surprising grace. He now remembered the path he had been taken forwards, and found backwards to be quite simple. *Like doing a Dame Coco dance in reverse,* Julian heard Vern's fleeting thoughts.

"We should go to the docking pod. I think there's things of mine there," Vern said, turning around. "Do you think that is all right? Do we have enough time?"

"What things of yours, Vern?"

"For my proposal in the aphotic, Eric sent along some of my assets," Vern said, plucking at his pearls.

"Your proposal, what the hell does that mean?"

"Contract, marriage, social media collab, I do not know. He was very strange," Vern said absently, counting lighting sconces. "...seven, eight, there we go, secret room!"

"You did not sign anything...?"

"No, *that* lesson is in my memory locked, Julian," Vern said, smiling as a door slid open behind him. "Docking pod! Boxes! Once-crispy snacks of an uncertain provenance! Welcome, brother, to my *salvation.*"

It was a docking pod, for certain, large enough to bear one person comfortably, crammed with boxes and chaotically wired technology that looked older than Vern, who was currently pulling a large box from under the control console with effort.

"Did you drive this thing here?"

"No, autopilot," Vern said. "As I have said, Florent Sage and Eric were tight. Ah, here we go. Map! You needed a map, right? Decoy map, which I created when I thought the first map might be important and was half mad from boredom. And um..."

He bit his lip. Julian waited, crossing his arms.

"What is it, Vern?"

"I do not know whether it is his er—or his, um," Vern said with a mincing precision. "It is *of Adrian*, I believe. But his kind, ah, it grows back, yes?"

"Vern, he is missing a *leg*," Julian snapped.

"As far as you know," Vern said under his breath, but grew serious when Julian glowered. "Eric was wearing it. I thought it must be important, so I rolled it off his spindly finger. It was only his *treasures* on INDRA-1, that is what he said."

He held out a ring, a curled tentacle on a handmade chain of paperclips. Julian resisted the urge to snatch it, or to vomit. Vern felt the wave of nausea from his brother and put the ghastly thing away.

"We have another problem," he said, glancing down the hall with trepidation. "Maybe it is above party security's paygrade to come down here and make sure we are not up to anything while the Champagne flows, but should we scale those stairs...Well, last time I tried they were rather rough with me and tied me up and knocked me out, and I did not like it even a little! I do not think they know who we are."

"That is *good*, Vern."

Vern huffed a curl out of his face.

"I do not want to do the whole thing again, the knocking out and throwing back into the cell thing," he said. "I would like to leave here now, though."

"What if I were sick?"

"Aren't you always sick?"

Julian stopped and explained from the beginning.

"I am pretending, this once, to be you. You pretend to be me, still and on the brink of death, right here in the hallway. They look you over, realize that you will die on their watch if you do not get help, halving our value and pissing off their boss…"

"And then we lock them in the docking pod and make our escape, excellent," Vern finished with good cheer. Julian paused and agreed. He had been planning on grievously injuring the guards with another page of good-bye but locking them in the docking pod made more sense. "Here, give me that delightful robe. This *will* be fun."

Vern lay with great pathos in the hallway, all shallow breath and hacking coughs, one golden eye drifting to the wall on the brink of unconsciousness. Julian watched the performance for a moment, nonplused.

"Very convincing," he complimented, and straightened out Vern's suit. "Maybe too convincing."

"Well, it never tricked *Adrian*," Vern said, hand to his forehead. "But it might be enough for the cream-faced loons at the door."

Julian walked to the door and rapped smartly on the window.

"Ugly man," he said in his best Vern voice. "My *brother* requires whatever meager assistance you can provide. He's sick and his medicine was confiscated when he was tossed down here like a wheel of cheese. So, if you please…"

"Ugh," one of the guards said. "One of the basement faggots is sick."

"The quiet one or the annoying one?" asked the other, long-suffering.

"Quiet."

"Ugh."

"If *you* go I'll suck your dick," the first one said, thinking it to be a bargain.

"Bro, you sucked my dick last time and it was *not* worth it. You don't know how to pull off, and this guy went to the opposite of charm school."

"Hey, asshole," said the guard with regrettable technique, turning around to face Julian, who kept his face impassive. "If you promise not to bite and scream and carry on this time, I will open this door."

"As if. I do not bite without planning to swallow whole. Unlike you, perhaps," Julian snapped, wrinkling his nose. "Time is of the essence, so once

149

more; my brother?"

"Fuck, okay. Please stop talking."

"Only because you said please," Julian muttered, and the door swung open.

Julian waited until the first guard was downstairs with a first aid kit before he lit another candle, pointing it to the sentry remaining at the door. Carbon monoxide pulsed in his veins within seconds and he crumpled without a sound. Downstairs, he could hear Vern's hissed exclamation after shutting the other man in the docking pod.

"Oh, Julian, you did slake your bloodlust after all," Vern tutted, clicking his tongue at the unconscious guard and toeing over him. "Well, it is a better end than being stuck in a room nobody knows about, with stale potato chips as a final companion. I suppose. Here's his key, let's go. But am I that aggravating?"

"Vern, you are a delight to know. Maybe too much of a delight for some."

Vern seemed satisfied by this.

They both hurried up the stairs, past another corridor. Julian, however, Saw something.

Run! Julian ordered. He took anything precious on him and handed it to Vern. *The other way! To the party. Adrian will know where to find you.*

Vern disappeared, scurrying the other way, but the footsteps grew louder.

Julian knew exactly who it was and who he looked like. In Vern's pocket there were no weapons. Along the walls he searched the magma torches and decadent doorways to bedroom after bedroom. He plucked one of the near-empty glass jars from a mirrored tray, its long handle meant to dip into some nauseating perfume, easy enough to conceal within his outfit.

Adrian, be ready, he thought, and he felt the room flash white, once, twice, before exiting. *This man who tried to sell my brother off, piece by piece! I will end his existence. I have sat on my hands for too long.*

He saw Florent. The man had long, blonde-pink hair, cropped on the sides with a razor. They wore a loose, long blazer in mauve, with matching pants. Their makeup was strange–it reminded Julian, for a moment, of the men Vern had met with, somewhere in his mind, he was already distrustful of them.

But they did not say hello and their thoughts ran like this: *Oh my goooddd, this is the guy Eric was talking about—stuck up bitch who would not put out for anything? Heh. Can't see how he survived on Earth. Ah well, a type for anyone! But this one should be shut in the fucking basement, with the other one, where I left them. Heh, too bad he's not here now…*

He lunged and missed, but Julian crumpled to the floor in such a way that he made the other think they had won. He picked up Julian like he was a sack of flour. Julian was smarter than this, even half-alive, he knew what to do; go along with it, do not fight, protect the glittering, short blade beside his hips from falling out…

Passive and good, too good—that is what they need to see, he thought. *If they do not…they will remember you are actually alive, a whole, complete being beyond that.*

Noiselessly, he shut his eyes and tried to feel where the room might be; black after black after black, the stream of shadows in his head spun; the smell of something bitter, but not a citrus or a flower, the dry heat of The Above; it was harder and harder to breathe the higher this man climbed; an attic? He thought vaguely, as they rounded another corner of stairs, water light and airy…

It was hard to breathe, but he would manage. He always did.

His body hit the floor with a thud. He cracked his eyes opened a bit and saw they were on the roof, the surface around them, their feet in shallow pools of water.

Help, he thought dully, but if the thought reached anyone, let alone Adrian, he knew not. He was too used to being Above and not having help. He was on his own now. The only thing that softened the thought was that Vern was alright.

Easy job—what was I gonna do without the other one? It's like a pair of bad earrings, dangling? Maybe I will tell them they attacked me. After what they did to Eric…told me at this party…Yes, the both of them. If they cannot be waved in front of a camera or reasoned with for commerce—what good are they for this cause?

Florent stood over his body, dragging him by his shoulders, so that he could not breathe.

We are the same. But to the above, we look so different. Or, they seduced me! They are, after all, Princes of the deep—and if words like that ever got out—who would they believe? I am soft and feminine—I can keep my position in The Shallows, in The Above, because I am good at being perceived—and they are creatures of the deep. Wild! Savage! Masculine! Strange. Yes, this one could succeed on his own Above, but two of them, lots of them, like rats from the sea, it is easier to spin a narrative about how dangerous they are.

They waited around, mostly. Thinking themselves clever. In the meantime, Julian reached for the handle, readying himself.

Yes, but first…

As Florent lunged, their hands unsteady and bejeweled, Julian braced himself and stabbed the perfume handle up; wrapped around it was one of the pages of Adrian's book, the flame dancing upon the glass, hot inside the man, blood rushing out. The fragrance combined with harsh Earth air made the flames dance higher and higher.

Julian had not burnt himself in the process, for the book's maker ensured some protection over those who lit it. With his eyes closed, and with help, he had bested the man. Florent lay sprawled on the sand. He laughed a little.

"What's the point of you? You will not kill me."

"I will not hesitate to do as I please," Julian wheezed, throwing himself down from the roof and plunging. He swam with great difficulty, fumbling for a nearby window. It was easier to fall back down this time, it was better than being dragged. He tried, with all his might not to cause a disturbance, but he knew better; a boy with blood on his hands, and a sharp hair pin might as well be a sculpture to debate—he floated in and slinked along the punch tables.

Everywhere, people stared.

He reached for a glass, hands shaking, when someone spilled a glass on him. Red hibiscus wine. It was Vern, in a masquerade mask, slip tied behind his curls. "Darling! The mess you have made…let's get you cleaned up, Sebastian."

Julian's legs shook. Adrian was there, too. They walked to one of the many restrooms and then fled down the nearest stairs to the docks.

What happened? Adrian asked.

Too weak, cannot…Eric takes bad, unchecked cheques from above. Creeps. Vern okay?

Yes, we are all…

Vern slid an arm under him but even with his help Julian could not move more than a few feet without seeing white. Adrian scooped him up as if he weighed nothing.

Where's Dimitri?

Sent them back to the ship. Realized we needed to go as soon as only one person came back. And…it was not you.

Julian groaned.

"I wish I could have told them not to worry, they must be so worried. I will be better when we get there. Promise…"

Adrian rushed down the stairs, Vern at his side. Once they reached the last platform, he put Julian down and Vern draped a cloak over him to better cover the stains. The coat-takers at the gates asked once more if they left anything—they smiled politely *No* and hurried on their way. All the way down the piers, the wobbling bridges so reminiscent of long-submerged and ghostly Venetian canals, Julian could no longer hear physical sounds. Instead, he heard the thoughts of the guards, lingering as they made their way down:

Foreign. Who let them in? And should they be allowed to stay? Florent sent a missal for folks that looked like them. Check their documents—were they from The Above or The Below? And if they do not belong here—we will send them

153

right back.

At the waiting ship, Batiste climbed up the anchor and rolled onto the deck, to the delight of Vico, who was playing jungle gym on the mooring ropes.

The party had been getting boring anyway. Batiste had overindulged on sundust and struck out like a clueless teenager with the most dazzling seahorse he had ever seen, possessed of a mane so lustrous Batiste would have been happy to braid and brush it for the rest of his days...clearly, he was out of his depth. It was time to get back to bed, and maybe into some work, and possibly let Dimitri court him some more. If Dimitri was not done with him at long last. That kiss on the dance floor between them and the Captain had been *hot* hot.

"Batiste, is not everyone over *there,* looking for *you?*" Pericles asked from the cushy beach chairs where he and Ernest had elected to sit and supervise Vico.

"Y'all could have just dropped a line if you missed me that much," Batiste giggled, standing and dusting himself off with aplomb. "The way the party was winding down, I bet everyone will be back soon. Anyways I am back! And I bring *gifts.*"

He discreetly checked to see if the packages he had been burdened with were in need of a crimping jet and a glass oven to dry out. But the backlog of letters for Pierre—from the *seahorse,* some people had all the luck!—was still safe in its protective package and the message bottle's cork was sealed with strong wax. *Good,* Batiste thought; he did not want to wade back for replacements, especially from a pill like Florent Sage.

Batiste really could not remember the last time he had seen that many armed guards at a little dance in a private home, outside of his home berth of Peusouci. In his not-limited experience, the excess of The Shallows did not extend to strongman displays like that. Things had been getting hairy the closer he got to the sun, just generally, to the point where he was canceling social engagements and giving continuous ship life more of an honest try. He *had* been happy to see his shipmates tonight. In small doses, he even loved them.

Maybe I have a funny way of showing it, Batiste thought. *But that is what they love about me.*

"Dimitri!" Ernest cried. "Back so soon?"

Batiste turned around, bright smile on his face and packages utterly forgotten. Dimitri caught his glance by accident and pivoted in their boots like they were ballet flats. Even after the party, they looked handsome and put together, almost aristocratic in their simplicity. It was putting thoughts in Batiste's head that he knew better than to try and action. He could take a seahorse's rejection, that was an honor. But getting dumped by *Dimitri* on the same night? Too much!

"Hi again, stranger," he said instead. "Where is the exquisite boy you came with?"

"With the Captain."

"And where is *he*?" Batiste pressed, not even trying to mask his curiosity. A Dimitri who kissed around at a party and danced everyone to distraction, only to end the night with an effortless French leave like some kind of debonair libertine, was unspeakably appealing in a way he could not put his finger on.

"Robbing them blind. What else?" Dimitri responded, looking over the wharf to the garishly lit party house. They had purple lipstick on their cheek, lipstick which was not the Captain's or the boy's. What, *what* was going on? "We have to be ready if there's trouble. Batty, you are a universal donor, right?"

"O-of what?" Batiste asked, flushing to his ears while Pericles and Ernest exchanged a look that meant they were talking about him in front of his face. Dimitri had never called him 'Batty' in front of anyone before. Not that he had asked them not to or anything, but…Dimitri looked at him properly for the first time since coming aboard.

"Blood."

Batiste, unsure if he could respond vocally, nodded before regaining some of his poise.

"*Si*," he said. "All boys are. Is it supposed to get bloody?"

Dimitri shrugged, and looked back out to the shore, waiting for something. Something *better*, Batiste was sure, while he started to knead the fine veins in his wrists. He needed to ghost the ship more often. Who knew what surprises would have awaited him in a year?

CHAPTER 20

The Clarel whirred as it departed the dock. The lights of the party seemed too harsh, too close even as they faded into the distance. Adrian gave the crew instructions for *where* to go next. Aboard was peaceful; the scent of chocolate chip cookies wafted, Vico was busy fencing with Henry and Batiste, having a whirl of it around the deck as soft polka music played from the painting room beyond…all of that hardly mattered.

Adrian ushered Vern into the nearest quarters to get Julian to bed immediately. When he returned to the helm, he saw Dimitri, grey as a corpse, pacing, *safe*. He marched up to them, hugging them hard and running a hand down their knotted up back, privately vowing to smooth every seized muscle. Dimitri stiffened like they had been struck but relaxed minutely in the embrace.

"Are we set to depart?" he asked, when he was sure Dimitri was unharmed.

"Yes, Captain." they said, breathing shallowly. "Are you alright?"

"Yes."

Vern strolled in, mask off. Still, in Julian's clothes. He was about to interrupt Adrian and let him know Julian had vomited all over him and Pierre before he collapsed. But it was too late, Dimitri was bolting towards him.

"I missed you," Dimitri murmured, face buried in the boy's curls. "Are you alright?"

"Dimitri, that is not—" Adrian said, too late.

"Oh no," was the response. "*You* are Dimitri?"

"That is the *other* one," Adrian said, watching Dimitri drop the boy in shock.

"Why would not you tell me so, Adrian? What the hell?" they snapped, pushing an aggravated hand through their hair, and looked down at Vern.

"Where is Julian, then?" Adrian asked.

"He is down the hall. It has been a trying evening and he needs rest. I was to run ahead and explain as much, before I was *intercepted* by this rude mechanical," Vern said, straightening out his clothes with a huff and turning to the Captain. "Adrian, what happened to you?"

"What the *fuck*," Dimitri said. "You cannot just ask that, little lord."

"Why not run down and collect Joules instead of presuming to dictate what I can and cannot ask Adrian, serf."

"Better do as he says," Adrian laughed. "He is a Prince, after all. *Serf.*"

Dimitri glared but exited to the hallway. Vern haughtily watched them go, and looked at Adrian, analyzing the familiar face. He did not seem much changed, Joules had overstated the catastrophe as usual, however…

"You used to be a master of the postscript," he said with great urgency. "Now tell me, does this simpleton Dimitri prefer for all to be expressed within the formal body of a letter? Or have you merely given up?"

"I have no idea what you are talking about, Vern."

"Do not play with me, man," Vern insisted. "I am not speaking to you as a Prince, but as Joules' brother and the occasional audience for your correspondence."

"Ah, the candle note."

"Yes, that doggerel."

"I am guessing Joules did not read you the postscript, Vern. Because it is none of your business. Would you please be nice to Dimitri?"

"How can I be nice to a man I do not know?"

"Julian likes them well enough, and so do I. Why not get to know them?"

Vern grimaced and crossed his arms.

"I cannot account for his taste. Or *yours*. And if a postscript exists as you seem to imply, I will hear it," he commanded, and pushed through despite Adrian's amused expression. "The possibility that Joules elected not to read it to me indicates to me an embarrassing and startling drop in the quality of your prose, and I…"

"Vern," Julian whispered from the door. Dimitri had hoisted him into their arms and his head rested on their shoulder. "Don't be naughty."

"He is hurt, Captain," Dimitri muttered to Adrian, panic thrumming in their shoulders. "And he already has a nasty fever. I gave him one of my white flowers, but we should get him medicine. Apparently, this one has the map?"

"Oh yes! I do have the map, yes," Vern confirmed, and produced the document to Adrian from the secret pocket in his jacket. "Joules, how did you know? I almost forgot."

"Darling boy," Julian said, closing his eyes as a sudden pain gripped his chest. "You have the stickiest fingers this side of the amphibian kingdom. Of course you have the map. As a general rule, if something important is missing one should check my brother's pockets first."

Dimitri shot Adrian a glance, for they had never liked sneak thieves on the ship, even though everything was freely given and so there was nothing to steal. Adrian warned them from speaking with a slight shake of his head. There was no time to question the stranger with Julian's face about anything important, and less time to assuage Dimitri's suspicions as to the boy's character. Dimitri blinked down and bit their tongue.

"Let's go then," Dimitri said gently to Julian, kissing another white flower between his lips. "Rest, your highness. See you on the flip side."

"Vern," Julian said drowsily. "Be good."

Vern squeezed his hand but said nothing, brow furrowed, watching Julian fall asleep as Dimitri took him away. Adrian could see he was scared, and wished he could speak to Dimitri through shared thoughts.

"Do you remember me, Adrian?" Vern asked in too jovial a tone as they walked to their vessel. "Or am I once again surrounded by strangers?"

"I will not lie to you, little Prince, even if it is a hoped-for lie," Adrian promised. "Except for what a wiser Captain wrote in the logs, I have lost Illyrial, and I have not been able to get it back. I have lost most of Julian, I have lost most of myself. And I have lost you."

Vern wiped at his eyes with the back of his elegant hand.

"Joules told me as much," he said with a deep breath, and looked down, gritting his teeth. "I'd truly hoped that he was wrong, *for once*. Thank-you for not lying. You did not deserve such a disaster to fall on your head. I fear in some part that it was my doing."

"I doubt it, lad," Adrian said, then sighed, bringing up what he could not in front of Dimitri. "But could I have the real map? An old sea Captain knows a forgery by fingertip."

"You are not so old, Adrian. But of course, I am keeping the real map. In case you or your ill-tempered navigator try to slit my throat."

"Dimitri is not going to slit your throat, and neither am I."

"I would not expect anyone to *announce* it. I am not a fool, and I am not a child, though I must play both when I am alone in this world. I do not know your heart, I do not know Dimitri's heart. I do not want to. I do know where the map is, however, which is a pleasant compromise for me. I am coming with you because my brother said I should, not because I feel safe, or wanted. You will receive the map when Julian is awake and well and can scold me for not giving it to you when I said I did. So do not press the matter," Vern said firmly, staring straight ahead. "Whatever you seek will have to wait until then."

Adrian said nothing more but walked close to the boy.

Pierre came out of where Julian resided and motioned for them to come in. Julian had already been bundled into the Captain's quarters; Pierre was pressing flowers under his arms, near the glands while Batiste, of all people, sat in a chair by the bed attached to an IV running from his wrist to Julian's. Dimitri was almost a posted sentry by the door and blinked when they saw Adrian and Vern.

"Captain, he…this is no place for the boy." They jerked their head at Vern. Batiste, having finished the transfusion, sidled out of the room, barely looking at Dimitri. He knew a scene and even more, knew when his exit was.

"I *know* my place," Vern snapped, and shrugged Adrian's hand from his shoulder with a hiss. "Know yours."

Dimitri's lips thinned and they put one hand on the handle of their sword. Vern glanced down, alarmed.

"Do not order me around like you are him, I don't fucking know you from—"

"You two must be crazy, to think of fighting here," Pierre snapped, taking the stethoscope from his ears. "Either shut your traps and let me take care of Julian or take it outside. Don't you dare give me more work than this. I will not repeat myself."

"You, stay. He needs you here, so straighten yourself out," Adrian said to Dimitri curtly. Worry made a clenched fist of Dimitri, and he could deal with them later, but they could not have tolerated Vern in this context, even if he had been still as a doll. He turned to the boy, who shrank under his gaze. "Your highness, come with me. *On your feet* or I will drag you."

"Do not touch me, I can see myself out," Vern growled, and stormed out of the Captain's quarters. Adrian paused for a moment, unsure of what to say to Dimitri, who was already biting their lip and trying to stay the tears, shoulders square and fists clenched like they were bracing for a blow.

"Get the fuck out of here, make sure I did not frighten the boy," they muttered, regretful. "I will apologize."

When Adrian left the Captain's quarters, he found Vern crying like a lost child in the arms of a woozy Batiste, who was whispering low reassurances into his damp curls and looking so confused.

"Captain, I think I am hallucinating?" he mouthed over Vern's shoulder. "There's *two of them*. A live pretty one and..."

"The one you have given blood to on an empty stomach, Batiste. Go find some cookies in the larder," Adrian interrupted, before Batiste could call Julian *dead*. "Tell them the Captain sent you. Er... welcome back. We were all worried about you."

"Just another day in paradise," Batiste slurred with an off-kilter salute,

161

and gave Vern a wee kiss on the forehead. "Chin up, beautiful. I am sure your little friend's been through some worse nights."

"If you have pen and paper," Vern said, once alone with the Captain. "I can draw you the map. I will not be staying. Of late I have become friends with boats and ships, and clothes and boxes and I have been so *happy* in this, because no dead thing has ever hurt me as much as something alive. And without my brother, I do not know if I am…*able* to be around men, or boys, or creatures."

Adrian did not know what to say to Vern, had not understood how different he would be from Julian.

"You want me to maroon you?"

"No. I do not know. Nobody is happy with me, whether I am here or there or anywhere, and if Joules dies, and I am walking about with his face, constantly reminding everyone, well," Vern laughed tremulously. "Our kind may be undying but between you and I, we might as well have killed him."

Adrian hugged the boy.

"I do not want to be an orphan again, Adrian. I am very bad at it," he whispered into his chest, looking up.

"Vern, I promise you whatever happens to Julian, you have a place here."

"I do not want that place," Vern shook his head. A place where everyone had loved Joules and a place where Joules was not anymore… "If I wanted that I would have stayed home, and I would not have *suffered*. I have suffered so much and it is not fun anymore. I just want my brother."

Dimitri emerged from Adrian's quarters. They hung his head, their eyes were shot with worry and fear and a sliver of something else.

"*Adrian.* it is not me he needs, it is you."

CHAPTER 21

"What do you mean?" Adrian asked, not letting go of Vern.

"Damn it, what could I mean except he *needs* you?" Dimitri pushed their hands in their pockets, but their scowl softened when they looked back. "Go to him. I will stay with Vern."

Dimitri pulled their sword out of their belt before presenting it to Vern, bare hand on the blade.

"It was unforgivable, what I said to you," they said. "I love your brother, so I love you. I follow him, so I follow you. And if I shame you, I shame him. I am so sorry."

"You are not forgiven," Vern said, and took the blade, slicing Dimitri's palm open. "But that *was* very sweet. Captain, please help my brother. If I am to be beset in such a manner by his masochistic thugs, I at least want the option to berate him about it after."

Adrian did not lose another second and rushed into the chambers.

Dimitri held up their bloody hand and bowed with wonderful grace before producing a handkerchief to wrap around their wound. Vern inclined his head in courtly approval, still holding the blade.

"Could you direct me to the larder? I am hungry."

"Certainly."

They walked in silence to the larder, already lit with soft sun panels. At a small table by the dry storage Batiste sat with a plate of pastries while young Henry, the pâtissier's apprentice, heated some dipping chocolate in the adjoining kitchenette. Vern caught Dimitri's panicked expression with a twisted satisfaction.

"I am sure I can find my own way back, *dear Dimitri*," he smiled, speaking a trifle louder than was his wont. "You can go."

The navigator was light on their feet for someone of such stature.

Vern tried to think pleasant Princely thoughts while he examined the jars of biscuits, the stacks of light and heavy pastries. But all his thoughts tended toward bloody, or remorseful. He settled on a cookie studded with chunks of chocolate and gelee cubes of gingered seagrass and leant against the wall with a sigh.

The nice boy at the table coughed pointedly.

"Do you want fondue for that?" he asked, once he was sure of Vern's attention. He shook his unbound scarlet hair from his face. "Henry's making fondue because I have been through it. And I have got an extra chair, though you look like you prefer a nice lap."

"Do not flirt with me. How common," Vern snapped. "I do not know what fondue is and I do not like to try new foods."

"What *old* foods do you like, sweetheart?"

Vern shook his head, suddenly overtaken by another wave of exhaustion at the prospect of trying to explain. Palace cuisine from Illyrial was not easy to find this close to the sun. The food in The Above had been delicious but his constitution could not tolerate most of it. Joules had been so much better at remembering what was good to eat in the absence of familiar. He sat where Batiste pointed, and lay his head on the table so he was shielded by his arms. It felt like he was in class and did not understand anything, forgetting something he had known just the other day.

"Your brother is not a textile merchant, is he?" Batiste asked, lips impertinently close to Vern's hair. Confused, he brushed off the other boy off in irritation.

"Who said he was in textiles? You must be thinking of someone else."

"Then are you in textiles?"

"I do not work. How absurd. I suppose *you* work?"

"Most people on the ship do not," Henry said with a guileless smile, and set a pot of melted chocolate on the table. Vern examined it seriously, and then looked at Batiste, annoyance throbbing his temple. "They work very hard at creating things they love, though…"

"Well, that is *chocolate*; why not call it that?"

"Still don't want it?" Batiste picked up a piece of fruit with a skewer and dipped it in the pot.

"Might be poison," Vern said.

"Who's poisoning textile merchants in your mouth of the river?"

"I am not a bloody *textile merchant*, and neither is my brother. That is a pernicious and odious lie. I will silence whoever started it," Vern said, and watched Batiste eat. He did not seem like he was being poisoned. "If I eat this, you must promise to share the antidote. It smells delicious and I want some."

"I only share antidotes on the second date," Batiste said. Vern understood it was a joke from his tone with a shaky laugh, before spearing a biscuit on his own skewer. "Forgive my confusion. 'Twas Dimitri who told me that your brother roughs his hands in the textile trade."

"Ugh, of course," Vern rolled his eyes.

"Of course, I did not believe them for a moment."

"Do they often lie?"

"Not at all dear, that is why it is easy to sniff out when they do," Batiste said. "I assumed they meant to protect your brother from scrutiny."

"If Dimitri *knew* anything they would know nothing protects us from scrutiny. It never seems to make a difference in my treatment, whether I am announced as Prince or pauper. Tell me, lovely boy, if I told you I was the ruler of a kingdom you have never heard of, only I cannot prove it to you the way such a ruler might because I am…momentarily embarrassed, what would you say?"

"I would be tempted to play along," was the delightful response. "Who does not want a world full of Princes and kingdoms yet to be visited or named? Should not we all be guarding our own kingdoms of the heart? But then, I am not a barkeep trying to settle a bill. Or a gold-sifter. Why do you hold Dimitri's sword?"

"They gave it to me, if you must know. And I do not want it, though it is well wrought," Vern said, looking at the ornate inlays of tiny blue jewels, the midnight wrapped handle, and the cross guard which looked like two outstretched wings, wings like birds from Above. Such a fine thing for a rough man… "Perhaps, I will keep them around for protection. If I ever get back to my kingdom…"

"The swords?"

"No. I cannot fight like that. I meant the person. At least, everyone will look good going down. Where was such a rare treasure obtained?"

"It is not stolen," Batiste said. "'Tis a rule, those who choose to wield a sword on this ship must receive a blade which would be worthy of the Captain. A blade which will not rust or chip, containing no defect that would betray its owner. *I* made that for Dimitri, according to their own specifications, which I had to wring from them in a delicate moment. No handguard, and shorter than the norm, but fast and light. Everything to make for a fast slice and a quick dispatch. Then their favorite stars and their birds in the pommel, to gaze upon if they are bested in battle and they have nothing else which is pleasant to behold in their dying moments. Wraps of silk on the hilt, which may be the only rich things they can bear to have on their person. And something secret embroidered on the innermost, written in gold on a cloudless night. That was not their request. That was for good luck."

He seemed almost remorseful. Vern resisted the temptation to unwrap the handle and see.

"But Adri- the Captain himself does not have a sword which matches this one."

"No," Batiste said with pleased certainty. "Captain's never let me make him one. He likes his nasty old cutlass, and his privacy."

"He would have to tell you…"

"Anything about himself, yes."

"What would I need to tell you, if I asked you to forge for me?"

166

Batiste tossed his head to the side thoughtfully, and his hand reached across the table. Vern let their hands touch.

"You would have to tell me what you have fought with before, all the hurts that you have had, what you can bear and what you fear," he responded. "You would tell me what makes you brave, and what would make you braver. You would not be able to lie, unless you wanted a sword which would fail you no matter your skill. So of course, there are many who would find it impossible to tell me these things."

"And what's the sword you'd make for yourself?"

Batiste laughed, a clear, low sound that reminded Vern so much of Julian, and he looked down guiltily.

"I was not laughing because it was funny," Batiste said, in no haste to explain.

"I did not think you were," Vern said. "I did not think you'd laugh at me."

"Ah, you do not want to have fun while your brother is sick."

"Well, that would be monstrous, and while I do not mind the appellation on my own steam, Julian has asked but one thing of me as of late; to be *good*. So, I should be waiting somewhere close in case he needs me. I have been gone for so long and he has had to do everything by himself and I…"

"But that is also true for you and yet, where is he?" Batiste reasoned, ripping out the line of logic like some unfashionable lace and replacing it with his own design. "Glutted on my blood and sweating out a luxurious fever. No doubt kissing the Captain *and* the navigator while they mop his sweaty brow."

"That is different, because this is all *my* fault, not his. He does not *like* to be sick, he just often is." Vern plucked one of the strawberries off the fondue plate, looked at it, then put it down, wrinkling his nose. "Do you think Joules kisses Dimitri?"

"He's missing out if not," Batiste sighed, and evaluated Vern's wrinkled nose. "Not fond of playing with man folk, are you, little Prince?"

Vern thought of the men he had met, and the men Julian tended to favor. He had understood *Adrian's* appeal, who was pretty enough and romantic and knew how to do a great many things which offset his inherent man-ness, the epitome of the *rough side facing itself.* All of the others, with rough hands and loud voices, condescending or cruel and not a sonnet between them. The work one had to put into a man, just to make him palatable! A pleasure for some, perhaps, but not Vern. Then, he thought he should not generalize—for the men down here were delights compared to any and all types of people he had seen Above. They were knights and gentlemen all, down to the last streetsweeper and uncouth drunk, compared to the true Kings of the land.

"No, not over-fond," he conceded. "I am certain I cannot imagine kissing one. And they play rough."

"They do play rough," Batiste said, dreamy. Vern frowned and dipped a part of cookie into the pot absentmindedly. It dispersed to sodden crumbs from the heat and he was left with melted chocolate between his fingers.

"Dimitri flashed the steel of this blade towards my royal person. Where I am from, where things make *sense,* that would have been met with banishment, and I would not have had to think of the wicked offense ever again," he said, more to himself than to Batiste, unsuccessfully looking for a handkerchief. "I am not a candle. I am not a flower."

"I have no idea what that means, sweet boy, though it sounds very serious indeed. What I do know is you should not put your fingers in fondue, if you do not want someone to lick them after."

Vern blushed.

Batiste's smile widened, his teeth sharp as the hooks in his wrists. "Ah, so brother Julian is brave in more ways than one."

"What?"

"It seems he gives all for those he loves, and you...you cannot imagine men because you have not tried to love them."

"You forget yourself!" Vern scooped the plate up and swayed as he stood, the next royal command thick on his tongue from fatigue. "Fair and most impudent youth, I need to retire to a bedroom—that is a room with a bed—If they have something like that in this hellhole. I would be much obliged to

168

you if you would graciously allow me yours, cramped and miserable as I am sure it must be."

Batiste moved, trying to keep up, and ushered him down the hallway. They walked in tense silence. Batiste threw open the door of the sprawling wardrobe room and armory. In the middle was a bed with velvet and daggers laced through the high headboard.

"And your love for your pearl-mate, is it—is it held all in reserve for him?" he asked, a spiteful grin illuminating from his features. "Is it such a paltry, finite love?"

Vern held the berry and then dropped it on the plate, sticky fingers and all. He deposited it on one of the nearest flat surfaces not covered in measuring boards, lace, or flatted sheets of gold.

"I have filled my days perfecting the art of *boyspeak* and *boysong*, and boy oh fucking boy, everything else! Kingdoms can be swayed without a sword, contracts and clams and banks full of commerce—rare books and rows of houses, all with proper words! If I deigned to use it on you, *you* would not recover."

"Then, why *don't* you? Or is understanding the act of loving through careful study the same as being loved for you?"

"I *understand* enough, do not take me for a naif. To illustrate, I just needed one look from them to know what you did to Dimitri. Or rather, did not do. And…"

Batiste's face fell. For the first time Vern could really see the indents in his arms from the hooks. Under the armory's lights, a little brighter than the rest of the ship, he could also see Batiste's own failings, Sight or not; all the extravagant materials in his hands, but nothing ever proved enough…even to the detriment of his own health.

"I could never stay in, you know. Never sit on my hands and rest. If I was you, and I'd been to The Above, I would have…made the same type of deal. Whatever it was."

"I did not tell you that. I have not told anyone that," Vern said, shivering.

"You asked me to make you a sword," Batiste said, as though that explained anything. "That means *secrets*, plain and simple. And you are here in my gilded lair, already asking how alchemy is performed in the mouth of a dragon…"

Batiste held one of the bolts of fabric up to appraise, a deep blue-green bolted with black pearls. He laid it up against Vern, then satisfied with the effect, let it roll out over the bed. He sat on it, ushering Vern down onto the sumptuous affair of pillows with him. Vern hesitated, feeling silly in his stocking feet, like the boy in pajamas on *INDRA-1*.

"I do not need a sword."

"No. You do not fight like that, and my blades are not decorative."

"I do not need *your* attention."

"Oh? Well. Then it is a simple matter for you to crawl into some other boy's bed." Batiste shrugged. He did not seem stung or hurt at all, to Vern's disappointment. He began to braid his long red hair for bed, tying in small, petrified anemones with care. "You could creep back to the larder like a thief until dawn or until your brother's fever breaks, whichever comes first. I reckon if you are a good boy like he's asked while he rests, he can give you the attention you need. Or you could let me look at you, just for a second, and then we could have fun. Unless it is also fun that we find *common*, your Grace?"

Vern sat gingerly, admiring the fabric under his hands, taking care not to tear it. Batiste smiled at him, and Vern glanced down reflexively, although it should have been the *commoner* who averted his gaze.

"Golden boy. You are afraid I will melt you down, to make something else."

Vern shook his head.

"I am afraid I would prefer whatever form you chose for me," he whispered, mouth dry from the stark truth. "I am afraid I do not know what I look like anymore. Without…without a looking glass, I am afraid."

"I have a mirror, if that is what you mean."

"That is not what I mean."

"Can I dress you?"

Vern considered the request. There was a bed, there were rich cloths and metals. There was Batiste, his forge and his blades, pins and drafting table, a drawer containing delicate chains of various degrees of function. Vern wanted to be dressed, and undressed, pinned like a butterfly or unwrapped like silk ribbon. He touched his collar.

"Do not take this off," he said, voice small. "It is not mine."

"If you want, it will be all that stays on."

Vern shuddered, and Batiste leaned in to kiss him. Instead, he held a hand up.

"You…may kiss me, and dress me, and serve fine at the palace," he said. "But your heart is not ready for mine. Yet."

Batiste's eyes widened. "Very well, your grace. I will get you dressed for dancing then."

Batiste hummed, picking out a loose, flowing lapis robe for Vern to put on. Then, he began working at the embroidery around Vern's sleeves with practiced fingers, lips and teeth.

The evening's din passed as Batiste busied himself over the bolts of fabric. Once, twice Vern asked if he wanted to rest. Each time, Batiste declined, insisting that such an interruption made him restless and sick. Vern understood and instead asked about the types of fabrics, the beads and gems, the swords that Batiste thought would be fit for Illyrial's royal armory. This made the boy much happier as he sewed and stitched and unstitched. He folded over many layers of gauze onto a bolt of linen, then cut it off. The velvet, yes! The linen was out. out. out. He ran to one of the looming closets filled with heavy grommets and tweezers and began rifling through…

"Batiste? May I… ask you about Dimitri?"

"Won't that spoil the fun?"

Vern yawned. He felt comfortable, sleepy, but not as though he was about to go out and have a party. Not after they had just escaped. He needed rest… he loathed the thought, but the more he saw Batiste, the more he knew he should.

"I was a coward, and I will atone for it, in my own way and time. Perhaps less for my own heart and more for how I have hurt them." Batiste said, surprised he was the one confessing over his own work, instead of Vern.

"What do you mean?" He was curious more than anything. He wanted to understand the strangers Julian knew. The ones he might come to know better, after all.

"The truth is," he answered. "I want someone who will make me want them, madly, madly, madly, someone I will drop everything for; someone who takes every shining inch of my attention and captivates it; no half loves, no solemn oaths without their blood, no filling in the blanks so the imagined lover is better than what's in my very hands to hold; I create too much and then my inventions, stand the test of time as men fall away. I will not force myself to behave dutifully for anyone I do not feel that way for."

Batiste ripped a sheath of gauzy fabric between the mouth of blades and began twirling it into a marvelous spiral. The process was done in a flash—like a magic trick, he had recreated a rose with petals opening, perfectly...

"It is all for the best," he continued, pinning the petals in place. "Besides, though I doubt they will forgive me, Dimitri seems *happy* despite it all. They have got their spot in a warm bed and a kiss on either cheek...would they have such joy had we stayed the way we were?"

"Do you still fancy them?" he wanted to believe Batiste, and his logic was sound *but...*

He heard himself, a little younger, before The Above and...he knew Batiste was not ready to be with him. They might be excellent friends and even more marvelous artistic comrades, but lovers were of a different nature. He thought of Julian pressed against him, *inside* him...how sure he was then, and knew he belonged elsewhere.

"I do not know. Not right this minute. I think they were so much more aware of me, than I was them."

"And could you have been, more so? What stopped you?"

"I do not know," Batiste said, threading a needle now, adding dark sequins in a row to a piece of chemise. "We passed like ships in the night, anchors drawn at different lengths; they, marooned, and I always adrift…"

He picked up another bundle of the glittering, flat disks and fastened them to the head of the roses. "What I *do* know is, I cannot stand to lock myself in the wardrobes and armory if I cannot go out dancing, wild and hardy and free."

Vern peered over at what he was making from the bed. He admired it already.

"May the dancefloors bring you all their heady pleasures, then," he commended. He would not judge Batiste too harshly. Although, he decided then, his own carelessness was not to be taken as lightly. At least, he would try. He was a Prince, after all—and he had not acted so Princely; he could see that now. Vern's head felt delicate. As he took a deep breath in, stretching, his gaze roved downwards, over the blood on his right palm from where he had cut Dimitri. For the first time in his life, he found himself tiring of parties and velvets and *pretty.*

"Batiste?" he asked, starting up with a shock, realizing he had lost half an hour. He took a moment to yawn, concealing it in the crook of his elbow. He could see the outfit now half made, but was not sure yet what it was…He felt his joints settle into the mattress, weak from all that time without rest. He knew he must sleep. He did not ask Batiste to take care of him. The clothes were enough. He would find someone with a medical touch down the line. *He would have to,* he thought, closing his eyes and falling on the heavy pillows.

"Wake me in another hour, please," he said, shuffling down onto the bed.

Batiste draped a tape measure over his shoulders. "Yes, your grace."

"And…"

"And?"

"I need you to make something else for me," he whispered, heart-thudding before dozing off. "A set of *somethings,* actually."

CHAPTER 22

Vern woke up long after the first turn of the glass. He heard the insistent bell which rang when someone forgot to turn it promptly on the hour, and jolted out of a dream that he could not remember, reaching for someone he could not place. Batiste, cursing at the drafting table, belatedly turned his glass and looked over.

"I am sorry to have disturbed you."

"You are forgiven," Vern said, courtly, and rolled off the mattress, flattening his bedhead. A missal fluttered from the vent over the drafting table and Batiste caught it, putting it on a pile of similar hasty scrawls. "What's that?"

"I told Pierre to send me updates on your Prince when he could. In case there was cause to wake you."

"Is he…?"

"He is out of danger. But he is very weak," Batiste said, and held the pile of updates to Vern, who shook his head; the writing looked closer to the wake of a water moccasin than anything he could possibly read. Batiste, thinking he needed to reassure him, put the papers down. "It is nothing bad."

"I believe you," Vern yawned, stretching. He did.

The paradox of grief allowing Vern sensuous refreshment was not lost to him in this moment, but he did not give in to a modicum of guilt. He had energy which for once was unurged by adrenaline or any of the million common impulses which had flooded him since his reconstitution from gold. He had Princely thoughts in his head, not the thoughts of someone clinging to the edge of the world in mad hope, or the clouded and selfish hustler of The Above. Vern was aboard a friendly ship, a ship which was no true stranger because he had heard so much about it. He was surrounded by gorgeous things, and interesting people. Vern had not killed his brother, or his brother's friends. Vern had been good and Vern was still good. For once he did not feel *bad bad bad.*

"Thank-you for the use of your bedchamber," he said to Batiste with a half-bow. "And for not waking me when I told you to."

Batiste smiled, amused.

"Little Prince, I do not think I could have roused you if I'd wanted," he said. "You will send me the specifications for your project?"

"Of course. All in good time."

Vern drew up the design in his head as he wandered down the long corridors. He did not feel pursued or watched, and when he put his hand on the ornate sun panels, he felt warmth and sturdiness. Unlike the cheap sun panels in other ships, which relied on zinc and thick glass walls to gather residual light and friction heat from passing through the ocean, these ones were opaque and far cleverer; he could not see himself in them even a little. He pressed his fingers against the honey panels and looked at the indent of darkness they left behind in delight.

"It will not break," someone assured, and Vern dropped his hand, feeling caught. He looked over and saw the doctor from last night, Pierre, and sloped his shoulders.

"Is my brother awake?"

"He is," Pierre said, and Vern anxiously waited for the other shoe to drop. It was never as simple as *Julian woke up, he can see you now, he feels so much better...* "Do you want to come with me? I have to pick oranges."

"There's no oranges," Vern said incredulously. In Illyrial there were oranges, it is how he knew Julian, but that was only because everywhere else... "There was a citrus blight and everyone got scurvy and it was very sad."

"Well *here*, there's oranges," Pierre smiled. "Your brother's keeping fine, he's got a devoted nurse."

What can't Adrian do? Vern thought, though there was no sting to it. Julian always felt better with his Favorite wrapped around him and sucking the poison out. He followed Pierre to the monstrous and overgrown garden in the center of the ship, which was humid and heady with the smell of citrus. He picked up a clementine from the ground and watched Pierre roll a ladder over to some of the impossible trees.

"How can this be?" Vern asked with unbelieving eyes, unsuccessfully picking at the fruit's peel and getting a fragrant yellow stain all over his hands. "When something dies Above it is gone forever. *Extinct.*"

Pierre laughed, bringing down a giant basket brimming with grapefruit and pomelos, lemons and blood oranges.

"It is certainly an interesting anomaly. I thought I'd got the deep sea dizzies for keeps when I saw it. But that is an orange in your hand, and there's been no blight on this ship."

"Who grew the garden if it was not you?"

Pierre looked around and shook his head with a puff of air through his lips without an answer.

"I am just on retainer until the real gardener gets back, I guess. Need help with that?"

Vern had been about to bite the orange like an apple but handed it to Pierre instead. He remembered oranges denuded of their pith and peel for him in the palace, how neither he nor Julian could ever start the peel. He wondered who peeled Julian's oranges these days. The pâtissier's apprentice came in and piled ten or fifteen precious lemons and limes into a satchel like they were mundane. Vern ate the tiny segments in his hands absentmindedly, trying to remember when the blight happened, when this ship could have been sailing to avoid the tragedy.

It is not breakfast yet. Have you got five more impossible things for me, mister caterpillar?

Pierre took out a pair of gardening shears and started attending to an overgrowth of gooseberries and its herb garden nearby. Into a wide basket with red beribboned handles went mint, sage and woody rosemary. From a

176

pollinator house installed in a dying tree, little insects and creatures buzzed, kissing flowers awake and nibbling their rightful harvest. And yet underfoot there was sandysuckle with its telltale pink berries, and mosses and algae spackled the walls and ceiling. Vern touched everything with his fingers and let his bare toes curl in the shaggy grasses.

"I need to send a message," he said. "How do I do that?"

"Got a desk, pen and paper behind the cacti."

"I need a scrivener, too. Please come with me."

Vern went to the writing area, full of prescriptions and half written formulas. He did not snoop but found a long scroll with less writing on it, holding it up to Pierre to make sure nothing important was on it. In a rush guided by the pictures in his head, he drew the blueprints for Batiste. Pierre wrote in his water moccasin scratch what needed explaining where he pointed, eyebrows raised.

"What's this for?"

"For a gift," Vern answered, though he knew that was not what Pierre asked. "And then through the mail tube? How does it know where to find Batiste?"

"You ask the most interesting questions. These circuits are a directory," Pierre said, pulling an apparatus forward on the desk that looked like a midi keyboard at a rave. "That is Batiste's button, see? And there's the Captain's, you can tell I use that one a lot because his name is rubbed out from my fingers. Kitchen, navigation, studio one and two, sick bay, everywhere I am needed. You press the button, and it shuttles the message through the proper path, most of the time."

Vern nodded and signed the blueprints. Each page received an ornate V, the r and n hidden in the capitals. Pierre rolled them into a bottle, set them on the tongue of the mail tube, and pressed Batiste's button. Vern watched it go with interest.

"Letters must be behind the sun panels," Vern pondered, and wandered off with oranges in his pockets, trying to discern more of the ship's hidden things.

What else was behind the sun panels, apart from the ocean?

Memories of Adrian and Julian sprawled on the royal bed over crumpled diagrams and specifications came unbidden to his head. He looked up, feeling somewhat surrounded by them, not in a bad way, at least he did not think *bad*. In a week or so it would be suffocating; he was sure he would be swimming endless laps and gnashing his teeth and ripping out Julian's hair, possessed by the foul mood to destroy and tear. He suspected that it was the inevitable product of his curiosity that once he had everything figured out, understood the purpose and intention of every beautiful thing he saw he wanted to *break break break* until it was useless, like him. But he could not stop pulling those threads. He collected mysteries like Julian collected lovers, maybe even for the same reasons.

"Oh, careful your highness," someone said. Vern looked up, and the polite creature addressing him looked abashed, bowed sloppily. "Your...other highness?"

"Just your highness, if you please. *The Prince* is still abed, but I will play along if you need me to be Julian," Vern said with an easy laugh.

"Charming," the man said, and appeared to mean it. "Perry, we have got company."

"And what have I told you about calling me Perry when we have got company?"

"I *forgot* my dearest," he said, beady black eyes clearly rolling. "Do not mind Pericles, your highness, you'd think he had be happy to be liberated of such a handle."

"Not all of us can be Ernest..."

"How could you tell I was not—" Vern started.

"If I may—" Ernest said, and when Vern nodded, he touched behind Vern's ear, pressing a single curl between his delicate fingers. "*You have* got a golden lock, whereas your brother is completely dark."

"*Really,*" Vern said, shocked. "Have you a glass?"

"Well, you might not be able to see it, *Ernie* has the most delicious color sense in the seven seas," Pericles said, extricating himself from an illuminated manuscript, and stopped when Ernest indicated. "Hm, I see it too, pure bullion. Oh, that is most intriguing. Let me find you a mirror, your highness."

Through two mirrors facing themselves, Ernest and Pericles were able to show Vern the yellow whorl behind his ear. Vern imagined this was what finding a first gray hair must feel like to the dying, a tangible mark of life lived, valorized as an honor in The Above just as surely as gold was, but he... he looked away, annoyed.

"I suppose your scissors are for fabric or paper, not hair?"

"You want to cut it?" Ernest asked, looking at the offending curl again.

"How could I not, what an eyesore it is."

Ernest and Pericles exchanged a glance, and Pericles went back to his desk and retrieved a small pair of scissors delicate anemones on the handle, as well as a green ribbon the width of a fishbone and a tiny, corked jar.

"Your highness, we would be so honored if you would permit us to keep such an eyesore," Pericles proposed. "Ernest has never seen this color in this value before."

"And if our request represents a unique psychic burden to you, we will simply excise the hair and not ask again," Ernest hastily rejoined. So courteous they were, and Vern knew what the Princely thing to do was.

"But it is just *gold*. Common and crass," Vern sighed. "If you remove it to the root, you may do what you will with it. It does not touch me, and I will think nothing of it once taken from my royal head."

"*Yes!*" Ernest hissed. Vern found he could not begrudge the creature's enthusiasm. "Thank you, your Grace."

Pericles tied the curl with the ribbon first so it would not disperse in the water. Then, with careful snips, he cut the lock from behind his ear and gently pushed it into the jar, giving it to his partner with a flourish. They were reefmates, Vern realized with a warm feeling in his tummy, bonded for life and constantly touching the other's thoughts. Nearly the same person, Ernest as much Pericles as Pericles was Ernest. Vern found it romantic, yet was too shy to say such a thing.

Vern rubbed the spot behind his ear to make sure none of the gold remained, and inadvertently touched his green fins, flattened as they were to his skull. He missed Julian then and walked around in a burst to try and stop from crying. There had been too many new people, kind as they were, and the feeling of waking up on a day with no school collided with the worry he had now that he was not at Julian's bedside, or that Julian did not want him there. He wanted to retreat into himself, shut himself away somewhere, but he was not sure where that would be, if quarters had been arranged before the pearl string of disasters he had brought in his wake.

"Your highness, are you well?" Pericles asked cautiously. Maybe Vern had been muttering. He looked down and nodded without a sound, before bolting from the beautiful studio of books and paintings and tints in jars.

If Vern were going to go mad, lose his marbles down to the last tucker, and be confined to a cushy Jungian settee for the rest of his natural life, he would not do it in an artists' studio. He would not do it in a garden. He would not do it in the larder or the forge, or the Captain's quarters or anywhere he could be *seen*, certainly not in the corridors lit so sweetly by opaque panels. He would have to do it somewhere secret, where nobody could find him by touch or thought, and where he could watch everything topple inside him and laugh and laugh. Where he could find the gold filaments residing in his veins and the finest hairs of his ears, all the ore deposits not yet strip-mined from him and just lay them out to say *There was a Prince, softer than anything and too much, too much—for the worlds above and beneath.*

Vern found himself back in Batiste's room, did not remember walking there, hoped he had been good but would not beat himself up about it if he had been bad. Tired from this light walk around the ship, he put the hourglass on the side, so no sand would run, and slept.

"Your highness," Batiste's hushed voice murmured, and tossed Vern from uneasy dreams.

"*What*," he asked, and flipped over, still so tired. Batiste was not at all stung by his capriciousness and continued as though he had greeted him properly.

"Your gorgeous helmets are finished, as per your instructions," he informed.

"Thank you," Vern said, and glanced over at the table.

"I have consulted with the logs," Batiste continued. "I have your room assignment. I thought it was ludicrous that nobody knew where you two go."

"Julian and I go where we please," Vern said, feeling a growl in his throat. Batiste held up his hands with a placating smile.

"Well then, if you please, there's a chamber in the keel assigned to you. Plum spot. I can show you."

"You may," Vern said, sliding out of the bed. "Bring those with you. And Batiste?"

"Yes?"

"Do not address me so familiarly. Who do you think you are?"

"*Yes*, your grace." Batiste flushed to the tips of his ears.

The assigned cabin was untouched; Vern saw no indication Julian had ever used it. He put the helmets on the desk and turned the panels to a low sunset before sitting on the made bed and staring at the ceiling, finally alone with his mysteries and his mystery. He wanted for nothing, and he could fetch for himself anything he needed, away from prying eyes. And if he needed to leave, he would, long gone before anyone thought to check.

Comforted by this, Vern went to the en suite privy and started the bath, a clamshell affair with nice deep sides and a table for reading or eating. He stripped and put the pajamas on the bench facing the tub before sinking in and laying his head on the cushioned back with a deep groan. Bubbles and medicinal vapors subsumed his body, the gauzy membranes flickering over his eyes, clouding the room most pleasantly. Lost in his thoughts, Vern listened to the sounds of the ship from his vantage point beneath delicate pipes. He thought of home, and wished he could see it again…

His eyes snapped open. *The pipes?*

CHAPTER 23

"You know, I do not believe we have ever been together alone," Pierre said, never one for small talk.

Batiste reclined on the couch behind the hibiscus while the third transfusion this week snaked from his arm. He shrugged with the peculiar grace of boys from The Deep.

Batiste was the first boy Pierre had ever seen, at first just as the siren songs described. Sailor superstitions and their accompanying prejudices meant Pierre used to feel the need to be cautious around such a creature, especially on a ship. Then he had watched Batiste at the forge, at dinner, around kids, and realized he was just another person as lost as he, if slightly more insufferable.

"I am sure you planned it that way," Batiste said without any trace of hurt. Pierre, caught out, did not respond, but set a fruit juice—pomegranate, orange and fresh-squeezed guava in that order into a coconut with hibiscus to garnish, as demanded—in front of the unusual donor. "How much blood does the poor Prince need? At the rate we are going, it almost feels like an allegory. *Gory* allegory..."

"I could ask his brother if it is getting to be too much for you. I just do not think he could sit still long enough for a full transfusion. It might kill him, and if not, it would absolutely kill me," Pierre explained by way of apology. "Boyblood is hard to come by, in any port. And, well, we are not particularly welcome at any port for the moment, so..."

Batiste's lips twitched indeterminately and he clamped down on the candy-striped bamboo straw instead of speaking. Pierre got the sense he did not like Julian's brother, though he could not imagine why. He had to believe that all boys could all get along, mutually braiding hair and hand-feeding grapes while indulging in their bewitching *boyspeak* until all the rough edges were smoothed…

As though just remembering, Batiste ruffled through his Basque linen robe and produced a parcel of letters, all opened.

"Do you have a *lover* at port, by any chance?" he asked with a sharp toothed grin. "Or are these for some other Pierre?"

"Batiste, you *read?*" Pierre retorted, snatching the pile. *What's with you boys and mail,* he thought to himself.

"Only smut, which…" Batiste trailed off, and let his head recline, suddenly woozy. "This Thaddeus sounds like a dreamboat heartthrob cocktease, which is the highest honor my kind can bestow. What in the seven seas are you doing *here?* I would have forgotten everything in my haste to return to such a creature, and you hardly go on Shallows-leave…"

Pierre did not answer, did not want to try, even while scanning the letters with an appraising eye. It made sense Batiste would have them, in a way. Thad was always cheap about sending mail underseas, and any middleman he could employ to avoid the fees and waterlogging insurance would have been too much of a boon to pass up.

"He seemed well? Thaddeus?" he asked Batiste, taking the intravenous out of his wrist and patching it up with a coral plaster, bright purple matching the other ones. Batiste really had been pricked all over these last few days, but apart from the summary fussing and fidgeting when Pierre had explained he was the only one whose blood Julian could safely take, he had been a dream. The hooks in his arms had been easy to avoid while Pierre had looked for a vein, maybe by design. He did not know what the fishhooks were for, always assuming it was a kind of *memento mori* body mod that deep sea creatures went in for. He found it grim, grimmer than Batiste.

"I am not a sea-horse-centaur biologist, but he was the most perfect shade of marigold I have ever seen. And that *mane*, what a catch. Wanna feed him sugar cubes and feel him nicker in my hand," Batiste murmured, and his beautiful eyes closed. "But *Pierrrrrre*, I have a rather urgent query; does the Prince *drrrrink* the blood or...?"

Pierre snorted at the question, taking it for a joke, but Batiste was already asleep. He pulled a heated blanket over the depleted boy before he carefully put the pouch of blood in a crystal box for transport. He had always had the sick feeling of dropping the precious fluid on the way over to the Captain's quarters but made it this time. The Clarel had borne the uneven seas with a strange grace lately.

Pierre knocked at the door of the Captain's quarters. Adrian himself answered, leaning a little heavily against the door. Pierre noticed he was not wearing his leg and resisted the urge to peek inside. He was not sure what Adrian's qualifications were to treat Julian, though the Captain had written with specifications for compounds and was consistently asking for his opinions on contra-indications. He was either a doctor in another life, an expert in royal diseases, or very good at pretending. Maybe all of those things.

"Boyblood," Pierre pronounced, as though there could have possibly been anything else in the transparent box. "Batiste thinks he's drinking it."

"Not quite," Adrian joked with the ghost of a smile. Pierre thought it was a joke. "Thank you. Thank him, too."

"Of course. Do you need anything else?" Pierre asked. Adrian looked behind him in the Gothically dark quarters, as though he were listening. Pierre could not hear anything except his own heightened heartbeat, and suddenly The Shallows sounded so good actually; marathon sex with Thad, the inevitable marathon screaming match with Thad after, grit under his feet and the glaring sun tingling his scalp...

"No," Adrian finally said, looking back at Pierre with his intense gray eyes. "Er, I do not think so. I will write when more blood is required."

"Aye aye Captain, and may I say, what a completely normal way to put that," Pierre said with a nervous chuckle. "Um. Dimitri..."

"What about Dimitri?" Adrian asked, frowning. "Are they alright?"

"They are peachy," Pierre said, feeling himself petering out. "Yeah, and I will let them know, uh, I saw you?"

"That would be *much* appreciated. Many thanks," Adrian smiled.

Pierre half-smiled back and made his rapid exeunt before the Captain could close the door. He had a letter to write before he would be emotionally prepared for Dimitri, who he was starting to suspect had never comfortably fit within the field of 'peachy' in their life. They had lately taken up looking windswept and widowed in the crows' nest, looking for those stars they could almost perfectly imagine without seeing.

Down the corridor, Pierre could hear the telltale banging underfoot which indicated either a fatal decomp breach or a Prince in the walls. Vern had taken up crawling through the mail shafts, causing bumps and creaks through the ship which were horrifying to hear and inexplicable until his bonny head would pop out through a vent, covered in dust and talking to himself at a spectacular volume, brandishing yellowed notes to incorrect recipients and disappearing again. Though he was the spitting image, Vern was not a thing like Julian, whose delightful curiosity had manifested as actually talking to people and kissing them a little bit. Vern, suspicious of oranges, kind words, and apparently mail tubes, had other methods.

Vern was growling somewhere near the brig and cursed expansively when he hit his head on something. Pierre had not heard the profanity Vern could command effortlessly, and he had been his whole life at sea. He would have to ask Julian or Batiste if *boyswear* was a thing.

"Say, are you all right down there?" Pierre called.

"I am fucking *fine* you ratfink bastard-physician," was the Princely response, amplified by the pipes. "Ask again only when you stop hearing me and start nosing me. Can you get that through your fucking head or should I write you a prescription? Interrupt me again and I will rip your tongue out of your rotting wordhole with my royal hands, and I loathe violence so do not you dare drive me to it..."

Pierre returned to his garden. Batiste was long gone, with his coconut, and to his surprise, Dimitri was there instead, gazing dolefully at the magnolias. When they saw Pierre they straightened.

"I need a couple of plasters," they said without preamble. "For um…"

They held up their hand, covered in a handkerchief completely saturated with blood. Pierre went to the coral bed and got a couple clippings.

"And how did you get this one?" Pierre gibed, grinding the coral down in his mortar and pestle before adding a touch of red seaweed. The dust would then form into a thick gel which stopped bleeding and held most creatures' skin together without discomfort; Pierre had learned this trick in the pastry kitchen but applied it to fins instead of flan.

"Knife catching contest?"

"At least you didn't catch it with your face this time," Pierre said, and Dimitri managed a small smile. "Speaking of, I saw the Captain."

"Good to know Captain yet commands this ship," Dimitri muttered, and sighed. "And is the Captain quite well?"

"Seems in fine fettle. He asked after you," Pierre said, and felt his heart clench at Dimitri's skeptical expression. He brushed the coral carefully onto the jagged wound and kept talking. Dimitri's particular quiet was so sad these days, and Pierre thought a couple of the main reasons for why were locked up in the Captain's quarters. It was not any fun being the odd one out. "Julian's still on the mend, but he is taking more blood."

"What's he doing, drinking it?"

"No, what—?"

Did deep sea kids just not know about blood transfusions? He wrapped a fresh algae bandage around Dimitri's newly knit palm and gave them back their ruined handkerchief. Dimitri put it in their pocket and nodded to Pierre as thanks.

"Try not to get into knife swallowing next, no quick fix for that," Pierre said, turning to his stack of letters. When he looked up again, Dimitri was gone. He shrugged and opened Thad's first correspondence. He had a bit of spare time.

Settling in, Pierre put on his glasses to read, but paused when he saw Batiste had left something behind in his haste to leave. He picked up the bottle, which was still sealed with wax, and looked curiously at the message. It was not Thad's style to mail by bottle, he was too economical for that and could not have known hand delivery was going to be a possibility.

Pierre chipped the wax off and let the rolled message fall into his hand, written on expensive waterproof and with a letterhead from Olive Branch.

"That is no good," he said to himself, trying to stop the full body shiver and failing.

Olive Branch was a familiar source of grief for just about everyone on the ship, up to and including the squirrelly little Prince who was one nut away from a full-fledged mental breakdown. If OBCO associates or the head honcho himself had been able to send this in the first place, despite the Captain's proven ability to avoid them…and who could he possibly tell right now?

Pierre set Thad's letters and precious weather forecasts to the side, with only a little regret. This was too important. He rolled the poisonous message back up into the bottle and set out to catch Dimitri before they disappeared on one of their sojourning swims around the ship.

In the artist's workshop, Ernest and Pericles were aflutter with their latest acquisition, oblivious to nearly everything else.

"Odd boy, to be sure," Ernest said for the second or third time, looking up from the tiny bottle of gold they had procured. "This is such an *expressive* gold. Not flat at all. Uncommon in all aspects of the word!"

"I do not think he was upset about the quality of gold per se," Pericles muttered. He had a single strand of the hair under his microscope, trying to determine how to disperse the pigment or else reproduce it.

"You think he was *upset*."

"Yes," Pericles said, and smiled when the hair finally melted into a setting dye. While Ernest could see every color including the imaginary ones, it was Pericles who could see the waves of emotion people exuded.

"That explains it a little more," Ernest said, and happily blinked at his bottle again. "I hope he feels better. What was his name again?"

"He did not mention, and I am afraid we did not ask."

"Oh Perry, we have to stop doing that, it is so rude. Though rather abruptly his quietus he did make, so…"

"We will make a point of finding out before we see him again."

They thought they would like to sit in the coffee nook on the top deck at first and grabbed a few pastries and tarts from the larder before the blinking ascent into the soft seas with all the blues and greens and grays and blacks they could ever want. Dimitri was there, rippling pure black and a rich purple as was usual, though Pericles had not noticed the ribbons of copper dust underneath before, and wondered what all that was about.

Are Batiste and Dimitri back together? he asked Ernest, and blanched when Ernest promptly opened his mouth to address the navigator. *NO ERNIE. If you do not remember, do not ask them!*

Ernest shut his mouth again and got lost in a lemonade's luster instead. *Not as gold as the GOLD but it is gold, anyway, see through gold and it is so pretty…*

"Rough morning for sailing," Pericles offered. Dimitri shrugged; maybe it was. "We have got new blues we thought you would like. For your depth charts. Divided black into black until we got a new black-blue. We'd love to have you by to see them."

"Thank you," Dimitri said distantly, and sipped their coffee, clutched in a death grip. There was an algae bandage wrapped around their right hand, flecked with a little blood, and their scabbard was empty. Ernest and Pericles simultaneously speculated on the possible games Dimitri was playing with the Captain, and with desperation scrambled to think of another topic more appropriate for breakfast before they were carried away by the fantasy.

"How fares the young Prince?" Ernest asked, and Dimitri blinked.

"I would not know," they said. "Why would I know that?"

Ernest looked at Pericles for help. *They are not reefmates?* Pericles shook his head and shrugged. He did not understand it either. There were many facts outside of their first home which threw them, and one of them was Dimitri, persistently solitary despite all that would commend them on the reef.

"We are very embarrassed," Ernest continued blithely. "We do not know his brother's name."

"Ah, you have met *Vern*." Dimitri said, tone light despite the periwinkle blooms that swirled around them. They did not offer anything to elaborate, and Ernest and Pericles started eating their breakfast, excitedly chatting about the possibilities of *Prince Gold* to each other.

Vico found them shortly after, as was his wont, and promptly stole one of Dimitri's sweets, the powdered cubes of seagrass they liked to eat. Dimitri smiled at him and ruffled his hair with the bandaged hand, which came away covered in paint.

"Vico, what have you been making?" they asked with half a laugh. Vico crammed the candy in his face and mumbled inaudibly through the resulting cloud of powdered sugar. "Pardon?"

"He's in his yellow period," Ernest explained helpfully. "We have been getting better at not eating the oils we find to be too beautiful though. Quite proud of that!"

"Vern showed me the other studio," Vico finally said, when his teeth were not glued together with stickiness.

"There are two studios?" Dimitri asked, nonplused, looking at Ernest and Pericles for clarification. "For…each of you?"

"No. There is our workshop, that of humble craftsmen, and then the atelier. For *les beaux-arts*," Pericles explained. "Canvas and frames and whatnot. Marble and other such luxurious ballast. *We* do not need that, 'tis not our bag."

"So who-?" Dimitri started, then paused. "Vern is there."

"Yeah, but it is *my* studio now," Vico said seriously, taking another cube of seagrass with paint-streaked fingers. "Once I get the clutter out. Just lots of paintings in there. Seascapes, nightscapes. *Boring*."

"I believe the Captain dabbles in there," Ernest finally mentioned, with a worried glance to Pericles after failing to read Dimitri's reaction. *Was I not supposed to mention the Captain to Dimitri?* Pericles did not answer. He had no idea.

Dimitri finished their coffee, long cold, and stood.

"Why not show me your studio," they said to Vico. "And then you can have the rest of my seagrass."

CHAPTER 24

Vern surveyed at the painting which dominated the atelier. It was probably good, but he was not sure what it was.

"What does it look like to you, Vico?" he asked, and frowned when he realized the child was already gone. "Blast. I am getting geographies, of um… desire? Is it from memory or fantasy? Both combined? Is it ultra-pointilisme? I do not…I do not like flat pictures, I wish there was something I could engage with in my own physicality…"

This kind of exhibit was Julian's bag, through and through. Vern sighed and sat on a half-finished sculpture, thinking. The disused studio door opened and Vico stood there with Dimitri. Eyes flashing, Vern glared until Dimitri turned on their heel and left. He was not ready for them, not yet.

"Little traitor," he said to the smudgy-fingered child without any anger. "You would sell me out for candy and head pats?"

"Yep," Vico said without any shame. "I am like ten years old."

"That explains it. What do you make of this?"

"Boring," Vico said. He had not budged from his earlier critique. Vern sighed again, trying not to agree.

"I do not think it is boring. I think I am just unable to access whatever the artist was intending," he suggested. "I do not connect for some reason. Maybe because the artist cannot connect."

"Who is the artist?"

"Adrian, sadly," Vern confessed, looking closely at the technique. "You can tell from the very delicate brush-and-sucker work here, on the waves and there, on the moonlight. He does not even need to sign it is such a specific and personal style. Executed well. Just to middling effect."

"Yeah, does he even know what he's painting?" Vico piled on with a mean-spirited grin.

"That is a thought-provoking question. *Does he even know what*...I do not know what he's painting, so he does not...yes, I think that is it exactly. He knew once, and then he forgot—and when he remembers, it will all make perfect sense," Vern said, and frustrated, considering going out the way he came, through the mail vents. "Thank-you for your insight, child. I am retiring to clear my head. Art is exhausting."

Vico did not answer, pulling a canvas out from the wall of raw materials. Vern knew when he was not wanted.

Vern ended up back in his quarters and rolled up in his bed not knowing if he wanted to try to read or scream or break. He ultimately ruled out all, exhausted by the day's travails, having run out of distractions, notwithstanding the inscrutable painting. But that was not a worthy mystery in his estimation, not at all like the letters and the sun panels. He was not hungry and entertainment on the ship was running thin. Usually when he was at such an alarming level of bored, he could bother Julian but that was not advisable from what he had heard through the mail vents. And nobody else was imminently botherable, except...

Vern screamed into his pillow and bit it viciously. Trapped! He was trapped in a gilded cage just like The Above, and even if it was Adrian's cage, that did not acquit his brother's Favorite of the placid boredoms he had uncovered. It would only be a matter of time before he was running as fast as he could into the walls until he was bloody and everything was ruined. He had met everyone and he could not do the same little conversations every morning over *tea*, or *cookies*, or *oranges*...He wanted to go home and all the wonderment he found here was flimsy consolation. Vern punched the benighted pillow a couple more times for good measure, and squeezed his eyes shut, flopping on his back. Hypoxia would be kinder. He could not think of anything else that would release him from these agonizing heights.

No, he realized gloomily, the *people here are strange and talented and not boring at all. But I…cannot focus. And I…am afraid to ask them for more than I already have. Hence why I relegate myself to this. This unendurable waiting! Maybe Julian is dead. The first undying boy to drop dead because…because of You.*

"Of course he's not," Vern protested in a strangled voice, hating the ceiling he had been assigned. "I would know. Someone would tell me."

Who can tell you anything? You are a fucking basket case.

"Ugh," Vern said, distraught and frightened and more annoyed at himself now. "Who even asked you?"

Did you give them the helmets? That is like the one thing you are supposed to do today.

"I have a lot of things I am supposed to do today," Vern wept, and turned over in his bed.

Vern wished he could focus, and was not paralyzed by the need to *do do do* things until he surrendered to a righteous sleep. It had always been that way in the palace; he would be so wonderfully set on one project or whim and then burst into inconsolable tears when asked to do anything else, be it eat or go to a lesson or even dance. It was not Adrian's fault, despite all. Adrian had just made a ship where he could flit about between his infinite varieties and never wither, the painter or the poet, the philosopher or the physician, the lover or the gentleman gardener. And it was *his* ship, it had to suit his needs before all else and be crewed by the people who were pleasing to him. Vern's mind did not skew that way, though he and Adrian were similar; Vern's ship would have been far smaller, with far fewer possibilities, and only people when he made port.

Except for one or two, he finally admitted to himself, looking at the helmets. *There are a couple who could stay at my pleasure during my exile. Until I could find my home berth. I almost know where I am going, I just need a map…*

Vern reached out with his quagmire thoughts, wondering if he would magically be able to do it Julian's way, just this once, if he was very good. He knew it was a fool's errand, but he preferred to talk to his brother than himself, even if it was just as one-sided.

Julian, can we go home soon?

There was a knock on the door, and Vern clamped a hand over his mouth so as not to shriek. He dusted himself off and vaulted from his bed, trying for presentable, and opened the door a crack, the inside chain still on. At his request, he had been given so many locks he nearly had to kneel to undo all of them. Dimitri loomed there.

"Oh," Vern said. "No, I do not think so. No thank-you. Thank-you for disturbing my rest. But no."

"Did not sound very restful," Dimitri countered, but stood there still before belatedly adding, "Your highness."

Vern pursed his lips. He was not bored anymore.

"Just a moment. I have a ridiculous artillery of locks on my door, I will feel foolish jiggling them while you watch. Do not try to burst in like some kind of armed guard," he commanded, and slammed the door a touch too hard on Dimitri's face. His hands were shaking by the sixth deadbolt, but the door finally swung open. Dimitri did not come in, respectfully glancing at the ceiling rather than Vern or his messy room. "Do you enjoy standing in doorways or is there something about mine in particular?"

"Batiste," Dimitri said, and looked so affronted at themself that they even had to start there to explain that Vern did not latch his fingers into their eyes for indulging in gossip. "Was mentioning that you are…"

"The soul of discretion he is. I will make him create his own self-clamping irons," Vern stormed, not caring if he made sense. "A further moment *if you please*. I must put something in a bag. And then you will take me to *your* quarters. This is dreadful."

CHAPTER 25

Vern walked up the stairs to the top deck. Dimitri followed him, skeptical and silent. As though the boy was their executioner, they walked three paces behind him; slow, steady, guarded and guarding; could they fear the boy so, and yet also want to protect him? How did these matters of the heart ever go? This…boy! Who was so lucky to have escaped treachery, completely unharmed. Who would go on to take Batiste and Julian and Adrian from the little company they might have shared. They noticed that Vern was now behind them and looked not vengeful or necessarily pissed…he was not holding a blade. This was a good sign.

Dimitri swung the door open to their quarters. The room smelled of ink drying and the subtle sting of peppermint and sugar from leftover tea. They looked at their maps, they wanted to place a few points on them before they forgot. If the boy needed nothing else, they could not be worried. Perhaps, he just liked to shadow people to annoy them. Or, when he was missing the person he really wanted to see…

They wondered if Julian and Adrian were okay. If they thought of them at all.

As they puttered, fixing the points of certain constellations they became keenly aware of the rocking of one of the floorboards. Its creak cut through Dimitri's own thoughts every so often.

Vern looked as though he might lunge at them after all.

"Alright, get it over with." Dimitri muttered. They turned and leant back against their desk, inviting the boy to slice into him.

Vern looked doleful. In his black satin nightshirt and pajama pants, the curls of his hair mussed from sleep, he reminded Dimitri of fish that preen before they poison, except...he did not strike. His eyes were tired. And the halo of sorrow around his bow-like lips made Dimitri want to, for the first time, reach out and ask if he was okay.

No, they thought, *I want to touch his lips and see where it hurts and touch and touch until I know. I long for his agony sealed in the axis of my grasp. Like stars exploding, brilliant crimson...*

Vern moved his hands out from behind his back and held out the helmet.

"I asked Batiste to make it," he explained, far too quickly.

Dimitri's mouth twisted and untwisted as they turned the metal over in their hands. They set the impossible object on his desk.

Why? they thought. They had never asked Batiste for something like this, they were always too afraid of the questions the armorer would inevitably have to ask. And yet, the very thing was so important that it entirely dissolved and left only them and Vern in the room.

"Above, maybe they think boys cannot hurt people who look like me..." they heard themself saying, slowly.

"Above, you would be eaten up like a fish on a plate." There was no malice in Vern's words.

"But would they filet me or just feed me to someone's cat?"

"My brother, he will never talk about it..."

"He is allowed his privacy, even from you. Do you wish for him to talk about it so you may feel seen or so that you may feel absolved by another's exposure?"

"Hm..."

Dimitri held their hands out as if to say something, to offer something, but could not determine what.

"He does not wake in the middle of the night, longing to see the stars, he already can when he closes his eyes." Vern explained carefully. "Not me. I took such a bad tumble I kept insisting that we were from some beautiful ringed planet," He shoved his hands in his pockets and pulled the papers out. They were filled with his scribbles. "This is all I used to look at and wonder, could I be happy there? Could I ever exist if I did not gaze up at the stars?"

"And did you find your answer?"

Vern spun a little on his heels and gazed around one of the many pinned up boards of the sky. Then, he looked at Dimitri, he looked and looked and there was no scrutiny in his gaze...

"Your maps...they are gorgeous."

"I am sure you and your brother have scores of cartographers to share. I hear you are a dab hand at it yourself."

"I am not trying to hire you." Vern whispered. He cast his gaze downwards. "I am trying to tell you how fucking *sick* I am of people looking at me. That, if you allow me, I will stay hidden in your map room any time my brother does not. That to be around someone like you, even *sometimes...*"

Vern held the side of the ship's walls as though he was using it to hold himself up. Dimitri, pencils long discarded, ushered him towards the bed. Vern wept and threw his arms over his face, mortified by the attention. He could not bear to be seen anymore.

"Batiste might come around to how we live, or maybe Batiste needs other things. Or, something else. But I am not worried about him. I saw him and I saw..."

"What you might have been?"

"What I think I was on earth, somewhat. What I do not want...down here. Not anymore."

And I would never force you to be any which way you do not want to be, he thought. *I would only gaze upon you as a confidante. So that we might chart the stars together, so that you are not so petrified when a hand touches your tear-stained cheek...*

Vern reached for his hand and slithered into his grasp. He took the sword from his belt and pushed their palms together. He took a long, deep breath in.

"My brother knows you do not wish to live forever, even though, you are possessed with this quality, like the rest of us–you cannot make it feel like a fact of life, let alone a gift," he said quiet and tender yet with the power of conducting a ceremony.

Dimitri tried not to cry. "So what? No one will notice me missing."

"If you let me spill your blood again, I shall spill mine, too. I will come to you when you are like that--we can feel it together. We can go up from the roof of the ship or the palace, tie a rope to our waists, and see the stars…"

Alright, they thought, and the thought itself was a marvel. *Alright, you are not the Prince who has captured every thought upon my heart—you are the Prince who has cut to the very quick of my blood, unbridled and starbound…*

The blade caressed each of their palms. It did not worry Vern. With their hands pressed together, Vern could see the wobbly, blurred images his brother could see with ease. Instead of trying to see, he closed his eyes and leaned back, Feeling; instantly it hit him, the waves of intense sorrow and despair and rage Dimitri contained; *why go on forever, no one's Favorite, no one's home, no one's 'how are you' each morning, why go on forever with this face, these skills, if I can never see what I long for, in a mirror, in a wave reflecting stars, so very far away…He felt the exactness of the maps being cut over and over, inside his mind, the agony of existing, perforated those same lines, and they could not be undone…*

And when he pulled Dimitri in for a kiss, touching them everywhere, the very sensation penetrated Dimitri twice, feeling what Vern felt as he kissed them; *how beautiful they were, how beautiful it is to be in their grasp and be known.*

Dimitri pulled away first, with a gentle hand on Vern's shoulder. They were about to say something, something important, when there was a knock on the door of the navigation room. They furrowed their brow; nobody ever came to the map room except Adrian, and Adrian never knocked.

But it was *Pierre*, looking worried. Without a word, Dimitri stepped out and shut the door, leaving Vern inside. They did not want to alarm the boy if Julian had taken a turn.

"We have a serious problem." Without preamble, Pierre held out a message bottle. Dimitri took out the scroll. "Eric knows where we are. He knows the Princes are aboard."

"No, how can that be?" Vern cried from the doorway. He did not ever stay put, Dimitri was starting to realize. "I thought he was…"

"Your highness," Dimitri interjected, already mentally charting a course far from here, to protect the people they held dear. "How would one get to Illyrial from these seas?"

"How indeed. Is that what he wants to know?" Vern asked, breath coming shallow, and took the message from Dimitri's hand before thinking. He scanned it and handed it back with a growl. "*I cannot read it.* What does it say?"

"Ships are not made to sail forever, and everything dies. Even feeble little boys and their sick fucking whores," Dimitri read the hateful missal, word for word. Pierre looked down; hearing it was worse than reading it. "Wish you were here. Signed, Duke Eric."

"Oh, he signed it, did he?" Vern said, and rubbed behind his ear. Dimitri nodded. "When can we change course?"

"Now. Where?"

"I do not know, but you might," he said, and pulled out the true map from his pocket before handing it to Dimitri. "*Please* do not be angry with me. I need help."

CHAPTER 26

Julian screamed. And screamed. And screamed. When he awoke, if he did awake, there was nothing to signify he was in the land of the living...Above or Below.

His mouth tasted of salt and sand. *Adrian,* he cried out, and he did not know how and why he was able to send the thought. He was attached to so many IVs and wires, he could only conceptualize them as plants, maybe weeds. Then, as time passed, those too seemed to disappear.

Adrian? The hours went by. Days maybe.

I am here, he said, at last.

I cannot see. It is hard to breathe. F-from the pain...

You are blind right now my boy.

Open the door. Step through. A foot off the bed his body floated. Adrian shrieked. Your very own floating, magical boy—what does it get you? Grief! Grief! Grief!

You are seizing...Fuck. Can you still hear me?

I am alight with pain—all my synapses, liquid on fire, and then...the terrible weakness will come. I have done too much and even when I do not, I am made this way, if I were not a Prince, I would be quite useless—all this sickness? What has it given me except a great capacity to understand others' pains, to touch you and want to help you, to be good to those even when I refuse to forgive them...

Julian, ever lost in his own head, began to swim in his thoughts. It was both a reprieve and a new horror. He could not tether to himself, but he could to Adrian. For here, in the place before Memory, he could Feel; Adrian hurting, Adrian worried, Adrian remembering more of himself in the caresses of his body against his…

Joules?

Adrian…my gills. Where you—

Julian, I am sorry. I have not been myself.

You need to do that again.

What?

You were not trying to hurt me. Not really.

Silly, besotted boy…

Listen to me. Please. I do not know how much time I have….

Adrian moved his hands up Julian's body to the state of his gills; he pushed, gentler, of course, kneading into the vents there; then, he pushed harder and harder, until the breath from Julian's body began to ease. He did it again. The action hurt his hands, and he wondered if he was able to keep going but he did; Julian gasped, over and over; the breaths came harsher, easier yet more strangled, air flowing freer from his gills.

He could breathe, but the pain that made him seize and shutter radiated down the planes of his arms to the very tips of his webbed feet.

My boy, you have already taken so much blood…

I must do this one thing. For you. And you will understand. Harder. Push harder there. Please. And…

He was not aware of how or why he saw it, but he did. He saw where Adrian was, the touch of his fingertips in the very path of his breath had colored every thought he saw and he knew where to find the very last of his dear Captain; better, he knew how to free him.

Your hair. It is burdening you, he thought.

Yes…it feels heavy. Why? But you are sick. Rest, damn it! Your vitals…

It is where Eric hid your memories. Your memories…will heal me.

Julian sat up, eyes open and unseeing, hidden by the veils of his third eyelids. The synapses that fired his eyes to his brain did not connect. He screamed at the searing, numb pain that drove his weak body to this. Shaking, Adrian held the scissors in his hands and folded his own over Julian's; *all of it, I want all of it off.* Something inside him screamed. He took the delicate, bronze shears to his hair and cut again; *I want you more than I want whatever I wanted before, I want to be free to love you, to save you from the very nature of your sickness; and we shall be sick together in the arms of comrades, in the arms of those who answer to no one but a kingdom of boys...* When the very last lock fell onto the bed, the door in Julian's head unlocked itself, too.

He fell back, wailing.

Adrian, still kneading at the gills on Julian's neck, began to feel dizzy. He was crying, copious tears soaking his beard, the dead hair on the bed and on the floor, meaningless all around them; he was ecstatic and afraid and...he was Julian's once more.

I remember, I am starting to remember, Joules! Oh, I am so sorry—Fuck, lay back, I have you my Prince. I have you, dear boy.

I know. You always do, dearest—my heart, my one true heart! You have returned. Do you know me now?

I tried to hurt you! He heard the unhealing anguish in Adrian's voice. Could he weep, even here? Could he gather him to his chest and press their flesh and scales together, until they merged back into one...*How could I do that?*

My heart, mignon—no more, we are found. Look at me, if we never found each other again...

Breathe!

We-we found each other. That...is all that matters, for all time.

Joules, I will end myself. I will end him too.

If you end yourself, I shall have no heart. Do you understand? Do you see yet, oh...I know you see what happened to me Above and I see what happened to you in the Shallows. I know had we been there for each other...I was out of my mind, worried something had happened to Vern and...I damned you. I damned us both.

No, no! You had no idea this vile creature...

I had no idea what The Above was like. How could I? I lived in a dream, for I only knew your love; totally surrounded and completely free.

My child, do you forgive me?

There's no need. I lived as a shadow Above, a renegade, a slave. Everything that happened, my body, my mind…I did it all to find him, to get back here. And I am only here because you never gave up on me. You saved me. Thank you, thank you.

But I am monstrous.

I knew that before—and I loved you! I love you! I love you!

And the way I behaved…

We tussled! We fought! As boys and men and creatures must! But under such a spell no one would be right…not even myself.

But I am more monstrous now—everything Eric has done…

Adrian, promise me as soon as I am stable, you will let Pierre treat you. Treat you, not cure, never cure. But you cannot go on like this. You will kill me. You and Vern, racing me to my death, then keeping me alive. Please, please, please. Promise me!

My Prince, I swear it. I fear it, but I swear it. But have I drowned you? In swearing my love, are you forever drowning with me, too?

We were always drowned. Now, we are in our element; drowning, swimming, chasing, splashing, caressing, kissing, dreaming with our blue lips curved into winners' smiles.

Winners?

You set out on our voyage without me…and all those times, all those waves of years— Adrian, to think your very name and be in the head of the one who made me; Adrian, Adrian, Adrian!

What are we going to do?

I am a boy, therefore I am monstrous. Always. My brother…he did not know the deal he made with this man. And neither did you. Soon, the monster sleeps, but then, then the monster wakes…

You mean…?

The difference is, this man almost killed you.

Julian saw it all clearly, before Adrian, and he knew he must rest, if only to make sure nobody laid a hand on his Favorite again. Adrian's name would not join the list of the brilliant and rare men killed for holding the hearts of Princes and kings in their common hands; the Gavestons, the Ashmans, the Hephaestions. He would protect Adrian from martyrdom at the hands of ignorant moralists who hated him for his extravagant devotions. He would banish every craven doctor who lay in wait for a diseased body to dissect, to analyze, who had no interest in attending to him in life with care and love, who *did no harm* but did not help. He would move Adrian off him, burly and statuesque as he was. He would move the entire ship, command the tide within his grasp; this tiny, impregnable boy; this creature smaller than the smallest whirlpools; nothing, he was nothing! A slip of bubbles through a funnel—he would rule and banish and fight with his last, shaking breath; he would rise in every tide…

My sweet friend, my most trusted mignon—I cannot forgive the world for how it has touched you, he thought, synapses alight as though touching fire itself.

He walked through the same door that Adrian had in his mind, pushed it open and fell back, blacking out for good.

CHAPTER 27

The slideshow projected on the automated blinds of Adrian's private hospital room summarized a half-life of hard partying and casual sex, disasters he had visited on his body daily and lesions the color of African violets on his arms and chest, milky circles obscuring his spine and brain in the MRIs. Adrian knew what it meant, or *thought* he did while his boyfriend explained with a laser pointer. Then the projector whirred to a halt and the fluorescent lights came up. Adrian still had a few basic questions, none of them had to do with the multi-hyphenate professional opinions, the unreadable portmanteaux for proprietary medicines all developed by the man standing before him.

"Am I going to die?"

Eric looked at him, and then glanced at the blinds like the presentation was still running and Adrian had missed something obvious.

"No, babe, you are going to be…I mean, *fine* is a bit of a stretch. But we have got everything under control for now and you are stable. You can't pull one of your famous disappearing acts anymore. This stuff you are on," he said, tapping one of the IVs. "It's for life. No skipping. It's not the Pill."

"What pill?"

"You're a funny guy, Dree," Eric said. "Always have been."

"Was I good at it?" Adrian asked, feeling at the cropped hair on his head as though it might bring anything back.

"Good at what?" Eric asked with a confused smile. Adrian blinked, now confused as well. "You mean the sex work?"

"Yeah, I guess. Did I make people happy?"

"I don't think you were in it for philanthropic reasons, Dree." Eric chuck-

206

led and Adrian could not imagine having ever loved this man.

"I guess that's you," he said instead, words thick on his lips. "Mr. Name on the Door."

"Hmm." Eric seemed thoughtful. "The difference between a whore and a businessman is…well, that sounds like the start of a pretty shitty joke. One of yours. For what it's worth you made me happy. Make."

For what it's worth, a voice in Adrian's head said, but he did not say anything else. It hurt too much to talk. But he had one more thing to ask. He licked his dry lips and forced the words through.

"Why did it get so bad, why didn't you, why didn't I…"

What did I do, that you were so ready to throw me away but decided against it at the last minute? Was it something I did right or something I did wrong? It does not make sense. If you love someone enough you end up killing them or saving them, you do not leave them in the middle. So why are you lying?

"I am sorry," Eric said. "It's my fault, I thought we were good, and we weren't. But I'm going to make it up to you, in dividends. You won't die."

Adrian pulled a venturi mask over his face to take in more fluids. He did not have anything in him for tears.

"I'm sorry they cut your hair," Eric added, with the first shadow of remorse Adrian had heard out of his mouth. "You've always been so Jo March about it, you know? You can grow it now if you like, they aren't going to cut in anymore. And the skinhead look does not suit you at all; you used to be such a pretty boy."

Got it, I will grow the hair, Adrian thought. He did not think he was allowed scissors anyway.

Eric did not kiss him before he left. Whether Adrian was too poisonous for his lips or too liable to be poisoned was unclear.

Adrian lifted himself into the wheelchair with immense difficulty, trying not to look at the stump, spotless white sock carefully folded over it. He rolled to the window with his drip frame and drew the blinds, squinting at the sun-saturated street below. This was way up even for The Shallows, some high street hospital he could not have the money for alone, even if he were a classy whore.

More like a courtesan, suggested the helpful voice in his head and he rolled his eyes at the absent friend.

"Like Favorites/Made proud by Princes," he explained to an empty room, then shuddered at the unanticipated self-satisfaction of the statement. How could he be *proud* of any of that? Anything that touched that? His body was broken, and he had blown holes in his mind, shrapnel through tissue, irreparable. He had let someone down. He had let *someone* down. He could not let people down anymore, this was a chance to make it right, with Eric with… whoever.

The hair grew, and Eric brushed it, filling him in on the goings-on of the world. He explained Olive Branch and how they'd met at an influencers' mixer up top and hit it off right away, even though Adrian ghosted him for long stretches and called him bad names and messed up a lot of potential business deals with his volatility.

"You know, cold fish stuff," Eric dismissed with an easy laugh, finishing a too-tight braid with the snap of a pastel elastic. "But you always turned up, sooner or later."

"Mmhm, I must have liked you a lot," Adrian slurred, a bit woozy from the heavy sedation that would get him through the night without screaming. The new leg was unwieldy and hurt where it was inserted into his remaining thigh muscle, but he was still learning to walk on it. He was getting pretty good at playing along with things that hurt him. He played with Eric's long black hair. When the light shone through it, it reminded him of seaweed forests and the rarer sunbeams of the deep. "Pretty hair."

"I am not the pretty one," Eric said firmly. Adrian grinned wide, licking the tiny ruby in his gold molar with the raw tip of his tongue so he would remember.

"But *I* am pretty."

"Sure Dree."

"Eric, why do you call me that?" Adrian asked, trying to stay hazy, trying to sound unfocused and sweet, not raising his voice in the way Eric found strident or shrill. Cold fish needed to be in slight torpor this high up, after all, or they got bit. Eric paused, then looked right at him with his dark shark eyes.

"You prefer Dree," he explained, as though it were true. "Or preferred. Is that tooth bothering you? It's some cheap grill you got on our first date, but I think I can get you a proper one that will not cut your cheek. Real gold."

"This one *is* real gold, pleb," Adrian snapped. "Hands off. After what you did to the *fucking* leg…"

It had come out of nowhere, but it was true; the grill was real gold, and it was not given to him by Eric. And his leg…his leg!

"Well, that was all you, honey," Eric said after a shocked pause. Adrian stared at him mutely, feeling so angry that his head might explode, and he wanted to remember, remember *what* they were and more importantly *why*, but he was nearly sure there was nothing, and it would not matter.

"Sounds like I had fun out there," he finally said. "If I am going to waste my life, I am going to do it my way."

"Yeah, you had lots of fun. You and your…"

"My *what*, were not we exclusive? Or did you have to pay?"

"Anyway, it is not just your life you would be wasting. The sheer amount of research you *represent* now, the experimental, I mean…it would be a lawsuit, not a party."

He straightened a bit, squirming, and for the first time, Adrian realized how easily frightened Eric was when he asserted himself.

"They cannot sue a dead man. I'm happy to leave you with the check."

Adrian stared at the ring on Eric's finger, as though for the first time; it must have been a wedding band, or an engagement ring; yet it looked gnarled and black, shriveled. Something was *wrong*. He blinked hard and pulled his head off of Eric's lap.

With both hands, Adrian grabbed the calf of his brand-new leg and unscrewed carefully below the knee. Eric watched him, the amused question on his lips answered by Adrian's mahogany foot in his face. Blood spurted all over the hospital bed and Adrian extricated himself from the mess.

"I am going to need my *things*, darling," Adrian said bluntly, all pretense of intoxication over with. He felt good, his lips were still numb, but he was lisping and hitting all his sibilants, like the flamboyant fucking *man* he was. His smile crooked against the scar on his lip when Eric cringed at the sound. "I had good clothes that were not fucking pastels. I had some documents of mine and I will not take your broke ass to court if you cannot produce them. I will kill you; I will fuck you up six ways to Sunday. But here's the punchline, lover! The difference between a whore and a businessman is, *I will give you fair notice before I do.*"

"It's all in the valise," Eric said, spitting out a couple of teeth and gesturing to his briefcase by the door. Adrian pointed.

"So, get it. Put it on the table."

Eric obeyed, wincing and dizzy. Adrian waited, watched Eric try all the panic buttons he had already disconnected, watched him try and reach someone with his smartphone, his smart watch, his smart glasses, though he did not try his smart mouth. Watched him struggle with the door handle, recently rendered un-smart. After watching, Adrian put his leg back on, and then got up, pulling Eric back to the bed with ease. He was strong. He had always been strong. He could remember that, even if he could not believe it.

"What's in this one, babe?" Adrian asked casually, indicating an intravenous bag on the drip frame marked DREE, full of pale blue liquid and still attached to his arm. "I thought maybe diazepam. Got a little tingle."

"That is...not diazepam," Eric said, eyes wide. Adrian laughed at his naked cowardice. Triumphant and unhinged, the brash noise was loud and rang off the white walls. Nobody came in to check on them. This man had been just as bad as he had imagined, and Adrian was going to get out of here.

"Sure hope it isn't antifreeze, for your sake. I hear that one's a hell of a comedown," he tutted merrily, and pulled the needle out of his wrist before sticking it right into Eric's. Purple blood dripped out onto the sheets, mingling with what was there. He hummed, pleased at the unexpected color, and shook out his arm while he held the needle in Eric's vein with a vice grip. "Sleep ti-ight."

"What a fucking waste of time. You never even gave up the stupid shell bed—but I can use this, you crazy slut! I can still use your fucking leg, whether you remember or not! I will make it all back in triple!" Eric spat as the IV kicked in, the drugs loosening his tongue. Adrian watched him go under, still smiling, only understanding a little. So, this whole thing had been a *shell game.*

The hospital was understaffed, even for nighttime, and he slipped out with ease. Adrian, in normal clothes, with Eric's suitcase and enough hair that he could tuck it behind his ears, did not look completely out of place with the nightlife outside. He kept walking until he saw the warning signs for shelf sea limits and then dove deep.

Muscle memory carried him to a peninsula where a wreck was docked, half scuttled on a coral growth the color of his boy's dark hair. *Not Eric, someone else…*Rich and dark like the real gold of his tooth, pure and shining…

His boy. The words sent a shiver down his whole body. He felt too alert and like he was dreaming all at once. Adrian blinked and took in as much deep-sea water as he could before swimming into the wrecked vanity of a ship. He felt better already. He had just needed to swim to feel better.

✳ ✳ ✳

A few months earlier, Adrian had docked the ship, restlessly searching for Julian. He still had the boy's letter in his hand: *I have no idea where my brother went and I am terrified. I have left looking for him. Please, only come after me if I am not back in a week. I miss you ever so. But…something's…something's wrong. Additionally, please, meet good people in my absence. I shall be furious if you do not have a harem of lovely creatures waiting upon my return, though I shall be furious at myself either way. Mostly, I wish to swallow the world whole. Now, as I leave—I want you to take me where no one else will ever ask a thing of me again. Ever yours, Joules.*

He sweated, hunched over the wheel. The crew was barely assembled, and people left and came as they pleased. There was no Pericles and Ernest or Batiste or Dimitri—the Captain looked more lost than ever.

He got off at the dock. He saw the Olive Branch Company's sign blink neon in The Shallows yellow-orange light. He felt sick. He was sick. He had always been sick, but it was closer to the surface now. No rest, stress, and the effects of shallow water were all eroding the buffers he could make for himself when he was more in control.

"May I help you?" The man asked with a grin. It made Adrian queasy.

"Yes, I was hoping to obtain information about someone in The Above. S-someone who...might be lost."

"You are looking for someone like *that?*"

"Like what?" Adrian asked bluntly.

Eric sniffed. "You do not look well."

"I am not," Adrian admitted, stupidly.

"Well, this is not a charity for the hysterical male, and we are fresh out of fainting couches. What's the problem?"

"Someone's missing and I think I can help with your...research."

"What could I need from you?"

"I can donate some stem cells from one of my legs. We can call it even."

Eric flipped through some papers. He held up a diagram.

"Do you know where this is?"

"No," Adrian lied. "And, if my offer is not good enough. I mean, it will make you rich to synthesize this and help people."

Eric blew a couple strands of hair out of his face. Adrian wondered what the point of such long hair was if he was not going to do anything with it. He stretched and yawned. "Sure, deal's a deal. I can help you find anyone pretty easy. So, let's get you a workup. Unless..."

"Unless?"

"You are too sick to help your little friend."

Adrian rolled his eyes. Explaining the cursegift to people who did not share his heritage was a chore.

"I have a wasting disease in my central brain which is common to my kind, but it does not affect the uh, regenerative properties of the ganglia," he said with a forced laugh and a wink. Easy pride, coaxed and prodded for so long by Julian, finally pushed through and he got serious; he was not explaining a bad thing after all, even if people feared sickness. "In fact, my disease makes them *possible*. By dint of its own disorder, it reorders the entropy of chance all central nervous systems must share. Others rely on being well to accomplish great things; I do not need that crutch. My disease makes me brilliant. It lets me help others. And without it I could not be who I am."

Eric moved from his silver and white shell-chrome desk and drank a shot of something. He was in the healing business, after all; maybe he was skeptical. Adrian shrugged. It was not his job to convert him.

"Alright, whatever you say. Just do not try to give me a bad deal. What's the name, entropic pretty boy?"

"Adrian. I am not a boy."

"You are not a…?"

"Obviously I am not. And for your part…drawing from my leg will be fine, right? It is…not going to damage anything else?"

"No, no, anything we do will be an out-patient deal, nothing that would harm you. Not to worry! Just sign here…."

Adrian went over the papers. He spoke to several nurses who assured him he would be just fine, that this was a standard procedure, who waved away his over-educated questions as a product of twitchy deep-sea hypochondria.

As they drew from his leg, Eric came in and they discussed the missing boy(s) in question. Adrian, was of course, ever careful to keep as little information revealed as possible, uncaring if Eric got the wrong idea about his position in the world. It did not do to explain things to someone who could not listen, and to Adrian there was no shame in being mistaken for a courtesan; any of his fellow administrators of the heart, whether they attended to Princes or carpenters, were worthy companions in reputation.

All that worried Adrian was that he had taken off without a moment's notice, and he wondered what the kingdom would do if something went wrong. No, he had to keep positive for Julian! He had to bring him home! And Vern too, of course. *Why the clam-bed?* He thought, *Probably just something interested in meeting them. Confused as to where the kingdom is. We should really put a statue up there. Get a map-maker. Directions could be helpful. Ah, new kingdoms!*

Adrian spoke but his tongue became heavier. He found his thoughts became more and more scattered, until…he panicked and panicked, and with a sick weight in his gut, he knew Julian could not hear his thoughts. Whatever they gave him…*Fuck, fuck, no—Julian! Save me! Save me! Please. Something's wrong…*hands reached for him in the white-out. hands cut, and pierced, and they were careless in their precision; *and if they did not know what conditions existed with the tentacles, do they know that severing one is just going to exasperate the whole damn thing? Shit, shit…Why can't I move! Where, where…Julian….*

When he awoke, groggy with agony, his leg (and sixth tentacle) had been severed neatly. He remembered nothing. Not his name, not his true nature. He tried to reach for a past, and what returned felt empty and hollow…

His heart had also been severed from its source, pumping sullen black blood into his body without direction. People talked to him, told him stories, fed him medicine. He took it all. He took it and thought it was punishment and protection at the same time. But whose? And what did men like him deserve? *Monster,* the thought came, and the thought did not stop. In the dark that night, he heard it beating, and he felt, he felt, he *felt;* he cried where no one could see him, and wanted to remember, but instead he felt [_] and the feeling was wild; heady, immutable, savage; memory would trickle in and he would keep it a secret; memory would fail him again and again; feeling got him back on the ship and sailing, sailing, sailing, never stopping, never giving up on [_]; he woke and he felt and it destroyed him, day in and day out;

to feel so much and not be able to remember was a hell that never ended; he slept and even as he slept and his dreams passed through him in waves of burgeoning, blazing flames; feel, feel, feel Everything a thousand burning needles through his heart coalesced, moving towards singular blue filament that would not go out; he felt and all he felt with no name became [Love.]

CHAPTER 28

The memories returned in a glittering array of lights and sound; Adrian became himself again. So did Julian. But there was one left, and it was one they had both puzzled over even after the many years together and apart had swept over them in this ceilingless room. The door had vanished now, and they were left at the iridescent purple seaflowers surrounding a shell bed. It was wide and white as a lace fan yet jagged and dark as the shadow which must accompany the undersea sunrise.

There were a few worried men, tutors from the look of their dress, surrounding the opal, glittering clamshell. It was large yet it looked perfectly in its place. The tutors were confused, unsure of what to do as its hinges creaked. They were crying. They were weeping with joy for what was to come—oh! To have a kingdom of boys! To be ruled and guided by them! To be brave enough to let them lead; how exciting! What a perfect kingdom this would be. If only...

Suddenly, it opened. A few of them gasped. One of them looked concerned.

The bed of the shell was iridescent, but when it opened the abductor muscles revealed a split of color; one side of the inside black, the other white. The black side was perfectly formed and ready to become a pearl. The other...did not move.

"It is sick," one of them suggested.

"That is alright..."

"Yes, of course it is alright...but he needs help!"

"Anyone, could you help us?"

216

The tutors looked around, signaling to passing ships, helpless. They wished the boys had been born already—oh, they would surely know what to do!

The white side wriggled and gasped, but could not push the flesh off his head; he could not breathe right...

Through the crowd, stepped a young man. He was weary and his hands shook, but...he wanted to help.

"I know what to do," he said, voice hoarse with worry. He sat by the shell for a few hours, arranging what needed to be arranged, answering as many questions to the learned men as he dared. He touched where the white side was struggling; he pushed and pulled and tenderly, he helped, pulling away at the jelly-like fluid with careful clean hands to clear the boy's lungs; he heaved, placing himself between the two abductors and...and he became the essence of the organic being, too; one that would become the heart.

The paler side gasped.

"There you go, my boy," Adrian whispered, cognizant that his was the first voice the tender ears could hear. Job done, he began to retreat before anyone accused him of diseasing the boy. But he felt as though the boy had his whole soul within his grasp, as though he could never extricate himself from that oozing, primordial mess.

Julian threw his shaking arms around him. "T-thank you, dear traveler. I am forever indebted to you."

With new, unsteady breaths he pressed his lips to Adrian and...Adrian kissed him, allowing the air to flow between their lungs; new, pure, alive...he had kept him there, in his grasp, until he was sure he could take the unfiltered sea air.

"Who are you, my Prince?" Adrian asked, amazed at the boy, all at once, before him. He wanted to take him away from the crowd and check his vitals, but there would be time, and these people were not like others Adrian had encountered...They knew that boys were precious. They would attend to their every need and let them rule thusly. Adrian's head spun–he checked to feel his hearts were beating and not only within Julian's now; the boy's dark curls and kind smile left a mark upon him that would never be severed; he was a part of him now, he had jumped in, haphazard and last-minute and every bit as laborious—and he, too, was born in that instant.

"I am Julian." He spoke, with a musical, sweet trill. "And you, are my heart. Thank you for saving me. For giving me life."

Aye, the boy's first words are thank you. Perhaps they really are in the best hands, Adrian thought. He had been around the seas for a bit now, and thought Illyrial was new…he suddenly wanted to stay. He knew he could not, not now. But…

"You are the ruler of Illyrial," he explained, examining the boy for signs of distress with delicate fingers. "And your shell has finally opened. The people have waited so patiently for your arrival."

"I see." He gave a little courtesy and smiled out at the crowd. He was surrounded by people! By boys! Oh…what a marvel life was!

"But I…" he turned to the shell.

"He is your…"

"I am technically the Prince, yes?"

"Yes, your grace."

"Then, I shall only take on a higher title when there is responsibility so as not to burden him. He shall be treated as my equal. From birth. For he is. Both of them are…"

He looked up at Adrian, then he wobbled over to the other side of the shell. Then, he plucked the black side from its cover. Vern struggled considerably less, and so, for the moment, they thought him perfectly healthy.

"I am your brother Julian. And you?"

"Vern," he said, stepping out with delicate steps from the shell bed. He threw his arms over his head as though yawning, merely getting out of bed and on with the fact that he had been born. He was sure of it as he said it and he flushed with boyish mirth. "That *is* my name. Vern, of Illyrial."

"Welcome, my dear Prince. You are home."

"The slightly younger."

"*Oh!*"

"I heard you, my dear, talking to…"

"Adrian," Adrian offered, and pulled the boy close to him.

Vern clutched at Julian and embraced them both. And Adrian of now watched the three of them, quivering in the shimmer of the Memory, gorgeous and fragile and fated as the forming of a rare pearl; and he knew where they were, where the very shell lay, and he knew how to go back, and he knew, with every inch of his being, how to care for Julian without a moment's hesitation; he watched the three of them, surrounded by so many new Illyrials, and he could see the whole sea; every wave surrounding them, leading back to where they had been created, the falling dust of a star, turning the shell to a place of wonder; the stray touch of Adrian, leading them to their iridescence; the horizon, the kingdom, the twin Princes and their Captain, bathed in the light of dawn.

✳✳✳

Julian walked to the en-suite privy and vomited twice more. A few days passed. He grew a little more stable. He would talk about what he saw with Adrian, in his head…he was still too weak for words.

One morning, Adrian's hands on his gills, moved up the plane of his cheeks and caressed his lips. Like the hinges of the shell, he massaged them until they opened and pressed his forehead to Julian's.

"*My Favorite, my creator, my heart…*"

Adrian pawed at his newly cut locks, then scooped the boy closer to him. "How do you feel?"

"A little more myself, a little more here…" *But I need you, like this, until I am better*—He thought, and Adrian understood immediately.

I am here, Joules.

I know.

Julian could see a little, in dribs and drabs of splashed color, but decided to close his eyes to avoid the pain.

Now that we are here, and free…I also remember this, Julian latched at the soft spot of Adrian's neck, and with his sharp teeth he sucked.

My Prince…you had a fever hotter than the desert sands Above.

I know. And now, I am here, and I am yours…

Adrian moved from his embrace and down the plane of his body. He was floating above the bed, only a little, but it made him feel more at ease, if anything…

Kneel for me, my Favorite. My dear Captain. Wrestle your body between mine. Sit with your hands tied behind your back. Love me, love me, love me.

Adrian knelt. His tentacles were out and reeling, pressing at the exposed, blue veins on Julian's ankles. He wobbled at first, the rest of his tentacles clambering erratically to compensate for the one that was gone, before he used one hand to brace himself. A soft, wrecked sound came from Adrian then, and Julian reached to him.

What pains you?

I have not held you in so long, it feels…new.

Why weepest thou for that?

Adrian could not answer, but Julian understood. He had changed, and Julian had…not. Not truly. Adrian still felt as though he were looking at a memory, at a long-misplaced longing, but he could not look at himself, could not bear to see the record of time described there. He felt lost and tired. He was safe now, but still battered, luster and braggadocio gone. He felt old, but without age, without wisdom, *without.*

You are not old.

I know, my Prince. I do know that. And t'would be no sorrow if I were, if only the time between had been spent in your arms. Yet, however foolishly, I yearn for how I was before. You have only increased in beauty and I…I did not even know how much I lost until…

The time he took from you is nothing. It might have been months or years, it might have been a day. But it is a bad dream now. And you are so, so beautiful.

Adrian sobbed, the *how* unspoken but present. In answer, Julian stroked his rough-shorn hair, under the ear, and his broad shoulders, then the subtle seam where his flesh turned slick and dark, those smooth strong tentacles. Julian took in his smell, sea-jasmine and coral salt, tasted his tears and skin and breathed deep, thighs trembling in want. How wonderful a form fate had chosen for his Favorite, quality wholly unimpaired by petty revenges and misfortunes, Above or Below! And yet Adrian could not see…

I will command you, and this time you will listen. You will move on me like I am new to you and you to me, but you will leave my crown in my pretty curls…

Yes, my Prince.

…Until I put it on your head.

I do not understand.

Julian pulled Adrian's hair, eliciting a sweet moan from his lips. The tentacles curling idly around his ankles tightened with a familiar velvety push and he smiled, guiding Adrian's head to the crux of his legs and letting another tentacle wind around his arm.

I think you must. Don't you want to be properly crowned by your boy? By your Prince?

As a response, Julian felt his hips lift from the mattress, felt Adrian's chin and lips and mouth on the inside of his thigh, felt the questing appendage on his arm wind behind his back and kiss the other shoulder so he was braced. His lips dropped in a shapeless moan, and he rutted up into Adrian's mouth, shoulders collapsing back into silky strength.

In my mouth too, like you used to, he thought, and felt Adrian's overwhelmed cry on his skin. *Keep me anchored and feed me with pleasure only. My mouth. Now.*

He opened his mouth wider to accept the longed for intrusion, gills flapping gently so he could without reprieve. Adrian moved him gently so he did not choke, so the curve of his neck was supported and his legs spread effortlessly. He could feel Adrian's chest against his and his hard cock leaking against his thigh, the rest of his tentacles lingering on secret spots that bruised novel pleasures deep into him, his tongue still pushed down like he was being protected from another seizure. He felt Adrian's head on his shoulder, mouth open and praise faltering into uncontrollable moans which started deep in his chest.

Yes, pull it from me, and then and then and then...

And then what, my sweet Prince?

And then do it again until I tell you to stop. Enter me so I can wrap around you as you do around me and let me take what's mine. Make me seek my rest, fix my restlessness by flooding me with yours...

Julian writhed in the sensation of being pushed open until he was full. Adrian whispered pleas into his ear and holding his face with both hands, like they were both on the verge of death. It had been too long, they were already crashing together, clamped around each other like drowned men and weighed down by pure lust. Engulfed by Adrian and yet engulfing him, Julian clutched harder and made him weep from the feeling and cry *thank you thank you* into his neck, until they were both falling and sinking and Julian could free his arms from lax tentacles and play with Adrian's hair, tracing his crown around his temples until he understood.

All mine.

All yours.

So beautiful, so worthy to rule.

Thank you, my Prince.

Worthy of my storied diadem. Worthy of my praise. Worthy of my protection.

Thank you.

Your hurts are nobly borne, beautiful man. They sully your attackers, not you. Never apologize again for them.

Adrian nodded in acquiescence, biting his lip, desperate to try and stop the sobs. He thought his tears were tiresome, still, but soon Julian would remind him that those too belonged to his Prince and would not be withheld.

My Favorite. Always my Favorite. I shall restore you to your rightful place, in my bed and by my side. I shall dress you and devote myself to you as your supplicant. I am your blind prophet and you are my only god. Let me worship you always. Let me worship you again. Now.

Adrian shivered, and once again Julian was wrapped up in roving, pressing tentacles, smiling and pulling his Favorite closer to him by the shoulders. He pushed his thumb into the closest sucker he could find and felt the crevice squeeze and push around his digit. Adrian's thoughts crackled like the first ice in a harbor.

I did not forget about that. Still feels good?

It is…

Julian pushed another finger in and Adrian writhed, the tip of another tentacle spasming around Julian's thigh.

I want to touch every single one and kiss and lick and lick. We spent days like that, until you forgot how to be polite.

I remember, I thought you meant to tame me.

Tame you? No. Why would I want you tame?

Julian licked up and pushed the tip of his tongue in, and cried out when he felt the first tentacle push inside. He felt around the tentacle in his hand, and realized with an ache it was the abbreviated appendage, nub striated with jagged scarring in this form. He pushed harder with his mouth, trying to slide down on the tentacle inside and whimpering when he felt Adrian hold him still around the waist, so the push would be slow.

Going to put more in? Or are you just playing with me?

Can't I play? What is a god meant to do while being worshiped? Be loved, be venerated? But what does he do apart from 'be?'

A delicate tentacle wrapped around Julian and he gasped at the sensation, almost too much. Adrian's other tentacles, the ones not imprisoned by his mouth and hand, flirted with his legs and tummy, exploring and divoting tell-tale rings all over him.

He does not have to do anything. Not a thing. A god can be silent to prayer, and never ever beg forgiveness and possess all with no acquisition or conquest and that is where his power lies. That is what I think a god must be.

Then I am no true god, Adrian smiled slowly. *I am false, and you, my dear boy, are damned.*

Julian's mouth dropped open, felt more tentacles push inside in concert. Everything in his head went white for a second before pleasure caught up with his overwhelmed body, lit up every point of contact within and without. Pushed and pulled all at once, he sank deeper into all of Adrian and screamed with his voice like he was being killed, or *sacrificed* and the bare thought made him splay out, allowing Adrian to take all of him.

Julian could not rightly determine how long he was held that way before the deep emptiness and warmth after, the kisses on his stomach, on his shaking arms, his hands and feet. He let Adrian massage the hollow bruises on his back and legs and run a finger over his swollen lips.

"Joules," Adrian whispered, and collapsed by Julian's side. He kissed him and Julian could feel him grin. They rested for a moment, still twitching and trembling before Julian felt a profound, expected cramp and urgently pulled on Adrian's arm.

Understanding and unphased, Adrian carried him to the privy and watched the boy heave. After, he bathed and re-clothed him and put fresh linens on the bed. He adjusted the blindfold so that it was loose enough not to agitate his head. Julian clung to him, pressing sweet words into the folds of his Captain's tentacles; *all will be well, we are together, made as we always were meant to be;* Adrian pulled the covers back and curled around him, a shell upon a pearl, unable to extricate from each other.

Then, Julian slept for two weeks, and Adrian adored him in silence and in thought. And not a soul dared disturb them.

CHAPTER 29

Two weeks passed. The ship bustled with sea-life. The weather had been smooth sailing, but sea-storms could happen at any time; some with great, forecasted warning, and others one blithely sailed into and hoped for the best. Many of the crew had elected to land at the nearest port when the true peril was explained to them, when the sharp and steel skies confirmed the ominous forecasts, and the ship could sail with more of a skeleton crew than currently commanding it. Pericles and Ernest and Vern steered the best they could without the Captain, hoping they were at least going in the right direction, if not the right location. Batiste had his many splendid armors and clothes to work on. Henry and Vico attended to the kitchen when they were not painting, playing, or making a general ruckus around the deck.

But Dimitri avoided life itself when they could help it. Or so it seemed. They could not fathom their absence from Julian and Adrian. They could not fathom the dark, sparkling kiss from Vern. They could not fathom the stars—far away and impossible, and for once, right within their grasp!

As the morning dragged on, Pierre gently made his way over to their spot at the kitchen nook. Dimitri looked at their cold coffee and then up at Pierre.

"Err how is…morning, I mean," Dimitri muttered, peevish sip following.

"He will see you now," Pierre gave a little bow. He looked worried, but not nearly as much as when they had docked from the party.

Dimitri thanked him, and forgot his coffee ever existed. Pierre was a blur. The whole ship might have caught on fire…it mattered not to Dimitri. Their stars were fated and lay in bed, trembling. They bolted, sprinting down the maze of hallways, then…they could not make their body move any longer. Oh, all this waiting…they thought, tearing themselves to pieces, a map without a destination; intricate, complicated, achingly gorgeous, and needing a guide.

They stood at the door. They could not make themself move! Oh, they felt as though they were a suit of armor, inanimate as stone, frozen in the sleepspell of a fairytale that forgot about them.

The door opened, as if on its own. They saw Adrian and Julian in bed. Adrian was looking very inky now, tentacles starting below his belly button, and seemed not to mind one bit. *Ah, so that is how the door had opened,* they thought, as they approached with caution. But Adrian seemed tame and Julian—oh *Julian!* It took everything not to run to him. He was dressed and fluttering about a bit, but he still looked weak, especially around the gills and fins, one could clearly see the boy had been on much needed bed rest.

"Why do you regard me as a stranger?" he asked and pursed his lips. "Is it because you fancy another?"

"No! I…"

"But you *have* fancied another—" He crawled over on the bed to hold their hand. "It is not working totally perfect, my darling—and I am fuzzy on thoughts. Who has your heart?"

Dimitri was confused. Was he not ready to replace them with Adrian? Just like Batiste, just like everyone?

"Just your own." they began, looking at the lines of the floorboards, calculating their angles instead of confronting a single feeling in their chest. "I have not…slept with him. I have only kissed him and felt…wondrous. And yet, somehow, I have betrayed you."

"*Betray?* You are my lover, not my pet."

"I am a man. There are honorable ways to go about such things. And my heart is well and truly…" Yours. His. And…Adrian's? And well…who else? Had Dimitri thought this would ever be the problem to plague them when they took this role on the ship? And to what end? A consort that looked like them! Hah!

"You have not done anything dishonorable to me. I sense what happened between you was special…not at all antithetical to how all of us feel, for each other."

"Your highness?"

"And the three of us, four with Vern, sometimes, if he likes…is quite perfect, don't you think? In addition to whoever else we please."

"I am not from your kingdom, my dear Prince. I thought you banished me so I might not be in your favor at all."

"Not so. You are not trained yet in taking care of me. I might have hurt you…or myself. Or both! We would not want that. A lot of it is quite violent, and not in the fun way. Over time, you will see…"

"We are both rather fond of you, Dimitri," Adrian said. "And if you stay now, you stay forever…"

Dimitri shook their head, trying to make sense of it all and failing.

"You and him loathed each other but are in love, him and I were supposed to be in love but loathe each other—and now, with Vern…all topsy-turvy! Is it like this in Illyrial, day is night and night is day?"

Adrian laughed and pulled Dimitri in with two tentacles. He kissed them gently on the cheek, trailing after their tears. Then, he kissed them on the lips. Dimitri brought a shaking hand to the back of his head, discovering with pleasure that his hair was shorter, way shorter, and they could scratch unimpeded down the nape of Adrian's neck.

"Actually, we have a semi-moonlit sky all the time." Julian remarked, looking at them both, smiling.

Dimitri pulled away, but found they fell back into Julian's grasp instead. "There's so much I do not understand as a man."

"Then, a boy must be your teacher." He kissed them on the tip of the nose and trailed a hand down the exposed flesh of their neck. "But you will call me by my title, and you will call your Captain by his, right? Like a good student. Take off your shirt."

"Yes, my Prince," Dimitri whispered, feeling the color rise to their cheeks again.

Once they had pulled off their shirt, Dimitri was suddenly overtaken by Adrian's many appendages until Adrian sat behind them and they were kneeling on the mattress. Julian played unencumbered with their hair and kissed down their neck, thigh between their legs so they could not squeeze them together. Dimitri bit back a gasp and tried not to look at the mirror across from the bed, certainly tried not to think of any vivid fantasy they had entertained regarding Adrian and his tentacles since that fateful duel in case Julian found them and…

"What vexes thee?" Julian asked. Dimitri did not understand until he tapped their forehead. "You are very quiet."

"It feels like being kissed," Dimitri breathed, and writhed as more tentacles wrapped around them.

"But you like being kissed, I have made you come just by kissing you. You are very dear that way. So whyever do you wriggle?" Julian asked with arch naivety.

"They like the wriggling too, my Prince," Adrian responded, almost as an aside. He was unbuttoning Dimitri's pants. "Might even prefer it, I wager."

"Adrian, you bastard—"

"Hmm," Julian said, practically on Dimitri's lap. "What is the sweet name you call them, *Captain*? When they need you to press them down on your bed and make them struggle so?"

Dimitri choked on a profane response, feeling something like a swoon enveloping their periphery. They could not survive this; they wanted it too much. Julian's hand was pushing their thighs further apart and Adrian's tentacles pinned them to position.

"I call them *Mitya*," Adrian said with a twitch of a tentacle around Dimitri's midriff that said *mine*. "And then they open for me like a flower."

Julian raised an eyebrow, glancing at Dimitri. Their lips parted while they tried not to buckle from the frank explanation, the pointed tenderness.

"I...yes," they admitted, and under Julian's gaze felt compelled to continue. "When the Captain calls me that, I feel like he can do anything to me."

"Do you like that he could do anything to you? Does it feel good?"

In trying to avoid Julian's eyes, Dimitri finally caught a glimpse in the mirror, and nodded, throat tight.

"Would you ever ask him to call you that? Have you? Or do you let the Captain choose when you get to feel good?"

Dimitri's gaze dropped. Julian pushed their chin back up.

"I suppose I must let the Captain choose, your grace," they said, voice thready and hoarse. "I have not once asked, but I have *wanted...*"

"He cannot read your thoughts," Julian whispered, stroking down Dimitri's bare chest. Dimitri shook their head in agreement, trying not to glance back at Adrian. He could read every other part of them so well. "And I do not understand them. Is it that you want the Captain to choose your pleasures for you? Or that you do not want him to make you feel so good?"

"*Your highness*, I..." Dimitri broke off again and bit their lip. "The former. But I fear it."

"You fear it," Julian repeated with a small laugh, not at all mocking.

"If such a *man...*" Dimitri forced the guarded words out and felt their mouth drop in a soft sound, unbidden. "Fuck! If such a man as the Captain chose so well for me, as he *does...* and if he knew I'd never quickly consent to a release from his choices, I am—I would be..."

"Hmm," Julian said again, inscrutable, and casually gestured to Adrian. "I forbid you to call them *Mitya* ever again. Unless they ask properly."

"Of course, my Prince," Adrian said with a courteous incline of his head.

No! Dimitri thought before they could school their thoughts. Julian smiled, hand still on their chin.

"*Yes,* Dimitri. If you do not want your Captain to choose, if you truly fear it, you will abide by my whims instead and we will see what you think of that. Unless you have something to ask of him?"

Dimitri moaned.

"Last chance," Julian prodded, thumb pressing on Dimitri's bottom lip. "Before I find another use for your lips. How do you wish to be ruled?"

"I do not want to choose. I want the Captain to choose," Dimitri finally said, and squeezed their eyes shut. "Please let him call me Mitya, your highness."

"Good man," Julian murmured, and pushed his fingers into Dimitri's mouth. "Captain, what do you think?"

"I'd like to speak to them, my Prince," Adrian said. His voice was a rumble against Dimitri's back.

"Mmhm, then they are all yours."

Dimitri felt their body being turned around so they were facing Adrian, legs still spread and mouth open. They cracked their glassy eyes open and whimpered when they met Adrian's gray gaze.

"There's a lad," Adrian said, a calming hand cool on their hot cheek. "What am I to do with you, Mitya? Do not you know I'd spoil you rotten if you gave me half the chance? The Prince and I both."

Dimitri squirmed, and gasped when they felt a tentacle prod between their legs. Adrian's hand wandered to their nipple and pulled the taut silver ring there before bringing them in for a deep, filthy kiss.

"My Prince wants to fuck you," Adrian explained gently when he broke away, and teased Dimitri's ass a little more. "The first food he's truly craved since he's felt well. All he wants is to climb atop and make such a mess of you. And I told him you'd let him, of course. That you need it as much as he does. Was this incorrect?"

"N-no Captain…"

"Good lad. I did not think so."

Dimitri felt something inside them cresting. They tried unsuccessfully to squeeze their legs together, to stave the sensation. Adrian watched them patiently, alternately teasing a little harder and pulling away when they were…

"Captain, I am going to come," they said, mortified.

"You do not want to?"

"It is too soon…"

"Mitya, do you have shame?" Adrian asked with a frown. Dimitri shook their head from side to side, mouth working silently. "Is it not a pleasing thought, being fucked by your Prince at your Captain's behest? Being worked open so you can take him properly?"

"It *pleases* me Capt-" Dimitri started, and cried out when Adrian's tentacle fucked into them, curling and pressing until they were spilling into Adrian's clever hand and unable to think of anything at all. "Fuck! Fuck, *daddy.*"

"Oh," Julian breathed in the aftermath, stroking himself hard while Adrian licked Dimitri's come off his hand and pushed another tentacle inside them. Dimitri was limp in Adrian's arms, trying to say words but only managing small kittenish sounds into his shoulder. "Oh, do that *again*. What lovely men."

"Daddy?" Adrian asked Dimitri with a quirk of his eyebrow. Dimitri swallowed. "You've not called me *that* in an age, Mitya. Quite forgot how it sounds from your mouth."

"Feels good in my mouth," Dimitri responded, dazed. "Feels like your cock. Daddy."

With thoughts Dimitri could not hear, Adrian smiled over to Julian. The Prince was already pushed flush against Dimitri's back, cock dripping.

"You want him in your mouth while I fuck you?" Julian asked sweetly.

"Yes my Prince, I do," Dimitri said, eyelashes fluttering.

Julian rocked his hips into the divots of Dimitri's. He was hard against their pink, puckering hole. He felt as though he was pushing his fingertip into a searose at the cusp of Spring. He felt as though he was driving a sword through a heart. He thirsted for purchase, the unslaking of this quiet man's existence; taking, taking, taking; back and forth, between the precious heat of their pleasure; the rise of his chest against Dimitri's back, heaving up slowly, slowly, Adrian coaxing him between them, tentacles swarming, rising from their knees, as though being knighted, until they were all three pressed together; tangling, the kisses bruising Dimitri's shoulders, Julian gasping frantic words against their skin until he was shuddering, over and over, conducting a small lightning storm of their own, striking.

Julian's head was not focusing, but he could hear Adrian and Dimitri's thoughts float into meaningless syllables, until they turned back into bright silver and golden strings of light.

Harder and harder, the touches came, and brighter the music played in his head. His hands clutched Adrian's over Dimitri's writhing waist and...as Adrian untangled himself a bit so Dimitri might breathe, he found he longed to stay inside, keeping him there...

More of a Prince now than before, Julian knew he would fight them both when they were back at Illyrial, that they three would wrestle forever in a way that could not be contained in his peripheral:

Y-your highness...

Mitya?

My dear Favorite—

Dimitri lay breathless and freshly conquered. Eventually, Adrian took a swig of the ginger beer at his bedside and poured a little into their mouth for good measure, fingers wiping it where it spilled on their chin and making them reach their tongue out to lick.

"And...Vern?" one of them asked.

Maybe both, at the same time. The sound had cut out of their ears for a little bit as they lay sprawled. Julian had laid next to him at some point, but Dimitri still felt...Julian nuzzled in the nape of their short hair, pressing another kiss to their shoulders.

"Vern's been, well...we have all been trying to figure out how to get back to where we need to be."

"The clam-bed?"

"The...the clam-bed. After we got that nasty letter from Eric..." Dimitri paused, eyes widening when Adrian and Julian shuddered at the same time.

"He's after us then?"

"Yes, Captain. And we really ought to–"

"Address your Prince," Adrian said with a stunning and carefree smile that Dimitri had never seen before, that made them lightheaded. They obediently turned to Julian. Their eyes met and Dimitri's heart felt out of time, their noses almost pressed together they were so entwined...

"*Your highness.* This man is dangerous."

"As are we all. Now, what is the trouble with charting the course?"

Dimitri looked embarrassed. "None of us know quite where it is. We found your painting room, Captain..."

"I know where it is!" Julian declared, stopping short of shouting in Dimitri's face. "Because *he* does. You must let Adrian write out the coordinates and deliver them."

Julian rolled over, opening the bedside drawer and handed it to Adrian. He turned back to Dimitri and squeezed their hand.

Dimitri, he needs medicine. I am so, so worried. It makes me want to fall back into bed and weep until I am ill if he is not thriving. I know you share this feeling.

Sometimes I think, 'Unfortunately so.'

Julian laughed and gave them a little wink.

He's been taking the wrong kind. Synthetic, it masks symptoms but it does not aid them. It estranges him from his true nature. It has been making him so upset. So unwell!

What am I to do for him?

He has consented to commission Pierre to make a remedy he used to take when we were in Illyrial. It helped, he had just forgotten...But Dimitri! Wait!

Yes?

Tell Vern to tell Batiste I need some of his finest swords. Ones to conceal. You understand? Made of glass. Something that can be lit on fire like a candle. Ah, fire! He will understand. I will let you know in my own time. Have him make it himself if he needs, but...

"...And get Pierre, or I shall make the pills myself." he finished out loud.

"Of course, your grace. However..." Dimitri nodded, with a tilt of the head.

"Yes?"

"We will never make it in time. What shall we do if he gets there first?"

Julian pulled Dimitri closer to him and Adrian.

"Never say never," he murmured, thinking.

"Never have the time with you."

"Adrian, as the Captain you know all about weather patterns?"

"Sure?"

"There's a storm approaching, yes? From a couple weeks back…"

"Hitting Illyrial soon, but we would just avoid it."

Dimitri turned. "So, if we speed up, we could cut through it…?"

Julian beamed. "Exactly."

"Would that destroy the ship?"

It was Dimitri's turn to look confused. Adrian scoffed and the delight in his eyes conveyed all he already knew:

My boy—are you very sure?

Oh, Adrian, we are going to need all the help we can get!

"Storms, ahem, have a certain power near Illyrial. Especially near the bed of Princes…we shall ride it! Properly!"

Dimitri flushed red as a seaberry. "You do not mean…"

"*All* of us."

"I do."

Over the boy's head Adrian shared a glance with Dimitri as if to say *Manic, the boy's off his head…*and *This might be wonderful, but what else is he planning? All these tricks of words and contracts—could make beasts fall apart at the hands of charlatans. And what a dangerous man to be in the wrath of—soft spoken and good on the outside—and totally rotted inside.*

"Bring everyone in, in their own time today, if we are to get to this ship home." Julian ordered.

After a few more rounds of lazy, lingering kisses, Dimitri stood and gathered themself. They dressed back in their clothes, Julian doing the buttons with tender, careful strokes and pressing a kiss to their forehead as he bid them adieu. Adrian tucked the coordinates into their capable hands with another kiss, and then he pulled Julian into his embrace. The afternoon passed in quiet, blissful peace. Alone with Adrian as he was alone with himself; perfect. And Julian felt well. Truly and fully alive.

As for the sword he requested, he would try to use his Sight to speak to Vern where no one else would overhear…

CHAPTER 30

Adrian lit the candles, testing his control. All around them the room glowed; soft, at first, and though they never lost the softness of their light, the flames grew higher; flames as blue as surface water on a clear day, hot, hot, hot; flames that did not take away oxygen nor snuff under the water's liquid embrace; flames round and flames vertical, flames dizzy and flames brilliant, flames that existed in some alchemical state of paradox; Beauty, lighting the way...

"When are you going to tell them, you can do this too..." Julian asked, marveling at the scene from his sickbed. He thought back to when they were in the palace and there was nothing keeping them apart; how infinite in nature was it to be; how they bound and wrestled and gnashed their many monstrous teeth; how there would not be held to anyone's standards but their own; how much he wished to push Adrian up upon the desk right now and have his way with him, to kiss the worry away that evaded his brow; *you are not old and though a rough man you might be, there is still a boy somewhere to be found...*

Pierre knocked and gave a little courtesy. Julian broke the tight grasp he had on Adrian's waist and waved him in. His long hair and beard were swept back a little neater and the green of his button-down accentuated his kind eyes. He carried a box full of glass jars and rattling pills and glanced over at Adrian.

"We want you to stay for tonight, Pierre." Julian said, as Pierre checked his vitals then attended to Adrian.

"What for?"

"Oh, we have found a way to get the ship to where we need to go. Then get back to Illyrial to refuel."

"Splendid! A second wind, as they'd say up top. What could it possibly be?"

Adrian gave Julian a look that needed no sharing of thoughts.

"Well, it *is* fun!" Adrian said as Pierre opened a few of the vials and crushed a powder down into his mortar and pestle.

"Adrian, are you sure about this?" Pierre asked, of the medicine. "Because I have no idea what it is going to do."

Pierre understood maybe a third of what he had been instructed to make, but what he knew was it was nothing like the compound that he had been making before, an elegant combination of gentle sedative, steroid, and coagulant. This new course of treatment included in part a spiky neurostimulant *and* an immunosuppressant, combined tersely with a strong bioreceptor, a magnet for the sleepy microbes everywhere under the sea. It sounded like Adrian was attempting to tax an immune system he had previously been appeasing. Which, for his kind of folk…

It was no great revelation that the Captain had inky heritage, even if he passed as vertebrate for the most part. To an old sailor like Pierre, the characteristic obsidian bolts which thorned around Adrian's pupils were a giveaway that even the most mantled inkman could not disguise, in any form. But that is where Pierre's knowledge of Adrian's kind truly ended, beyond the folktales about an octopus's sickness, his trickiness, his fickleness. Sick-tricky-fickle, ick ick ick. There was the bulk of conventional wisdom about any deep-sea creature, and Pierre had long learned not to pay it any mind, especially when the best people he knew were cold fish. If this was what Adrian needed to feel better, then he was going to listen.

"It does not make a lot of sense," Adrian conceded, looking nervously at the compound. "But I have to start trusting myself."

Then he did something Pierre had never seen this far below the surface, in a hybrid environment of air and water. He took Pierre's mortar, put it on the table, and lit a candle, dropping it into the mixture with a quick shake of his wrist. Pierre stood and found the door handle with one blind hand, eyeing the impossible flame.

"*Fire!* What the…" he stopped himself when he heard Julian hush him, though the hairs on the back of his neck were standing on end.

"Come on Pierre, what did you think the sun panels were?" Adrian asked with a twinkle in his eye. "*Zinc?*"

"Yes, I did? Zinc is the ocean standard, it is what *everyone*…you really are half-mad, if half is whole and whole is more," Pierre said, consuming fear suddenly overwhelmed by his curiosity. "But how the devil does that *work?*"

Adrian shrugged and squeezed the charred oxblood mixture in the bowl to a lump between his fingers before putting it in his mouth. Pierre looked at Julian to see if any of this was registering the same alarm and only saw puppy love. *Great.*

"Good thing I am not a doctor," he finally said. "I wash my hands of this."

"But I just looove that you are not a doctor, Pierre. I hate doctors. Hate 'em! So go ahead and *wash*," Adrian said with a permissive gesture of one lazy hand. He smeared more ash on his lips and licked. Little glowing microbes, previously dull and falling listlessly like snow up top, were already floating his way and he wafted them towards him. He rolled up his sleeve and attached the vintage pulse rate monitor to the crook of his elbow, picking it up from the bedside table and lounging on the bed, head in Julian's lap, loopy like he had just consumed a party drug instead of bombing his immune system. Adrian held the pulse monitor like a stuffed animal while Julian unbuckled his leg and gave it to Pierre to put in its case. Pierre felt insane. "Pretty, pretty hair. Pretty."

"He's going into a torpor state," Julian explained to Pierre, not trying to bat away the fingers in his curls. "He will be all right in a few hours, but if the screen blinks yellow, he needs adrenaline, *tout suite*. You brought adrenaline, right?"

"You do this a lot, Julian?" Pierre asked, voice high even to his ears. He clanged through his box to find the adrenaline and checked its expiration date, best practices still drilled in him despite all. "Because I am wigging out right now."

"Just have the adrenaline ready," Julian commanded. "Do you know where the branchials are?"

"What's wrong with the main heart?"

"Joules, *he cannot*," Adrian whispered, eyes cracking open in a fleeting panic. Julian stroked his hair reassuringly, and fixed Pierre with a steely, regal glance.

"*No*. The main heart is too delicate, and it fuels the other two, along with everything else. If it takes the injection while his immune system is compromised, Adrian will go into total cardiac arrest. So, only inject in the branchials," Julian explained firmly, caught Pierre's clueless look and hastened to explain. "You will have to inject right through the neck, either side. But it is an easy shot, you cannot miss it."

"The two of you are something else when you party. The two of you and *Dimitri*," Pierre said, feeling a little sick while he watched Adrian's pulse rate drift to a hibernal level. "Stabbing and burning and torpor and I bet a bit of light poison on the weekends."

"Only if I am very good…" Adrian trailed off as he fell asleep. A couple of tentacles unfolded from wherever they liked to hide, twining Julian's hair in the same dipsy way as his hands. Green glowing clusters of microbes lit on Adrian's parted lips and eyelashes and Julian was rubbing oblong circles on his forehead, cleared of its lines in true repose. Pierre thought about Thad with a pang then, and looked down at his box of medicines.

"Is he very sick?"

"Oh, *very*. But who is not sick, who must live beneath the ocean?" Julian replied sweetly, not vexed by the question. "We are open; open creatures and open systems on the open seas and we are so sick all the time because we are open. There's no denying such a thing and coming out alive. Adrian was in whale fall trying to keep it closed. Trying to shut the illness in and losing all of the good things of himself instead. He did not know any better. Nor did the man who tried to cut it out."

"Eric."

Julian's expression turned dark then and Pierre tried to change the subject. Adrian's pulse had stabilized to a dreamy single digit BPM; the two twin hearts calling and responding at leisure while the sluggish main thumped at sporadic intervals. The microbes were settling in with him for the rest. It was too peaceful to speak of such things.

"Captain was mentioning something 'fun,' in relation to the upcoming storm. I am almost afraid to ask."

"Let's say it powers the currents. It will ensure we get there before Eric."

"New type of engine?"

Julian shook his head.

"Did you know, under the correct conditions, a Prince may function as the eye of a storm?"

"Must have missed that one in school," Pierre admitted. Julian smiled again, tentacle draped around the back of his neck, letting his golden eyes linger on Pierre. "I...I see. I think. You are going to be well enough for that?"

"Which of us?"

"Either. Both," Pierre said, then felt foolish. He realized suddenly the precise nature of what Adrian and Julian had been up to this entire time, why the expanse of Dimitri's neck and shoulders had half-moon marks lurid as new tattoos when they'd passed by the gardens with Adrian's new requisition and a terrifying level of good cheer. The ship had not encountered any trouble this entire month, despite the weather patterns tightening around their location like a noose. Bedridden but also bed-riding, now that was one hell of a cure, and apparently a potent navigation aid.

"It is a happy matter of adding, multiplying," Julian assured, eyes glinting fondly on a memory. "In Illyrial, we are never beset by storms when I open my royal chambers and welcome all. I never needed to direct a storm to get anywhere before, but there's a first time for everything. And it is a wonderful way to bless ships before a long voyage. Champagne should be for drinking, after all…"

Adrian's branchial pulses heightened for a split second before lapsing back into the languid rhythm of torpor. Julian nodded as though he had said something, and the stray tentacle dropped onto his lap. The microbes had started turning into the varied colors of a meadow in their glow. Julian urged them closer to Adrian's mouth with careful fingers.

"They like him."

"Of course. He's warm and safe and when they gather around him, take refuge inside, he feels better. If he remembers to eat and rest, they will not leave him again," Julian murmured. "They needed a reminder that he can be their oasis. A beacon of ash and flame."

"How does he do that?" Pierre asked, newly jolted by the memory of the fire Adrian produced without a thought. "How *can* he? I just do not understand, water is wet, oxygen is precious, and fire is—I have not seen fire underwater since they were still using burnt power in decomp chambers. That was all chaotic, dirty, and so dangerous. I still have nightmares about…But his fire is *beautiful.* How?"

"I do not know how, Pierre," Julian admitted. "And I have not met anyone else who can. He figured it out on his own, on a whim."

"A whim," Pierre repeated. It made no sense, but he did not press the matter in case he got tiresome.

"We all have whims…"

Pierre nodded.

"But do you often have nightmares?" Julian asked, after a long and comfortable silence that settled in the cabin like a blanket. Adrian's pulse remained steady and he was showing signs that he was about to come back to them. Julian rubbed his wrists and his tentacles methodically to urge his waking. Pierre, thrown by the unexpected question, started sorting the medicines in his box and tried to look busy.

"Aye, I do not sleep easy," he responded after a moment of consideration. "Better here. She's a friendly ship. Or closer to The Shallows. It is the depth, the weight of water that gets me. Feels like…well, not to offend you, I know you are from deeper. I feel I have been buried at times, and it takes me for a spin, if I let it."

"I am not offended," Julian promised. "You have never offended, dear fellow."

Julian was still holding Adrian's head in his lap while they spoke, legs bracketing the Captain's waist like they were the only thing keeping him weighted to the bed. Together they were gorgeous, complete yet also…beckoning, the way beautiful things had to be. Pierre suddenly did not feel like a doctor on a call. He felt like an interloper, or like he was ogling with a man's eyes…

"I imagine you sleep better when you share your bed," Julian continued.

"I'd imagine so," Pierre answered.

"But you do not?"

"Ah," Pierre said, seeing what Julian was driving at. "I have not often had occasion. I think he's coming around."

Julian smiled down at Adrian, whose eyelids were twitching.

"Hello, darling. How do you feel?" he asked, unstrapping the pulse monitor. "Do you need the basin?"

Adrian shook his head and managed to open his eyes.

"How long was it?"

"It is nearly evening."

"Feels like longer." Adrian managed to prop himself up on an elbow. His tentacles retreated into his mantle, and he appeared as just a man once more, though it threw him off whatever remaining balance he had. He laughingly tried for a kiss so badly aimed that his head landed square in Julian's chest with a thud.

"Did you dream?"

Adrian shook his head, seemed thankful for it. Julian nodded and looked

242

up at Pierre.

"Are you hungry?" he asked both of them and pulled a box of sweets from the bedside table, hand delivered by Henry earlier before the child was excused from his duties for the night. "Adrian gets an awful sweet tooth after this, every time."

"I *do not.*"

"And you forget, every time," Julian scolded. The residual microbes in the shells of Adrian's ears glowed a fading pink. "But there's nothing those wee beasties love more than sugar. Even if gritty sea Captains must drink blood and eat hardtack on the wrong side of a knife, so come on…"

From the beautifully decorated box, Julian pulled out a truffle the size of a marimo and rolled in shredded coconut which got everywhere. Pierre watched the Prince hand feed Adrian dessert with wide eyes; they really must have known each other for forever and a day…

"You cannot just stand there like a revenant, Pierre," Adrian said to him, glancing over. He had a bit of coconut on his nose. He looked so happy. "It is such a big bed. I do not think Thaddeus would mind."

"Pierre! Who's Thaddeus?" Julian asked, delighted, and patted beside him. "Tell me about *Thaddeus.*"

Pierre could not resist anymore and banished the earthly thought of Adrian and Julian contained by a frame while he stood before them in a museum. The *beaux-arts* canvas rippled, and he was sitting with them in their bed, explaining about Thad. He felt like he had always belonged in the Captain's bed, somehow, even while he missed the bedroom and the garden that were kept manicured for him in his absence. And Pierre realized that they were all looking for a home. But they—he, Julian, and Adrian—all knew where *home* was, which made the search that much more desperate, more painful. To say goodbye to what had been *home* in the meantime was a special kind of hardship. And then there was the other fear; that he would find something he liked better and never want to come back. That the mere act of wanting would make him an exile from his own heart.

"You two try everything, huh?" Pierre said quietly. "I think I have stopped trying things. It is not good. It hurts more, but it is the hurt I am used to."

Adrian and Julian exchanged a glance, but Pierre felt as though they understood, would understand if he...

"My body can withstand so much pain because it embraces pleasure," Julian finally said. "His too. And yours. Why would you gate yourself from any of it?"

CHAPTER 31

The rest of the late afternoon passed between Pierre, Adrian, and Julian and soon it was evening. Having secured the deck against damage from the weather in their methodical way, Dimitri returned to the Captain's quarters. They were a little roughed up by the start of the storm and shirtless, as was their custom when they prepared for bad weather, tying all that was precious to the deck and dodging debris hurled from across the seas. Pierre had slipped out earlier to retrieve a few things from the gardens and Dimitri was glad for it; curling up by Adrian's side after battening down the hatches was a peculiar intimacy they were not yet prepared to share with anyone outside of Julian.

"Feel alright? The medicine, I mean?" they asked, though the Captain seemed *fine*, better even than when they'd left him. Adrian traced the half-moon bruises all over their shoulders.

"I should be asking you that. I seem to recall you took part of the mast to the head last time you went top deck during a storm."

"You mean the *whirlpool*; yes, I did. I have not forgiven you," Dimitri corrected, not at all angry. Adrian had found the raised scar from the mishap on the back of their skull and stroked it with gentle fingers. "Rougher seas then. No real harm done."

"There was harm done nonetheless," Adrian countered, and kissed Dimitri's knuckles like they were the Prince in the bed. Dimitri turned pink and cleared their throat; the absurdity of a chivalric kiss causing scandal in their heart was not lost on them.

"Excited to kiss my brother again?" Julian asked cheerily, coming out of the bathroom, dark curls glitter-dusted and wild. A sprig of pearl-shock laurels tucked on one side of his fins, splayed out and ready to be touched. He wore a few gauzy sprays of green-blue tulle, draped around his shoulders, the paludamentum was encrusted in lines of thin gold and shimmering shells, and though the fabric covered him as a cloak might, he was entirely naked underneath for all to see. Dimitri choked and Adrian laughed. "I know I am! Oh, I do love a storm…"

Excited for me to kiss Vern or for you to kiss Vern? Dimitri thought. Julian did not answer, examining himself in the mirror and smiling back at them through the reflection.

Deep sea thunder rocked the ship. Adrian rose from the bed and produced tapers and candles of all types. Dimitri noted with confusion that they must have been salvaged from The Above, for they contained wicks, and only understood when Adrian produced flames from a small good-bye book in his pocket. The quarters lit up with gorgeous colors and the cold in Dimitri's bones from their earlier travails was singed away by the licking flames. They smiled at the feeling; in the candlelight the cabin no longer seemed cramped, but properly spacious and suited to purpose.

"Could you always do this?" they murmured, watching Adrian create multicolored sparks that he guided into the clear orbs delicately suspended from the bedposts, so their light danced and morphed on Dimitri's body.

"Not always. And not always so well," Adrian said. "Do you like it?"

"I love it," Dimitri said.

I love it because it comes from you. Teach me how, they thought wistfully, even if Adrian could not hear. *I want to know your secrets and keep them with you.*

There was a knock on the door, which swung open of its own accord without its heavy bolt. There was Pierre, with a heavy case different from his medicine box. The gardener blinked at them as though seeing them for the first time and Dimitri sat up, feeling timid all of a sudden, under the firelight and shirtless.

"Had not realized how far down the tattoos go," Pierre admitted, setting the case down on the bedside table like it was a host gift at a dinner party. "Or how beautiful they are."

"Oh. Thanks," Dimitri said, looking down to see how fire changed the designs and the way they lay upon their skin, how it made them dance. They looked back up and met Pierre's eyes, surprised by the compliment, by being looked at to begin with.

"I have not done anything like *this* before," Pierre continued, not bothered by the fact. Dimitri did not need to ask what 'this' was.

"No, me neither," they admitted with equal ease. "I don't think anybody who is not from Illyrial has done anything like *this* before."

There is one Illyrian who has not, Julian interjected, and Dimitri's eyebrows raised, looking over. Adrian was helping Julian into a last piece of his outfit. Music played as Adrian dipped his fingertips into a half shell of dust the color of desert sands and blew the excess away. It set off the deep blue of his nails, all the smooth rings of black opal he had chosen for his fingers, and when he touched Julian's cheek, it left a saffron kiss there.

"*Captain*, you shine up. And Julian, your highness I mean, I will have your tailor's name before the night is through, if nothing else," Batiste said, fluttering in. He was wearing an orange shimmering cape, matching teddy with a corset inset underneath. Aquamarine thigh highs and no shoes, to Dimitri's surprise; they thought he liked the extra height. His hair had been teased and dusted with sequins that were sure to get everywhere. He glanced at Dimitri as though they would turn him to stone. "Dimitri."

"Batiste," Dimitri said, and flashed their teeth. It felt like a lifetime since the complicated flirtations and agonizing slights. "Pretty cape."

"Why, you can have it. You seem cold," Batiste responded with a laugh and a toss of his head that set off his many earrings. "Though maybe it is more sensible to be underdressed for this kind of party."

"What kind of party was this again?" asked Ernest, pulling Pericles in. They were both dressed for dinner.

"Navigating party," Pericles said wisely. "BYOB."

"Navigation? In the Captain's tastefully appointed boudoir? Navigating *what*, precisely? Glad we left Vico with Henry."

"Well, I am just glad we were invited, I fear we are getting a reputation as shut-ins…"

The two chatted cheerily amongst themselves and immediately began monopolizing a couch. Ernest unbuttoned Pericles' shirt and skirted a hand under the waistband of his trousers. Dimitri met Pierre's amused gaze.

"They waste no time!" he said. "In faith, I know not how these things start."

Dimitri, a little hypnotized by the color display suddenly erupting from Ernest's hands and cheeks, did not respond. Had Ernest's nails always been that sharp? Pericles did not seem concerned…

"Dimitri," someone muttered, and an irritated hand waved in front of their face. Dimitri blinked at Vern. Before they could say anything else, he took them by the hand.

The sparkling lights were softer and lit the bed-scene as though it were a theater. Julian braced against the back of the headboard, one arm above his head while he clutched a sturdy rope strung from one bedpost to the other, his other hand gripped to the back of Adrian's head. Adrian, without his mantle and tentacles spilling from the bed like blackest ink onto parchment, wrists wrapped behind his back in lurid purple satin. Julian fucked into his mouth with a hooded glance downward, at the Captain first, then at the crew. He was playing both sacrifice and high priest, Dimitri thought, dizzy with want. He was the weather and the sky and the sea but also their opponent, shaping all to his own royal will. And if Dimitri believed in him, they could surely ride this storm.

The first Prince of Illyrial issued a discreet command to the crew, and each man heard it as though it had been whispered into his ear. He pointed to the sky whilst looking below, then pushed his Favorite deeper onto his shaft and released all from his spell. Now he sunk into the pile of pillows and many, many arms which awaited him, a hungry boy once more.

They understand now, Adrian thought, chest heaving, mouth a mess, still sweetly tied. *It will be a good storm.*

One for the ages, Julian thought, with the power of prophecy still thrumming his veins, and kissed Adrian, tasting himself. He was not immune to the night's enthrallment, now that he had wound the charm up, and he was hardening again. *Spoilt for choice,* he thought idly, and the responding hum of satisfaction from Adrian made him lick his lips, his sharp teeth. *And of course, you are built to spoil.*

Julian unwound Adrian's bonds, tying the long sash around his thigh with a bow, while a thick tentacle slithered around his ankle and tugged him from his stage. He stepped down gracefully, and joined the crew, found Dimitri and Vern first in their pillows by the corner. Right where he thought he would find them.

Too soon for this, my boy. You will do your part of the ritual, Julian thought of Vern. He noticed with fondness that Adrian's thoughts were a deep monstrous grumble of *mine mine mine,* Dimitri the subject therein.

Ours my darling, do not be jealous.

Mine! We two are one. So Dimitri is mine.

Julian could not argue with that, felt the fraught hunger for Dimitri along with a spate of delicious Adrian-memories that snaked into his mind and made their home there as surely as the tentacle up his thigh.

And I have to share. But not just now, they both thought, vibrating with intense erotic need to mark and fill the navigator so there was no confusion about it.

"Vern," he said, bangles jingling around his wrists. "You are quite a good host."

"Thank-you, your highness," Vern nodded, still concerned with Dimitri. Julian stood silent, waiting pointedly until his brother met his eyes.

"Trip no further, pretty sweeting."

"Journeys end in lovers' meeting," Vern responded, eyes wide. The meaning was clear to him, though he could not discern it. He stood and let Julian kiss

him.

You dare try and usurp me on my sickbed? You can have them when I say! If I say! Not a moment before, Julian commanded, smiling eyes growing inky. Vern swallowed and nodded, squeaking when Julian claimed his lips once more, feeling a tentacle glance on his thigh. Moaning into Julian's mouth, he glanced over at Dimitri, and his knees buckled. Dimitri was half hard, lips parted as though deep in thought, sipping from their shared glass. Julian broke away, and brushed Vern's hair from his face.

"Go on then," he said with a laugh. "We will find you later."

"Nngh," Vern responded eloquently, and wandered into the fray like an amnesiac.

"My Prince," Dimitri said, properly in awe. In response, Julian swept down to them, so he was straddling them, aided by a silky tentacle around his waist. Adrian's clever appendage encircled them both and Julian unbuttoned Dimitri's pants, shoving them down with surprising force.

Mine mine mine my Mitya, he and Adrian thought or growled, and Dimitri gasped at the unfamiliar incursion in their head, instantly recognized as their Captain. They kissed Julian hard and responded *your yours all yours* with no lie in their heart.

Ernest saw the gold Prince in his periphery and paused from his careful work. Pericles spasmed helplessly in another orgasm wrung from his body, crying for more-nomore in the most delicious way, and did not even register the reprieve. His hands were cuffed securely to either side of his collar, which he always wore but was not always employed so helpfully.

"Good evening, your highness," Ernest said, wiping green blood off his chin.

Vern was dressed beautifully for the night, layered black sequins like rare scales or chainmail on a bodysuit which swept under his chin with royal reserve, yet finished at a gleefully inviting four-inch inseam. He could not possibly know the refracting starlight colors Ernest parsed from the ensemble, catching and twinkling with every gentle breath. The draping body harness was an additional fascination, of a noble metal that did not rust, matching rings around each thigh clasped shut with interlocking black gems, strategically broken and then hinged with that same mysterious metal. He had dressed to fascinate, to be beheld but also to be undressed. And here he was, taking off long gloves of fishnet and inset winking gems.

In thought, Ernest reached out to Pericles, as beautiful in his ruination and as rare to behold. The thread of their thoughts had long felted into one hard knot of want, but Ernest could still talk and think and decide.

You have caught a pretty Princeling's eye, he informed with only a shadow of a taunt. *Can I let him partake of the quarry, if he asks?*

Pericles responded with several emphatic yeses and exclamation marks and thank yous and pleases and every foolish pet name he had ever had for Ernest. He was deep inside himself, and Ernest was pushing him deeper. After so long just thinking about it, there was no stopping it now.

"I hardly wish to intrude, but could I...?" Vern inquired, gesturing to Pericles as though he were a buffet froid.

"What lovely manners," Ernest said. "It is an intrusion we welcome. Can you believe he keeps them hidden away like this? Would you have known just by looking at him? Back home he was not so modest. I fear he's forgotten to be wild, and it requires stern correction. Oh, your highness, may I?"

Vern had grasped one of Pericles' twitching cocks with a loose grip. Ernest, upon receiving the Prince's hesitant nod, guided him to a tighter grasp, until Pericles twitched. Vern licked his lips and looked at Ernest.

"And then you, the other one?"

"I like your thinking, your highness," Ernest praised. "I like to start on one when he's about to come from the other, so he's just inconsolable, but perhaps this will black him out. And then I can put something inside him without all the crying. Perry, honey, can you hear me?"

Pericles sobbed in response.

From the other side of the room, Batiste watched, lingering.

"Are you faring well, you beautiful creature?"

251

Pierre had finally managed to extract himself from the beardy round of heavy petting he had engaged the Captain with, looking dazed and dear. Batiste blinked.

"Me?" he asked, looking around theatrically. "I am quite alright. How does the Captain kiss?"

"Like a fucking god," Pierre said, letting the unvarnished thought pass his lips without thinking. Batiste's mouth dropped. "Or else I have been too long at sea. I care not, I'd like to kiss him more before the night is through, if he is not otherwise engaged. What have you been doing?"

"Just biding my time, taking it all in. It is…"

"You are waiting for Dimitri?"

"No!" Batiste said, too quickly. "We are um…I do not think they are on my dance card tonight."

"Oh! I did not mean to assume, I suppose I thought you'd be…"

"No, we have never, beyond their little prologues. Charming though they were."

"Really."

"Is it really *such* a surprise?" Batiste asked, only realizing he was tugging an earring nervously when he sharply snagged one of the fishhooks in his hair, stiff from spray and sequins and wider than he was used to. "Why Pierre, I could tell you I was once loved by a glittering fellow who haunts our dreams and prances on screens, but you would not believe me."

Pierre reached over and helped him dislodge the hook with gentle fingers. He took his hand down and rubbed the skin around the wound.

"Thank you."

"I have something for you," Pierre said. "But no need to be scared. It is not a bouquet."

Batiste laughed a little and watched him take out his suitcase and start rummaging through like a salesman. It was a pot of glowing algae, swaying a little bit and the color of shallows coral. Pierre pulled one of the fronds by the root and massaged its broad side with his fingers until it exuded beads of gel.

Batiste held out his arm instinctually, knowing a medical wrap when he saw one. Soon both his wrists were wrapped in the algae and Pierre tied them off with a small kiss to either side.

"It is very sweet, but I would have preferred...oh," Batiste breathed, feeling the ever-present pain turn to something a little less jagged but just as deep. *"What is that?"*

"It takes the edge off bone pain, I have a couple of 'em on too, storms are murder on my joints," Pierre said, pulling up his shirt (which was still on, how was this possible?) to show a couple of the algae wraps on his arms and elbows. Batiste reached out to touch without thinking, and they ended up in a slow kiss. Pierre pulled away, looking like he needed to explain further. "Generally, they uh, loosen things up. Were you in need of loosening?"

"I think I have nightmares like this," Batiste admitted with a nervous giggle, unbuttoning Pierre's shirt, a very fine linen for gardening or whatever it was he did in the garden.

"Do you want to get out of here? Are...are we allowed?"

Batiste considered the option seriously, finding that he fit perfectly on Pierre's lap while he did. Adrian's body had become gradually more multitudinous during their brief conversation, and tentacles which were wide and heavy crept across the floor, stuck to the wall and guaranteeing an awkward exit. Every time Batiste looked over to the extremely busy bed, Dimitri and Julian were in new positions unimaginable as they were enticing; it would be a shame to miss any of *that*, if just for the sake of sweeter dreams.

"If anything, it would be very selfish of me to deprive the whole crew of the ship doctor at such a crucial time," he finally sighed.

"Uh..."

"I am sorry," Batiste apologized, surprised at his own sincerity. "You hold some measure of courtliness. You are such a gentleman to your seahorse suitor by the seashore, after all."

"He is not really my *suitor*," Pierre corrected gently. "Guys like me seldom have suitors. That is the courtly stuff you boys go in for. Me and Thad are...

very old friends."

"Not all of 'us boys' are into the pretty words behind the shoji, you know," Batiste said with an easy toss of his head, raining sequins onto his carefully discarded cape. "I suppose you thought I was going to eat you when we met, sailor-man."

"I will admit it crossed my mind. I do not think that anymore, have not for a long time. Turns out it was *Ernest* I had to watch out for, is this…?"

"Yes," Batiste promised, voice unsteady as Pierre pushed more fabric away. "Do you have a lot of f-friends you avoid when you are on shallows leave?"

"Not really. Just Thad. We are, well it is mostly a me thing, unfortunately. Thad's great."

"But?"

"No buts. He's great. We going to talk about Thaddeus all night or…? Both are good with me."

"Well, I thought you might," Batiste paused, trying to think of a synonym which would not offend Pierre's tender ears. "Pollinate?"

Pierre laughed "We will get there."

"Yes, what else do you have in your suitcase?" Batiste asked, reaching over curiously and giggling when Pierre swatted his hand away. "Oh? You need to ambush me for this to work?"

"That is what foreplay is. Can I put your hair up?"

"*I* can put my hair up, thanks," Batiste said. He unsnapped a bangle from his wrist and gathered it all into a high ponytail. "*Comme ça?*"

"*Tu as des cheveux spectaculaires,*" Pierre responded, twitterpated despite himself while he rummaged. "Why do you dye it?"

"Why *don't* you?" Batiste retorted, self-conscious. Was it so obvious, in the candlelight?

"Same reason, I imagine," Pierre said acquiescently, and found what he was looking for. "Well, no, I know I do not dye my hair because it is too much work, whereas you…"

"In my heart, I have always been a redhead," Batiste explained with gravity. Pierre nodded and held out a length of soft rope.

"Hands behind. Do not want you to hurt yourself," he said in a quiet, strong way that Batiste could not put his finger on. There was no rush, there was no need to do, well, anything. He was not dizzy dancing in the arms of strangers, but he *felt* dizzy being stilled. Batiste's lips parted and he obeyed, whimpering when Pierre pulled him to his chest and tied him up so his wrists drifted behind him in a kind of prayer. "There you go, so beautiful. Damn, how tight did you cinch this thing?"

Batiste blinked down and watched Pierre tangle with the laces on his corset, pursing his lips to stop the moan as some of the stays loosened. Pierre let him grind on his lap for a minute, fiddling with a tube that looked like lipstick in his hands.

"Have not tried this before," he said. "Uh, except on Thad."

"What is it?"

"Are your nipples sensitive?"

"No."

"They will be," Pierre said by way of explanation.

In their periphery, they saw Vern float by. He was covered in a watercolor palette of bodily fluids, otherwise completely bare, dreamily observing them. He had learned much this night, and was looking for someone, though his head was so full of reef-mate fancies that he was fuzzy on who that might be. His contagious thoughts filled Batiste with remorse, and he struggled to shake it out.

"Whatever, I am sure he just wants to tug at my pigtails," Batiste muttered to himself, trying to be brave. "Virginal castle brat. Still annoyed with me about *Dimitri's* feelings. I did not make a move on the man. I may have tempted them with a few kisses but…Oh, I cannot imagine being so bothered over it, when it seems to have turned out in his favor specifically!"

"I do not take Princely words as law," Pierre said, trying gallantly to console. "Nor am I from his neck of the river, and I do not care what he thinks is true."

"Do you care what I think is true?" Batiste asked and cringed when the truth of the matter came out without an ironic twist, when Pierre heard all of it unvarnished. "*Oh no.*"

Batiste wished he could hide his face and think of the sword he would make to filet a Prince instead of crying. He thought of Pierre instead, and the intention melted; water in the molten metal warped the shape before he could draw it from the mold. He let Pierre hold him like someone precious, someone who could be hurt.

"The little Prince is correct, of course," he admitted after a moment, fidgeting out of the soft rope and scared to meet Pierre's eyes. "I was very unkind to Dimitri, for no good reason. I would be unkind to you, if left to my own devices. But not because I need you to be *any other*…"

"I know," Pierre said, and pushed an errant curl out of Batiste's face. "You want your perfect visions; your swords and armor and elegant ballgowns with every last sequin in place. You are a vision, too. It takes time."

Batiste turned his head, his cheeks, wet with tears, pressed against Pierre's.

Pierre's hands treaded the delicate waters of his locks and he placed his own greying ones into Batiste's. He waited, slow and precise, before capturing Batiste's lips, parting them natural as the bloom of petals, opening; sanguine and honest and utterly poisonous.

Batiste kissed him, and decided then, tonight would be dedicated to something new; to finding out who Pierre was, and who he would become in the unfolding of his many, languishing embraces.

CHAPTER 32

Vern stood by the porthole, watching the incoming storm as though it were a painting. He smiled at nothing, and there was an accompanying glass of nothing in his hand. Still possessed of the lovely and frightening things he had seen and done, he felt enchanted and cursed, touched and untouchable. Maybe it was fleeting, and tomorrow he would be as he had been yesterday, he thought lightly, but who knew when tomorrow would arrive, if ever? They could be wrecked in this storm and fall downward drown down drown but they would be gripped by such *pleasures...*

"Vern," someone said, and he turned around, oddly expecting to see himself. He was not sure if he did or not.

"That is my name. Hullo," he said with great courtesy. "Are you having a nice night?"

"Yes, sweetheart, I am."

"And am I having a nice night?" he asked with an easy laugh, and a phrase passed through his lips on the way to his head. "Black-browed knight..."

"Your *hand*, dear boy."

"I got bit," Vern nodded, not upset. "Then he kissed it better. Then I bit."

The boy chuckled and took the empty glass out of Vern's bloody hand, leaving it on a ledge and leading him away from the porthole.

"I saw. I have never seen you do such a thing before," he said. "Did you like the taste?"

"He *was* tasty," Vern assured, letting the other boy lay him down and wrap his hand. "But in his blood, the marvelous creature is possessed of a most subtle poison against which I have not been inured. I am learning my lesson now."

"What lesson is that?"

"I do not know yet, I am learning it," Vern said, watching the sparks in a glass orb dance and bounce. The boy kissed his forehead and that was sparks too. Vern wiped at the tingle before he realized it was the feeling of remembering. "Hullo Joules! I have been poisoned!"

"Yes, you were explaining how," Julian smiled. He was so beautiful, covered in scratches and marks of his own. The purple sash around his thighs was tattered.

"I have always been so frightened of poison, but I think for the first time it went remarkably well," Vern said, gripping Julian's shoulder against the swimming sensation. "What other silly things have I been frightened of?"

In response, Julian kissed him on the mouth with a hand around his neck, where *anyone* could see. And there were quite a few anyones, Vern realized with a heated groan into his brother's mouth, quite a few anyones who were certainly watching...

"I know not where my clothes went," he confided when Julian released him, only a little troubled by this.

"I do not think your clothes exist anymore, Vern. Furthermore, I do not know if I shall allow you to be dressed ever again," Julian said. Vern could not discern if he was serious or not, but he had a mad hope for such a command, and reached a hand between his own thighs at the thought of Julian, finely accoutered as ever, keeping his brother sat by his knee, bare and hard...

Julian's power lies in giving and I always thought mine must be in withholding, he thought giddily, stroking harder. *How much nicer it would be to only be given when he says...*

Then Vern remembered something rather urgent and tried to sit up again, looking for...

"Dimitri is just over there, darling. Do not worry that envenomed little head," Julian reassured him, glancing just over Vern's shoulder. "Let me attend to you while Adrian takes care of them the way they like."

"What's the way that they like?" Vern whispered, feeling color rise to his cheeks. He had not imagined Dimitri in such a state of undoing, not truly. Perhaps he had tried not to, worried that Dimitri would sniff it on him and find it crude.

"With Adrian?" Julian prompted, kissing down his chest. "With me? With you?"

"With *anyone,*" Vern replied. "I want to know *everything* they like, even if I cannot give it to them. I would never tire of such lessons, Joules, I would be such a good student if Dimitri were my subject."

"Mmhm, your wanderings tonight have convinced you of this?"

"Precisely," Vern sighed, remembering Ernest and Pericles in their gory petty mort.

"And would I be equally convinced, if I were to look in your heart?" Julian asked, raising his head from the fluttering trail of kisses on his chest to look at Vern with an appraising eye. "Or do you only wish to know so Dimitri may please *you,* not the other way around?"

"I…" Vern faltered and swallowed. "I do not know what you would find there to convince you one way or the other, but I am only ruled by you, and I submit to your judgment. You are wiser than me. And older."

"Pretty words!" Julian said haughtily. "Maybe too pretty. Let's put you to the test. *Adrian.*"

"Upstart."

"Brat," Adrian retorted, with fondness. He inched closer to Vern. "Let me explain something to you, once. I am less patient than Joules and I will not repeat myself, so please do try and focus. If you want to answer back and make me be firm with you, that is your Princely prerogative. But do you think *Dimitri* acts like such a willful child under my instruction?"

"W-what do you mean?" Vern asked, fists bunching the sheets as Julian tied him down.

"If you truly wish to know their pleasures, you should be patient and learn from one of their teachers," Adrian proposed, and his dancing gray eyes crinkled at Vern's expression. "Do you understand now?"

"I can be good, if that is what you want," Vern spat between gritted teeth. He was close, far too close already. Adrian was right beside him and all around him, and Vern was pinioned further by his full attention.

"No, you cannot," Adrian said with a shake of his head, and wrapped a hand around Vern's cock without asking, without needing to ask. "I'd fuck your brother again if I wanted *good*."

"Oh!" Vern cut off when he came, gripping the sheets tighter so he did not fall flat on his back. Adrian pulled a handkerchief from the bedside table with a flourish and wiped his hand.

"There you are, your highness," he said, and smiled when Vern moaned. "You see, it *can* be a pleasure to obey. Do you require another example or shall you learn by rote?"

"Do not be mean, Captain."

Vern hid his face when he realized it was Dimitri who spoke. Dimitri, who was totally bare, ravaged and triumphant.

"You don't like it?" Adrian asked. Dimitri shook their head, and kissed Adrian on the cheek.

"*I* love it," they said, stroking Adrian's hair. "As well you know. Permit *me* to be the boy's companion for a spell and luxuriate awhile with your Prince."

Vern slumped onto the bed, freed from tentacles and hands, and Dimitri pulled out the handkerchief with a soft smile.

"Adrian will play you like a fiddle if you let him," they said.

"I was not going to *let* him," Vern denied, wiping his mouth. "Maybe I was going to let him a little. But don't you? Let him play you, I mean."

"He plays with me," Dimitri said, parsing the delineation with a careful hand. "But Adrian and Julian are both fully in their power now, and they will be united in their cloudy thrall until we pass into the eye of the storm. Any of our petty tussles hitherto seem chivalric and chaste compared to tonight. Most wondrous…"

They held out a hand so Vern could finally attempt sitting up. Their tattoos glowed and danced in the candlelight, and Vern reached out to touch before feeling shy. Dimitri smiled at him.

"You can," they said. "I do not mind."

"I am not like Julian," Vern said softly. "I cannot do as he does. Flood your mind with marvels and wants."

Dimitri took Vern's hand and pressed it to the shimmering ley lines between their elbow and heart.

"You don't think you have done that?" they asked after a moment. Vern opened his mouth, then closed it with a shake of his head.

"*Ta gueule!* I will not forgive you if you have waved off your Captain's attention from me simply so you could flirt," he warned with a giddy grin. "It would be most retrograde to my desires. I hate hate hate a flirt."

"Fussy," Dimitri smiled. "And fancy free."

The ship rocked suddenly, shot up in a maverick wave, and Dimitri's arm braced around Vern's waist. A wobbly thought passed between them and Vern felt frustrated all of a sudden; why should it not be that he and Dimitri could luxuriate in the cloistered congress of mutual thoughts as Julian and Adrian could do without effort? As Ernest and Pericles did, to offset the catastrophe of their star-crossed desires when made material? Why must *he* alone have to say with his animal mouth the things which seemed too precious and circumspect to break with rhetoric? A Prince of Illyrial, literary and learned capital, glistening with glossy spired shells and *boyspeak*, and yet he could not speak to his desires as any of his subjects might, in the arms of a beautiful man, on a stormy night.

Dimitri brushed his hair from his face.

"I am not flirting," they promised. "I am not good at that sort of thing."

"How could I believe that?" Vern scoffed. "You command these disparate hearts so effortlessly."

Dimitri's mouth twisted and they laughed, a deep and addictive sound. Shyly, Vern looked at their tattoos again, flummoxed by the jumping scrawl.

"What do they say? I cannot read them," he asked, running his curious fingers up the one which wound around Dimitri's bicep. When Dimitri did not answer, he looked up, feeling silly. "It is not that I *cannot*, it is just…the writing has to be big letters in a stronger light."

"They are coordinates," Dimitri said hoarsely. "Rendered in the antiquated longform. A poem for a place. They used to do it that way so sailors without book-learning could hear and remember."

"Why did they *stop?* Poems are so much easier," Vern said, taking it as a personal slight.

"The world became too big to be mapped via verse," Dimitri said with palpable sorrow. "The sky became too wide, and the oceans became too deep. Or so I have been told."

"And *this* poem, where…" Vern trailed off, and met Dimitri's eyes. "You do not know?"

"I know the poem, not the place," Dimitri replied. "I often imagine it was the place I was made."

Oh. Vern felt as though he had opened a door he should not have, like a thief in the night, or maybe the private investigator hot on his tail. He withdrew his fingers, feeling poisonous, and set his hands on his folded legs in retribution.

"I will not pry you apart. Even if you would welcome it, I will not interpret you like a poem," he murmured, bowing his head. "Not while the purpose of such a disarticulation remains a mystery to me."

"If I could divine your purpose, would you?"

Vern *wanted*. He wanted it, but shook his head, hands clenched in fists.

"If I said please?" Dimitri finally said, lips crooking and far too handsome.

"You invite your destruction?"

"Yes. If indeed it is destruction I am inviting. I would invite it. And I would say please. The destruction of the stranger you fear to break. The destruction of the man you think to cherish by keeping your desire at an arm's length," Dimitri said. "I would invite such destruction on myself, without hesitation. Then you would learn what I already know."

"What's that?"

"It is not truly me you would destroy."

The room had been tilting subtly, the ship caught as it was on a wave. Vern was so tightly clung to the mattress in the raw fear of pitching forward and finding himself in Dimitri's arms by fate's design instead of his, he did not realize he had torn the sheets. He looked at Dimitri to see if they had noticed, and they had, and on the knife edge of a decision, he shut his eyes, asking for the water and the waves to take him where they willed.

Dimitri gathered him in their arms, and he was drowned all at once, gasping in foam and salt as he grasped blindly with his hands, kissing Dimitri's face until he found their lips. He let them lift him off the bed and wrapped his legs around their waist and kept on kissing. He fancied he could know Dimitri as he knew the world, the source of all understanding but the root of every mystery he would never unpick, vast and beautiful because he was lost in them but would never be gone from them. The enormity of such a thought hit him like a wave and he gasped into Dimitri's mouth, winded and falling. He could not open his eyes, his hands were clasped around Dimitri's wrists and somehow they were beneath him now, breathing hard into his mouth and he needed them to know but did not know what it was...

"I know you. I do not know you," he wept. The twin statements were true and he marveled at it. "Please. Divine my purpose."

"You wish to find me here. You wish for me to find you," Dimitri answered with the surety of a knight confronted by any curse, who could walk untroubled through lonely forested paths. "You tire of the chase and you wish to rest with me."

"Yes," Vern breathed, nodding emphatically.

Dimitri sat up so they could kiss him while he stayed straddled on their legs. He shook at the feeling, suddenly scared, but Dimitri was careful and firm, warm hands down his back and then pressing hot touches into his thighs. They pulled away and guided Vern's hand to his own cock, inviting him to stroke while they continued to learn by touch, voice low under his ear.

"Sweet boy. You may rest by my side as long as you like and watch the clouds go by over our heads. And we will kiss as new lovers every time we meet. But we will meet over and over, if that is what you command."

"I do not wish for us ever to be new lovers," he said, and groaned as Dimitri's hand replaced his. "I-I want us to have always been and to always be. No fumbling first times because we have always been entangled and writhing. I do not care how mad it is, show me how we have loved before, how we will love again, show me..."

Dimitri was patient and damnably careful, but their fingers were thick, they pushed and spread Vern in ways he had never felt before. He wanted Dimitri to go faster but could not work a word from his open mouth, arms thrown around their shoulders while they thrust their fingers deep and made him twist.

"Please," he cried, a long-sustained sound he heard as though from a distance. He felt like he was singing, it did not hurt to scream. He wanted to slide forward and slip onto Dimitri's cock all at once, he wanted to be so full that he could not move on it unless he was guided by the hands on his hips... *"Dimitri. Please."*

Dimitri finally pushed in with their length and did not stop until they were fully sheathed with a moan that Vern could feel in his own chest. He shook, eyes wide and unsure if the thunder he heard was from the ocean or from his head. He opened his mouth, full of more pleas, but Dimitri captured his lips in a deep kiss and then started moving deep within him. In Dimitri's embraces Vern no longer was aware of his body so much as the rhythm of Dimitri's, so much as the strange mixture of their togetherness. He had not understood the night going into it, and here, he began to understand even less; and how marvelous it was! Outside the storm had indeed come. The sea-skies were ripe with drifts, dizzying currents, torrential of heavy waves. They would pass through the storm, riding faster and faster, until they became the very beats of the storm itself; lightning and thunder, and so many slick, wet sheets of waves, raining down, swirling…

And as the grey light of the storm penetrated the sea, he found their arms extending, all their kisses breaching upon the laurels of each other's loves; all of them, here Ernest's tail twining into the fronds of Batiste's algae lined wrists, Pierre kissing the side of Dimitri's tattooed arms, Vern brushing Julian's delightful, open-mouthed commands, Julian delighted in swimming through, pulling Pericles in, Pericles pushing against Adrian's tentacles, and Adrian feeling clear and himself, his tentacles wandering through the field of these such creatures, tentacles stroking fins, tentacles pulling hair, tentacles, caressing cheeks, tentacles, prodding and sliding the heels of nervous glances into their rightful places; tentacles, squirming, summoning, searing; the fire from the sky, and the fire from the sea, and the fire in his heart; blue flames roaring, smoke-singed hyacinth sweat, sounds of opera and symphony, harpsichord, violins, and chimes; the metaphor, the metronome, the meandering will with no shame; the tentacles writhing in ecstasy, alive and dying, sick and well, and oh! All of them, reaching, coated in bright, shimmering come; squeezing, squeezing, squeezing…

The storm broke and the gray sun reached the ship even in the depths of the ocean, in broken lines and glowing filaments no brighter than the guttering candles surrounding the Captain's bed. Safe and unburdened by its passage, the ship plunged forward at lightning speed just as Julian had planned. And yet, the Clarel also rocked the crew like it was a cradle; all aboard slept like lovers in an Athenian field.

CHAPTER 33

Batiste slunk out of his quarters at half past noon. He adjusted the silk of his robe around his shoulders and smiled. *Last night was…different,* he thought. It struck him as stranger than some of the parties he had been to. More intimate, yet initiating nothing that was not asked for. And Pierre…Oh, Pierre! Everything was different now. *Was this growing?* He watched the pink-grey light of day float over the water's blue. The hours danced in front of his eyes, thread upon thread, and he remembered the feeling of Pierre's shirt in his and he knew Pierre found it strange that they should fit so well together.

The others piled onto the main deck. Ernest and Pericles provided the sample, perfectly replicated. Julian sat down. Batiste took the dye applicator and tried not to fumble when he brushed hands with Pierre. First, he applied the liquid and made sure to stop when it matched the color. Then, he scrubbed at the lock of curls so that it would look brand-new. As though it was not a dye job at all, but something done from the very acrid nature of the air to the sea. He would know. He had dyed his own bright curls so many times, ashamed for the roots to be so dull and gray, even as a boy, that the process felt as easy as cutting the pattern for a pirate's loose blouse.

"That is perfect," Julian said, as he finished, and thanked him.

Adrian steered and Dimitri charted. Julian could hear their thoughts. He knew their worry.

As Batiste ushered him and Julian into his quarters to dress, he instructed them.

"These blades, designed for hidden wounds," he said, dressing Julian as Vern would dress. "Flammable, too. Remember."

Then, he threw a stack of daggers to the side. "Those will not inflict hidden wounds, and I am giving them to Adrian and Dimitri in case Eric pulls any tricks."

"I do not want…"

Batiste smiled. "They are armed at Vern's request, your grace."

Julian looked at Vern and sighed. Vern did not back down, crossing his arms petulantly.

"Alright, but last resort—and unnecessary precaution."

He did not dress Vern as Julian was dressed. No, the play was not to see double. At least…not yet.

He handed Vern a variety of powders and liquids that he knew what to do with.

Vern moved around in Batiste's quarters, preparing, lingering, floating in his own nervous way. He began to fidget, feeling both better and worse, fingers splaying along the many shining threads, feeling, feeling, feeling…

The ship moved through so many dark, deep waters; green-blue waves, tipped black, that became brilliant in their darkness the further they navigated. Past one of the windows Julian could see Illyrial in the distance, could think of it before he saw it; and he wanted it, he wanted it, more than he wanted to turn his head away and not think of anything at all. He turned his head and saw the shining palace in the distance, and he shed tears, in his own quiet, proud way. The distance grew, a few miles away, in some indeterminate direction to anyone who was not Adrian on this ship.

Adrian knew where to go. Julian knew what to do.

And Vern…

From the other side of the bed, Vern reached out and touched his hand. Julian gasped. It might not have been sudden, it might have been Vern looking at him the whole time. He would not have known. It worked. Yes, he understood for a moment how well their plan would work. It must. Together, they embraced, and wept freely:

My Prince, my Prince, we are going home no matter what.

CHAPTER 34

The meadow of kelp shrouded in dark seemed to be pierced by a ray of golden-white iridescence below it. The shell bed, protected by so many natural strands of seaweed, was surrounded but not hidden, protected but not kept. Nothing could naturally uproot something so precious. If one were to come across such a thing, they would immediately know not to disturb it. Unless, of course...

Eric was already there, singularly focused on reaching the bed.

Adrian's ship docked, amidst the seaweed, it was not obvious it was there. Those who stayed aboard stayed aboard.

Julian swam towards Eric.

"Will you tell me you discovered it first?"

"Ah, Vern!"

Eric stood by the bed, looking coiffed and perfect as ever. He smiled and waved as though spotting an old friend by happenstance. It was chilling. Julian laughed, waving back with a couple of wiggled fingers. The grating tension of the scene felt strange and threatening...but *more* strange than threatening. Julian looked for some sign of him knowing how to disconnect parts of the shell. He seemed flummoxed, as though the shell was an art installation he might mistake for a garbage receptacle.

He does not know what to do with it. With any of us. With...me.

"Do you even know what it is?" Julian asked.

"I know what it *could* be. It is a great resource. The pearls inside of it, the bed itself, I mean, make and remake themselves...in such a way, that—that," he reached for his sword. "You going to fight me?"

"A first fight *before* the wedding cake? I am just trying to understand your terms. You seem to…want something that is not yours?"

He listened for this man's thoughts: there were none.

"I want what we agreed, in your contract. What does it matter if you did not sign it, there is still power in a verbal agreement."

"Yes, that is right," Julian answered. He purred a little for good measure. "But once you have an acquisition that is so precious, you ought to know what to do with it, am I right?"

"Yeah."

"So?" Julian cocked an eyebrow. He practiced his speech to a fault. The way Vern could charm and leer and crack into someone with a single word.

"I will sell it off! Stem cells, maybe, maybe some other application, beauty's been a beast, but I hear that space exploration is the new deep-sea extraction…"

"*We will*, darling—remember?" he simpered, and batted his eyelashes. He loathed this man. Eric rolled his eyes and launched into what was surely the first of many diatribes.

"I do not know about that, Vern. After *INDRA-1*…last fucking thing I needed. Awful amount of scandal. Sticks to everything. Also, I nearly died without *actually* dying, so thanks a lot for that. Surviving was a really unpleasant experience all around, and *no*, I am not going to tell you how, you beautiful psycho. Let's just say I have got an inquest and a grotesque amount of debt waiting for me when I finally get back to civilization. I look like a total idiot and it is all your fault. Like, what kind of crazy did I agree to? Are you even the Last…"

"Pah! Cold feet. That is all. No need to call it all off. Let's set another date, on *INDRA-2* this time. Everyone will forget the particulars of the unpleasant engagement, do not you know nobody throws a party like me?"

"Your parties are great."

"We will be laughing about this Last Boy on Earth nonsense before long. You just have to make me your Man."

The poisonous language of the marriage contract seemed to appease Eric, if only momentarily. Julian felt bile pushing up in his throat but forced it down. Instead of convincing or wooing or romancing, Eric used words like a cudgel, set them down on waterproof to contain every intention and make it last forever. And the feats he wished to immortalize—stem cells retrieved from the singular and brilliant and unconsenting, patents of wondrous inventions perverted by their acquisition, assets all hoarded by an agreement made with no passion or friendship—presaged a world of rhetorical imprisonment for everyone who ever dared to speak or write or read two words: 'I do.'

"But..." Eric finally said, having mulled it over with hideous lassitude. "There has to be a Last Boy on Earth—how else will we market you? How else will you be useful to society? How else will we make sure there are never any others, so that you can remain...?"

"Stuck? Frozen? Alone?"

"Valuable?" Eric suggested. "Value requires exclusivity, scarcity..."

"Maybe in your world. My value is not in my scarcity, even if I am singular. My value is beyond your comprehension."

"Exactly! I mean, look at you. You are stunning, when you walk into a room, you are all people can see."

"A-huh. But the bed...?"

"The bed needs to be researched and quantified so we can sell it to our benefactors."

"So, you can get out of your debt?"

"Yup! Literally I owe the debt people my life now. And then we can...do whatever you want?"

"But this is where *I* was made. It is not yours, not even as a wedding gift."

It seemed to blindside Eric, who looked at the bed and tried to put it all together, boy from pearl, pearl from shell. He looked back at Julian with an ugly frown.

"You knew where it was and did not tell me from the start! You lied! By omission, but still...Tricky little boy, aren't you? Why Vern, why all this trouble? Are you still mad about *Adrian*?"

"Pardon? Adrian?"

"Yeah, your, um…special friend? The bed warmer? The geisha-groupie thing. What *is* the sugary name for a professional companion where you come from? Though I wonder what a boy like you even wants with someone like that. You seem so vanilla, and I mean if you have to haggle for sex, what hope is there for the rest of us? Have you seen him lately? I hear he does not even pretend to be respectable these days, limping around with a crew of shoreline abortions, playing rape and pillage out there in the outskirts," Eric said, and rubbed the inside of his wrist. "*And* he gave me the fucking clap…but that's just water under the boat."

Julian breathed deeply; he knew none of it was true, just more vicious lies. A clueless smile plastered on his face instead of the rictus of rage he felt in his heart. He did not want a lecture on his dreamy nature of Revenge. No, he knew what Princes were made of. He knew what he was made of.

"Haggle? I do not know what a haggle is."

"Pay. Commerce. Trade. What the hell does Illyrial run on?"

"Beds fascinate you that much, huh?"

"Sure. Profitable beds."

"When you close your eyes and lay in one," he began, inching closer to Eric. "Do you feel like you are being watched? Can you stand yourself at the end of the day? Do you love yourself, even when you are alone?"

Eric reached for his sword at the shallow offense, laughing sardonically. The sound jerked through the water. Julian held his hands up with an equally infuriating Vernesque chuckle.

"Hey, I just want to know what kind of deal I am going into."

"A deal's a deal."

Eric stepped back further. Julian advanced. Imperceptibly small advances…

"Then seal the deal. Tell me what you will do when you have the bed without the pearl."

Forward.

"The bed without the…pearl?"

Forward.

"An empty bed. A bed ravaged by the oppressor. A bed sold and commodified. A bed you extract and extract from but cannot determine what it is for. Not really. Sometimes, you do not even know you do not know. If you do, if you had a slight idea, you might tell me this is 'the bed I must rise up against, or surely you will take it from me.' You cannot take it from me."

Forward.

"Fancy words! You poncy fucking boys with your purple fucking prose!" Eric drew his sword this time. All he could see was Julian. Julian, blinding and bright and everywhere. It enraged him.

Forward.

Julian knew he must turn his head. That this time, the sword meant nothing at all. Violence for the sake of violence, without the lust and drama, did not move him. In the easy context, it also did not protect him any better.

"You are already insignificant to me. You cannot take what has always been mine since the very moment I was born. You cannot uncrown me, darling."

But all of us, all of us can only ever go back.

Eric's foot stumbled. His sword shook in his hands. His eyes grew wide; *No, no I am not what you are about to say.* He heard the words, somewhere, inside his head and he felt as though he had heard a ghost. He lost his balance. He sliced and sliced. He used his fists where he could not use his words. It did not serve him well; for it had no true passion behind it, only a self-serving nature of cowardice.

Julian ducked, underwhelmed and unbothered. Eric had never been a worthy opponent.

"Y-you are the…pearl? The last boy—"

"I am not him," Julian said, and he smiled as he did. He was so very glad he was not. "But I know him well."

Eric fell back onto the bed. The shell's top was strong. It did not crack.

Vern, cloaked in a nearly-invisible netting that rendered its wearer more not-there than here, jumped behind him, and caught him in a chokehold. Eric had not seen him at all. Something in Julian and in Vern knew, he never would.

"So, thou mayst say the king lies by a beggar," Vern sung, breezily.

"If a beggar dwells near him," Julian agreed. He slid some powder onto the blade and touched the very tip to Eric's forehead. He did not slice. In his other hand was Vern's, completing the ritual.

"How quickly the wrong side may be turned outward," they finished together.

And Eric, entirely calcified, did not strike.

CHAPTER 35

"I hear obsidian is very sharp, when it breaks," Vern said hesitantly, looking at the statue. He remembered how he, too, had been transformed, though the agony on Eric's face, veined with white perlite deposits because of the haste of his transformation, was not at all part of that memory.

"We will not break it," Julian promised, suddenly weary. "He will not cut anyone. He will stay there. A warning to others."

"I would like for it to break," Vern admitted, and looked so remorseful that Julian gathered him into his arms. "Oh! You are bleeding."

"It is nothing." Julian assured him. "But it is enough."

"Even a scratch is too *much*."

Vern frowned. He looked at the hood of the shell bed. Later he would have to ask Julian to please move the statue someplace else, away from the miracle of their first making, when they were compressed to life from exquisite nacre and a fallen star. The interior sharpness of obsidian worried him too much. For now, however, he could abide by Julian's poetics of revenge. It was fitting for the day.

Dimitri and Adrian emerged from the seaweed forest, swords at their belts. Vern kept a hold on Julian until Dimitri swam over and looked them both over with worried, frenetic efficiency, starting with Vern and neutrally asking him the standard questions of field medicine instead of anything from the flurry of relief in their head. They'd known how scared Vern had been of this confrontation, and it was not something to brush off on their way to Julian this time, but...

"Do you feel sick?" they finally asked. "Panicked? Did he...?"

"No, Dimitri. Dimitri, I am *fine*," Vern promised, meeting Dimitri's eyes, gripping their hands and jolting them out of it. "Look at me. All of my fingers and toes, see? Not even a hair out of place. I am perfectly well, you wonderful creature. But Julian got…"

"That is a lot of blood, Julian," Dimitri gasped, eyeing the wound in Julian's midriff. Adrian was already ahead of them, trying to pull Julian together– arms out and ready!

No. I know what I need. Do not treat me. Not now. Not here. After. First, I need to rest. I need to go to my own, true bed. I need my brother.

Adrian and Dimitri maneuvered Julian into Vern's hands. Vern helped Julian into the bed. His blood oozed out onto the sheets, blue and beautiful. Vern curled around him and kissed him.

His body was seacool, and he twined his fingers with Vern's, his side coalescing under the fleshy layers of the shell's open mouth. It had not housed them within its hinges in quite some time. And yet, they still fit, like they had only been gone a day. Julian beckoned with a hand and Adrian came to his side; on Vern's, swam Dimitri. All four of them were joined for a moment, and then the shell accepted the twins back into its folds.

Julian's head filled with perfect boysong:

Lay me down/in the hour of your love/let it last
now is the hour of/my death/is it my death/really
here/no, there is no boydeath/because I have
decided/to live/I have decided I am born
from the chambers of your heart/your heart/
your heart/your heart/your heart/your heart/
your heart/your heart/your heart/your heart/
your heart/your heart/your heart/your

heart/overflowing/down the ventricles
and atriums/glowing/down the hearts

of others/like me/unlike me/without me/
with me/the heart of peace/becomes

the heart of the centerfold/hinges
and clasps/and unclasps/the mouth
a stage to dance upon/the song a
ballet to dream/the underwater deluge/

resisting metaphor/leaping from the
tongue/to the tips of your fingers/
the first pose/the repose/the position
of your hips/to his waist/the pinctada/

the nacre/the double of the boytoboy/
the mantoboy/the boytocreature/the boy
to mancreature/the creatureboy to man/
the man to boy/the creature/a boy/running

towards/every toostrangegrotesquebeautiful
thing with eyes open and yearning/all
the world is my own/darling/when you

come into my kingdom/when I beckon you
come into my kingdom/I promise you—

You are also coming home.

The shimmering flesh gasped and churned around the twins. Julian clung to Vern in some unconscious state; Adrian laid down, and the four of them, for all the weathered journeys that had brought them here, felt wounds begin to close; Julian writhed and the sound was not pain; it was love; Love

276

from the ones who loved him, forming and reforming, constantly changing, ever stable, shaping, arranging, atomical, metaphysical, diaphanous and flowing…his lungs filled with fresh seawater and he yawned as though waking from a dream; he was tired, then he pushed through the tired, and found he was awake…

Julian rose from his shell bed. So did Vern. They helped Adrian up last and watched as the hinges held the heart. Dimitri embraced them, and found themself, somehow, in the center of everyone's affections. The shell twinkled in the dark of the ocean floor as they swam away, back to the ship. From one of the portholes Julian could see its outline as they sailed away.

The bivalved shell lay there, rooted and whole—Yes, the shell bed would remain untouched unless it was opened at their behest; closed, safe as a story when the book has been shut.

CHAPTER 36

The ship sailed upon the horizon. The water was briny-clear and bubbling, as the wooden hull was pursed by the waves. A few more turns of the sundial and they came into a clearing. There, amidst the large plains of seaweed, was a kingdom. Even the outskirts were lush and verdant, seaflower filled and thriving. From the reaches for the natural came large, looming coves, and shimmering spires topped with marvelous gems. The palace was breathtaking. Julian could remember the outline, but not the details—they hit him sharply and all at once; wide roses and sea hyacinths blooming from the cavernous windows of conches and clusters of spiky-smooth shells; the rooms twisted, turned and felt almost too much to look at; circle upon circle upon circle, a labyrinth of a celebration; an existence.

"What if you did not give them enough?" Pericles asked. Ernest threw a spool of yarn his way. Pericles caught it with ease.

"Enough? What does enough look like, did you feel, did you want, were you born—that is more than *enough*."

"These are my words. They are not a pile of trauma for you to dissect and decide upon– that too, is over in my life. In my boyhood, you see…"

"What will they say, when it is finished, *if* it is ever finished…?"

"They must read for the pleasure of reading, the way one loves for the pleasure of loving--it must come to them when they are ready."

Vico skittered in.

"Are you guys still making that thing?"

"Mhm, sure are."

Vico rolled his eyes and raced out of the room, a set of thudding footsteps followed after; Henry trailing behind with a wooden kitchen spoon and a colander on his head. Shrieks of laughter clattered onto the deck. Pericles looked ahead. He did not say a thing. Ernest laughed, cocking an eyebrow:

I can tell why he favors us as someone to take care of him. Him and Henry will have many, many adventures of their own…

Pericles and Ernest continued to roll the thread until it was time to pack up some of their things on the ship. Pierre was choosing clippings he most likely wanted to introduce to Illyrial *right away*. Batiste--already packed of course--lingered needlessly around the botanist, asking questions for no good reason about what he *might* be doing when he arrived in Illyrial, if he *perhaps* needed some new threads for his gardening. If Mr. Snorsky would be writing to him once they landed, and if he could hang around in the rose bushes with him when he--of course--was not very busy making armory and wardrobe for everyone. Of course, Pierre said, with a smile that crinkled to his eyes *We shall see how you behave, my dear. But I would enjoy your company greatly.*

Meanwhile, Dimitri found Vern in the mail vent by their chambers, looking despondent.

"We are about to make berth, your highness," they said with a small bow, as though Vern was holding court and not covered in dust, distractedly trying to open a cleverly locked envelope.

"I think Adrian meant for this to reach you," he responded. "There's an issue with the mail where the corners are too sharp in the vents and letters get lost."

"Ah yes, that is one of his," Dimitri smiled, pocketing the little square marked *Mitya*. That was for later, when they were alone; they were coming to find that Adrian's love notes were potent and unpredictable, just like him. "Thanks for finding it."

"Of course," Vern said tremulously, and then burst into tears. Dimitri, nonplused, reached a hand through the vent to extract the young Prince. Vern took their arm and let himself be hoisted out.

"What's wrong? Aren't you happy to go back?" they asked cautiously.

"They are all going to be so cross with me," Vern wept. "I hurt my brother and his Favorite so much and I left without telling anyone and, and…everything is ruined! I cannot go back because I have been so *bad*."

"Oh," Dimitri said. "Are they often cross with lovely boys when they have been bad?"

Vern wiped at his cheeks and started weeping anew.

"I do not know," he said. "Nobody in Illyrial has ever been as bad as me."

"Are Julian and Adrian cross with you?"

Vern shook his head haltingly.

"I have not been to Illyrial before," Dimitri continued. "But I have heard if one is bad there then they must be banished. You have already done that part, in a way."

"Oh *yes*. And it has been so long, longer than any banishment."

"So why should they be cross with you, if you have already done as they would have asked?" Dimitri reasoned. "And are coming back all the wiser for it? I think such a sweet Prince must be sorely missed from his castle."

Vern's lip quivered again but he smiled instead. Then he wrapped his arms around Dimitri and held them tight. *He makes a truly rotten runaway,* Dimitri thought with a pang, *everyone wants to be his home.* They could not hold it against Vern though, nor could they imagine anyone else would either.

As he embraced Dimitri his thoughts shifted to Julian; Julian was thrilled watching the kingdom come into view as Adrian docked the ship in one of the palace's gardens. Julian was breathless, exchanging kisses with Adrian, pushing him up against the console, teasing, silly, giddy! Oh, his whole life was ahead of him! Finally, had such a day ever come before? And would it ever come again? He could smell the sweet sea-waters of Illyrial, and as he and Adrian began to disembark, discussing in a flurry to his (very worried, though elated) tutors what had happened, Julian thought what Vern thought and knew *This would be so much, so enchanting and bountiful, could we even stand it?*

And then he *felt* as Vern felt, and he did something he did not know he could do; he sent the thought back as feeling; and Vern clasped Dimitri closer and said *Thank you, thank you— I want everything we will become.*

CHAPTER 37

It turned out when the tutors were left to their own devices, the rooms of Vern and Julian's boyhood instruction turned to archives arranged by an architecture of desire and mystery only. Temporarily embarrassed, the tutors pushed all the scrolls on tables and chairs to the floor for later perusal and indicated to the Princes and their odd retinue to sit at their leisure. Refreshments were briskly passed around while the tutors consulted amongst themselves. Vern, happy to finally see palace food, took an overflowing jam tart topped with torched meringue and started eating with determination. The taste was just as he remembered, to his intense relief. Julian smiled and sat in the high-backed chair he had chosen for himself, head resting delicately against his hand.

"Your highnesses, where have you been?" Daniel, one of the tutors finally asked. There was no malice in his voice, for in Illyrial none were truly scolded. Rather, he seemed worried and curious, and the former was quickly draining from Daniel's good-natured features. "Well, there's Adrian, welcome back dear lad! I have something I need to ask you about…but do not mind that right this moment, just a trifling matter touching acoustics! Who are your new friends?"

"They are all my guests, and my brother's," Julian said. "They may stay in Illyrial at my pleasure and are to be treated as the royal family while they remain in the castle. I am sorry to have been gone so long. How is the kingdom?"

"The kingdom fares well," Daniel assured. "All the general populace lacks is the pleasure of our Princes…"

"And they can certainly wait another week or so for any general address," added the court doctor, Malory. "I daresay your highnesses' travels require rest and medical attention as answer."

"I feel well," Julian said, marveling at the truth of it. "I will be happy to retreat into repose. But I feel well."

"It surprises me to say it, Prince Julian, but I am not immediately concerned with your royal constitution. I meant that of your younger brother," Malory responded with a half-bow, and turned to Vern, who was about to take another tart. "Your highness?"

"What did I do?" Vern asked, eyes wide.

"Nothing, my dear boy," Malory assured. "Only you seem quite peckish."

"Well, I *am*," Vern said petulantly. "But I am not sick."

"*Vern*," Julian prompted, but Vern crossed his arms. He did not want to talk about the gold deposits he feared were in his body, not on the day of his homecoming. Julian nodded, looking back at the doctor. "Through no fault of his, my brother unfortunately found food to be a difficult obligation during our travels. Illyrial and its bounty will be the remedy for this."

"Thank you, your grace. This is a welcome comfort to me," Malory said with another bow.

"Aside from myself and my brother, our companions are weary from the voyage. It is therefore our general order that rest, and fussing is duly required for all, and shall last a fortnight. This will be followed by a joyous reprieve from rest," Julian ordered. "Please prepare the guest rooms and provide attendants for all according to their need, in true Illyrian custom."

"Who rests with you, your highness?" asked the keeper of the chatelaine, Isebeau. Julian looked at him, uncomprehending until the rotund man with beautiful freckles and delicate hands clarified. Julian never had a head for the protocol of the castle, and was so close to bed that he could hardly hear the question. "I mean which persons of your party are to fill the guest suites near the Princes' wing?"

"My Favorite. And my brother's Favorite," Vern responded smoothly to general surprise: *Vern* with a *Favorite?* "Adrian, of course. And Dimitri."

"Which is Dimitri?" Isebeau inquired politely. Dimitri glanced at Vern, coloring just slightly. Vern looked up at them with a grin and took another tart.

"The handsome fellow by my side, Isebeau. Do not be coy. They have not been to Illyrial before, so please make sure their suite is properly attended to. No skimping. I do not want them to get a bad first impression."

"*Never* been to Illyrial?" Isebeau asked, looking Dimitri up and down. "Are you quite sure, your highness? Aren't they just…?"

"I am always sure and hardly ever wrong. For all the others of our friends, please see that they are within reach in the adjoining rooms by the Princes' wing," Vern said, and stood. The tutors all stood with him and the staff made a swift exit to execute his orders. "There's room for everyone."

Vern pulled Dimitri away with him, down the hall, and the others dispersed, following insistent and helpful attendants. The tutors dismissed themselves as well, and soon it was just Julian and Adrian in the mess of the tutorial atrium. Julian could hear musicians tuning up and the bell-like sound of the gardens nearby, meeting Adrian's equally misty gaze.

"Like we never left," Adrian managed to say, wiping away a tear.

Julian nodded.

"A fortnight of rest?"

"Mmhm. I need to make sure it is not a dream. I cannot think I am dreaming when I address my people."

Adrian looked out the window, holding his own arm tightly.

Do you suppose they will understand what you have to say? he thought.

It does not matter. I need to say it. Illyrial is too precious for me to be some chief sycophant.

Other kingdoms would go to war.

Not ours. Revenge is for banished boys, or Princes. Or both.

I know.

In the adjoining chambers, Batiste fell face first into the softest bed he had ever had the pleasure of meeting and rolled over. An attendant insisted on struggling with his suitcases, heavy with weaponry, clothes, and other necessaries.

"What's your name?" Batiste asked.

"Ivor, of Illyrial."

"Charmed. I am Batiste. Ivor, you know I carried my kit in," Batiste said pleasantly. "I can continue to watch you if it is your pleasure…"

"It is the Princes' pleasure that you watch me at my vocation, Batiste. And mine, if I may be so bold," Ivor puffed, and *down* went the shields and bejeweled escutcheons into the corner with an almighty clatter. Batiste shrugged, staring at the elaborately painted ceiling. He was not quite sure if he could get used to this, but he was willing to give it a fair shake.

"Do you know where everyone else has been put?" he asked casually.

"Well of course! Am I to arrange a tryst? I will pack the picnic. There is a fine spot by the…"

"Thank you, Ivor, I was just wondering if Pierre has a room down the hall or if I have to do stairs."

Ivor looked up from his trifling business with a hatbox and pressed a button. One of the walls slid open and there was Pierre in the next room, apparently having had the same conversation with his own attendant. Batiste wiggled his fingers, feeling awkward.

"So, no stairs," he said.

"No, my younger master was very particular," Ivor smiled. Oh, Vern was going to get it… "Let me know if you need that tryst set up, you two!"

Suddenly, they were alone. Pierre coughed, and gestured to the suitcases, neatly unpacked and stowed now.

"Expecting a siege?" he asked with a small chuckle. Batiste twirled his hair 'no.' "You want to take 'em up on that picnic tonight?"

"Picnic sounds nice," Batiste said with a blush. A moment passed, and he realized he was not speaking. "Should I, um, *wear* something?"

"Dealer's choice," Pierre responded, raising his eyebrows with the clear insinuation. Batiste scoffed and hid his red face.

"Why Pierre, you are such an *awful* flirt," he rebuked. "Come here right now and I will wear whatever you pick out for me tonight."

Ernest and Pericles were swimming around each other in their chambers, the thrill of the chase compounded by their mutual thoughts turning into a ribald white froth of teeth and kissing.

And in the Princes' wing, Dimitri watched the attendants unpack their things with a bemused expression which was close to a smile. Someone else was fitting them for proper court attire and Vern was there, explaining that their chambers were adjoining to his and there was a secret door in between.

"...and Julian's rooms are just upstairs, all you have to do is go through this secret staircase," Vern said, pushing another button on Dimitri's headboard to demonstrate. "For whatever it is you and Julian et al do."

"Vern, does anyone use the non-secret staircases?" Dimitri asked with a laugh. The tailor gently pushed their arm up to get a measurement, and they gracefully complied, noting the attendants paused from their busy work to watch.

"Well, *they* do," Vern said, indicating to the staff, and looked at Dimitri nervously. "The secret staircases are just for us. So we can get to each other quickly in case...Is that all right?"

"More than all right, it is very tender, your grace. I expected nothing other from your kingdom."

"*Charmant*," breathed an attendant, who was arranging flowers with great care. Dimitri looked at him suspiciously, and then back at Vern.

"Everyone *out*," Vern said with a slight raise of his voice. "And monsieur tailor, stop fondling my Favorite with such impetuosity. You must see Dimitri's clothes are court-ready as they are. All they require is for their boots to be blacked and a short cloak of starlight, to hang from the back of the epaulets."

"Like in the book?" the tailor asked.

"I have already drawn it. Now leave and have the boy send up the completed piece when you are done."

"Are people in Illyrial generally free with such kind praise, or is it just the palace?" Dimitri asked, sitting on the bed with Vern.

"Dimitri, do you think I keep courtiers around to compliment me and my friends every hour of every day?" Vern asked, then held up a hand. "Do not answer that. Yes, obviously I do. I am their Prince. But...and oh, I hoped Joules or Adrian would explain...well."

"Explain what?"

"Your allure," Vern said, desperately uncomfortable. "Do not laugh. I am not the person who should have to explain. There is a...oh for heaven's sake."

He went to his bookshelf, pulled a thin tome from it, and threw it on the bed.

"I imagine this must be a surprise," he said, with no trace of irony. "But in between their other divertissements, brother mine and his Favorite sometimes put their little heads together and write narrative poetry. Have they *never* mentioned this?"

"Vern," Dimitri said, opening the book and scanning the elaborate verse. "What do you mean to say?"

"There are many boys in Illyrial who have read *The Itinerant Heart* in their youth," Vern sighed. "And I have come to suspect they will look at you and find you to be close to their imaginings of Roderigo."

Dimitri laughed outright.

"Sure. I have a literary doppelgänger haunting the pages of this book," they said. "Pull the other one."

Vern primly thinned his lips.

"I pull nothing, Dimitri. I wish only to give you fair warning as my Favorite."

"Oh good, you are settling in," Adrian said from the secret staircase. He had changed into something akin to sleep clothes, an oversized shirt that fell over one shoulder and linen pants. He had his spectacles on, to Dimitri's surprise. "I thought perhaps they did not have anything for you to change into just yet, Dimitri. These are some of mine."

"Thanks, Captain. The crown Prince just dismissed the tailor for mysterious reasons known only to him," Dimitri said, smiling at Vern's outraged tut.

"I am just *Adrian* here, darling," Adrian said airily, and kissed Dimitri on the lips. Dimitri kissed back, letting their hand tangle in Adrian's hair, newly soft from washing and a green ribbon tied into a braid. Vern watched from his cavernous bed with pie eyes.

Dimitri pulled away first, taking the clothes and pulling off their shirt without a thought. Adrian picked up the book on Vern's bed curiously.

"One of mine!" he exclaimed, with pleasing vanity, and flipped through. "*The Itinerant Heart!* I *remember* this, what were we thinking with the cantos? Sonnets too? Haibun and haiku? Joules and I did this one in a month! I thought I was going mad ..."

"Dimitri was curious," Vern said archly. "What is it about?"

"Brooding and winsome lad by the name of Roderigo loses his mind in the pursuit of Beauty and Love, two handsome boys who desire him equally but must always be apart. They mop his brow and nurse him back to health once he takes leave of his senses in the most delicious way, but they can never do it together. Finally, he embraces his madness and manages to trap Love in Beauty's garden. The end," he explained with a little laugh. "Dreadful allegory. We tried to refine it and focus on the language."

"But what does Roderigo look like?" Vern nudged. "How is he described?"

"Oh, you know," Adrian said, suddenly abashed. Dimitri froze, shirt half buttoned, and glared at Vern to be quiet and let Adrian dig his hole. "Handsome. Er, dark. Graceful, remarkable poise despite his demons. Dab hand with the sword and so stoic, but witty, head easily turned by a pretty face, though only out of undying loyalty to beauty and love, not churlishness. You know, *Julian* would know more about...we both had...hmm!"

He was looking at Dimitri quizzically, as though he had never seen them before. Dimitri's eyes widened and Vern giggled, sorting through a gilded box of combs and hairclips.

"Adrian," Dimitri said. "My Prince is possessed of the notion that I have an uncanny resemblance to a character in this work."

"Generally speaking, a Prince's notion is law in Illyrial. Things are simpler that way," Adrian said noncommittally and cleared his throat. He was *blushing*, a pleasing soft lavender.

"I see," Dimitri said with a slow smile, letting Vern button up their shirt with an infuriating grin. They still fought the feeling of being made fun of, but the *notion* that even so far away from their kingdom, even having lost each other, Adrian and Julian both desired as they once had, and both lit on Dimitri independently. It flattered but it did not cloy.

"Vern, do not frighten Dimitri," Julian said, coming down the stairs as though it was his own room. "My love, did you say *The Itinerant Heart* is a dreadful allegory? It was *your* idea to call the boys Love and Beauty…"

"You wanted to give them names without rhymes," Adrian sighed fondly.

"The true poet creates rhymes for the names which are too sweet to be without," Julian said. "And you kept Roderigo as he was. What rhymes with Roderigo?"

Adrian conceded loss of the well-picked creative bone, and Julian took the book from his hands before leading him to the bed with Vern and Dimitri. Vern showed Dimitri hairclips the size of his little fingernail in the shape of stars and planets, glittering with the luster of the skies.

"This one or these for your hair?" he asked, soft cheek on Dimitri's shoulder while they perused his treasures. "Or none of them, and we commission the jewelers for something better?"

"I cannot rightly say. Is this how it always is here?"

"It is how the days of rest must be. Secret staircases, nothing serious to discuss except the loveliest nonsense. An exercise in intellectual forbearance which leads to great feats of creation. You seem nervous about it."

"I am nervous. I am terrible at resting but I do not wish to disturb."

"Me too, me too, me too! Oh good. What should we do instead of resting?"

Vern and Dimitri made their plans. Adrian and Julian made absolutely none. Soon all four slept, tangled in each other's arms and thoughts until late into the night, when Vern tugged Dimitri's sleeve awake with an indiscernible mumble. He carefully squirmed out of Julian's hold around his waist and stood.

"I have plans now. Come with me," he whispered.

Dimitri followed Vern though the quiet castle, through passages and antechambers that Vern stepped through with mincing surety. Soon they were outside, and Dimitri blinked in the semi-moonlit night.

Vern held out a helmet.

INDRA-1 stood firmly planted in the palace's gardens. It had been a surprise to Vern how simple it was to find her for salvage; his photograph had automatically generated the coordinates of her location. By Vern's command, she had been pulled by a stronger ship to Illyrial, carving a sandy, disappearing path through the ocean floor until she was gently lifted to her final rest, behind the palace. She would be retained as a planter, of sorts, unburdened of Vern's valuables, now safely tucked in the palace, restored, and then…Vern would take her out, when he chose.

For now, she rested on her side, two sturdy woven ropes tethered to the side of her metallic frame. Dimitri attached one to the clip on Vern's waist, and then to their own. They were a stronger swimmer than Vern, and took him in their arms, marveling at the ease with which they could ascend through Illyrial's clear waters.

Before bursting the surface, Vern looked at Dimitri, lips already clamped around the tube which would make a reservoir of the seawater from beneath while they glanced above with their helmets. There was no storm to toss them upwards by chance, the skies were clear. Dimitri would behold the stars in stillness and peace. How had they come so close, so quickly, Dimitri thought with wonder, but did not pursue the mystery, did not need to in the face of the true riddle above their head. They put their helmet on and joined the Prince above the mirror sheen of the sea.

The moon made quicksilver of the water dripping from their visors for a moment, but soon they could see the stars, as clearly as though they were flying. Dimitri could feel tears, could feel time unwinding like the coils of rope which kept them tethered to Illyrial and to Vern. They could stay here forever, or for just a second, and be satisfied in full.

If it was forever or a second, it passed, and Vern held Dimitri's hand, ready to make their slow descent, bundling their tethers as they did, speaking softly though there was nobody to hear. With the castle in sight, Vern produced a packed lunch, wrapped in a cloth the color of midnight with yellow starfish drifting. They ate in silence, Dimitri's legs wrapped around Vern's waist so they would not drift apart too much.

"Do you think anyone is worried?" Dimitri asked. Vern shook his head happily. "I am used to not being missed, but a Prince?"

"I told them where I was going this time," Vern murmured. It meant something more.

Eventually they came down, resting atop *INDRA-1* to watch the gardeners. To their surprise, Dimitri could see Adrian in what was clearly the medical garden, taut in its planning and function compared to the ornamental plots and orchards further afield. With a wide basket in his hands and small scissors that looked more suited to a haberdashery than a garden, Adrian retrieved clippings and roots, lying on his side and chatting with cheer that carried, though his words did not. Julian watched him with palpable pleasure, perched on a broken statuary. He was ensconced in a long white robe whose vaded luster and opalescent embroidery forbade gardening, tied closed with a wide black belt. He held a book in his hand and a beautiful pen, hollowed out coral producing a shimmering ink nearly impossible to read except by the writer. Dimitri suddenly became aware of watching Julian's watching in an odd way, and turned back to Vern, who was delicately struggling with an orange and, in trying not to make a fuss about it, became even more conspicuous.

"Here," they said, and started the peel before returning the fruit. Vern caught their hand and kissed it. "Your highness."

"It looks an awful lot like work down there," Vern giggled at the scene below. Dimitri watched Adrian's basket fill with leaves, berries, roots, watched him lightly prune something that had got overgrown in his absence and wipe a dirty hand on his forehead. Julian seemed enchanted.

"I suppose they get antsy, too."

Vern shook his head, and gestured '*look again.*'

With a heavy gaze, Adrian was watching Julian, not the other way around. The young Prince was taking off the impossibly clean robe, shrugging off its shoulders first. Now bare chested, he took up his notebook and his pen again, but it was a clear tease. Their conversation grew low. The belt came off last. The notebook was abandoned and so was the basket. They were in the dirt together, kissing, Julian having descended from his statuary in Galatean style. Dimitri looked away and met Vern's distracted glance.

"Not work after all," Dimitri proposed.

"Evidently. And there will be no getting them out of the bath after this, either," Vern said with a snort. "The poor fullers. Shall we join them? Or do you wish for the indoors? I have been flooded with sky and stars and all else, and I fear I crave a pillow."

"The indoors, I think. I'd like to draw some of what I have seen," Dimitri said. Quite pleased by the prospect, Vern nodded.

"Let me show you, I know just the place."

Vern showed Dimitri a studio of inks and parchments close to the greenhouses, with a glass ceiling of its own. He pulled out a rolling bed from under a desk, bundling himself in the provided quilt and letting Dimitri stroke his hair until he fell to an easy nap. Dimitri sharpened some pencils and looked in all the drawers with care, finding bottles of pigments filled with more blue than they'd need in a year of making maps, liquid golds and deepest blacks next. They looked up and noted the blue circle of glass to indicate the position of the morning star. It was an observatory then, made with the intention of seeing stars that should not be visible so close to the bottom of the ocean. Dimitri did not understand...

Vern murmured in his sleep. Dimitri straightened from the barebones grid of their first Illyrian map, ready to rouse him in case it was a nightmare. They touched him and Heard. Vern was at peace, and Dimitri realized he was singing, a bell-like, glittering sound they had not ever heard:

Who will be my baby, tonight, Who will get to know me, get to show me how to feel loved... dance the hours away, who can say, what an hour means when it is shared?

Dimitri smiled, letting the starsong serenade their happy work. They worked, but soon their hands drifted to the cord of string with a tiny, black shell under their shirt. They would show Vern, in some way, that they understood.

Vern, half-awake now, pulled him in and kissed him. Folding their bodies together, twined like perfect, green stars in a distant sky, Vern felt what they could not say; all the years of wandering, all the ways Dimitri was made, so very different, all the shadow-gloom places they had traversed had lead him to their arms.

Vern pulled them closer and wrapped around Dimitri and together, and felt this through his Favorite's caresses

All of this was here for you, my darling friend, so that even the impossible light could touch your design...

CHAPTER 38

The next afternoon, a flurry of tutors surrounded Adrian. The first Favorite's health was of paramount importance and Adrian could not wave them off despite his best excuses, not when he was missing a leg; after all this time he had forgotten that it must be a shock to those who remembered him otherwise.

The infirmary wing was sunlit and beautiful with high ceilings and mosaics on the walls, and it almost did not feel like a hospital. Nonetheless, Adrian was jumping out of his skin and his arms were crossed over himself while he sat on a bed and let the court doctor prod him, nervously watching the nurses. Dimitri stood nearby, leaning against the wall, having insisted on being his companion when it became apparent that Adrian would not be able to be seen elsewhere for this visit. If they were wearing their sword and smiling at the nurses who drifted a little too close to their Captain, then surely it was out of habit.

"Adrian, what *happened?*" Malory asked. "Was there an infection? An accident?"

Adrian shook his head and pulled his leg from the doctor, wrapping it back up with tight, agitated movements. He grabbed the prosthesis with shaking hands, then discarded it altogether onto the floor. He would be like this always now, and it would be his even more monstrous form that everyone would need some getting used to, never mind the missing leg.

"It has been quite some time," the doctor elaborated. "And you have been my patient since the Princes' arrival in Illyrial. If there was something missing from your history and it impacted your care, Adrian, it would weigh heavy on me."

Adrian sighed and pushed his hair out of his face, still tight-lipped. His eyes flicked over to Dimitri, and they did not need to share thoughts for Dimitri to know that he desperately wanted to leave, to do anything except to speak of it. It was only Julian's worry that gave him pause, or the possibility of continued interrogations every time he visited the infirmary.

"Does it really change the options for treatment?" Dimitri asked the doctor, brisk and to the point. "How it happened, I mean? Is it Adrian's responsibility to explain such an awful thing for you to help him?"

"No, of course not," Malory said after a moment, and turned to Adrian. "I apologize. I spoke out of curiosity and not concern."

"Did you get my gardener's notes?" Adrian asked, to the floor.

"Your gardener…"

"The um," Adrian took a box from his bag and opened it. Overstuffed papers and samples spilled out, and he looked at Malory, worried. "It seems a little mad, off the ship. It is not mad. I am not mad. Unless Dimitri says I am…"

"You *are* mad," Dimitri promised. Adrian was brilliant and would not be tricked into believing otherwise anymore. "But not madder than me."

Relieved, Adrian hummed and sorted out a couple of the envelopes before placing them together with a bottle for the doctor.

"There's one less leg, so one less brain," he explained. "Regeneration is not viable, but the ganglia do not know. They understand it less when I am mantled. This causes overproduction of hemocytes. Just like the usual problem, you see, but it is worse because it does not self-regulate as it did when I had all my…I could suppress hemocyte production before, but it is not something I can depend on anymore, not since excision. The solution has been— or it *could be*—simply to cause a crisis which justifies the level of hemocyte production, and head them off by making them too busy to cause mischief. Er…sayeth my gardener."

"To be too sick for you to attempt regenerating the leg," Malory said, looking concerned at the implication. "To be sick forever?"

"The alternative is regeneration," Adrian muttered. His fingers plucked at airy threads he was trying to follow even as he tried to reason through. "My body will try to make a new leg and a new *brain*, younger and undeveloped. A pretender welcomed as the prodigal by my body. I have suffered for years from the effects of neuronal dislocation and I understand why now. Regeneration took my mind hostage, wrecked my faculties more than the amputation. It was not something I could mitigate or control, despite my kind and capable crew. If I am to be a suitable companion to my Prince during his travels, or the suitable company of any good man, then this is the path I must take."

There's no going back, and there's no stopping, Adrian did not say. He wanted so to leave the infirmary before the inevitable panic attack he could feel burrowing in his chest, knowing Dimitri would whisk him back to their shared chambers if he asked. But he stayed while the doctor left briefly to make a few compounds from his detailed instructions, still hugged around himself.

"I am sorry," Adrian said. He could not bear to look at Dimitri, who would never have him at his best and somehow persisted in staying. "I do so want it to be fixed."

"I know Julian would spurn such an apology, so do not insult me thus," Dimitri rebutted with a frown set on their pretty lips. "There's nothing which needs fixing. I am only glad I never met the man responsible for this immortal wound. I would have killed him without a thought, and it would have debased me. But you would have remained just as you are now and as I have always known you to be. Innocent and brilliant and mad."

"Innocent," Adrian repeated. Dimitri did not revise the sentiment and did not elaborate. The doctor came back with medicine and set it on the table, along with new eyeglasses which he took with a sigh.

How could I think of you as anything other than innocent, Dimitri thought, *given the circumstances of our meeting? When you told me you were sick of searching for something you could not name without a map? How readily you shared everything you had with me, a stranger, even your desire and the restless hopes you did not understand... When you did not cast me away upon finding what you had missed so dearly, but embraced me tighter and brought me here. What word applies except innocent?*

They wandered back to Julian's room, empty for now while Batiste had whisked the Princes away for a fitting, the previous tailor for the time being having been supplanted by their shipmate, who could not rest! Not when there was so much to do and such lovely fabric to play with in Illyrial...

Adrian took off his leg and shed his mantle with a relieved breath out. Dimitri watched his tentacles release and settle over their lap with lovely grace. They stroked what they could of the stretching limbs absentmindedly, as lost in thought as Adrian, humming and speaking of trifles to dispel the remaining nervousness from the infirmary.

Vern came in through the secret staircase, delicately toeing around Adrian's flowing tentacles, and the chaise of Julian's that he favored most. He seemed positively calm compared to Adrian and held one of Dimitri's new maps in his hands, lounged on his stomach and sighing as though the depth chart was a sonnet.

"Ernest and Pericles send their fond regards, but otherwise they are a horror and only have eyes and teeth for each other. They will not be joining us for dinner," he said by way of conversation. "I have never heard such an inspired ruckus. I have never seen such a sight as them. Are they like that all the time?"

Adrian and Dimitri laughed.

"I think they are trying to be good guests," said Dimitri. "That is *better* than their usual."

"In truth, I was worried. They were in a bit of a dry spell when you met them, Vern," Adrian added. He was reclining across two chaises now and as inky as a Beardsley illustration, looking just as wicked too. "If they stopped their antics and descended into domestic complacency and reef-death, it would be terribly sad."

"What would be sad?"

Pierre walked in through the door, not the secret staircase, with Julian and Batiste, who turned immediately to Adrian as they entered.

"Captain, you have to let me dress you just *once*," the armorer said, eyes bright. "Vern fired the tailor, so you have to let me."

"I *have* to, do I?" Adrian asked with a slow raise of his eyebrow.

"Do not tease him, my love. He cannot take it," Julian said with a soft kiss to Adrian's forehead. "You know it is sheer nonsense that Batiste has not made anything for you the entire time you have been at sea. By my royal decree, let him take a look."

"You will be absolutely shining," Batiste promised with the brash confidence that he and Adrian shared. Adrian smiled and obligingly let Batiste drag him away from his duties as Dimitri's lap pet. In turn, Julian brought Dimitri to the comfortable bed and curled around them, chatting idly in their head.

Pierre, comfortable in the opposite end of the chaise that Vern lay strewn across, looked out onto the balcony, twirling a stray thread from one of Batiste's embroidery hoops in his hands. His ear was turned toward the window, the curtains billowing in strange noise.

Adrian entered, resplendent in the obsidian and emerald coat Batiste had been dreaming for him for years, finally made manifest. It was adorned with spare sachiko threading that revealed anemone fractals in the shoulders and so full after the waist, cinched with a deep velvet belt, it appeared to be one and the same with his tentacles. Shards of dark-veined jade and teardrops of ruby and tiny gold chains festooned his ears, interlocking with the existing piercings. He looked the part of a royal Favorite, though everyone still greeted him as Captain. Dimitri simply grinned at the vision, too busy laying in Julian's arms.

"Mitya? Do you hear that?"

"No."

"I do," Pierre agreed.

Vern, lost to the world, humming and tracing his Favorite's map, said nothing.

Julian beckoned Adrian over. Adrian kissed his hand, then sat on the edge of the bed with them.

"Dimitri said it went well, and that you were brave."

"It went as well as it could," Adrian said, glancing at Dimitri thankfully. "I managed to speak of it."

And one day I will find it in me to speak of it to you. I am sorry if I make you worry. But have they worked you up yet?

Yes, and no. When they give me the full one. Well, it will be a doozy.

They will not have anything more concrete than last time.

Perhaps a stern warning to rest. Perhaps some more tests. I will do what I can, what I wish. So that I am well enough to always travel with my dear Captain.

Adrian nodded, pressing a kiss to Julian's head, before kissing Dimitri's, too.

"About that noise your highness," Pierre asked, a note of humor in his voice. "Did you think, perhaps, people wanted to see *you* in Illyrial today?"

"I doubt that. We have left everyone in terrific hands! Why would they miss us?"

"Do you think people would not miss you if they were deliriously happy every day? Do you not think your absence would somehow mean there is still something dear to miss?" Dimitri pressed.

Julian bowed his head. "I confess...As long as I leave one in good hands with good intentions, I do not always..."

Adrian's tentacle curled around his wrist with a gentle, assuring touch. "That is the words of a silly boy whom I had to return to this very kingdom. Who left without his Favorite."

"But if you are to be careful with us, we must be careful with you, your grace." Dimitri added.

Vern turned to him and he sent out a warm, lush feeling across the room. Julian felt it shiver down his spine.

"You, Julian. They have missed you."

Pierre stood at the windows, peeking the balcony behind the shades. He could see the crowd below.

I know how to do things perfectly and still not expect someone to praise me beyond well done. It is just my nature. No matter how shining it is. My own heart critiques and critiques—I am thy own jousting partner so many times!

Beyond that?

Beyond that, I will have to trust you, all of you, that The Above knows nothing of hearts—and that mine is worth it, in infinite shades of blue blood, all of this love. After all, who could I deny such a thing? And why would I deny it of myself, especially when I am surrounded by those who are dearer to me than any gem in the sea?

"I…" Julian wandered from his perch on the bed. Dimitri held his hand, following him, with Adrian not long behind. In case he was too weak, in case the shock was too great…so that he might stand…

"Well, they could all be looking at you. To know you are here." Pierre offered.

"Me?" Julian repeated again, shocked.

Julian walked to the long, oval balcony window and opened it. The opening of the sash kissed him with the memory of each and every one of Adrian's long-awaited returns and he almost knelt to weep. He remembered all the sweet wonders of boyhood until his memories were no longer memory itself but present and future laid out before him, iridescent and bubbling, rising within and around; he would not grow old, he would only go on, radiant in his pursuit of all the things he loved…

Adrian?

Yes?

Can you, Dimitri?

Yes, sweet lad? Are you alright?

I…just want to let you both know, I am fine. Thank you. For everything.

Then, he pushed the doors open. Outside, the sea was wide and blue and smelled of a new season. The seaweed was lush and the gardens around the palace were blooming; not coming into bloom, but full and fresh and fragrant. The seas above were mild and the kingdom itself, while beautiful and strong, held so very little interest to Julian now. Instead, it was crowds of Illyrians, all shapes and sizes gathered in the square just outside the palace; sitting upon fountains, having picnics in the squares, reading poetry in the fields–some were waiting with bouquets or chocolates, others with extravagant cards and letters. Others, standing up or sitting, were there plain and simple, as if just waiting to ask *Are you okay?* and *We wanted to see you. We hope you are well, dear friend.*

He was wearing one of the soft, sensory-finessed robes that Batiste had helped design. He worried his fine hands on the fabric to calm himself. He found, despite any prior contempt he held to Batiste for how he treated Dimitri, he would be sending a basket of desserts for even more sincerest thanks for the garments he was now wearing—anything else and he simply might have been too overwhelmed.

*I imagined once, going home. And then I said, I never could. Today, I have done this one impossible thing. I have…*the thought resounded in Julian's head. Adrian heard it. Dimitri heard it, too. He realized Vern felt it. Pierre, and down into the hallways, everyone else began to…

Julian cleared his throat. He grasped one of Adrian's tentacles tighter.

"I imagined once, going home. And then I said, I never could. Today, I have done this one impossible thing. I have…for so long, I thought I would not get to tell it. Not really. Not how I want to. How do you tell people the things you want? And will they listen if only you present yourself as you are? I have been Above, but do not worry or gasp—for there is no horror that lives in my heart upon seeing all of you, being *here. Now.*" Julian smiled. "There is only the news of our insatiable travels. There is only tales of forever in a boykingdom under the sea."

He heard Adrian thinking a bouquet of thoughts to tell them all later. His Favorite stood at his side caressing him. Vern was there too, next to Dimitri, on his other side. Yes, there would be time for more statements later. From anyone who wanted to. There would be time for sweet words, true words, words with no meaning and every meaning.

Julian thought of them in repose, later that night. He thought of them sleeping like how they slept in their shell bed; Adrian around him, Vern beside him, Dimitri adored by all. He thought of the marvelous castle which would at last open and remain open. He had been born of Love and all was for Love's sake. Inspired, he turned to Adrian and kissed him.

The crowd cheered: it was a gorgeous, deep-blue sound that reverberated back, with the welcome of a proper jubilation. At last.

"And I hope you want," he said, throwing open his arms. "With profound passion, I hope you want beyond reason and beyond hope. That is where you discover exactly who you will become. I want you to find me there. I swear it. I want you all to be there, too."

END